NIGHT SCHOOL
Legacy

BY C. J. DAUGHERTY

Night School
Night School: Legacy

NIGHT SCHOOL
Legacy

C.J. DAUGHERTY

www.atombooks.net

ATOM

First published in Great Britain in 2013 by Atom

Copyright © 2013 by Christi Daugherty

The moral right of the author has been asserted.

A CIP catalogue record for this book
is available from the British Library.

ISBN 978-1-907411-22-9

Typeset in Bodoni by M Rules
Printed and bound in Great Britain by
Clays Ltd, St Ives plc

Papers used by Atom are from well-managed forests
and other responsible sources.

MIX
Paper from
responsible sources
FSC® C104740

Atom
An imprint of
Little, Brown Book Group
100 Victoria Embankment
London EC4Y 0DY

An Hachette UK Company
www.hachette.co.uk

www.atombooks.net

To Jack
My navigator

One for sorrow
Two for joy
Three for a girl
Four for a boy
Five for silver
Six for gold
Seven for a secret
Never to be told

Untitled, Old English Nursery Rhyme

ONE

'Isabelle, I need help!'

Crouching in the dark, Allie whispered urgently into her phone.

For less than a minute she listened to the voice on the other end of the line. Occasionally she nodded, her dark hair swinging. When the voice stopped she fumbled with the phone, snapping off the back to remove the battery. Then she yanked out the SIM card and ground it into the dirt with her heel.

Scaling the low brick wall around the tiny square of London garden in which she hid, almost invisible in the moonless night, she ran down the empty street, slowing only long enough to drop the hollow phone into an open rubbish bin. A few streets away, she threw the battery over a tall fence into somebody's garden.

Then she heard something above the sound of her own feet

pounding on the pavement. Ducking behind a white van parked on the side of the road, she held her breath and listened.

Footsteps.

Her eyes darted around the quiet residential street lined with terraces of homes, but it offered few hiding places. She could hear her pursuer running – she didn't have much time.

Dropping to the ground, Allie wriggled her way under the van. The smell of asphalt and oil filled her nostrils. Her cheek rested on the rough tarmac, cold and damp from a rainstorm earlier that day.

She listened hard, willing her heartbeat to quiet.

The footsteps grew closer and closer. When they reached the van, she stopped breathing. But without slowing they passed her hiding place.

She felt a rush of relief.

Then the footsteps stopped.

All sound seemed to be sucked from the air and for a moment Allie could hear nothing at all. Then a muffled curse made her flinch.

After a moment she heard a quiet male voice whispering. 'It's me. I lost her.' A pause then, defensively, 'I know, I know ... Look, she's fast and, like you said, she knows this area.' Another pause. 'I'm on ...' his feet shuffled as he moved to look '... Croxted Street. I'll wait here.'

The silence that followed stretched on for so long Allie began to wonder if he'd somehow tiptoed away without her hearing. She never heard him move once.

Just as her muscles began to ache from lying so still, a sound made her spine tingle.

More footsteps.

These rang out crisply in the cool night air.

As they neared her hiding place the hairs on her arms stood up. Her heartbeat thudded in her ears. Her palms were slick with sweat.

Calm, she thought fiercely. *Stay calm.*

She practised the breathing techniques Carter had taught her over the summer – focusing on slow breaths in and out helped stave off the panic attacks that would otherwise be uncontrollable.

Three breaths in, two breaths out.

'Where'd you see her last?' The low, menacing voice drifted above her as she breathed quietly.

'About two streets back,' the original voice replied. She could hear the rustling sound his jacket made when he pointed.

'She probably turned off somewhere or ducked into a garden. Let's backtrack. And check behind the bins – she's not very big. She could hide behind them.' He sighed. 'Nathaniel's not gonna like it if we lose her. You heard what he said. So let's not, shall we?'

'She's fast as hell,' the first man said, sounding nervous.

'Yeah, but we knew that already. You take that side of the street. I'll take this one.'

Their footsteps moved away. Allie didn't budge until the sound had completely disappeared. Even then she counted to fifty before carefully slipping out from beneath the van. When she was on her feet, she hid between cars and looked as far as she could see in every direction.

No sign of them.

Hoping she was headed the right way, she ran, faster this time.

When things were normal she loved to run, and even now her feet automatically adopted a smooth, easy rhythm. Her breathing steadied as she moved.

But things were not normal. She fought the urge to look over her shoulder, knowing that tripping and injuring herself could mean discovery. And who knew what might happen then?

In the dark the houses flew by as if they were moving, rather than her. It was late – the street was quiet.

Motion detector sensors became her enemy; if she ran on the pavement porch lights clicked on as she passed them – simultaneously blinding and exposing her. So she kept to the middle of the street, although there the street lights harshly illuminated her.

Suddenly the street ended at a junction and Allie skidded to a stop, panting as she looked up at the signs.

Foxborough Road. What did Isabelle say? She rubbed her forehead as she tried to remember.

She said left on Foxborough, she decided after a moment. *Then right on the High Street.* But she wasn't certain. Everything had happened so fast.

As soon she turned left, though, she saw ahead the bright lights of the High Street and she knew she'd been right. But even as she ran towards them she wondered whether the presence of the taxicabs, buses and lorries rumbling down the road meant she was safer. She was out in the open now.

Without slowing, she powered right down the High Street looking for the place Isabelle had told her about.

There! At the garishly decorated sandwich shop on the corner Allie veered right and found the little alleyway where the headmistress had told her to wait. Without looking back, she dashed into the shadows between two massive metal rubbish bins.

Leaning back against the wall, she paused to catch her breath. Her hair hung into her eyes, clinging to the sweat on her face, and she shoved it back absently as she wrinkled her nose.

What the hell is that smell?

The bins reeked but there was also some other awful stench around that she really didn't want to think about. Focusing on her rescue, she kept an eye on the entrance to the alley. Isabelle had said she wouldn't have to wait long.

But as the minutes ticked by she grew impatient. Even here in the dark she felt too exposed. Too easily discovered.

If I were looking for me, this would be one of the first places I'd look, she thought.

Frowning, she chewed her thumbnail absently, until a strange shuffling sound drew her attention. Glancing down, she saw a discarded sandwich box moving by itself. At first she couldn't register what she was seeing then her mouth opened in startled astonishment as the box crept slowly towards her from the far side of the alley. Only when it moved into a pool of light did she see the thin, prehensile tail dragging the ground behind it.

Allie covered her mouth with her hands to stifle a scream.

She was crouching in a rats' nest.

She looked around desperately but there was no place to go. As the sandwich box made its uneven way towards her, she could feel her heart flutter with fear and she struggled to stay still. She had to remain hidden.

But when the rat-box bumped against her left foot it was too much – she tore out of the alley as if she'd been scalded. When she stopped, she found herself back on the street with absolutely no idea of what to do now.

At that moment a sleek, black car skidded to a stop in front of her. Before Allie could react, a tall man leapt out of the driver's side door and whirled to face her, all in one smooth move.

'Allie! Quick! Get in the car.'

She stared at him in astonishment. Isabelle had told her she'd send people to help. She hadn't said 'I'll send one guy in a posh car.' He looked very much like the men who'd chased her earlier – he wore an expensive-looking suit and his dark hair was cropped short.

Allie raised her chin stubbornly.

No way am I getting in that car.

But as she turned to flee two figures appeared out of the darkness on Foxborough Road. They were running straight for her.

She was trapped.

Looking back at the man with the sleek car she saw that he was watching her worriedly. He'd left the car running and it purred like a tiger, spotting its prey. As she took a hesitant step away from him, he stretched out his right arm, his hand turned sideways. He spoke rapidly and without punctuation.

'Allie my name is Raj Patel I'm Rachel's dad Isabelle sent me to get you please get in the car as fast as you can.'

Allie froze. Rachel was one of her best friends. Isabelle was the headmistress at Cimmeria Academy.

If he was telling the truth, she was safe with him.

With only seconds to make up her mind, she searched for a sign to tell her what to do. Any indication that he was who he said he was.

His extended hand was steady; he had Rachel's eyes.

'You do not want those men to catch you, Allie,' he said. 'Please get in the car.'

Something in his voice told her he was telling the truth. As if he'd said the magic words that somehow made her function Allie sprang towards him, scrabbling at the car's unfamiliar door handle and then leaping in. She was still reaching for her seat belt when the car took off.

By the time the catch clicked into place they were doing sixty miles an hour.

TWO

The thing was, the night had started out so well.

Allie had gone out with her old friends Mark and Harry for the first time in months. These were the guys she'd hung out with back when she was always getting into trouble – she and Mark had been arrested together just a few months ago.

Her parents loathed them both, so she'd expected a bit of pushback when she announced her plans for the evening. But they hadn't appeared cross at all.

Her mother said only, 'Be in by midnight, please.' And that was that.

Ever since she'd come home from Cimmeria Academy that summer they'd treated her differently. With respect.

It felt weird to go out without a row.

Weirder still was going back to the park where they used to hang out together every night to find Mark and Harry still swinging on the exercise bars in the dark like overgrown children.

'You lot need to get a job,' she said, striding through the gate.

'Allie!' they'd roared, running across the dark playground to her.

She was so happy to see them she couldn't stop smiling. And they'd seemed thrilled to see her again – pounding her on the back and shoving a can of lukewarm cider into her hand. But once they'd settled down, the two boys on the swings and Allie perched at the top of the slide, the conversation lagged. All they talked about was skiving school, sneaking on to the railway lines to tag, nicking stuff from Foot Locker. The same things they always talked about.

Only now it seemed ...

Boring.

Just two months had passed since she'd last seen them, but Allie felt like she'd aged years; so much had happened during the summer term at Cimmeria. She'd helped to save the school from fire. She'd nearly died. She'd found another student's dead body.

Remembering that, she shivered.

She felt sure they wouldn't understand if she tried to explain what Cimmeria was like. When they asked her about school she replied in vague terms: it was 'kind of crazy', but 'pretty cool'.

'Are all the people there, like, total toffs?' Harry asked, crushing a cider can in his hand and throwing it into the park. Allie studied the can as it glinted amid the soft green leaves of grass.

'Yeah, I guess,' she said, still staring at the can.

But, she thought but didn't say aloud, *I really like them.*

'Do they treat you like the hired help?' His voice sympathetic, Mark was trying to read her expression. She avoided his eyes.

'Some do,' Allie conceded, thinking of Katie Gilmore and her group. But by the end of the term, she and Katie had been working together to save the school from fire and they'd developed a grudging respect for one another. 'But they're not so bad,' she finished.

'I can't imagine going to school with a bunch of toffs.' Harry stood up on the swing's seat and launched it into the darkness. His voice floated to them as he swung by. 'I'd tell them where they could go and then get kicked out, I reckon.'

'Like they'd let you in in the first place,' Mark scoffed, shoving the chains of Harry's swing until it gyrated sideways.

'You going back?' Mark asked, looking at her with sudden seriousness.

'Yeah, my parents say I have to. And I kind of ... want to, you know?' She held his gaze, hoping he'd understand.

Mark's background was different from her own – his dad wasn't around and he lived with his mother in a tower block. His mum went out to nightclubs and bars with her friends – she didn't act like a regular parent. After Allie's brother Christopher ran away two years ago, Mark had been as much like a brother as anybody could be. She knew he'd missed her since she'd gone away to school. But the truth was, after the first couple of weeks at Cimmeria she hadn't thought about him much at all.

'I'll write you letters,' she promised now, guilt making her more fervent.

Mark's sarcastic smile reminded her fleetingly of Carter.

'Yeah?' He popped open another can of cider and jumped up on to the swing. 'I'll write you notes on the Hammersmith and City line.'

He shoved off with his feet and arced out towards Harry, who was singing nonsense songs to himself as he swung.

Allie sat on the slide and watched them joke around – jerking at the swings as if they wanted to rip them from the metal frame. Her expression was thoughtful; the can of cider sat untouched next to her.

It was nearly midnight when Harry's phone rang. After a brief conversation, he conferred with Mark before turning to Allie.

'We're gonna hit the bus depot in Brixton – give it a bit of work. You coming?'

After a pause Allie shook her head.

'I promised the rentals I'd be home early,' she said. 'They're still treating me like a criminal.'

Harry held out his fist and she butted her own against it. His bag rattled when he picked up.

'Later, Sheridan,' he said, heading out of the park. 'Don't let the posh bastards get to you.'

Mark lingered behind.

'If you want to write those letters, Allie,' he said after a long second, 'that'd be cool.'

'I will,' she promised, determined to do it.

At that, he turned and ran after Harry. For a little while she

11

could hear them talking and laughing in the distance. When the sound faded, she climbed down off the slide and picked up all the empty cider cans, depositing them in a rubbish bin. Then she flipped her dark hood up over her head and walked back towards home, her feet moving slower than her thoughts.

She was almost there when she saw them – four men standing outside her house. Their suits were perfectly tailored; haircuts short and neat. One wore sunglasses in the darkness; as she stared at him her heart began to pound. His athletic stance and intense focus reminded her of Gabe.

She stopped in her tracks. That was her first mistake – she should have just walked into Mrs Burson's garden and sneaked out the back.

But she didn't.

When her footsteps stopped the one closest to her swung around. She was half in shadow but he seemed to recognise her. He gestured in her direction.

'Hey,' he said quietly, snapping his fingers twice.

They all turned towards her.

Allie took a cautious step backwards.

'Allie Sheridan?' the first one asked.

Another backwards step.

'We just want to talk to you,' another one said.

Allie whirled around and took off. Leaping over Mrs Burson's low fence, she ran to the back gate she knew was always unlocked and tore through it. Behind her she could hear the men swearing and struggling to get through the gate in the dark as she pounded back to the park, across the slippery grass and through the fence on the far side.

Twisting and turning her way through the neighbourhood, she ran until she couldn't hear them behind her. Then she jumped a garden wall and crawled beneath a hedge.

When she hadn't heard footsteps for what seemed like an hour, she pulled her phone out of her pocket with shaking hands.

Now she sat on the smooth leather passenger seat in the black Audi, watching as Rachel's dad manoeuvred through traffic on the South Circular at speeds well over the allowed limits. It wasn't that she didn't trust him exactly, but she kept her distance, leaning against the door, one hand resting on the handle.

Rachel kind of looks like him, Allie thought. But his skin was darker and his hair was coarse, whereas Rachel's was all glossy curls.

He didn't speak until the rows of houses around them thinned, then faded away, replaced by dark pastures.

'You OK?' he asked then. His question was abrupt but she could hear a touch of fatherly concern underlying the words.

'I'm fine,' she said, sitting straighter. 'Just a bit ... freaked out.'

'Thank you for trusting me,' he said. 'I wasn't sure you would at first.'

'You look like her,' Allie said. 'Like Rachel, I mean. So ... I believe you.'

For the first time he smiled, his eyes on the road. 'Don't tell her that. Her mum's the pretty one in the family.'

He looked nicer when he smiled, and Allie felt herself relax a little.

'What happened?' he said. 'We left your house two hours ago and everything was fine.'

'You were at my *house*?' Allie tensed again.

'Not inside.' He seemed to sense her anxiety and his voice was calming. 'Just nearby. Isabelle asked me to keep an eye on you. One of us has been there – one of my guys – every day.'

Rachel had told her he ran a security firm – one so respected it was used by presidents and business executives. Other than that she didn't really know anything about him, except that he went to Cimmeria when he was a kid.

As hard as she tried to remember seeing him or anyone like him on her street, Allie came up with nothing. The idea that she'd been watched all the time gave her the creeps.

'Everything was fine,' she said. 'There was nobody outside when I went to the park. When I came back, though, those guys were just standing around my street. They recognised me.'

'Did they try to grab you?' He glanced at her.

She shook her head. 'They said they wanted to talk to me. But I didn't believe them,' she said. 'I ran. They never touched me.'

'Good girl.'

Hearing approval in his voice, Allie felt a flush of unexpected pride.

'I'm surprised you got away from them, though,' he said. 'They're very good at what they do.'

Her shrug was modest. 'I'm kind of fast. I ran where I thought they might have trouble following me.'

'And you wore black,' he said.

14

'Isabelle told me to wear it at night, just in case.'

He pulled on to the M25, glancing into the side mirror to make sure the way was clear.

'I'm sorry she was right,' he said.

'Me too,' Allie replied, slipping further down into her seat, and watching the cars slip behind them as he sped up. Now that she was warm and safe, all the adrenaline drained from her body. Her eyelids drooped.

'What about my parents?' she asked, weariness making her voice thick.

'Isabelle will phone them and explain,' he said. 'They'll know you're safe.'

Allie rested her head against the seatback.

'Good,' she murmured. 'I don't want them to be scared.'

In a few minutes she was asleep.

A cool breeze woke her some time later. She sat up with a start.

The car wasn't moving. The driver's side door was open – she was alone.

The night around her seemed unnaturally quiet after London. There were no sounds of traffic. No sirens. She could hear low voices nearby – a man and a woman talking quietly.

Sitting up, she ran her hands through her mussed hair.

'You're certain no one followed you?' the woman asked.

'Positive,' Rachel's dad replied.

'Poor thing. She must be exhausted,' the woman said. 'I didn't wake Rachel; we can tell her in the morning.'

Allie opened the car door and their conversation stopped.

Mr Patel was talking to a woman with light brown hair and

fair skin. She wore jeans and a long blue cardigan, which she'd belted tight across her torso.

'Um ... hi,' Allie said, uncertainly.

'Allie,' Mr Patel said, 'this is Rachel's mum, Linda.'

It was so dark around them, Allie could see very little. She could just make out the shape of a building behind them – one light on in a ground-floor room. An open door.

She was still trying to orient herself when Mrs Patel put her arm around her shoulders and ushered her to the house. 'I think it's a cup of hot chocolate and bed for you, Allie. I've put a few of Rachel's things in your room – they might be a bit big but you should be able to make them work. It's only for a short time anyway.'

A steaming mug was placed in her tired hands then Mrs Patel led her up a flight of stairs to a spacious room with thick cream-coloured carpet and pale yellow walls. The lamp by the bed cast the room in a soft light and the double bed, covered in a lemony duvet, was made and turned down.

'The bathroom is there.' Mrs Patel pointed at a door. 'And the clothes I've left you are in the dresser. Make yourself at home. Rachel will come to get you in the morning and bring you down to breakfast. Sleep well. We'll talk it all over in the morning.' With a reassuring smile, she closed the door behind her.

Allie sat on the bed for a long moment. She knew she should get up and wash her face. Find something to sleep in. Figure out where exactly she was.

Instead she kicked off her shoes and lay back against the pillows. Then, rolling on to her side, she curled up into a tight ball and counted her breaths.

THREE

'**W**elcome back.' After running lightly down the old stone stairs in front of the intimidating Victorian brick building that held Cimmeria Academy, Isabelle le Fanult pulled Allie into a warm hug. 'I'm so glad to see you in one piece!'

'It's good to be whole.' Allie grinned at the headmistress.

After the London rescue, she'd spent a few days sheltering with the Patels, which consisted mainly of hanging out by the pool and, memorably, riding a horse for the first time.

Clearly seeing a girl in need of a parent, Mrs Patel had overfed Allie and fretted about her safety, while Rachel's younger sister, Minal, followed them everywhere, eager to be included in everything they did. In some ways it was bittersweet; the Patels were the kind of family Allie had always wanted. The kind of family hers had almost been once.

But Rachel's father and Isabelle had decided they'd be safer at Cimmeria. So even though school didn't start for another ten days, Mr Patel had driven the girls back.

The school looked the same as it had in the summer – huge, solid and intimidating. The three-storey red-brick building towered over them – its slate roof a range of Gothic peaks and valleys where wrought iron finials thrust into the sky like an armoury of dark knives. Symmetrical rows of arched windows seemed to watch them as they pulled their bags from the car.

The headmistress had pulled her light brown hair back tightly with a clip, and wore a white Cimmeria polo shirt over a pair of jeans. Allie couldn't remember ever seeing her in jeans before.

'Thank you for sending Mr P. to save me,' Allie said. 'I don't know what would have happened without him.'

'You followed my instructions perfectly.' Even on a cloudy day like today the headmistress' golden-brown eyes seemed to glow. 'You were very brave. I can't tell you how proud of you I am.'

Blushing, Allie looked down at her feet.

'And Rachel, my star student.' Smoothly deflecting attention, Isabelle turned. 'Thank heaven you're back; the library needs you. Eloise will be so glad you're here. Hello, Raj.' As she shook Rachel's father's hand she arched one eyebrow. 'Or should I call you, Mr P.?'

'If you must.' His smile was wry. 'I seem to have no say in the matter.'

Turning back to the stack of luggage beside the car, Isabelle said, 'I assume most of these hold your books, Rachel? You *can* leave them here between terms, you know. We won't throw them away.'

Grinning, Rachel picked up one of her bags and heaved it over her shoulder. 'You know how I am, Isabelle . . . '

'Indeed I do. Well let's get you settled in. Everybody's busy with the repair work, so we're more on our own than usual.'

The headmistress picked up a bag and walked briskly to the door. The others lumbered themselves with luggage and followed her through the grand entryway with its stained glass window, dull on this cloudy day with no sun to illuminate it. Allie noticed the fanciful unicorn tapestry usually found hanging near the door was missing. And it soon became clear much more had changed since she'd last seen the school on the night it nearly burned down.

'Carter, Sylvain and Jo are here already.' Isabelle's voice echoed as they walked across the stone floor towards the grand hallway. 'Jules will be back in the next few days, as will Lucas and a few of the older students, but we'll be a small group until term starts.'

In the wide, main hallway, the wood floors were covered in an inelegant carpet of dirty canvas dust sheets. The dozens of oil paintings that usually brightened the glossy oak wall panelling had all been removed. Without them the space felt oddly naked and, to Allie, disturbingly impermanent.

Ahead, Isabelle was still talking cheerfully but Allie noticed how high-pitched she sounded; she could hear the strain the headmistress was trying to hide.

'Because some rooms were damaged in the fire, classes and bedrooms are being shifted around.' Isabelle's sensible, rubber-soled shoes gripped each step with firm assurance. 'We must be ready by the time the rest of the students begin arriving in ten days. I think you'll find volunteering to help is compulsory.'

At a brisk pace, she led them up the wide staircase, where the Edwardian crystal chandelier overhead was draped in a filmy, protective fabric that looked like a gigantic spider-web. As she trotted after the others, she could hear hammers banging somewhere, workers shouting orders and the sound of something being dragged.

She'd known repairs would be needed. Even though she'd left the day after the fire, she'd seen enough to know the work would be substantial. But somehow she hadn't envisioned the school so . . . damaged. Stripped of the art and details that had made it feel like a fairy tale castle it seemed wounded, and she trailed her hand softly up the wide, polished oak banister as if to comfort it.

At the top of the stairs they turned on to a narrower staircase which led them to another hallway and then a second set of steps. The acrid smell of smoke was stronger here and Allie's stomach churned as she remembered the night a few weeks before when she'd seen her brother, Christopher, standing down the hall, a flaming torch in one hand, as he set fire to the school.

As if she'd expected this reaction, Isabelle was by her side in an instant, putting an arm around her shoulders and turning her away from her room.

'Your room had smoke and water damage, Allie, so we've moved you down the hall.' She steered Allie past her usual door to one marked 371. 'Your things have already been moved.'

'Hey, that's right next to mine!' Rachel said, throwing open the door marked 372. As she walked in Allie heard her say, 'Hello small, rectangular personal space. How I love you.'

Isabelle opened the door to Allie's room. 'I thought you might feel better living closer to Rachel.'

The plainly furnished room smelled of the sticky-clean, chemical scent of fresh paint. Allie stood in the doorway as Isabelle fussed with the arched, shutter-style window, pushing it open to let the watery grey light flood in.

The tall bookcase was lined with the familiar spines of her small collection of books. The bed was covered in a fluffy white duvet, and a dark blue blanket was folded neatly over the footboard – just as it had been in her previous room. Everything was exactly the same.

Isabelle was already heading out of the door. 'Your parents sent some of your things over; I've put them in the wardrobe. Once you're all settled in, come and find me. Let's have a chat.'

As the door closed Allie's heart gave a happy flutter. She was back where she belonged.

This homecoming was so different from last term, when she first arrived at Cimmeria. Back then it had seemed intimidating and hateful. Most of the students had treated her like a gatecrasher at an exclusive party. Her parents had been so angry with her at the time – she'd just been arrested – they told her nothing about the school. They just drove her here and dropped her off. When Jules, the perfect, blonde prefect, showed her around on her first day she'd felt like an idiot. It was only then that she discovered its bizarre rules – all electronic devices were banned, and nobody could leave the school grounds – and the elite group known as Night

School, which gathered secretly after curfew and took part in strange training rituals other students were forbidden even to watch.

But despite all of that weirdness, only two months later, this felt like her real home.

She opened the wardrobe and lugged out the small suitcase her parents had sent. She'd been quite specific about what they were to include. Several books, all her notebooks, a few changes of clothes and ...

She smiled.

There they are. Right on top.

Her red, knee-high Doc Martins.

She caressed the scuffed, dark red leather with one hand; with the other she held the note her mother had put in the case.

'Cimmeria provides your shoes, so I don't know why you need these ...' it began.

'I know you don't, Mum,' Allie muttered with mild irritation. She scanned the rest of the note – it said nothing about what had happened in London that night. Nothing about Isabelle or Nathaniel. Nothing that *mattered*.

So they were back to pretending again, then.

Sometimes Allie felt as if she'd been accidentally scooped up from her rubbish, ordinary world and dropped into the middle of somebody else's life. A life in which everyone was at war. Now she was in the line of fire but had no idea who was doing the shooting. Although she was beginning to learn who to trust.

She hurried to empty the rest of the suitcase but it all seemed to take too long, and the case was still open on the floor when she ran out of the room. Rapping her knuckles with impatient force on Rachel's door, she walked in without waiting for an answer to find Rachel sitting on the floor surrounded by stacks of books, with an open text in her lap.

During the few days Allie had spent with Rachel's family, she'd felt as if she had the sister she'd always secretly wanted. As they'd splashed in the pool and wandered the family's well-guarded horse pastures, they'd talked about everything: Carter, Nathaniel, Allie's mother, Rachel's father. Allie felt that she could tell Rachel everything and not be judged. And she could tell her anything and know that she could trust her.

'Let's unpack later.' Allie hopped from one foot to another. 'Don't you want to see the library?'

'You mean, don't I want to go with you to find Carter?' As she closed her book and climbed to her feet, Rachel's smile was indulgent. 'Of course I do.'

On the ground floor, things were bustling. A clatter of hammering emanated from the classroom wing, and through the open door they could see workers tearing out damaged plaster. Blackened panelling leaned against a wall awaiting removal; a scorched desk was discarded nearby. Workers hustled in and out in a busy stream. Scaffolding scaled the walls in silvery mesh.

Elsewhere, though, things looked better. The dining room was undamaged, and the common room looked just as it had before the fire.

Stepping into the great hall, they saw that it was in good shape but so filled with furniture they could only just squeeze inside. Clearly furniture was being stored here from rooms being repaired.

Rachel made her way gingerly past the legs of a chair which rested on its side under a desk. 'I wonder where ...'

At that moment, the door flew open and Sylvain rushed in carrying an Oriental rug rolled into a long, heavy tube. He was so focused on getting his awkwardly shaped cargo through the doorway that for a second he didn't see them. Then he glanced up and his vivid blue eyes met Allie's. Startled, he lost his footing and the rug swung wildly. Allie and Rachel ducked out of the way as he struggled to regain control, finally dropping the rug on to the floor with a dusty thud.

In the silence that followed, Allie noticed how his dark wavy hair had tumbled over his forehead. His tawny skin glistened from exertion. Then she wondered why she'd noticed that.

She nearly jumped when Rachel spoke. 'Hi, Sylvain. We didn't mean to startle you.'

'Hello, Rachel. Welcome back.'

Hearing his familiar voice with its elegant French accent, Allie felt an indefinable surge of emotion. As if she'd moved, he turned back to her.

'Hello, Allie,' he said quietly.

'Hey, Sylvain.' She swallowed nervously. 'I ... I mean ... How are you?'

'I'm well.'

His oddly formal vocal cadence made him sound more sophisticated than his seventeen years, and when Allie had first met him just a word could make her melt.

But that was then.

'How are you?' he asked. As their awkward conversation continued, Rachel backed towards the door.

'I'm just going to ...' she explained vaguely before dashing out.

When she was gone, Allie took a step closer to Sylvain, trying to read his guarded expression. 'I'm ... OK.' Her throat tightened and she swallowed hard. 'I ... just ... I never got a chance. To thank you, I mean. After the fire.' She reached towards his arm. 'You saved my life, Sylvain.'

When she touched him, a spark of electricity shocked them both. Yanking her hand free with a yelp, Allie jumped backwards, tripping over the rug. Sylvain grabbed her arm to steady her, but quickly let go and stepped away from her.

This wasn't at all the way Allie had visualised this meeting. She'd wanted to be cool. Not a clumsy oaf stumbling over rugs and electrocuting him with her *skin*.

The colour rose in her cheeks. 'I'm sorry. I have to ... go and ...' Without finishing her sentence she fled the room.

When she was safely around the corner she stopped and leaned back against the wall, squeezing her eyes shut.

Replaying the scene in her mind, she banged her head rhythmically against the wall behind her.

'Hi, Sylvain,' she muttered sarcastically between thumps. 'I'm a complete moron. You?'

With a sigh, she straightened and stepped out into the hallway, running straight into Carter's arms. Laughing, he lifted her off the ground. 'I heard a nasty rumour you were back.'

His shirt was covered in paint spatters and his hair was a mess. A smudge of white paint marked his forehead endearingly. His hands were strong and warm on her waist. After her awkward encounter with Sylvain, just being with Carter was like a balm for her soul.

'Bad news travels fast,' she said, raising her lips up to his.

The kiss spread warmth through her body, and she parted her lips to his, tightening her arms around his shoulders. After a moment, he leaned his forehead against hers, whispering, 'God, I've missed you.'

She smiled into his eyes, still holding on to him. 'Right back at ya.'

'You look great,' he said, straightening. 'Are you great? When Isabelle told me what happened in London. I was ...' His voice trailed off and a muscle worked in his jaw. 'Well, by the time she told me about it we knew you were safe but ... You're really OK, right?'

'Yeah, I'm good,' Allie said. 'Rachel's dad came to my rescue. He's ... I don't know ... a rock star.'

'Yeah, he's supposed to be the real deal,' Carter said, smiling. 'Even Zelazny talks about him like he's Batman.'

At the mention of her least favourite teacher's name, Allie made a sour face.

Jokingly, Carter shook his finger at her. 'You two need to learn how to get along, Allie.'

'I know, I know,' she muttered. 'But it's not my fault – he hated me first. I just hate him back.'

'That,' he laughed, 'is the lamest excuse I've ever heard.'

She couldn't believe she was here at last – sparring with Carter. She squeezed his hand with sudden happiness. 'I really have missed you, you know.'

Pulling her into a nook behind the main staircase, he kissed her again, more passionately this time. His lips trailed down her jaw to her neck, raising a Braille pattern of goosebumps.

She pressed her fingertips tightly into the lean muscles of his shoulders and he gave a small gasp of pleasure, raising his lips to hers.

'Oh, Carter. There you are.'

At the sound of Isabelle's voice, Carter spun around. Smoothing her hair, Allie tried to look innocent but Isabelle's knowing look told her she wasn't fooling anyone.

'Eloise is looking for you. And, Allie, she would really appreciate your help, too,' the headmistress said. 'If you're not busy, that is.'

She walked away without another word.

Allie's face flushed at her tart tone but Carter's shoulders shook with repressed laughter.

'I don't see how that's so funny,' Allie said primly, but Carter just laughed harder and pulled her gently in the direction of the library.

'Come on, Al. You know Isabelle's cool. She's not going to give us detention for a bit of snogging.' When she continued to pout, he tickled her until she laughed and pulled away.

As soon as they neared the library door, though, her mood changed. Dropping his hand, she slowed her steps, finally coming to a halt.

A step ahead of her, Carter stopped to look back, concern in his dark eyes.

'Have you been back there since the fire?'

Her eyes locked on the door, she shook her head mutely.

'You want to go in there now?'

She shook her head again. 'Nope. Not one bit.'

He reached for her hand.

'You don't have to do this, you know,' he said gently. 'You could give yourself some more time.'

Not taking her eyes off the door, which seemed to loom before her, she nodded.

'I know. But the thing is, the longer I wait, the harder it's going to be,' she said, her eyes flickering off his and back to the door. 'I need to get it over with. I mean, I can't just not go to the library. This is where they keep all the knowledge.'

Her weak joke didn't fool him and he held on tightly to her hand.

'Well. Just keep breathing, OK?'

Her eyes still focused on the heavy, oak wood of the door, she nodded. She knew perfectly well that it was just an ordinary door with an ordinary room behind it. But it was the room where she'd nearly died.

Watching her expression, Carter reached for the door handle. 'Ready?'

Her heart thudding in her ears, she nodded.

The door swung open.

'Oh my God,' she whispered, covering her mouth with her hands.

Everything at the front of the once-beautiful room had been destroyed. All that was left of the tall, old librarian's desk that had stood near the door for decades was a scorched square on the floor. Rows of tall bookcases were gone, too, and a section of the eighteenth-century wood panelling with its elaborate carving had burnt to ash. The acrid stench of smoke hung in the air.

'It looks bad, I know,' Carter said, 'but, trust me, it's a lot better than it was.'

An unexpected wave of grief washed over Allie. Before the fire, this had been one of her favourite places at Cimmeria. It was always crowded with students sitting in its deep leather chairs, resting their feet on soft Oriental rugs, reading by the light of the green-shaded lamps.

All gone now.

The furniture had been removed and the bare, scorched floor looked old and abandoned.

'It's ruined,' she whispered.

'I had the same reaction when I first saw it.' Eloise Derleth's voice was sympathetic. Her long dark hair was tied back in a ponytail, and her white T-shirt and jeans were as paint-stained as Carter's. She even had paint on the frames of her glasses.

'Hello, Allie,' she said. 'Welcome back.'

'Eloise, I can't believe it.' Allie's voice was thick with emotion as she turned to the young librarian. 'Your beautiful library!'

Eloise looked around the room, her expression stoic. 'It isn't as bad as it looks. In some ways we were quite lucky.'

She walked to where her desk used to be. 'We lost all the records that were kept here and that's a tragedy because they dated back a century. But the older records are stored in the attic and they're safe.'

Gesturing at a burnt area where a row of bookcases had towered to the ceiling, she said, 'The books here were the newest acquisitions, which meant that they had the least value. The ancient Greek, Latin and other antiquarian books were across the room, and almost all of them survived the fire, although quite a few have water or smoke damage. But we've hired one of the best restoration companies in the world and they're doing all they can to save them. So you see?' Her smile was tight with grim determination. 'Things could have been worse.'

All Allie could see was disaster but she wasn't about to say so. She knew the fire must have broken Eloise's heart.

She forced a smile.

'It's totally fixable. What can I do to help?'

FOUR

'I can't quite get to that spot, there.' Allie pointed to a smoke-stained section of library wall, just out of reach of her scrubbing brush. 'Even when I stand on my toes.'

Bob Ellison glanced at it over the top of his wire-framed glasses. 'Just reach up as far as you can. The ladder crews will be in later and they'll do high walls and ceilings.'

Normally the school's groundskeeper, Mr Ellison was now overseeing the day-to-day organisation of the repair work. He'd put Allie in among those who were scrubbing the library walls to prepare the room for painting. Wearing bulky, bright yellow rubber gloves that stretched up to her elbows, she dipped a scrubbing brush as big as a brick into a bucket and scrubbed until dirty water ran down the wall on to the dust sheet below.

'This would be more fun with an iPod,' she muttered, scrubbing fiercely. Cimmeria allowed no modern technology – no computers, mobile phones or televisions.

'No it wouldn't.'

At the sound of the familiar voice, Allie spun around to see a slim girl with short blonde hair smiling at her with uncharacteristic shyness.

'Nothing could make this fun.'

'Jo!' With a splash, Allie dropped the brush into the bucket and ran over to her. 'I'm so glad to see you.'

Caution in her eyes, Jo held her gaze. 'I wondered if you would be.'

Jo's breakdown at the end of the summer term had thrown Allie's already shaky world into turmoil. And it had been Jo's boyfriend, Gabe, who killed Ruth at the summer ball. Jo had handled it all very badly, covering up for Gabe, even when she knew lives were in danger.

But Allie had been arrested three times herself; she knew all about bad choices. 'Of course I am.' Noticing the bucket and brush at Jo's feet, she quickly changed the subject – now wasn't the time to delve into all that had happened last term. 'You're on bucket brigade, too?'

Jo nodded.

'You can be my iPod. Mr Ellison.' Allie turned to the groundskeeper who was busy with his clipboard. 'Can Jo work with me?'

'As long as you do as much working as you do talking.' The gruffness in his voice was betrayed by the amusement in his eyes and Allie smiled broadly.

'Awesome sauce.' Jo set her bucket down a few feet from Allie's. 'When did you get back?'

'A couple of hours ago. We took one look at the place and . . .' Allie waved her scrubbing brush.

Jo pulled on her rubber gloves with a snap. 'Rachel's with you?'

'Yeah – she's at the back going through books with Eloise and the guys from the restoration company.' Allie scrubbed the wall in loose circles. 'I think she got the better job.'

'Totally,' Jo said. 'Hey – I heard about what happened in London. You OK?'

'Hey, it takes more than four big muscly guys in suits running really fast to hurt me,' Allie joked.

'That's what they say about you.' Jo smiled.

But after a moment she looked more serious. Lowering her voice, she said, 'It wasn't Gabe, was it? I mean, he wasn't one of them?'

Shocked, Allie nearly dropped her brush.

'Oh, Jo, no! I promise. These guys were older – like in their twenties or even older than that. Definitely not Gabe. I'd never seen any of them before.'

'Good.' Jo returned to scrubbing, nodding to herself as if this was what she'd hoped to hear. 'I just can't bear to think . . . ' Her voice broke and she scrubbed harder, turning her head so Allie couldn't see her face.

Allie scrubbed the wall absently as she tried to decide what to say. 'Have you . . . heard from him since that night?'

Jo shook her head vigorously, and she looked so sad it tugged at Allie's heart.

'Are you OK?' she asked.

Jo's brush stopped moving but it was a long second before she replied.

'I don't know.' She spoke slowly. 'When everybody left

and there were just a few of us here and everything was burnt it was . . . bad. I felt,' her voice was so low Allie could hardly hear it, 'responsible, you know? Like I could have stopped it.'

Before Allie could decide what to say to that, Jo continued, only now her voice had changed and she spoke briskly, as if she were repeating something she'd memorised. 'But Isabelle and Eloise were great, and I'm seeing this counsellor. And it's all helping. Everyone keeps telling me I'm not the worst person ever in the history of the world, but I still feel kind of . . . I don't know . . . Like the worst person ever in the history of the world, I guess.'

Her laugh was as brittle as thin ice. At that moment Allie wanted to forgive her. After all, she wasn't the one who'd killed Ruth. Gabe did that. But she also hadn't gone for help when she found out what Gabe had done. Even after he threatened Allie's life.

And that's where it all gets a bit twisted, she thought.

But Jo was looking at her with expectation in her crystalline blue eyes. She had been Allie's best friend before everything went wrong. And she wasn't a bad person, really. She was just . . . What had Rachel called her? Fragile.

When she spoke, Allie chose her words carefully. 'Listen, Jo. Gabe did this, not you. Gabe is the murderer, not you. Gabe is the worst person in the history of the world. Not you. OK?'

Allie was talking as much to herself as to Jo, and the relief on Jo's face was her reward. She only wished she was certain she meant it.

*

'Help,' Jo moaned. 'I think I'm in a coma.'

It was seven o'clock. The library walls were scrubbed clean and Allie's neck and shoulders ached whenever she even thought about raising her arms as she sat on the dust sheet next to Jo.

'Do your arms hurt?' Allie asked, rubbing her shoulders.

'God yes.'

'Then you're not in a coma.' Gingerly Allie stretched out her legs. 'Jesus. What have I got myself into? Rachel has a swimming pool and horses. *Horses*, Jo. I could be floating in a pool and petting soft pony noses if I were still at her house.'

'Here.' Jo turned to face her. 'My nose is soft. You can pet it.'

Allie stroked her nose tiredly. 'Wow. This is just like being at Rachel's. Where's the pool?'

'No pool,' Jo said. 'Showers.'

'Sucks.'

'Totally.'

'Are you two just going to lie there complaining? Or are you coming to dinner?' Allie looked up to see Carter standing above them, studying them doubtfully.

'Jo's in a coma,' Allie informed him. 'She no longer needs food.'

'Wait. Did you say food? I think I'm actually awake.' Jo scrambled to her feet.

'My God,' Allie said mildly. 'It's a miracle.'

'You've only been doing this one day, Sheridan.' Carter reached down to pull her up. 'You can't be tired already.'

'Everything hurts,' she said. 'Shoulders, arms, back ...'

'Legs, feet, head ...' Jo offered helpfully.

'Ankles. Shins. Name a body part,' Allie said. 'It hurts.'

Carter didn't look impressed.

'Food will ease your pain.' He steered them towards the dining hall.

'He's very wise,' Allie told Jo.

'Clearly,' Jo replied.

With most of the students still away, only a few tables were set up. Eloise sat at one with Jerry Cole, the science teacher, and a few others. At another, Sylvain sat alone.

Allie felt her heart sink. She hadn't thought about sitting at meals with both Carter and Sylvain.

This is going to be weird.

But Jo saved the day, sinking into the seat next to Sylvain. 'Help me, Sylvain,' she said piteously. 'I hurt.'

'What happened?' Rachel appeared, pulling out the chair next to Allie's. 'Why does Jo hurt?'

'We worked ourselves into a coma,' Allie explained.

'Tell me about it. I've loved books all my life but why does this school need so many?' Rachel groaned, stretching. 'How much learning do we really need?'

'Can we go back to your house?' Allie asked. 'It was nicer there.'

'You are all infants.' Carter sounded exasperated. 'I've moved furniture all day. All you did was wash walls and pick up books.'

'Whatever,' the girls chorused.

As if on cue, the doors at the end of the room opened, and staff appeared carrying trays of food. Steaming bowls of pasta were placed at every table.

'Oh good,' Carter muttered sarcastically. 'Pasta again.'

'Awesome.' Jo brightened. 'Is it the cheesy kind?'

'Why did you say "again"?' Allie asked as bowls of food were set on the table.

'We've had it almost every day.' Carter lowered his voice as the waiters passed. 'Cooks are too busy helping out with repairs to do much else.'

'Did everybody hear about Lisa?' Jo changed the subject, as bowls of food were passed around the table and a low buzz of quiet conversation filled the room.

'What about her?' Allie asked as she served herself from a heaped bowl.

'She's not coming back.'

Allie dropped the serving spoon with a bang.

'What?' Everybody seemed to say the same word at once. Then they talked over one another. 'Why not?' 'What happened?' 'Is she OK?'

Jo held up a hand for quiet. 'Her parents decided, after all that happened last term . . . ' She shrugged. 'She wants to come back but they've forbidden it. They're sending her to some school in Switzerland.'

A stunned silence followed.

'Well, I can't say I completely blame them.' Rachel's expression was sober. 'I doubt she'll be the only one who doesn't come back.'

'Maybe next year they'll let her come back– it's our last year,' Jo said.

'You mean,' Rachel's tone was wry, 'if nobody gets killed this term maybe they'll let her come back?'

'Basically,' Jo said.

A long, awkward silence fell, then Allie held up her water glass.

'Here's to Lisa. And nobody getting killed.'

The others raised their glasses, too.

'To Lisa,' they chorused.

'And not dying,' Jo said.

At the end of the meal Carter caught Allie's eye when nobody was looking and tilted his head towards the door. Something in his expression made tingles of anticipation dance in her stomach. But they'd only made it halfway across the dining hall when Isabelle intercepted them.

'Oh, Allie, good. I was looking for you. Shall we have that chat now?'

Allie met Carter's gaze for one desperate second before hurrying after her.

Isabelle's office was just beyond the main staircase, its door so smoothly integrated into the polished oak panelling it was hard to see if you didn't know it was there. As Allie dropped down into one of the two leather chairs in front of her desk, Isabelle switched on the kettle in the corner. As she busied herself making tea, Allie noticed that the normally neat and elegant office was dishevelled. Papers were stacked high on every surface, file cabinet drawers were half open and a cardigan had been tossed on to an empty chair atop an open briefcase.

A frown creased her brow but before she could say anything, Isabelle pressed a steaming mug into her hands, cleared the mess of papers from the chair next to her and dropped into it with a tired sigh. Up close, Allie could see dark circles under her golden brown eyes – she looked thinner. But her demeanour was as soothing as ever as she lifted the glasses off the top of her head and set them down on the table beside her.

Allie expected her to start by talking about what had happened that night in London – they'd already discussed it briefly on the phone but she was sure Isabelle would have more information for her now. So the headmistress' first words took her by surprise.

'So, tell me. While you were home, did you have a chance to talk with your mother about Lucinda?' Isabelle's tone was brisk, almost businesslike.

'Yes.' Allie held her gaze. 'And now I know.'

'Tell me what happened.'

It had only been a week ago but it felt much longer since she'd sat down with her mother at home in London and demanded an explanation. For everything.

'I told her you said she had to tell me.'

Isabelle watched her closely. 'And what did she say?'

Allie remembered the way her mother's lips had tightened, and the sad look on her face, when Allie said: 'This Lucinda person . . . She's my grandmother, isn't she?'

For a fleeting second she'd thought her mother would lie, and if she had she would never have forgiven her. But after a second her shoulders had drooped. 'I always knew you'd find out someday. Especially after you went to Cimmeria. Yes, Allie, Lucinda is my mother – your grandmother.'

Since she'd been so confident that this would be the answer, Allie should have been ready to hear it. Instead she felt as if the air had left her lungs. She'd grown up thinking all her grandparents were dead.

And now I have a living grandmother.

She leaned back a little on the chair and stared at her mother as if she'd never seen her before. 'Why? Why would you lie to me about something like that? We could have got to know each other . . . '

'I know it's hard for you to believe this,' her mother kept her voice gentle but firm, 'but everything I have ever done was to protect you. To keep you safe.'

'But you let me believe she was dead. All my life you let me think that.' Allie had stared at her mother, hurt and disbelief making her chest ache. 'How could you do that?'

Her mother took a sharp breath. 'It is . . . it *was* a terrible thing to do. And I am sorry. I just didn't know what else to do. Maybe I should have just told you the truth. But I was afraid if I did you'd insist on meeting her, and then everything would have been ruined.'

Allie was baffled. 'How would my knowing my own grandmother have ruined everything?'

'Because then she would have had you,' her mother said without hesitation. 'And I would have lost you.'

Dropping her chin to her chest, Allie closed her eyes and fought for calm.

Another non-explanation. Another random statement.

This time she wasn't going to let her mother get away with this stuff.

'What?' Her voice was sarcastic. 'She would have kidnapped me?'

But her mother didn't back down. 'You don't understand, Alyson. You've never met her. Lucinda ... your grandmother is a powerful and dangerous person. She gets what she wants – it's just how she is. Nothing gets in her way. I ... ' She'd stopped and thought for a moment; when she started again, her voice was quiet. 'When I was your age, I was very different from her. She is a very controlling person, and she dictated my life down to the most elemental detail. What I wore, who I knew, what I studied, where I went – everything was decided by her. At first I accepted it, but as I grew older I rebelled. I didn't want to be like her. I didn't want to be rich and miserable. I didn't want what she had. I wanted to be myself. To make my own decisions.' She looked at Allie searchingly. 'I should think if anyone would understand that, it would be you.'

And Allie did. But it still didn't make sense. 'Fine. If she was like that, then running away was the right thing to do. But lying to me about it wasn't right. I have to make my own decisions too. Just like you did.'

A bitter smile curved her mother's lips. 'Isabelle says exactly the same thing. But neither of you is Lucinda's daughter, so neither of you knows what she's really like.'

'Mum, who is Lucinda? And why are you so scared of her? I get that she's some huge bigwig. But who is she really? The Queen? God?'

She hadn't liked her mother's ironic smile.

'Not quite,' she said. 'But close.'

Allie studied her warily. 'What does that mean?'

Her mother spoke very deliberately. 'Her last name is Meldrum.'

That time Allie couldn't pretend not to be shocked. 'No. Way.'

'My grandmother is Lucinda Meldrum.' Allie said now; Isabelle inclined her head very slightly, as if to confirm that information.

The words still felt odd in Allie's mouth. How could it be? Lucinda Meldrum was the most famous woman in British politics. The first female Chancellor, and now head of the World Bank, she advised presidents, prime ministers and kings. Even Rachel had been impressed when Allie told her.

'Thank you for convincing Mum to tell me about Lucinda. I don't know if she would have admitted it otherwise, and it meant a lot to me to know the truth.'

'It was time for you to know,' the headmistress said. 'Past time.' She straightened in her chair. 'Allie, I know you'll have more questions about what this means for you and your place in Night School, but first I need to talk to you about the incident in London, and explain what's going to happen next.'

Although Allie didn't react, a rush of excitement sped her heart rate.

'As you know by now,' Isabelle continued, 'there should have been somebody watching your house that night – somebody was always there while you were home.'

Allie nodded.

'But the guard left shortly after 11 p.m. after receiving a panicked text from his wife telling him their child was critically ill. He called Raj to warn him – he actually spoke to Raj, who personally authorised his departure.'

When Isabelle paused, Allie felt goosebumps rise on her arms. Before the headmistress said her next words, she knew what they would be.

'Except Raj never received that call. He never spoke to the man. And the guard's wife never sent the text. There was no problem with their child.'

'Nathaniel,' Allie breathed.

Isabelle nodded. 'The guard's phone records bear out his story – he did call Raj in a phone call lasting several minutes. That call was diverted.'

Remembering that night – the footsteps thundering after her – Allie wanted to punch something.

'*Why?*' She set her mug down with a bang; the milky tea sloshed dangerously. 'Why is he doing this, Isabelle? I don't understand. What is so important that he would try so hard?'

A long moment passed as the headmistress seemed to struggle to decide what to say.

'The history of Nathaniel's obsession is long,' Isabelle said. 'And if I try to explain it now we'll be here for hours. But you should know that you are not what he really wants. What he really wants ... is me.'

'You?' Allie stared. 'I don't get it.'

Isabelle rubbed her fingertips against her temples. 'It really would take me ages to tell you the whole story but, suffice it to say, he and I have very different views on how the world should be run. But I have Lucinda's ear, so my views hold more sway. She doesn't always do what I tell her but she listens to me.' She picked up her teacup and took a reflective sip. 'And that is what Nathaniel is trying to change.'

Her brow creased with thought, Allie tried to put the pieces of the trouble together. 'I'm sorry but I still don't understand. What exactly does he want?'

'Don't apologise. Nathaniel's obsession is a kind of madness. So not understanding it is logical.' Isabelle's smile was sad. 'He doesn't want Cimmeria. He wants to use the school as a stepping stone. You see, what he really wants is the larger organisation of which Cimmeria and Night School are just a small part. Lucinda is head of that organisation. And I am her closest advisor.' She studied Allie as if trying to ascertain if she understood the import of what she was saying. 'We are a powerful group, Allie ... and he wants it all.'

'How would Cimmeria help him get the organisation?'

'It's hard to explain, but the Cimmeria is where it all began – it's the heart, if you will, of the group. The Cimmeria Board doesn't just run the school, those same people run the entire organisation. We are at the core of it all.' Isabelle made a sweeping gesture with her arms. 'So if he can get rid of me he can then eliminate Lucinda. Then he thinks the board will put him in charge. It's a mad plan but he believes it will work. That's what he's working on, that's what he's been doing – trying to make it appear that I can't even control a school or protect my students ...' The tendons in her throat tightened as her voice trailed off. 'Well,' she said after a second. 'You get the idea.' She reached over and straightened a pile of papers at the edge of her desk. 'You are a pawn on his playing board. And I am the rook. Protecting the queen.'

'Queen Lucinda,' Allie murmured, thoughtfully. She looked

up at the headmistress. 'Why does he hate you and Lucinda so much?'

Isabelle's gaze was chilly. 'That,' she said with finality, 'is a conversation for another time.'

'But,' Allie persisted, her mind whirring through the possible escape routes, 'surely Lucinda can stop him? If you tell her what's happened and that I'm in danger . . . She wouldn't want bad things to happen to me. Surely she'd help?'

An uncomfortable pause fell.

'Lucinda is aware of what's been occurring.' Isabelle's tone was careful. 'And she is not willing to become involved at this time.'

'What?' Allie couldn't believe it. 'Why not?'

The headmistress shot her a warning look and when she spoke she used her most authoritative tone. 'I know you want to know everything, Allie, but just trust me when I tell you, this is complicated. Now, we must protect ourselves and not wait for a rescue from Lucinda or anybody else. So I have hired Raj and his company to protect the school. He knows more about Nathaniel than anyone. Except me.'

She said the last words so quietly Allie hardly heard them as she stared at her hands. She felt mutinous. Once again, her safety was being entrusted to other people. Once again, she was powerless. When she glanced up, Isabelle was studying her as if she knew what she was thinking.

'And you have a role to play, Allie.' Her voice was gentler now. 'In London you showed tremendous calmness under pressure. You were innovative and fast. You followed my directions perfectly in a situation where very few people would have been able to do so. Based on that, as well as your vastly improved marks over the summer term, I have recommended that you be accepted into Night School on an accelerated training module.'

Allie was so excited she quit breathing. 'I . . . I . . .'

'Training this term will focus on self-defence, and you'll work very closely with people who are highly skilled.' As Isabelle reached for Allie's hand the intensity in her eyes was almost frightening. 'What happened to you in London should never happen again.'

FİVE

Allie hurtled out of Isabelle's office into the hallway, fairly dancing with excitement. She turned right, then left, then stopped and spun in a circle, giddy.

Carter, she thought. *I have to tell Carter.*

She ran across the canvas dust sheets thinking about how great things were going to be now. She and Carter could train together. He could give her tips. They could spend loads of time together.

And we won't have to keep secrets from each other any more.

He wasn't in the common room. And when she yanked open the dining hall door, the empty room echoed with the ghostly sound of dishes clinking in the unseen kitchen.

As she rounded the corner towards the classroom wing, she barely avoided colliding with Rachel who was coming the other way with an armload of books.

'Oh hi,' Rachel said, unruffled as ever. 'What's up?'

Allie meant to be cool, to say nothing about her new status. Besides, she was forbidden to talk about Night School. But it all burst out in a tangled rush.

'I just had a meeting with Isabelle! I'm going to be in Night School! Advanced training module! Have you seen Carter?'

'Oh.' Instead of looking happy for her Rachel looked as wounded as if Allie had slapped her. But all she said was, 'No, I haven't seen Carter.' Then she turned and walked away.

For a long second Allie just gaped at her back, then, as if she'd only just realised she could move, she ran after her.

'Rachel? Hey. Don't run off like that. I've just broken like ninety-seven rules by telling you and you seem . . . ' Catching up with her, Allie touched her arm. 'What's the matter?'

'I just . . . I can't believe after everything that happened over the summer, you want to be part of that.' Holding the books against her hip, she shoved an errant dark curl out of almond-shaped eyes filled with anger. 'I thought you were smarter than that.'

'Hey,' Allie said, wounded. 'Ouch, Rach. Don't be mean. Let's talk about this.'

'You think I'm mean?' Rachel shook her head in despair. 'I'm trying to save you, Allie. Night School isn't just a school thing – crazy times to look back on later when we're old and boring. It's for life. I've seen what it did to my dad, Allie. *They own him.* This is his whole life for ever. You shouldn't be a part of it. But if you are . . . ' She took a step away. 'Well, I'm not in it, so we can't talk about it any more. You could get in trouble – a *lot* of trouble – if you talk about it to me or anybody else who's not in it.'

Rachel walked away, and this time Allie let her go, glancing to either side as if there were people next to her sharing her bewilderment.

What the hell just happened?

Muttering to herself, she climbed the stairs to the girls' dorm. As she opened her bedroom door, she was so deep in thought that she didn't notice the light was already on until she saw something move.

Jumping back, she gave a small scream.

'Hey,' Carter said sleepily. 'Don't call the cops. It's just me.'

Still upset about her encounter with Rachel, Allie glared at him, her panicked heart slowly returning to normal speed.

'What are you doing in here?' Even though the wing was virtually empty, she lowered her voice to a whisper out of habit; boys weren't allowed in the girls' dorm. 'You scared the crap out of me.'

'Sorry. I was just waiting for you to get back so we could talk.' Carter's dark hair was rumpled and his face was flushed. 'I guess I dozed off. You were ages.'

'Yeah, well, first I had to talk to Isabelle and then Rachel was pissed off with me.' Her voice sounded more snappish than she intended but she couldn't seem to stop it. 'That stuff takes time.'

'Rachel was pissed off?' Carter cocked his head to one side. 'What happened?'

Without thinking, Allie launched into her account of their encounter in the hallway. 'I told her I was going to be in Night School and she ranted at me about how it would ruin my life and I was stupid and it was evil ... What's the matter?'

Carter's hands had dropped to his sides as he stared at her. 'You're going to be in Night School? Isabelle actually said that?'

Nobody was reacting the way she'd thought they would.

Where's the joy at my big opportunity? Where's the 'Yay Allie'?

'God, what's wrong with everyone?' She threw up her hands. 'Why isn't anyone happy for me?'

'I'm sorry ... I'm just surprised.' Carter seemed unsure of what to say. 'I didn't think ... We hadn't really talked ... ' He pulled himself together. 'It's a big deal, Allie.'

'I know it's a big deal. I'm not a complete idiot.' Her voice rose sharply. 'And I was all excited about it until I started telling people and everybody acted like I'd just told them I had *tuberculosis*. Now I'm all, like ... What*ever*.'

Fully aware she was the picture of self-pity, she flopped down on the bed.

After a second, Carter sat next to her and took her hand, twining his fingers between hers. Even in the midst of her misery, she liked the way his hand felt – warm and strong.

'Look,' he said, 'I'm glad you're excited. I just need a couple of minutes to sort of process this. What exactly did Isabelle say?'

'She said I'd showed, like, grace under pressure, or something, in London, and that I was ... I don't know ... I had good marks. And that I needed to be able to protect myself so she was putting me in Night School on an accelerated training module.'

Carter gave a low whistle. 'Accelerated module? They never do that. Are you sure?'

Allie nodded so vigorously her hair bounced.

'Bloody hell,' he said, mostly to himself.

'What does it mean?' she asked.

'She didn't tell you?'

When she shook her head, he exhaled loudly.

'It just means you'll skip the early stuff that we all spend the first term doing, and you'll train with the most senior people.' He studied her with curious eyes, as if he was trying to figure her out. 'You'll go straight in at the deep end.'

Something in his tone made Allie nervous, and she was glad when he changed the subject. 'So, what exactly did Rachel say that pissed you off?'

Pulling her hand free, she twisted the hem of her shirt tightly around her finger, frowning with thought. 'She acted like it was this evil thing, and like she thought I was stupid for joining. She was really angry.' She added worriedly, 'Rachel never gets angry.'

He didn't seem very surprised. 'You know she doesn't approve of Night School, right?' he said. 'I mean, she's told you that. Everyone knows she's been asked to join several times and turned it down. And, I mean, *nobody* turns Night School down. It's a big thing between her and her dad.'

Allie's head shot up. 'What ... really? She never told me that. She just said her dad wanted her to do it and she didn't want to.'

'Yeah well ...' Carter said. 'She really hates it.'

'But why?' Allie asked. 'Why does she hate it so much?'

'Rachel's a genius, you know that. She's got political objections to it, which are totally reasonable. Night School isn't fair.

Never has been. It makes things easier for rich kids – like they need things to be easier for them.' He stretched out his legs. 'But I think there's more to it than that. Something to do with her dad. You should ask her.'

Worry twisted Allie's stomach. 'I hope she's not too mad at me. I didn't mean to be thoughtless. I just ... wasn't thinking.'

Carter barked a laugh then grew serious again. 'Al ... '

His tone was so hesitant she looked up at him with concern.

'I'm glad you'll learn to defend yourself, and obviously that's a good thing, but I have concerns, too. You know I don't trust the people running Night School – we've talked and talked about it.' When she opened her mouth to object, he rested his finger lightly on her lips. 'I know I'm in it and I'm a total hypocrite, but I had my own reasons for joining. But that doesn't mean I want you to get caught up in it, too. It kind of scares me that you're going to be right in the middle of it now.'

'Here's the thing.' She pulled his hand away from her mouth and held it against her cheek for a second before dropping it. Then, sitting straight, she filled him in on what her mother and Isabelle had told her. When she'd told him everything she finished by saying, 'I think I've been in Night School my whole life. I just didn't know it until now. And now maybe it can help me ... I don't know ... stay safe. Stay alive.'

For a long moment Carter looked away, lost in thought. Then he turned his dark eyes back to her.

'OK.'

'OK what?' she said cautiously.

'OK Night School.' His jaw was set in a grim line. 'You need to learn to defend yourself. So, welcome to Night School. I hope you don't like it too much.'

SIX

Somewhere in the dark distance she could hear voices calling her name. But she was running fast – as fast as she could.

Soon the voices faded into silence.

The night was clear – a full moon turned the forest into shades of blue as she hurtled down the footpath.

She didn't know where she was going or why she was running, but she knew she couldn't stop. Her breathing was ragged – her lungs burned. Still she ran.

Then, out of the corner of her eye, she saw something move through the trees.

It seemed to flit, like a bird, but she knew it wasn't a bird. She stopped, effortlessly.

'Who's there?' she called into the darkness then gasped when she saw someone move again. Just slow enough to be seen. Just fast enough not to be recognised.

'This isn't funny,' she called out. She'd begun to tremble. Something wasn't right. It wasn't right at all. Where was she going anyway? And why was she outside so late at night?

Suddenly, from behind her, a low, threatening growl.

With a muffled scream Allie sat bolt upright in bed. Clutching the covers to her neck, she looked around the dark room in panic. At first she was disoriented. The room wasn't familiar. Nothing was where it should be.

Then she remembered.

'Cimmeria,' she murmured, lying down again. 'I'm at Cimmeria.' She closed her eyes. 'I'm safe.'

After rushing through breakfast the next morning, Allie made an excuse to Jo and headed to the library in search of Rachel. She had to make up with her. Fighting with Rachel was absolutely not on the agenda for the first week back at school.

Just inside the library door, painters were setting up a metal forest of ladders with a clamour. Big cans of paint and fluffy pale blue rollers leaned about like fallen trees; the air already had the acrid petrol smell of white spirits.

Hurrying past them, she made her way down the long room. A wide metal table had been set up along the back wall where Eloise and Rachel were filling cardboard boxes with books. Each layer of books was separated by sheets of crisp tissue paper, and they nestled the heavy old leather tomes in as if they were fragile pieces of crystal.

Pushing her glasses back up her nose, Eloise looked at her enquiringly.

'Can I talk to Rachel for a minute?' Allie asked.

Eloise glanced back and forth between them; Rachel avoided Allie's eyes. With a sympathetic look, the librarian slid a box across the table.

'Why don't you two take this out to the truck together? It's too heavy for one person alone.'

With Allie holding one end of the box and Rachel the other, they manoeuvred through the bookcases to the back door. Outside, a white van waited, its back doors open. The driver stood a few feet away talking into a mobile phone. He paid no attention to them.

The damp morning air left a sheen of moisture on Allie's skin, like oil on water. It was quiet and grey, the only sound the crunching of their feet on the gravel drive and the driver's non-committal, monotone voice as they slid the box on top of another just like it in the back of the van.

'I'm sorry,' Allie said suddenly. 'I didn't think about how you might feel about . . . anything. I was just being selfish and . . . '

Relief filled Rachel's eyes and her words flooded out in a rush. 'Me too. You have to do what's right for you. I can't expect you to be me.'

'It's just . . . ' Allie drew a line in the grey gravel with her toe. 'I really have to do this, Rach. Not because I believe in what it all stands for, but because of what I'll learn. I'll be able to protect myself. I'll find out more about my family if I'm on the inside. They won't be able to hide things from me any more. Maybe I'll find out what happened to Christopher, because I think they know and they're not telling me. Can you see my side of this?'

'I can.'

But Allie could hear the reluctance in Rachel's tone.

'I just wish there was another way . . . for your sake. Because I think you'll get more than you bargained for once you're inside, Allie.'

Out of the corner of her eye Allie checked on the driver. He was still talking on his phone.

Seeing her glance, Rachel tilted her head towards the door. As they headed back inside she changed the subject. 'Are you working with Jo again today?'

'Painting.' Allie nodded. 'Because I'm serious about my art.'

Rachel snorted, but her expression was serious. 'How is she, do you think?'

Allie thought about Jo laughing and scrubbing walls yesterday. 'Better than I expected. She's sort of . . . fine, I guess.'

'A little too fine, maybe?' As soon as Rachel said the words, Allie realised she was right.

'Do you think she's faking it?' Allie whispered. 'I mean, Isabelle's making her see a shrink and everything.'

Rachel didn't seem reassured. 'I don't want this to sound mean, but Jo's a master at manipulation and deception – anybody who grew up the way she did would be. And she's just had this huge awful thing happen in her life yet she's still normal, bubbly Jo.' She shrugged. 'Something doesn't seem right. She could have one of her meltdowns. So, just . . . keep an eye on her.'

Allie nodded. 'I will.'

'And be careful with all this,' Rachel gesturing vaguely, '*stuff* you're getting involved with. Watch your back.'

'It's not like I'll be alone,' Allie pointed out. 'I'll have your dad to look out for me.'

She didn't like the look Rachel gave her.

'Just because he likes you, don't think he'll treat you any differently from anyone else. He's tougher than you think.'

'I'm ready,' Allie promised, wondering if she was.

'Welcome to Cimmeria Academy. All new students please line up on the left. Returning students on the right.'

Isabelle stood on a small white platform at the far end of the great hall. She wasn't shouting, but her powerful voice somehow soared above the din of two hundred chattering students. It was the first day of the autumn term, and Allie and Rachel stood in the queue on the right wearing identical crisp, white, long-sleeved shirts with dark blue crests, tucked into short, dark blue pleated skirts.

'God, I can't believe I'm saying this, but it's good to be back in this stupid uniform,' Allie said, straightening the hem of her skirt.

'I hear you.' Rachel wrinkled her nose. 'And yet I disagree.'

The two studied the new students in the queue across from them.

'They all look so young and nervous,' Allie said. 'Did I look like that when I started?'

'Of course not.' Rachel flipped her long, curly ponytail over one shoulder and quickly changed the subject. 'The place looks incredible, doesn't it?'

'Totally.' Allie followed her gaze up the walls, panelled with oak, and out into the hallway, where the polished wood floors shone and the chandeliers sparkled without a speck of dust. 'I can't believe we did it. All that work . . . ' She flexed her fingers and admired her healing blisters. 'There's still loads to do but at least the main stuff is finished.'

'And can I just say, TFFT,' Rachel replied. 'I've had enough book sorting and stacking, painting and sweeping to last a lifetime.'

The last ten days had been intense and non-stop. Walls had been scrubbed and painted, heavy Oriental rugs taken away to be cleaned then returned, floors polished, and furniture moved in and out of rooms endlessly. Each day involved a haze of work that had left her too tired at the end for anything except tumbling into bed. Many rooms were still being worked on, but enough of the building had been restored to allow the term to start on time.

'Allie.'

She turned around to see a girl studying her expressionlessly as the sunlight highlighted her long red hair and illuminated her milky white skin.

'Oh,' Allie put her hands in her pockets and tried to look casual. 'Hi, Katie.'

Katie seemed uncomfortable – she fidgeted with the hem of a dark blue jumper that Allie was certain must have been tailored to fit her so annoyingly perfectly. 'Can I talk to you for a minute?'

Allie and Rachel exchanged an intrigued look. 'I'll hold your place.' Rachel nudged her.

Allie followed Katie to a quiet corner.

'You know what happened last term, with you saving everybody and everything?' Katie said.

Thinking of a thousand sarcastic responses, Allie nodded and kept her face blank.

'And we worked together and it was all good?'

Another nod, this one suspicious.

'Well, it was important, and I'm really glad we did it, but I don't think we should be friends, OK? I mean ... despite that stuff. It was great, and you weren't as big a moron as you usually are but I can't really hang out with you. I don't really like you, to be completely honest. Well, most of the time, anyway. So what I wanted to say was, please don't expect us to be best mates or anything.'

Speechless, Allie tried to decide how to respond. An unwelcome thought crossed her mind that it seemed wrong that someone could be so pretty and so ... awful.

A long uncomfortable silence passed. Then finally, shaking her head, Allie turned and walked away. 'What*ever*.'

When she returned to her place in the queue, Rachel's eyebrows shot skyward, but Allie shook her head in disgust.

'Anyway,' Rachel said, 'where were we?'

'I think we were talking about what amazing workers we are,' Allie said, but then the absurdity of her conversation with Katie overwhelmed her and she burst into a sudden bout of uncontrollable giggles.

Rachel looked puzzled but soon was laughing along with her. 'I don't know why I'm laughing exactly but I have a pretty good idea.'

'She's just,' Allie gasped, crying with laughter, 'such a bitch.'

That sent them off again. They were still giggling as they walked up to the registration table a minute later, but Allie's smile faded when she saw Zelazny sitting rifle straight, flipping through papers on the table in front of her.

'Sheridan. Patel,' he barked, glowering at them. 'Keep it down. Patel, here's your course schedule and reading list.'

'Thanks, Mr Zelazny.' As she took the papers from him, Rachel's tone was just a little too polite to be believable.

'Sheridan,' he snapped before Rachel had finished thanking him. 'Your schedule.' Allie started to thank him but he fixed her with an icy glare. He continued, 'You have been assigned extra-curricular classes this term. You are expected at twenty-one hundred hours tonight. The location is on your sheet. Tardiness is not acceptable.'

Glancing at the paper, Allie saw the words 'Training Room One' scrawled across the top. A cold finger of fear brushed her spine. She wasn't taking PE, and she'd signed up for no extra activities. There was only one reason they would want her in a training room.

It's all starting, she thought. *It's really going to happen.*

Just after noon, Allie raced into the dining hall, stopping suddenly as a wall of noise hit her. The room was packed. The tables were all evenly spaced, filling it from one end to the other. Each surrounded by eight heavily carved chairs. The noise made by the mass of exuberant students was daunting.

Jo was waving at her enthusiastically from a table near the massive stone fireplace.

' Over here!'

Allie made her way across the room to the table where Jo sat ignoring the students around her, none of whom Allie recognised.

She patted the empty seat next to her. 'I saved you a place so you wouldn't starve. It's mad in here.'

Feeling a bit stunned, Allie swung her arm to take in the room.

'Where did they all come from?'

Jo laughed. 'I know! How different is this from summer term? The place is packed. The cheeky buggers even took our table.' She pointed at the spot in the middle of the room where they usually sat, now occupied by fresh-faced fourteen-year-olds eating in awkward silence. 'I didn't have the heart to move them.' Jo's smile was beatific. 'They're just babies. I'll get Lucas to break the news to them later. Gently.'

'You mean you'll have Lucas threaten them,' Allie said, sliding into her chair.

'Of course.'

Mindful of Rachel's belief that Jo was faking normality, Allie had been watching her closely for days, but she seemed completely herself – bubbly, chatty, silly – just as she always was.

Maybe Rachel's overreacting.

Jo dipped her spoon into a china bowl filled with soup of an oddly deep red colour. 'As long as they're out of there by tomorrow they get to live. How's it going with you anyway?'

'What is that? Tomato?' Allie was still trying to figure out Jo's soup.

'Yes, but I think it has beetroot in it.' Jo wrinkled her pert nose. 'It's the colour of carnage. And it tastes of dirt. Or maybe poison.'

Cimmeria's kitchen staff were usually good but sometimes their experiments didn't work out. Nonetheless, after taking half a sandwich off the tray in the middle of the table curiosity won out and Allie ladled some of the soup into a bowl. Dipping a spoon in it, she sniffed its contents suspiciously before taking a careful sip.

'I don't think it's poisoned,' she said.

'Oh good. Still,' Jo nibbled her sandwich, 'I'm not taking any chances. Hey, what's your course schedule like? Are you in my classes?' She held her hand out, palm up. 'Hand it over.'

Allie shoved the last quarter of the sandwich into her mouth and dug around her bag until she found the white slip of paper.

'Here,' she mumbled through her food.

'You're such a lady,' Jo said, then she squealed with excitement. 'We're in three classes together this term! History, biology and French. This is awesome.' She blinked at Allie over the top of the paper. 'I wonder if I could convince Isabelle to move us together for everything. I could promise to be good. For the first time ever.'

'You'd get sick of me,' Allie said. 'I snore.'

'That is so not a surprise.' Jo handed her schedule back.

'Hang on,' Allie said looking up from her soup, 'how can we have French together? I thought you were in advanced French?'

Jo leaned over to pick up her bag. 'I think you'll find that you, too, are in advanced French, *ma petite chou*.'

'No way.' Allie looked at Jo with suspicion.

'And in advanced history, biology and English.'

'No. Way.'

Jo rolled her eyes. 'Allie, haven't you looked at your own timetable?'

'Advanced my arse,' Allie muttered scanning the page, but Jo was right – almost all her classes were advanced.

She grinned triumphantly – for two years her marks had been sliding down a steep slope towards failure, but all her hard work over the summer term had paid off.

'Unfortunately, you're still in normal baby maths,' Jo said, with a smug smile. 'Which is lame.' She stood up. 'Well? Are you coming?'

'Maybe,' Allie said. 'Depends where you're going.'

Jo was already walking away so her reply floated back over her shoulder. 'Common room. To pee around my favourite sofa so the little ones don't try to steal it too.'

Grabbing another half-sandwich to eat on the way, Allie followed her out.

After the clamour of the dining room the hallway was a peaceful oasis. Everything was back in its place. Sunlight glimmered off the oak-panelled walls, and the old oil paintings had all been returned to the spots where they'd hung for centuries. Her rubber-soled shoes stuck a little to the recently varnished wood floor.

To Allie it all felt right again. Like the fire never happened. And Cimmeria was safe.

The common room, reached through a door virtually underneath the grand staircase, was filled with bookcases and deep leather sofas and chairs. A glossy, baby grand piano dominated one corner.

After making her way to the middle of the room, Jo plopped on to a sofa with a satisfied sigh. 'None of those pesky ankle biters are getting my spot.' She stretched languorously. 'I can't believe classes start tomorrow. We just never stopped working this summer.'

'Oh, stop complaining.'

They glanced up to see Rachel walk in, smiling, with a tall, slim boy whose light brown hair fell forward across his brow.

'Hey, Rach. Hi, Lucas,' Allie said.

'Did you fight your way through the crowds of newbies?' Jo asked, reaching out to take a magazine from the low coffee table.

'There were too many.' Lucas dropped into the chair across from them without ceremony. 'We retreated.'

'With honour.' Rachel sat on the ottoman beside him. 'They are legion.'

'It shouldn't be allowed,' Jo said, flipping through the magazine without really looking at it.

'Allie,' Lucas said, 'we saw Carter in the hallway outside. He was looking for you.'

Allie climbed to her feet with a yawn, and headed for the door.

On the way out, she passed a group of new students who stood in the common room doorway looking lost.

'No TVs,' one of them said. 'I might die.'

'No computers,' another replied in tones of quiet desperation. 'Seriously. What the hell will we do?'

Allie was nearly out of earshot when she heard the third one sigh. 'I hate my parents so much right now.'

SEVEN

Carter stood leaning against the door to the great hall reading, one foot propped behind him. Lost in his book, he didn't notice Allie standing in front of him. His straight dark hair swung forward as he read. When he pushed it back absently with a characteristic gesture she loved, she sighed.

His head shot up and his dark eyes met hers.

'Hey,' she said.

His eyes traced the outlines of her face. 'Hey back.'

He had this way of studying her that made her almost nervous – as if nothing could escape his gaze.

'What are you reading?' she asked, to get him to stop.

As he reached out his hand and pulled her closer, he held up the book and she saw the name on the spine. 'Vonnegut? Who's he?' She frowned. 'Are we assigned that this term?'

His crooked smile made her insides melt; when he shook his head his hair had this way of flopping . . .

'No, I just like it. I'm reading everything he ever wrote. He was awesome.' Tucking the book under his arm, he reached back and turned the doorknob, leaning hard against the door at the same time so that they both tumbled laughing into the great hall.

As they regained their balance, she saw that most of the furniture that had been stored in the vast space had been cleared out. It was just a ballroom again, with tables and stacks of chairs scattered at the back, awaiting the next party.

'What are we doing here?'

He cast a sideways smile so sexy it made her shiver. 'I thought we could just, you know ... hang out for a while. And I know this room is always empty, so ...' As he spoke he set the book down and then walked backwards, pulling her gently across the room. She followed without resistance, her gaze locked on his. 'Last night turned into something completely unromantic,' he continued. 'And we can't have that.'

When they'd nearly reached the back wall he stopped, pulling her into his arms, one hand behind her back, the other holding her hand. Instinctively, she placed her free hand against his shoulder. Through the crisp cotton of his button-down shirt, she could feel his muscles move when he spun her in a circle.

'What ... Are we dancing?' She laughed up into his eyes.

'Can't you hear the music?'

She cocked her head to one side. 'No.'

Pulling her closer, he swirled her in a circle, making her giggle.

'I don't think you're really trying,' he whispered very quietly in her ear. His teeth brushed her earlobe – her whole body tingled. 'Try harder.'

She tilted her head to one side to give him free access to her neck, as his lips travelled down as far as the collar of her prim cotton uniform blouse, and then up behind her ear to the downy hair at her temple, then back along the sharp edge of her jaw. It was a long, exquisite torture, and by the end, she was leaning into him; willing him not to stop.

When he reached her lips and whispered. 'Can you hear it now?'

'I think ...' Her voice came out hoarse, breathy. But she wasn't really thinking any more. She was feeling.

Standing on her toes, she tangled her fingers in his silky hair and pulled him harder against her. As her lips parted to his, she felt all his muscles tense, and then his arms tightened around her. He held her so tightly she couldn't breathe but she didn't care. She wanted him to touch her everywhere, to kiss her everywhere.

As if he'd heard her thoughts, his arms loosened and his hands slid to the waistband of her skirt. Without lifting his mouth from hers, he began pulling her shirt loose.

Trembling, she slid her hands down to his chest. She felt his heart race when his fingers made their way under her shirt to the warm skin of her back.

'You're shaking,' he whispered, his eyes dark as smoke. 'Are you OK?'

Not trusting her voice, she nodded against his neck, breathing in his scent of sandalwood and fresh air.

'Your skin is so soft.' His voice sounded wondering as his

hands stroked her back, sending shocks of sensation through her. 'I want to kiss you there.'

'I want that too.' Her voice sounded so faint she wondered if she'd said the words out loud.

But she must have, because he groaned deep in his throat and pulled her down to the floor until they knelt, facing each other, still kissing.

'I don't want . . .' He pulled her tightly against him – so close that she could feel the heat radiating from his body. 'I don't want to hurt you.'

A frown flitted across her face. 'You wouldn't ever do that.'

With one finger he traced a line from her forehead, down her nose, along her cheekbones and then back to her lips, which he lightly circled.

'I just . . . care about you, Allie Sheridan,' he whispered, looking at her lips. 'A lot.'

Her breath caught. 'I care about you, too, Carter West. A lot.'

With her right hand still resting against his chest, she lifted his hand with her left and placed it against her heart so he could feel it pounding.

'See?' she said. 'We both feel the same thing.'

His eyes darkening, he kissed her so hard she fell backwards, and they both tumbled to the polished wood floor. They rolled over until she was on her back, looking up at him. His fingers came to rest on the first button of her shirt. His eyes held hers.

Asking.

Wordless, she nodded, and he carefully unbuttoned it, kissing the skin until goosebumps rose beneath his lips. Her breath came in short gasps, as his fingers rested on the next button.

She was breathless to the point of dizziness. *Are we really going to do this?*

At that moment, someone opened the door.

Allie thought her heart might have stopped. Carter's eyes warned her to stay still, not that she needed more incentive. Lying half stretched across her body, he was like a reclining statue – his breathing so shallow she could hardly feel his chest move.

She couldn't see who it was – her view was blocked by a table and a stack of chairs. Then she heard Jerry's voice – he was talking so quietly she could only make out snippets. Hearing no one else, she realised he must be on the phone.

'. . . can't talk right now . . . situation is serious . . . Raj Patel is providing security . . . I don't see how anyone . . . No!' His voice rose on the last word.

Carter's eyes widened, but he didn't move.

Jerry was speaking again. '. . . all we can. The grounds . . . secure.' A pause and then he nearly shouted. 'I'm not going to argue with you. You can take this to Orion . . . ' As if realising he could be overheard, he lowered his voice to a harsh whisper, and after that they couldn't make out what he was saying. They remained frozen in place, barely breathing, communicating with their eyes, until he stopped talking.

A few seconds later they heard the creaking sound of the door opening. Then the soft thud as it closed.

Carter lifted himself up to see over the stacked chairs to take in the expanse of the room then he flopped down on his back next to her.

'He's gone,' he said.

Allie could breathe more easily without his weight on her chest. She could think more easily, too, with him further away. Even though she hadn't wanted Carter to stop, some part of her was glad they were interrupted. She cared for Carter. Maybe *loved* Carter. But she wasn't sure she was ready for what might have happened if Jerry hadn't walked into the room. It all seemed to happen so fast. They'd gone from kissing to something more *just like that*. And suddenly it had been like a merry-go-round spinning too quickly for her to jump off safely. She'd had her chance to jump when it was going slow at the beginning but she hadn't done it. So what did all this mean? Could she jump off now, and go back to just kissing? Or was she required to stay on for the entire ride?

A worried frown rumpled her brow. When he noticed, Carter reached over and smoothed a hair from her eyes.

'He wouldn't have been too cross,' he said, with a lazy, unworried smile. He clearly believed she was just fretting about nearly being caught. She let him think that's all that concerned her. Now wasn't the time to talk about sex. Was it? 'But he probably wouldn't have been very happy either,' Carter continued. 'He'd have taken us straight to Isabelle. And she'd have forgiven us after a lecture about safety.'

Imagining Isabelle looking at her with disappointment, Allie flushed and sat up. 'It's fine, though,' she said. 'He didn't see us.' For the first time, she thought about what they'd overheard and turned to look at Carter. 'What was that all about?'

'Sounded like another angry parent.'

'I didn't know teachers had phones,' Allie said.

'Some do.'

71

Stretched out on the floor he watched her, his eyes serious, as she re-buttoned her shirt. Feeling suddenly shy, she looked down until her hair swung forward to hide her face.

Sitting up, he pulled her against him so her forehead rested against his, and she looked into his eyes.

'Everything is OK,' he whispered. 'I promise.'

'Where the hell am I?'

It was just before nine o'clock as Allie hurried down a narrow basement corridor. Carter had given her thorough instructions to the gym and training rooms but it all seemed to be taking too long and she had the sinking feeling she was lost.

The basement gave her the creeps. The ceiling was so low it felt like a long coffin; the harsh green-yellow fluorescent lights made everything look like a television crime scene. The corridor was lined with closed doors – most of them unmarked. A thud that seemed to emanate from the wall beside her made her jump.

Just the pipes, she told herself, having no idea at all why pipes would make such a noise.

When something creaked above her head a few seconds later, she refused to look up.

Just someone walking upstairs. But her heart thudded in her ears.

Then a skittering sound from just behind her and a rush of air. Before she could react, someone flew by her at speed, knocking into her hard and stepping on her foot as she passed.

Already jumpy, Allie recoiled, bashing into the wall.

Ahead, a slight girl with a brunette ponytail paused and glanced back at her.

How could something so small cause so much pain? Allie thought, grabbing her foot and hopping in place.

'Hey!' she snapped. 'Like ... Ouch?'

Bird-like, the girl tilted her head to one side, studying her for a quick second.

'Sucks to be you.' Her voice was high-pitched and unsympathetic; Allie gaped as she dashed around a bend in the hallway and disappeared.

'Bloody, bloody, *bloody* hell,' she muttered, limping after her.

She followed the girl around the corner, only to find an empty hallway stretching on for what looked like for ever.

'Where in the name of holy hell is this useless, pointless, stupid gym?' she muttered.

As if she'd summoned it, a set of double doors appeared on her left, with opaque glass windows with the word 'Gym' written above them in faded letters.

'Oh.'

Carter had said the training room was across from it. Turning in a circle, she saw a door marked only with the word 'One'.

Training Room One.

Taking a deep breath, she turned the handle.

The room was dimly lit, small and crowded. About thirty students stood around on the blue exercise matting.

She was just closing the door behind her when the rumble of conversation diminished, and Zelazny, at the centre, of the room, shouted, 'Quiet please! Let's get started.'

Noticing Allie standing in the doorway his expression soured.

'Nice of you to join us, Sheridan. One second later and you'd have had the shortest Night School career in the school's history.'

Some of the students turned to stare and laugh. Allie's cheeks flamed, but she said nothing. Standing with her arms wrapped around her torso, she calmed herself by thinking of ways she'd like to hurt him. Then she noticed Sylvain a few feet away. He was frowning at Zelazny.

'As I was saying,' Zelazny resumed, 'welcome back. I know you are all fully aware of what happened here over the summer. As you can imagine, our work is changing this term because of what occurred, and we will now emphasise self-defence and security over strategy.'

Now Allie's eyes were adjusting to the gloom and she could make out more faces. She saw most of the people she'd expected. Just beyond Sylvain stood Jules, the girls' prefect. And she thought she saw Lucas standing at the back. But she couldn't find Carter.

Zelazny's tone changed and she tuned back into what he was saying.

'To help us, we've brought in an expert in security who will teach you the principles behind the world's best security. And I do mean the best – his skills are called upon not just by corporate executives but also by world leaders. The person I'm talking about is your new specialist instructor, Raj Patel.'

A murmur swept through the group and they clapped respectfully. Rachel's father stepped out from the shadows to stand beside Zelazny.

Just seeing him there made Allie feel better. She smiled at him and waved, but he didn't notice her.

Things won't be so bad with Mr P. here. He'll look out for me.

'Thank you very much for that warm welcome,' Mr Patel said. 'I'm happy to be back at Cimmeria again, even under such serious circumstances. As Mr Zelazny mentioned, we're refocusing this year on self-defence tactics. We're also adding a new element, something we've never tried before. Now, I believe you have all been briefed on what happened with Gabe Porthus.'

At the mention of Gabe's name Allie felt some of the oxygen leave the room. Mr Patel didn't seem to notice.

'Because of Gabe's actions, this term we'll address the concepts of betrayal and trust. A key question I have is, should you have known that Gabe could not be trusted? After all, many of you counted yourselves among his friends. Were there clues that he had switched allegiances? Clues that we should have seen? And, most importantly, is there somebody in this room we can't trust?' He moved like a panther, his footsteps silent, getting close to students and looking right into their eyes as if he could see into their minds. 'Is there somebody in this room right now who plans to betray us?'

A shocked hiss followed his words, as if everyone let their breath out at once. Looking around, Allie could see they were all as thrown by this as she was. Her head swivelled back to Mr Patel. He seemed cold and distant. Not at all the way he'd been at the Patel family home.

Her heart sank. Maybe Rachel was right. Maybe she didn't really know him that well after all.

'Now,' he continued, 'my people are screening everybody at the school – every kitchen cleaner, teacher and student. If one of you is lying about who you are or what you're doing here, rest assured we will find you. But I've decided that you should handle one element yourselves. You see, I'd like you to investigate each other.'

Someone gasped but Mr Patel was still talking.

'You'll be trained in how to detect signs of deception,' he continued. 'And then you will interview each other and report back to me. And, know one thing: lying in your interview is forbidden. If you lie we will find out. And then you will be expelled.'

With that bombshell, he turned to Zelazny. 'Over to you, August.'

'Quiet!' Zelazny barked, glaring at the students, although Allie hadn't heard anyone speak. 'We'll start today by appointing training partners – each one of you will have a partner with whom you will work throughout the term. This person will be your backup – the other half of you as far as Night School is concerned. You will be scored the same as your partner, so if your partner isn't working hard I suggest you inspire them to try. If your partner fails, you fail. Your partner assignment is non-negotiable.' He paused to glower at them again. 'Do not even think about asking to have your assignment changed. There are no exceptions to this rule. Ever.'

He flipped a page on his clipboard. 'Henderson! Your partner is Mitchell.' Allie saw two boys she didn't know walk to each other and silently high-five. 'Richeau, your partner is Smith-Tivey.' A girl with long dark hair walked over to a stocky, muscular boy. Allie chewed on the cuticle of her thumbnail and listened to her heart pound until he said, 'West!'

She held her breath, hoping to hear her own name.

'Your partner is Matheson.'

Allie's shoulders slumped. *Carter's partnered with Jules?*

Although Allie was less intimidated by the girls' prefect than she used to be, Jules still had a way of making her feel insecure – she was so perfect. So Cimmeria-insidery. And such an old friend of Carter's.

If Allie'd been partnered with him it would have been so perfect. They could have helped each other. Now she'd be with some stranger, and knowing Zelazny it wouldn't be a very pleasant stranger . . .

She was so lost in self-pity when Zelazny finally read out her name she didn't hear the name of her partner.

Panicked, she tugged on the sleeve of the person next to her. 'Did you hear what he just said?' she asked a tall, blond boy. 'Sheridan and who?'

He gazed at her blankly.

'He said Glass.'

The chirpy voice came from behind her. Allie spun around to see the small, ponytailed assassin from the hallway.

'As in Zoe Glass,' the girl said, cocking her head sideways. 'That's my name. Don't wear it out.'

'No!' Allie turned to the younger girl in horror. 'It can't be you.'

'Great.' Zoe rolled her eyes. 'Trust between training partners is super important. So I'm glad we're totally starting out on the right foot.'

'There you are.' Lucas and Carter walked up together. Allie gave them a helpless look.

'I can't believe it.' Allie looked at Carter for help. 'I can't be her partner. I just ... can't.'

He held out his hands helplessly.

'I don't think she likes me.' Zoe stood with a hand on one hip, obviously unbothered.

Ignoring her, Allie turned to Carter. 'Could you believe what he said about us investigating each other? That's just —'

'Enough chit-chat, people.' Zelazny's chainsaw voice cut her off. 'You have your partner assignments. Training starts now. I want to see a five-mile competitive run on the usual path. Then Raj will run us through a defensive training drill.'

Everyone rushed for the door at once. Allie turned to Carter, her expression blank. 'What's a *competitive* run?'

Grabbing her hand, he pulled her after the crowd heading down the corridor to a side door. 'It's a timed run – last one back is punished. Hurry!'

'Punished how?' But she ran after him.

'Does it matter?' Lucas asked, speeding past them.

Outside, a soft rain fell as the cadre of students took off into the darkness at speed. They all seemed to know to run down a footpath towards the edges of the school grounds.

'Shouldn't we warm up first?' Allie asked as Carter set a fast pace. 'We could all get cramp. And I can't see where I'm going. Can you see where you're going?'

Out of the darkness, Zoe appeared right beside them.

'Does she ever shut up?' she asked Carter before turning to Allie. 'Do you ever shut up?'

'Yes ... I mean ... What?' Allie stuttered. She was so taken aback she tripped over a root and pinwheeled off the path. Grabbing her arm, Carter kept her on her feet.

'Bloody hell.' Zoe looked baffled. 'What is wrong with you?'

'Talk about,' Allie panted, 'me shutting up. Why don't you ... give it a try ... Shorty.'

Increasing her speed, Allie focused on getting as far away from the girl as possible.

'I wouldn't use up all my energy so early,' Zoe called after her.

'No talking!' Zelazny's voice seemed to come from nowhere,

as he ran up behind them. 'Anyone found to be talking from this point on will be punished.'

'Oh just sod *off*,' Allie snapped, but she said it quietly enough so no one could hear.

Still, she knew Zoe was right. Five miles was a long run and she was already tired – she wouldn't make it if she didn't pace herself. But she certainly wasn't going to let Zoe see that.

So after a half-mile or so she slowed her pace to a more reasonable rate, shaking her shoulders to loosen the muscles that anxiety had tightened into knots. Soon, even though her thoughts whirled, her footsteps entered the steady, hypnotic rhythm of a regular runner.

As always, the exercise calmed her and, even as her heart rate increased, she could feel herself relaxing into the pace. Now she could pay more attention to the world around her. Clouds blocked the moon but her eyes were starting to adjust to the dark – she could see the pine trees all around her, swaying in the breeze, and the path ahead.

Only now did it occur to her that she hadn't just lost Zoe when she sped off, she'd lost Carter and Lucas as well. She was completely alone. But she didn't mind – the endorphins had kicked in and she ran with confidence and grace. The only way she could be certain she was still on the right path was that occasionally she'd pass another runner, then they'd fade into the background behind her.

The problem of Zoe occupied her thoughts, although she was calmer now. And the way Raj Patel had acted – tough and ice cold. Was this the side of him that Rachel had warned her about? The side she hadn't been able to imagine before?

She guessed she'd run about two miles when she reached a deep patch of the woods where the path was so dark she had to slow her pace to avoid tripping. The darkness here was so intense it almost had a weight – she imagined she could feel it pressing against her skin.

As she moved at a slow jog the wind picked up; the sound of thousands of trees swaying in unison was like a roar – like waves pounding against a pebble beach.

Then off in the distance a vixen shrieked a blood-curdling scream that made her skin crawl. She was sure it was a vixen. It definitely wasn't a girl being murdered and screaming for help.

Definitely.

Thoroughly unnerved, she picked up her speed but found it hard to get back to her previous easy rhythm. Every sound made her jumpy; she kept looking over her shoulder, thinking she heard footsteps behind her. Hoping another runner would catch up with her.

When she noticed she was nervously counting her footsteps, she ordered herself to stop. Having a panic attack now in the dark, all alone, would not be cool.

Don't freak out, Allie. Don't freak out, Allie. Don't freak out . . .

She was telling herself not to freak out for the thirty-seventh time when she saw someone standing in the woods.

It happened so fast she was past him before what she'd seen fully registered in her brain, then she skidded to a stop. Spinning around, she looked back – the woods were empty. Carefully, she backtracked down the path, squinting into the darkness where she'd seen a man in a suit standing under a tree. Staring at her.

But she was completely alone.

The sharp retort of a twig snapping behind her made her spin around, but she could see nothing but inky darkness. Then the wind blew through the trees again with a rush, and she assured herself that the roaring sound of branches brushing into each other was all that she'd heard.

But she didn't really believe it. So she ran.

Willing herself not to turn around, she ran as fast as she could. There was somebody back there – she knew it. And she could imagine them following, their footsteps in time with hers.

Right behind her.

Her breath burned in her throat as she hurtled pell-mell down the footpath through the trees, ignoring the protests from her muscles. Only when she rounded a bend and the forest thinned enough so she could see students running in the distance ahead of her did her nerves steady enough for her to look behind her.

The footpath was empty.

The end of the run was signalled by a student with a pale blue fluorescent light stick silently waving the runners to the school building. Limping down the stairs to the basement, Allie clutched at the stitch in her side with her hands as she headed straight to Training Room One and Raj Patel, who stood talking to Zelazny at the back of the room.

'Saw,' she gasped. 'Man. Woods.'

Bending over double, she put her hands on her knees and

watched her sweat drip on to the dark blue padding covering the floor. She closed her eyes to try and steady her nerves.

'What?' Zelazny's voice was sharp as a razor. 'What is it, Sheridan? Out with it.'

'She said she saw a man in the woods.' Mr Patel's voice was too calm, and Allie turned her head sideways to see his face. He was watching her alertly. 'Get your breath, Allie. Can you describe him?'

'Short ... hair,' she panted. 'Wore ... suit.'

Mr Patel stiffened, and she knew she'd said something important.

'Did you recognise him?' As he spoke he reached out and gestured to somebody behind her. Her hands still on her knees, Allie shook her head. 'Too dark.'

She was catching her breath now. The pain in her side was subsiding. The intense attention he was paying to what she'd seen made her nervous – it had been dark and she'd been spooked. What if it was all her imagination? But she didn't know how to say that without looking like a total flake.

Two muscular men in running clothes and a woman whose long blonde hair was pulled back in a braid flanked her, facing Mr Patel expectantly. He didn't introduce them. 'Allie saw somebody in the woods,' he told them. 'Wearing a suit.'

They exchanged glances as he turned back to Allie. 'Where were you precisely?'

She described as best she could the location. When she'd finished, he nodded to the others and they slipped out of the room as quickly as they'd appeared.

'If anybody's still there they'll find him.' Mr Patel's words were a kind of dismissal, and Allie walked back to Carter and dropped down on the mat beside him.

'You OK?' His face was flushed from exertion as he handed her a bottle of cold water. Beside him, Lucas, Jules and a boy she didn't recognise were sprawled in various poses of exhaustion.

Holding the cool bottle to her forehead, she nodded.

'What were you and Patel talking about?' His eyes studied hers. 'It looked a bit intense.' As she told him about the man in the woods, his lips tightened. Jules and Lucas moved in closer to listen.

'You didn't get a good look at him?' Lucas asked before she'd finished.

She shook her head. 'It was super dark there. I only saw him for a second. When I doubled back he was gone.'

'And you're sure it wasn't just your imagination?' Carter asked. 'Nobody could blame you for being a bit paranoid after all you've been through.'

His question revived her own self-doubt and she felt a twinge of defensive anger. 'I can't be certain, Carter. But I had to tell Raj what I saw.'

'Carter's not saying you did anything wrong, Allie.' Jules adopted a soothing tone. 'I think he's just trying to decide how worried to be.'

'Well, don't be worried.' Allie knew she sounded snappish but she couldn't seem to help it. If somebody else had just seen the freaky banker in the woods they wouldn't be having this conversation. Everybody would just believe it. 'Raj sent some of his manimals out to look for him.' Her gaze skittered off Carter's. 'And we're all here, safe and sound.'

'Everybody up.' Mr Patel stood in the middle of the room. His tone brooked no opposition and the students climbed to their feet, groaning. 'Find your training partners and prepare for basic self-defence techniques.'

Carter bounded to his feet but Allie didn't move. 'He must be joking,' she said.

Across the room Mr Patel snapped, 'Right now, people!'

With a sigh, Allie stood gingerly – all her muscles ached.

'You're sort of out of shape.' Zoe's piping voice came from right behind her; Allie paused to take a calming breath before turning to face her. She looked none the worse for wear after the run. Her ponytail hung limply down her back and a sheen of perspiration covered her face, but she looked as energetic as ever.

'No,' Allie said. 'I'm not.'

Zoe shrugged, doubt clear on her face. 'Are you ready?'

No, Allie thought.

'Yes,' she said curtly.

'So you've done this before?'

Before Allie could reply, Mr Patel spoke again. 'Each pair choose one to act as an attacker, the other is the attacked."

'I'll be the attacker,' Zoe volunteered.

'Awesome,' Allie muttered.

'The attack will come from the left side,' Mr Patel called, walking around the room to study the students' preparation. 'The attacked will attempt to throw the attacker to the ground and subdue them.'

This all sounded very bad to Allie, who had no idea how to throw an attacker to the ground. But then, Zoe was little. How hard could it be?

'In three,' Mr Patel called. 'Two . . . '

Allie braced herself, shoulders stiff. Zoe stepped out of her sightline.

'One!' Mr Patel called out.

Hands grabbed her arm. When Allie tried to pull free the room whirled and she landed flat on her back looking up at the ornate plaster ceiling. Zoe's foot rested on her abdomen.

'Pathetic.' Zoe lifted her foot and stepped back.

'What the hell . . . ' Allie groaned, 'just happened?'

'I dropped you.' Zoe's tone was matter-of-fact.

'Good!' Mr Patel said to a pair across the room. 'Now . . . Switch!'

Allie looked up at Zoe in confusion. The younger girl sighed. 'Now you try and attack me.'

Allie scrambled to her feet. For a second she looked around the room desperately to see what everyone else was doing. Her eyes met Sylvain's and she saw concern on his face.

Focus, Allie, she told herself.

Taking a deep breath, she tried to figure out what Zoe had done when she'd attacked her. Then she lunged at her.

The room whirled again. She hit the ground hard.

'How?' she gasped. Her ribcage felt assaulted.

Standing with her hands on her hips, Zoe looked down at her as if she were a maths problem she didn't know how to solve.

'Why aren't you better?' she asked.

Mr Patel appeared above Allie, his head blocking the fluorescent ceiling light.

'Nice job, Zoe.' Mr Patel leaned down to help Allie to her feet. 'Now why don't you try teaching instead of just hurting?'

'I don't get it,' Zoe said, cocking her head to one side with the alertness of a robin.

'This is Allie's first class,' he explained. 'She's never done this before. I didn't pair you with her so you could put her in hospital. I paired you with her so you could teach her.' He turned to Allie. 'Zoe is one of the best in the class – she's a natural – so I thought it would be good to put you two together. But she's never taught anyone before.' Turning back to Zoe, he said, 'Stop hurting her and just help her, OK? You win when Allie learns.'

'Ok.' Zoe's voice held no rancour. She turned to Allie. 'Want me to show you how to knock me down?'

'God yes.' Allie spoke through gritted teeth.

'Put your hands here.' Zoe pulled Allie's hands into place on her own arm as Mr Patel walked away. 'Then you just do this . . .'

But Allie was not a natural. This became apparent almost immediately. Although she tried very hard to flip the smaller girl over, all she managed was to drag her around a bit. Once or twice Zoe fell to the ground helpfully to illustrate how the move should work but, despite the fact that she was small and slim, Allie couldn't seem to flip her.

Looking around, she saw other students performing the move to perfection. In a corner, Jules flipped Carter without obvious effort. He laughed as she helped him up and she patted his shoulder warmly. The longer she was unable to perform what she knew must be a simple move, the more anxious Allie became. Her chest tightened and she tried to keep her face expressionless. But by the end she was panicked; breathing in small, desperate gasps.

'OK, everyone.' Mr Patel's voice stopped the torture at last. 'That's enough.' He moved to the centre of the room. 'That's pretty easy for most of you, I know. But tomorrow it starts to get harder. If you had any trouble with today's exercise, I suggest you start practising. This is just the beginning.'

Allie kept her eyes on the floor. She was the only one who hadn't been able to do it. That message was for her.

As the others began leaving the room she lagged behind, bruised and defeated, hoping to slip out unnoticed. She didn't hear Mr Patel walk up to her.

'If you want some extra help, come in early tomorrow,' he said quietly. 'I think Zoe will be a good partner for you. But sometimes it takes a little time for a partnership to gel. You'll both learn together.'

Biting her lip, Allie nodded. She didn't trust herself to speak.

I will not let them see me cry, she told herself. But she could feel tears burning her eyes. Across the room she saw Carter looking at her with concern – but that only made it worse.

So she walked away before he could see her face and know how miserable she was. Blindly, she stumbled down the hall and up the stairs to the ground floor. She wasn't sure where she was going or if anybody was following her. She really didn't want to talk to Carter right now. Or Mr Patel.

Or anyone.

It was just all so embarrassing.

She shoved open the back door and darted down the foot-path.

One hundred and twelve steps. One hundred and thirteen. One hundred and fourteen ...

After a minute, though, her exhausted muscles protested so loudly she slowed her pace. The night was cool – the rain had stopped and the clouds were clearing away. A glowing crescent moon dusted the landscape in silver.

Through the trees she caught a flash of something white. At first her breath stopped. Then she remembered.

The folly.

She'd forgotten all about the little gazebo where she'd hidden with Jules the night of the fire, but now she made her way over to its hiding place behind a line of trees.

The dome-roofed white structure was encircled by narrow columns. The moonlight illuminated the statue at its centre – a girl in a silky gown dancing eternally, arms above her head, a stone veil slipping through her fingers.

On the cold marble step next to the statue's bare feet, Allie rested her head on her knees. But now that she wanted to cry, tears wouldn't come. She felt empty.

Maybe I'm not cut out for it after all, she thought wretchedly. *Maybe I'm not good enough for Night School.*

She tried to imagine what it would be like to fail at Night School completely. What would Jules think? Or Lucas? Would they want to be her friend if they knew what a loser she was?

Jo was kicked out, she reasoned. *And it hasn't totally ruined her life.*

But Jo was different. She travelled in the same social circles as Lucas and Katie and Jules. Her family was important. They'd all like her no matter what. Allie was an outsider. Her parents were nobody. She would never run into the others on skiing trips in Switzerland or shopping on Bond Street or Fifth Avenue.

Because she'd never be in those places.

Except I'm Lucinda's granddaughter. The very thought was heady. *So maybe I should be.*

'Allie.'

At the sound of the distinctive French voice, Allie looked up. Sylvain stood at the foot of the steps, his expression unreadable in the dark.

'Hey.' Allie put her head back down again. 'What's up? Seen any really rubbish new Night Schoolers lately?'

He sat down on the step beside her. 'I wanted to make sure you were OK.'

'Yeah well.' Allie sat up. 'I'm a total loser. But otherwise I'm fine. So . . . move along. There's nothing to see here.'

'I saw what happened.' His vivid blue eyes met hers; colour crept across her cheeks as she turned away.

Shrugging to show how much she didn't care, she said, 'I hope it was entertaining.'

'No,' he said. 'That's not why I'm here. I know what went wrong. I can help.'

'I know what went wrong, too.' She didn't meet his eyes. 'I couldn't do a really simple move. It was pretty obvious. I just . . . failed.'

He ignored her self-pity. 'Zoe is very good but she is young. She's never taught anybody before. She was showing you the right things but she missed some details. Your hands were in the right place but your feet were wrong every time. If your feet are not right it will not work. I can teach you. If you let me.'

She studied him out of the corner of her eye. She couldn't see any sign that he was making fun of her – his voice was steady and calm. And there was something about him that made her feel comforted. Maybe he could help. She couldn't bear another nightmare session like the one she'd just had.

As she hesitated, though, one thought nagged at her the most.

Carter wouldn't like this ...

But Carter wasn't here. And she had to practise.

'OK,' she said. 'We can try. But be aware: I totally suck at this.'

His smile was confident. 'I promise you can do it.'

He led her to a nearby clearing where the pine needles lay thick enough on the ground to make a springy mattress.

After kicking stones and fallen branches out of the way, he turned to her.

'Now, stand as if you were about to attack me,' he said.

Allie crouched down and tried to look tough, her arms bent at her side, hands curled into fists. Amusement flickered in his eyes; he struggled to contain a laugh. 'OK, that is all wrong.' He walked closer to her. 'Look, you're a runner, so your strength is in your legs. Stand up straight.'

Over the next few minutes he explained to her how to arrange her body into the correct posture – legs straight but knees soft, arms loose at her side, feet shoulder-width apart. But something still wasn't right.

'Turn your feet this way,' he said, demonstrating. When she tried to emulate him, he shook his head. 'No, that's not quite right.'

Crouching down beside her, he reached out for her leg. Instinctively, she flinched away from his touch.

He stopped, his hands still outstretched. He looked up at her, moonlight turning the blue of his eyes to glitter.

'May I?' he asked.

Allie's stomach tightened. It would be stupid not to let him touch her *ankle*. He was being helpful.

'Yes,' she said. Her voice sounded small and she cleared her throat, watching as he carefully took her ankle in his hands to reposition her foot. His hands were warm against her skin.

If he noticed her anxiety, he didn't show it. When she was in position, he demonstrated how she should grab him. Again, he asked permission before touching her. This time, though, she said 'yes' with more confidence.

His body pressed lightly against hers as he moved one of her hands to his shoulder, and the other to his elbow – sliding her fingers gently into place. She stood stiffly but his light touch spread goosebumps across her skin.

I'm trying to throw him violently to the ground, she told herself. *Surely that's OK, even after everything that happened?*

Stepping back, he demonstrated how to shift her weight when she made her move. After she'd practised a few times they decided to do it for real.

'OK, so . . . Now I will run at you,' he said. 'Just do what you practised and it will work perfectly.'

'I'm ready,' she said with false confidence.

I'm going to screw this up. I'm going to screw this up. I'm going to . . .

Then Sylvain ran at her and the circular thoughts stopped. Her mind went still. Grabbing his arm, she shifted her weight as he'd taught her.

He landed on his back at her feet.

She gave a small cheer and waited for him to tell her how brilliantly she'd done, but he said nothing. In fact, he didn't move. He lay still on the ground, his eyes closed.

'Sylvain?' Her heart thudded with sudden panic as she dropped to the ground beside him. She couldn't tell if he was breathing. 'Sylvain? Are you OK? Have I killed you?'

Then she noticed his body shaking with laughter. His eyes flew open. 'I knew you could do it,' he said.

'Don't *do* that!' Allie chided him, but his laughter was infectious and she jumped to her feet. 'I did it! I did it!' Dancing through the trees, she clasped her hands above her head in a pose of victory.

Suddenly she stopped in front of him. 'Hang on a minute. Sylvain, did you actually play a joke on me? Like, an actual *joke*? Or did I just dream that?'

'What are you talking about?' He feigned surprise. 'I have a very good sense of humour.'

'Uh-huh.'

'OK . . . Seriously.' He led the way back to the clearing. 'You did very well. I would make a few small adjustments but it was good.'

'Teach me.' She could hear the fierceness in her own voice. 'I want to learn it all.'

Something in his face told her that he understood how she felt. But he said only, 'OK. Let's start with an attack from the right. You need to adjust your stance slightly.'

Over the next half-hour he taught her how to handle attackers from different sides — how to pivot into position with no warning. How to fight back. By the end, they were both sweating despite the cool night air.

He was so professional and polite in his approach, she soon forgot her hang-ups about him touching her. He was teaching her how to elude a neck-hold, his arms wrapped around her from behind, her hands on his wrist, when Carter walked into a pool of moonlight and stood looking at them in disbelief.

'Allie? What the hell is going on?'

NINE

Surprised, she stared at him wide-eyed for a long instant before she was able to react.

'It's just ... you know ... we ...' she stuttered, unable to think of an explanation.

As she spoke, Sylvain dropped his arms and stepped back. With a sick feeling, she realised how it must have looked. Carter's eyes were fixed on Sylvain – tension crackled in the air between them like electricity.

'Sylvain was teaching me how to flip people. It was just ... practice.' Her voice quivered before slowly fading into silence.

'I don't get it. Didn't we just have an hour-long lesson from Raj?'

'Yeah but ...' Heat rose in her cheeks. 'I don't know if you noticed. It didn't go very well.'

'I could have helped you.' He was pale with anger.
This is bad.

'Hang on. You don't under— It's not like I asked him. We sort of . . . I don't know. Ran into each other.' She avoided looking at Sylvain, but a strange mixture of panic and resentment flooded through her. He'd just spent ages helping her. And she still had the right to choose her own friends. Didn't she?

She shot Carter a warning look. 'It's not like you're the only person who can help me. We're not chained to each other at the ankle. You and Jules seemed to have a good time working together and you don't see me freaking out about that.'

'You know that's not the same thing,' he snapped. Hectic spots of colour appeared in his cheeks, and tendons bulged on his neck like exposed wires. 'I can't believe you'd come out here with him after what he did to you.'

Instantly images of the summer ball flashed in Allie's mind. Sylvain shoving her against a wall, kissing her hard. Refusing to let her go even as she fought.

It was Carter who had found them. Carter who made him stop.

Just remembering that night made her feel sick. She swallowed hard.

But Sylvain had spent months trying to make it up to her; he'd rescued her the night of the fire. She believed he was truly sorry.

Was she just being naive?

'This is stupid, Allie.' Carter sounded impatient, but she could see the hurt in his eyes. 'I'm not going to stand here arguing with you in front of Sylvain. It's after curfew. Jules was wondering where you were and she sent me to look for you. You need to get back.' Then he turned on his heel and strode back towards the school building.

Watching him disappear through the trees, Allie stood very still but her thoughts were chaotic and confused. She was surprised by her own anger – it was as if he'd thought she'd been cheating on him with Sylvain just because she was working out with him.

As if he didn't trust her.

Suddenly the night felt empty and quiet; she took a deep calming breath of the cool air and for the first time noticed the stars, like silver frosting on the dark sky.

She was glad Sylvain hadn't said anything, hadn't made things worse. For a second, she thought about saying something to him about that night. About maybe forgiving him for the bad things and remembering only the good. About being friends.

But she didn't.

And as they walked back towards the school building in awkward silence, she thought about the things she *should* say. The things Carter would want her to say.

I really appreciate your help, Sylvain. But we can't ever do it again. Carter wouldn't understand and he really doesn't want me hanging out with you. Or speaking to you. Or breathing the same air as you.

But, instead, all she said was, 'Thanks for helping me.'

As he held the door for her his eyes were as blue and enigmatic as the smooth surface of a lake. And all he said was, 'You're welcome.'

The next morning, despite the late night, Allie woke before her alarm went off and couldn't get back to sleep. Giving up on rest, she sat up slowly, feeling the new aches in her muscles.

Everything hurt.

With a groan, she climbed out of bed and draped a towel over her shoulder before trudging down the silent hallway. The bathroom was mostly empty, although she could hear water running in one of the showers.

The last cubicle in the row was her favourite – it seemed bigger than the others, and lighter. Setting her slippers on the teak bench, she hung her robe on a polished brass hook set into a wall tiled in cream-coloured stone. The long, hot shower loosened her knotted muscles, and by the time she padded out of the cubicle she felt like herself again, but she was no longer alone. Another girl, swathed in a white Cimmeria robe identical to Allie's, stood at a sink.

To give them both privacy, Allie chose a sink well away from her. But as she studied herself in the mirror and scrubbed up a toothy foam the girl spoke.

'Excuse me. Are you Allie?' The accent was French. The voice light, musical.

'Yes?'

The girl moved closer. She was tiny, Allie saw now. Barely five feet tall, and delicate, with enormous brown eyes and ludicrously lush lashes. She looked strangely familiar but Allie couldn't place her.

'I thought so.' The girl seemed pleased. 'I've heard so much about you from Sylvain. I am Nicole.'

Allie had never heard of her – Sylvain had never mentioned her.

'Oh yeah ... I mean ... ' she said through the toothpaste. 'Of course. It's nice to meet you.'

Nicole blinked up at her. 'He talked about you so much over the summer term in his letters – I feel that I know you.'

She even blinks prettily, Allie thought.

She wasn't sure what was happening here. Was Nicole Sylvain's girlfriend? One he forgot to mention? And even if she was, what did that matter?

She really needed to rinse her mouth.

'Last night, he told me was going to check on you after training.' Nicole seemed completely unaware the Allie was drooling foam. 'He could see you were upset. Did he find you?'

Colour crept into Allie's cheeks. *Night School. That's where I saw her. And that means she saw me totally fail.*

'Yes. He did find me.'

'And he helped you.' Nicole said it as if there was no question anything else could have happened.

'He was very helpful,' Allie said stiffly. Then she turned around and spat out the toothpaste.

After rinsing her mouth, she turned to gather her things, but when she looked up Nicole was still watching her.

Her giggle was musical, like water trickling in a stream. 'I am sorry to bother you without . . . warning.' She wrinkled her pert nose. 'It is just nice to know who you are.'

'And it's great to meet you at last,' Allie said with false enthusiasm as she hurried out the door. 'After hearing so much about you from Sylvain.'

'Who is Nicole and why is she so pretty and French?' Allie cast a sideways glance at Rachel.

'Ooh. Sylvain's off-and-on girlfriend. Very sophisticated, annoyingly gorgeous,' Rachel said. 'Why?'

'Are they off now?' Allie asked. 'Or on?'

Rachel arched one questioning eyebrow. 'Off . . . I think. But who knows with those two? Why?'

They were walking down the hall between classes. Allie longed to tell her everything that had happened last night, but she knew full well that, not only could she not mention it, but Rachel really wouldn't want to hear about it anyway. She hated that suddenly she couldn't tell her best friend everything. It felt uncomfortable – like an unspoken lie.

'Oh it's nothing, really.' Allie shrugged. 'She just talked to me in the bathroom this morning. Freaked me out.'

'I hate being talked to in the bathroom,' Rachel commiserated as she dodged a crowd of giggling girls. 'What did she say?'

'Just that Sylvain told her all about me. It wasn't weird or anything. It was just . . . weird.'

'I understand completely,' Rachel said, shaking her head and staring at Allie as if she were mad.

'I know,' Allie sighed. 'It doesn't make sense. It's nothing. I have a more important question.'

'Hit me.'

'What's the story with this Zoe creature?'

'What?' Rachel looked confused. 'You mean Zoe Glass? When did you two meet?'

Allie shrugged non-committally and Rachel shot her a knowing look. When she spoke again her tone was brisk. 'Right. What do you want to know?'

'What's her story?' Allie asked. 'She's strange. Like ... I don't know ... a really violent robot.'

Rachel didn't laugh – she didn't find anything related to Night School funny.

'Zoe is your basic prodigy. She's thirteen but she's studying at our level – actually above our level – she takes college courses with a tutor—'

'Wait. Seriously?' Allie interrupted her, stopping so abruptly the person behind her ran into her. 'Sorry,' she said, glancing over her shoulder as the nervous first-year boy shuffled by without meeting her eyes. 'She's *thirteen*? I knew she was younger than us but ...'

'Seriously. She's like a genius.'

This was not at all what Allie expected to hear. But Rachel had more to tell. As they climbed the stairs to the first floor of the classroom wing she reeled off the basic Zoe facts.

'Her dad's a lawyer; her mum's a journalist, I think. She's from London like you. Her parents are older. Like, maybe she was an accident. Anyway, until she came here she was homeschooled by her grandparents. So until then, she'd never spent time with kids her own age.' They reached the landing and slowed their pace as Rachel continued. 'She's totally socially awkward. It's like she was raised by wolves. I think she's probably a bit Asperger's ... but the good bit, if you know what I mean.'

'That's a nice way of saying she's psycho, right?'

Rachel shot her a disapproving look. 'Don't be mean.'

'Sorry.' Allie held up her hands.

By then, though, Rachel had already moved on. 'She doesn't accept new people easily – she doesn't like change. So, good luck with that. But if she does accept you, she's so loyal it might drive you crazy.'

They stopped on the landing.

'*If* she accepts me,' Allie muttered.

Rachel nodded. 'There are people in this school she ignores completely, like they don't exist. She'll run into them if they stand in front of her. It's like they're invisible to her.'

Somehow this didn't surprise Allie at all. 'Does everyone just . . . accept her?' she asked. 'I mean, she's really odd.'

Rachel's brow creased. 'Some don't get why she is the way she is – they think she's rude because . . . Well, she's rude. But she doesn't mean to be. I'm mean, she's not, like . . . cruel. She seems rude because she's honest. And people aren't used to honesty.'

Allie felt a ping in her chest, as if Rachel's words had physically touched her.

Glancing at her watch, she winced. 'Look, I'd better run. My next class is with Zelazny. Tardiness is not an option.'

With a quick wave, Allie hurried down the hall to history class, where Jo had saved her a seat; she slid into it just before Zelazny walked into the room. He surveyed the students darkly.

'I see you all made it on time.' He marked a sheet of paper and put it back in a folder. 'How kind of you. Welcome to ancient history. This term we'll be focusing on the classical civilisations of Greece and Rome.'

As he spoke, he walked around the room putting a textbook on every desk with a deliberate thud.

'Class participation counts towards your overall grade,' he said, setting a book down on Jo's desk. 'So I expect you to be engaged and involved in classes. This is advanced history – there will be no slacking.'

As Zelazny moved across the room, Jo wrote diligently in her notebook. When he was well away from them she turned it sideways so Allie could read it.

'THIS IS GOING TO SUCK DONKEY BALLS.'

A laugh burst out of Allie before she could stop it. She feigned a coughing fit to disguise it, but Zelazny turned to glare at her. She slid down in her seat, fighting to keep a straight face as Jo gazed around the room innocently and flipped to a clean page in her notebook.

By the time Allie made her way to Isabelle's English class that afternoon, her bag was heavy with books and her to-do list filled a full page in her notebook. When she was going to find the time to do that work was a mystery to her. She had Night School at ten, so everything would have to be done before then. Somehow.

She was walking down the hall with her head down when she bumped into someone.

'Sorry,' she said automatically, before looking up into Carter's dark eyes. 'Hey!' Her face lit up and she leaned in for a kiss but he took a quick step away from her.

Confusion and doubt roiled her. 'What's wrong?'

He looked furious.

'Wait, are you still pissed off about me training with Sylvain?' She couldn't believe it. 'You can't be serious, Carter.'

'Am I still pissed off?' He stepped out of the hallway traffic flow and lowered his voice. 'Of course I'm still pissed off, Allie. Wouldn't you be? Put yourself in my shoes. You had a bad lesson and instead of coming to me you went straight to Sylvain for comfort. How would you feel if I did that with one of my ex-girlfriends?'

He had a point, but she wasn't about to admit it.

'That's not fair, Carter. I didn't go looking for him. He was just checking to make sure I was OK. Then he offered to help.'

'Oh that's so much better,' he snapped. 'And did you ask yourself why he went looking for someone else's girlfriend?'

'Carter, seriously.' Anger fired inside her – hot and dangerous. She fought to stay calm. 'First of all, I'm not just "someone's girlfriend". I'm Allie Sheridan, Person. Second of all: Nothing. Happened. You have to trust me.'

'Do I?' he said. 'Would you trust me in the same situation? In all honesty, if you found me in the woods practising with Clair, would you trust me?'

Allie winced; Clair was his ex.

'No, because Clair's not in . . . well, *you know what*. So that would be weird.' He rolled his eyes but before he could interrupt her she added, 'But if you were practising with Jules? Yes. I'd be fine with that. And if you were studying with Clair? Yes, I'd be fine with that. Because I trust you.'

'Oh really? Well, I might just put that to the test,' he said, stalking off.

'Carter,' she called after him but he didn't look back. With a sigh, she heaved her bag on to her shoulder and followed him into class.

Isabelle always arranged the desks in a circle for what she called her English 'seminar'. Carter sat moodily to one side avoiding her eyes, his long legs stretched out towards the centre.

She was trying to decide whether to sit next to him when Zoe bounded over, her brown eyes bright. Dressed in her school uniform, with prim white socks and loafers, she looked more like a little girl than a martial arts expert with personal boundary issues.

'Allie!' she said. 'I looked all over for you last night.'

'Yeah,' Allie said vaguely, 'I . . .'

Without waiting for her to finish, Zoe continued in a low voice. 'I had a long talk with Mr Patel and he explained what I was doing wrong. It was totally my fault you were so lame at it. He told me not to hurt you any more.' She winced. 'He was kind of firm about that. Did I hurt you?'

Allie thought about how her back had ached when she climbed into bed last night, and the humiliating experience of finding herself staring up at that stupid ceiling over and over again. Then she looked into Zoe's curious eyes.

'Nah.' She shrugged. 'I'm still in one piece.'

'Aces,' the girl said with clear relief. 'I won't hurt you tonight. I've been practising.'

'Me too—'

'Take your seats, please.' Isabelle's words interrupted their conversation.

Just as Isabelle started the class, Sylvain walked in. His eyes met Allie's and for a second she froze, terrified he'd sit next to her. Her eyes darted to Carter, who stared at them both with narrowed eyes.

But Sylvain slid into the seat next to Nicole, who Allie hadn't noticed before. She leaned over to whisper something that made him laugh. Watching them made Allie feel strangely hollow.

105

'This term,' Isabelle said, walking around the room putting a book on each desk, 'we're focusing on early twentieth-century literature. Our schedule is tight – we will be reading four books. The first is Edith Wharton's *The Age of Innocence* ... '

As she talked, Allie couldn't resist glancing over at Carter. He was studying the book cover so intently he might have been trying to memorise it. He didn't look at her.

'So far, so painful,' Jo said, sipping from her glass of water. 'I've got enough prep for a week and it's only the first day.'

'Me too,' Allie sighed. The others agreed.

They were sitting at their usual table in the crowded and boisterous dining hall. Around them the roar of conversation ebbed and flowed in a tidal pattern.

When they'd first walked in, their table had again been occupied by younger students, but Lucas had leaned over to have a quiet word with them.

'Now,' Jo had said with satisfaction after the young students left in a rush, 'it's ours for ever.'

Rachel and Lucas sat across the table, laughing. Allie liked how much time they spent together these days. They looked cosy. She kept hoping they'd get together properly. Rachel had liked Lucas since her first day at Cimmeria. But nothing except friendship had ever happened between them.

Carter walked up shortly afterward, taking a seat next to Jo without a word to Allie. Noticing this, Rachel glanced at Allie and artfully arched one eyebrow.

Allie shook her head and mouthed, 'Later.'

Allie's eyes drifted to the table next to them, where Sylvain sat next to Nicole. Maybe Rachel was wrong and they were 'on again'. They were always together. He smiled at something Nicole said, then, as if he'd felt Allie's gaze, glanced up. When their eyes met, he looked at Allie curiously, as if he wondered what she was thinking.

Flushing, she dropped her gaze to her plate.

'So, is everyone going straight to the library after dinner?' Rachel asked. 'I've got, like, no option.'

'Oh yes,' Jo said airily. 'We'll all be there. The educational torture of Cimmeria Academy has begun.'

'Did Zelazny assign everybody else essays?' Allie asked, and the others nodded.

'Two thousand words.' Lucas took a bite of bread. 'The man's a sadist.'

'We should revolt,' Jo suggested. 'An uprising of the privileged.'

'A reverse revolution? I like it,' Rachel said.

While the self-pitying conversation continued, Allie looked around the crowded dining hall. The room was set up much the same for dinner as it had been over the summer. White table-cloths covered each round table. White china with the dark blue Cimmeria crest sat at every place setting, and the crystal glasses sparkled. The huge chandeliers glowed overhead. But there were no candles anywhere. Isabelle had announced they wouldn't return until new, flameproof tablecloths and curtains arrived. At the moment the windows were bare . . .

Allie's breath caught in her throat; her fork fell from nerve-less fingers, landing on her plate with a clatter.

It was still very faintly light outside. And Gabe was stand-ing outside the window. Staring right at her.

TEN

Everyone turned to look at Allie.

All the air seemed to be missing from her lungs as, pointing at the window, she struggled to speak. 'It's G ... G ...'

The word wouldn't come out.

The others looked where she pointed but when Carter looked back at her he was clearly puzzled. 'What is it?'

'Gabe,' Allie said clearly. 'Outside the window. Watching.'

'What?' Jo jumped to her feet so quickly she nearly upset the table. A glass fell over with a crash and Allie heard water trickling to the floor.

As soon as she got the words out, Allie could feel the pressure on her chest ease. They all turned to look out the window. But Allie could see he wasn't there. Outside there was only darkness and trees.

'Are you sure, Allie?' Carter's eyes were serious.

God, how she wanted to say no. That it had been a trick of the light. But she'd seen his face, as clearly as she saw Carter's now.

'Positive.'

Allie looked up to where Jo had been, but she'd run to Isabelle's table and was gesturing frantically. Even from here, Allie could see that she was hysterical. She watched as Isabelle at first frowned, trying to understand Jo's rapid-fire delivery, then rose to her feet, waving for the teachers to follow. Jerry Cole ran from the room, presumably to notify Raj Patel's security team. Putting her arm around Jo, Eloise led her out of the dining hall.

Glancing around the room, Allie saw that the other students seemed unaware of the drama unfolding. Most were eating and talking, although a few watched curiously as Isabelle approached.

'Allie. With me. Now.' The headmistress' voice was sharp. Allie rose and followed her to the door; the others were right behind them as they walked into the silent hallway.

'You're absolutely certain it was Gabe?' Isabelle's voice was calm, but Allie could see the tension in the way she held herself. 'It's getting dark. It would be easy to make a mistake.'

'Maybe you imagined it.' Jo looked at her, tears of fear in her eyes.

Gabe had held such power over her when they were together, Allie thought. *The idea of him coming back must terrify her.*

'It was him. I'd know him anywhere. Even in the dark.'

As she spoke, a muscular security guard dressed all in black walked up to the group. They all stepped back to make space for him. Turning towards Isabelle and Zelazny, the security guard blocked Allie and the other students out of the conversation with his body.

'My team is outside the dining hall now.' He lowered his voice. 'There are no signs of him. The ground is soft but we found no footprints outside any of the windows. We'll continue searching the grounds, just in case.'

He thinks I'm lying. Heat rose in Allie's face. She tried to control her temper as she appealed to Isabelle. 'Is that guy . . .' She pointed at the security guard. 'Is he saying I'm making it up?'

Carter rested a hand on her arm, as if to calm her down, but he said nothing and his gaze evaded hers.

He doesn't know whether or not to believe me.

'No, Allie,' Isabelle said. 'I asked him to make a report and he's making it.'

She turned back to the guard. 'Thank you, Paul. Keep looking and let us know immediately if you discover anything.'

With a curt nod, he strode to the door.

Zelazny turned to the headmistress. 'It's your call, Isabelle, but if it were me, I'd send them back on their normal patrols. She probably imagined it. She imagined something similar on a run the other night.'

'I did not imagine it!' Allie protested.

'Did anybody else see him?' The history teacher's tone held a challenge as he looked at the other students.

Rachel, Carter and Jo exchanged looks. Allie glanced up at Carter imploringly, but he shook his head. He had seen nothing.

'I don't ...' Frustration made her inarticulate. 'You believe me, don't you?'

Carter looked uncomfortable. 'I believe you think you saw something, Allie. But ...'

Stricken, she stared at him. *How could he not believe me?*

Reading her expression he held out his hands. 'I looked, Allie. There was nobody there. Isn't this just like the other night in the woods when you thought you saw someone?' She opened her mouth to argue but before she could speak he continued, his tone gentle. 'Nobody can blame you for seeing things. You've been through a lot.'

'It. Was. *Him.*' She emphasised each word, anger making her voice ring.

'Enough.' Isabelle sounded angry. 'Come with me, Allie. Everybody else get on with your evening unless we call for you.'

Her shoes tapped a furious staccato beat on the polished wood floor as they hurried down the hall to her office. Flipping the light switch, she pointed at a chair. 'Sit. I'll come back for you in a few minutes. Do not leave this room.' Then she closed the door behind her.

For what seemed like a long time, Allie was left alone with her thoughts. Over and over again she tried to recall exactly what she'd seen. What if she'd been wrong. But it had been so clear. She was sure it was Gabe.

Dropping her head to her knees she thought about the way Carter had looked at her – the doubt on his face. How he'd talked to her like she was losing it.

Thinking about it made her feel sick, and she jumped to her feet and paced the small windowless room, trying to think about something else. Maybe by now they'd found Gabe. Maybe that's what was taking so long. Then they'd all apologise and everything would be OK again.

Her pacing journey took her to the door, and she leaned against it to listen. She could hear footsteps and voices – nobody sounded agitated or concerned, so whatever was happening, it wasn't too dangerous. Then she paced again.

From the wall with the tapestry of a maiden and a white horse to the back wall was seven steps at a diagonal. She'd traversed it one hundred and twelve times when she heard Isabelle speaking to somebody outside the door. Allie pressed her ear to the door to listen.

'I know you're busy . . . '

Sylvain's voice.

'I am. What is it?' Isabelle's tone was short. She sounded stressed.

'I heard what Paul said earlier – that he found no footprints in the dirt outside the window.' Sylvain's French accent was thicker than usual. It got that way when he was upset. 'That doesn't mean Gabe wasn't there. Remember how well trained he is. He would know where to stand in order not to leave footprints. There is a narrow ledge of stone at the base of the wall, he could have—'

'Thank you, Sylvain.' Isabelle's clipped voice cut him off; Allie ground her teeth in frustration as she pressed her forehead against the door.

What he was saying made sense. Why . . . ?

At that moment, the door opened with a jerk, and she jumped back.

Her expression unreadable, Isabelle gestured for her to follow. 'Please come with me.'

In tense silence they retraced their steps down the now-bustling hallway; Allie watched the headmistress' inexpressive back with growing concern.

Isabelle held the dining hall door open for Allie then closed it behind her. Now empty, the room was still redolent of dinner; smells of roast pork lingered unpleasantly. But the tables had been cleared and Allie could hear faint voices from the kitchen as Isabelle led her back to the table where she'd sat earlier that night.

'Now.' To Allie's relief, the headmistress didn't sound angry any more. 'Let's go over this again without everybody telling you what to think. Where were you sitting?'

For a moment, Allie's mind went blank. The emptiness of the room was disorienting. With a steadying breath, she forced herself to calm down and visualise the room full.

She pointed to one of the seats facing the row of tall windows.

'There.'

'Sit please,' Isabelle said, 'as you did during dinner.'

Allie perched on the edge of the chair, watching as Isabelle walked across the room to the windows.

'Tell me again. In which window did you see the face?' Isabelle asked.

'That one.' Allie pointed. 'Third from the left.'

'This one?' Isabelle stood in front of the window and Allie nodded.

'And where in the window?'

'Lower left hand corner,' Allie said.

Isabelle studied the glass, lightly touching it in one spot with her fingertips before turning back.

'Now. What was Gabe doing when you saw him?'

Allie's heart leapt. 'You believe me?'

'There's a clear mark on the other side of glass. He got too close – he pressed his nose against the pane.' Isabelle sat down in a chair near her. 'What was he doing?'

'He was just ... watching us.' Closing her eyes, she visualised his face, his eyes fierce with concentration. 'Me and Carter and Jo.' Her eyes flew open. 'Isabelle, how could this happen? How could he get through security to get so close?'

The headmistress pinched the bridge of her nose between her thumb and finger as if she were fighting off a headache. 'Somebody on the inside is working with Nathaniel. Somebody with ... access.'

Allie's mind flashed back to what Mr Patel had said in Night School. He believed some students had supported Gabe, maybe even stayed in touch with him after Ruth's murder. But he hadn't suggested anyone else might be involved. Or that they were still helping Nathaniel.

The investigation we're doing in Night School, she realised with sudden horrible clarity. *It's real.*

Her throat went dry. 'A teacher?'

Isabelle met her gaze. 'Perhaps. Or an advanced Night School student. Someone close to me. Someone I trust.' She let Allie process this information for a moment before continuing. 'I think Nathaniel is using Gabe to scare you and Jo. He knows it will upset you to see him, more than anyone else he could send. It would all make a kind of horrible sense. Tell me, how did Gabe look?'

Allie looked at her blankly. 'I don't . . .'

'I mean, what was his expression? Did he look different than you remember? What was he wearing? Could you see his hands? Was he holding anything?' She paused before adding, 'Anything you can remember could help.'

Closing her eyes again, Allie described what she recalled.

'I couldn't see his hands. His hair was shorter and neater than it used to be. He looked . . . older. He wore a suit.' As she realised what she'd said, her eyes flew open.

'He wore a suit and tie,' she repeated, 'like the man in the woods. And the guys at my house.'

When Allie left Isabelle in the dining hall, she didn't know where to go. She had a huge stack of homework but it all seemed so meaningless all of a sudden. Her first instinct was to look for Carter, but he was still angry with her and she didn't want to fight. She knew Jo would be freaked out, and Rachel would want to know everything that had happened. But she didn't know how much she was allowed to say to either of them. And the truth wouldn't make Jo feel any better.

For a while, she just walked, with no particular destination in mind. The common room was packed with students chatting and playing games, but she didn't feel like playing.

The next obvious place to go was the library. She stood for a long moment with her hand on the door. The others were probably in there. And they'd want to quiz her about everything that had happened.

She could tell Carter and Lucas everything – they were in Night School. But the others ...

Whirling, she ran down the hallway, and then dashed up the grand staircase. It was crowded with clusters of chatting, slow-moving students, and she darted between them. She was halfway up when she saw Sylvain coming down the other way. The surge of relief she felt upon seeing him took her by surprise. Sylvain knew everything – she didn't have to keep secrets from him. And he believed her.

When he saw her hurrying to reach him, he quickened his step and they met in the middle of the staircase.

Her words tumbled over each other in a rush. 'I heard you ... talking to Isabelle I mean. Gabe was there. He really was. Thank you. For believing me, I mean. I don't know if anyone else did.'

She was sure she sounded mental, but he didn't look as if he thought so. He looked serious and concerned.

'I merely told her the truth.' Like jewels, his cobalt eyes refracted the light from a nearby window. 'It seemed obvious to me that ... ' A younger student passed them on the stairs; Sylvain lowered his voice. 'Look, where are you headed? Perhaps we should get off this staircase.'

Together they climbed to the sweeping first-floor landing. Once there, he stepped out of the stream of traffic into the rel-ative privacy of a window nook. After a split second of hesitation, she followed him. But when they were alone, neither of them seemed to know what to say.

'So, are you OK?' he asked after a moment.

For some reason the question made her grumpy. Why

116

wouldn't she be OK? All she did was see Gabe through a window. It wasn't like she was in real danger.

'Of course I'm OK,' she said. 'But I'm scared and I'm pissed off. I don't like being spied on and I don't like being called a liar.'

His lips quirked upward. 'Sorry. I assumed you were fine but I didn't actually know what else to say. The circumstances are bizarre.'

'Yeah, well,' she said, mollified, 'at least you didn't call me crazy, and I appreciate that.'

'You are many things, Allie, but crazy isn't one of them.' His smile was contagious and she found herself smiling back at him, despite everything that had just happened. But the seriousness of the moment returned and her smile faded.

'Sylvain, Isabelle says somebody here really is on Nathaniel's side. Somebody high up. That Night School investigation thing ... It's real.' Searching his eyes, she saw no surprise, although he hesitated before replying.

'We've known for a while,' he said, 'that somebody – one of the teachers or the Night School instructors or senior students – is working for Nathaniel.'

His words made it seem real, and goosebumps raised an icy path down Allie's arms as she tried to imagine Zelazny or Eloise working for Nathaniel. Or Jo or Lucas. 'I don't believe it,' she breathed. 'I can't believe one of us would do that.'

'None of us can.' His voice low. 'That's the problem. It must be somebody we trust. That makes it worse.'

Wrapping her arms around her torso, Allie looked up at him. 'Why are they doing this, Sylvain? Do you know? Nathaniel and the people working for him – what do they want so badly?'

His eyes darkened and he glanced out the window before meeting her gaze again. 'Things we can't give them.'

Without thinking, she grabbed his arm. 'You know, don't you? You know what's really going on.'

His eyes flashed up from her hand to her eyes, momentarily unguarded; his expression made her breath hitch in her throat.

Dropping her hand, she lowered her lashes. When she dared to glance up again, that look, whatever it had been, was gone.

'I know things you don't know, Allie, yes,' he said. 'But I've been here longer. My family are involved in all of this in a way you wouldn't understand.'

'Oh really?' She'd had enough secrecy. Enough lies. And his vague words infuriated her. As she stalked away she said, 'I wouldn't be so certain of that.'

When she arrived at Training Room One that night, the room was already filling, but it was less crowded than it had been the night before. She didn't see Carter or Sylvain anywhere.

She dropped on to the mat and stared off into the distance, thinking about her conversation with Sylvain; she was so lost in thought when Zoe walked up she hardly noticed.

'I can't believe you saw Gabe at dinner. You're so lucky.'

Allie snorted in disbelief. 'I don't feel lucky.'

'You should.' Zoe dropped down beside her and stretched. Allie had to admire her flexibility as she easily lowered her head to one knee, her hands wrapped around the arch of her tiny foot. 'Everyone's looking for him and you're the first one to see him. That's awesome.' She moved over the other leg, bending lithely. 'Some senior students are out with Raj's team searching the grounds now.'

That was news to Allie.

Raj stepped to the centre of the room. 'We're going to start with the same flip-and-drop move we practised last night. Please stand with your training partners.'

Allie liked how his quiet voice carried authority. He didn't need to shout in order to be respected. And he didn't seem shaken by what had happened earlier. It was just business as usual.

'Left side attack first.'

Zoe stepped towards Allie. 'We should go over this first. I did some things wrong last night.'

'It's OK.' Allie cut her off. She hadn't forgiven her yet. 'I practised last night. I think I've got it.'

'Are you sure?' Zoe sounded doubtful. 'We could go over it from the beginning. I could show you . . . '

'Let's just try it first.' Allie kept her expression blank. She didn't want Zoe to know how much she was looking forward to this.

Zoe shrugged. 'It's your funeral.'

'Ready,' Raj called.

Zoe stepped out of Allie's sightline.

'Now!'

As she had with Sylvain last night, Allie sensed rather than saw Zoe's flying approach. She planted her feet. When Zoe's hands gripped her arm she flipped her on to her back with ease.

'Crikey,' Zoe gasped as Allie helped her up. 'That was brilliant! Who taught you that?'

'Let's just say I had a private tutor.' Allie couldn't suppress a triumphant smile.

'Switch,' Raj called.

Allie prepared as Sylvain had shown her – standing straight with her knees slightly bent, arms at her side. But ready – like a coiled spring. She tried not to be cocky, but the success of her first move had filled her with confidence.

She knew could do this.

'Now!'

Grabbing the younger girl by the arm, she used the moves Sylvain had shown her but Zoe stayed solidly on her feet, crouching low and resisting all Allie's efforts.

'Good.' Raj stood nearby, watching them. 'Well done, Zoe. Allie, your moves were perfect but Zoe is well trained; what would you have done next in a real situation?'

'A chokehold,' she replied without hesitating.

'Correct.' He looked pleased, and she beamed. 'Great progress, Allie.'

For the next hour they practised self-defence moves until Allie's muscles ached.

At the end of the session, Zoe studied her appraisingly. 'Huh. Maybe you aren't completely crap after all.'

'Thanks ... I think, anyway.' Realising she should praise Zoe, too, Allie added, 'You're very good at this.'

'I know.' Zoe seemed puzzled that Allie felt it necessary to say something so obvious.

Allie was still smiling as she turned away to see Carter standing in the doorway watching her, his expression dark. She hurried over to him.

'Hey.'

'Hey back,' he said, but his voice wasn't warm.

She tilted her head at the door. 'Any luck out there?'

He shook his head, his lips set in a thin line.

With all that was going on, their fight seemed so petty. Allie shot him a glare. 'Oh for God's sake, Carter, enough with the moody act.' She grabbed his hand, pulling him through the door. 'Come on. Let's sort this.'

She was afraid he'd refuse, but he followed her outside to the terraced garden behind the school. At the very back, hidden amid the boxwood hedge, Allie sat on an old bench, tugging at his hand until he sat down beside her. The wood was cold and clammy from the earlier rain. 'OK,' she said. 'Talk to me.'

His eyes narrowed. 'Why should I? You won't listen.'

'Hey!' He'd practically spat the words at her, and she recoiled from his vehemence. 'Carter, bloody hell. This isn't like you. Talk to me.'

'I'm sorry. That was ... ' Leaning away from her, he ran his fingers through his hair. 'But sometimes it's like you think this is all a game.'

'That's not fair.' She fought to stay calm. 'I wasn't "playing games" with Sylvain, I was learning to fight. And I'm sorry you were worried about me. I was upset and I wasn't thinking straight. But I was safe the whole time. I mean, I was with Sylvain, after all.'

'Do you think that makes me feel better?' He nearly shouted the words, and Allie winced. He lowered his voice. 'Jesus, Allie. You're hanging out with Sylvain again after everything that happened.' A muscle worked in his jaw, and his wounded eyes met hers. 'You're supposed to be with me.'

She put her hand on his arm. 'I was just *training* with Sylvain. It's no big deal.'

'You know I don't like you hanging out with him, right?' With reluctance, she nodded. 'So why do you do it?'

Her own confusion about how she felt towards Sylvain made this worse. She didn't know what to say. Everything sounded weak. 'I guess ... because he's sort of my friend.'

'Your friend who practically molested you at the summer ball.'

His words hit her like weapons and a flare of anger fired in her. 'I was thinking more along the lines of my friend who saved my life,' she shot back. She could tell by the way he winced that she'd hurt him but anger was taking over now and she didn't care. 'And yeah, he did something that was wrong and gross, and I hated him for that for a long time. But he's sorry and he's been trying to make up for it ever since. And you can see that, too – I know you can. Bloody hell, Carter, this is *my life*. I can choose my own friends. All I'm asking is for you to trust me.'

With a jerk he stood up; all his muscles tense. 'Allie, you're not listening to me. I don't want you spending any time with him. At all.' He spoke with tired dignity, as if she were being completely unreasonable.

For a long second she just stared at him. What was the point in arguing when he ignored everything she said?

'Wow,' she said. 'You ... really do hate him, don't you? So I guess there's no way you'll ever believe he just wants to be my friend?'

His gaze didn't waver. 'No. So, it comes down to this: you're my girlfriend and I don't want you hanging out with Sylvain. Ever.'

'Oh come on.' A wave of confusion threatened to subsume her anger. 'This is stupid. You don't actually think you can tell me who to be friends with just because we're dating, do you? This isn't, like ... the past. I choose my own friends.'

'I'm not telling you what to do. It's your choice.' He didn't flinch from her disbelieving gaze. 'But if you want to be with me, you can't hang out with Sylvain.'

As she realised what he was saying, her heart felt heavy in her chest. 'Are you saying if I'm friends with Sylvain you'll break up with me?'

He didn't reply, but his expression made the answer clear.

'Oh Carter.' Trapped, she dropped her head to her knees.

If I say no ... do I lose him?

It was hard for her to breathe, to think. But she didn't have a choice. And she knew that. He was the most important person in her life.

I can't lose Carter.

She looked up at him, her grey eyes troubled. 'OK,' she said unhappily. 'I guess I won't hang out with Sylvain then.'

Triumphant, he grinned at her, then pulled her up off the bench into a tight hug. 'I'm sorry we fought,' he whispered, his breath warm against her hair. 'I don't want to be a complete bastard but I can't bear to see you with him.'

Her head resting against his chest, Allie didn't reply.

ELEVEN

All the next week, Allie worked so hard she barely had time to think about Gabe or her argument with Carter, although a nagging worry about the argument never really left her. Avoiding Sylvain wasn't difficult – she was too busy for anything except work and sleep. The whole time, though, the idea that one of her teachers, or one of her friends, could be working with Nathaniel plagued her thoughts. One of them was spying on her. Watching her.

But which one?

Every time she talked to Eloise, she would think, *It can't be her. She's too nice. Nobody could be that great an actress.*

She hated Zelazny of course, but it was impossible to imagine that he'd work for Nathaniel. He was dedicated to Cimmeria beyond any sense of proportion. Isabelle was of course out of the question, and then there was Jerry Cole, the science teacher. A nice, geeky man who got excited about atoms and genuinely loved his students – impossible.

It couldn't be Raj Patel, or Sylvain, Carter or . . .

Her thoughts always ended in the same place: it was impossible to imagine anyone she knew in Night School betraying Isabelle and the students like that.

But somebody was.

When she wasn't running on the school grounds, studying or learning defensive techniques, she was trying to convince Zoe to like her. But all her efforts backfired. The harder she tried, the more suspicious the younger girl was of her motives.

Zoe's strange, emotionless way of talking and her almost mechanical approach to work and problem-solving made her hard to like. It had taken Allie a while to truly accept that behind the wireless robot facade and almost scary intelligence was a thirteen-year-old girl.

Zoe hated small talk. Allie's attempts to engage her in chit-chat always ended with Zoe staring at her with blank fierceness, as if she were trying to figure out what it was about Allie that was so annoying.

One day when Allie was talking about their science assignment, Zoe interrupted her mid-sentence.

'You talk too much,' she said. Then she got up and walked away, leaving Allie staring after her, open-mouthed.

But when they were training, Zoe was a good partner. Whenever Allie quickly learned a move, Zoe would try to compliment her, although it usually came out as, 'You learned that quicker than usual. What's wrong?'

But there was something vulnerable about Zoe that made Allie keep trying.

'She's kind of like a pet . . . person,' she'd told Rachel.

Rachel smirked. 'I wouldn't let her hear you say that.'

'Like a cobra-kitten hybrid,' Allie continued, undaunted. 'Cute and vicious at the same time.'

'Or a python-puppy,' Rachel offered. 'But if you tell her I said that I'll call you liar *to your face*.'

'I wouldn't dare.' Allie shivered. 'She'd hurt me.'

By the time Jerry Cole assigned them to practise surveillance techniques on an unseasonably warm afternoon in October, Allie had begun to believe she'd never win Zoe over. As the two struck out after their surveillance subject, Allie kept saying in dramatic tones, 'It's Night School by day . . . day . . . day', adding an echo effect to the last word as Zoe glowered at her threateningly.

Their assignment was to follow a Night School student named Philip for three hours without being discovered. They had to track his every movement and record them on a form.

When they got their assignment, they both thought it sounded kind of cool.

It was unbelievably boring.

First Philip spent an hour in the library studying alone. Then he went into the boys' toilets. *For ages*.

They were in the hallway arguing about whether or not to go in and check on him when he emerged so suddenly he almost ran into them. Luckily, he seemed distracted and hurried outside without noticing them. Upon following, they watched as he joined a group of friends playing football.

While he played, Zoe and Allie hid in the woods, spying on him through the trees.

'He's intercepting the ball!' Zoe announced, watching Philip through a shield of bracken. 'Oh no. He's missed again.' Turning to face Allie, she sat with her back to the game. 'He's rubbish.'

Holding a thick leaf of grass between her thumbs, Allie blew on it until it made a squawky trumpet sound. When she tired of the noise, she let the grass float from her hand.

'God, this is dull. Why couldn't he do something interesting? Like get in a fight or ... anything that isn't this?'

Eventually, they decided to play games to pass the time. First I Spy then, when that grew dull, Cloud Animals.

'I see a minotaur,' Zoe said, as they lay on their backs staring up at the sunlit blue sky.

'No you don't.' Allie, who saw nothing but shapeless blobs, leaned over to squint at the cloud Zoe pointed at. 'That's nothing.'

'It's a minotaur!' Zoe insisted. 'Look. Two horns *there*, and a freakishly muscled torso there. And a kind of tail thing. It's a minotaur.'

'Minotaur,' Allie mumbled to herself. 'Well, I see a duck.'

'Really?' Zoe looked where Allie pointed. 'I don't think that looks like a duck. Looks more like a rabbit.'

'Fine,' Allie sighed. 'Then it's a rabbit-duck. A dabbit. Or a ruck.'

A bird fluttered from the trees to the ground nearby, cocking its head at them before changing its mind and flapping away. Allie barely noticed it out of the corner of her eye as she looked for a more interesting cloud to challenge Zoe's minotaur.

'Oh no,' Zoe whispered to herself. 'Just one.'

Allie was still staring at the clouds. 'Yes. Just one dabbit, Zoe.'

But Zoe wasn't talking about dabbits any more. She leapt to her feet and stared up at the trees, panic-stricken. Allie squinted to see her against the bright sky.

'One for sorrow; there can't be just one. There must be two. One for sorrow, *Allie*.' Zoe's voice was urgent as she turned back to look at her. 'Help me find another!'

'Find another *what*?' Startled, Allie scrambled to follow her but the younger girl had already run into the woods. When she found her a few seconds later, Zoe stood in a clearing, her eyes roaming from tree to tree. 'Find another what, Zoe?'

The younger girl pointed up, to where the fat, glossy magpie balanced on the branch above her head, its tuxedo colouring strangely out of place. It darted a look down at them before something else caught its eye.

'There can't be just one,' Zoe was muttering to herself. 'There can't be just one.'

Still confused about where all this had come from, Allie scanned the surrounding woods for a bird – any bird. 'There.' She pointed across the treetops to a tall horse chestnut tree far away where one could just be seen on the highest branches, swaying in the light breeze. From here there was no way to tell what kind of bird it was but she hoped it would look like a magpie to Zoe. 'Isn't that a magpie?'

Doubtful, Zoe stood on her toes, peering into the distance. Then she gave a squeal of happiness and clapped her hands.

'Yes! Two for joy!'

Startled, the first magpie flew away.

Without another word, Zoe ran back to where they'd been playing Cloud Animals earlier and lay down again, looking up at the sky as if nothing had happened.

After a second, Allie sat beside her, a puzzled frown creasing her forehead. 'So,' she said carefully, 'magpies?'

Frowning, Zoe scanned the clouds. 'There can't be just one, Allie. Ever.'

'Because of the poem?'

Zoe nodded.

Allie remembered it vaguely. Her mother had sometimes recited it if a single magpie crossed their path. *One for sorrow, two for joy, three for a girl, four for a boy* ...

She knew some people were superstitious about the birds, or considered them to be bad luck, but she'd never seen anyone react like Zoe. As she considered this, Allie glanced absently towards the football players – but the lawn was empty. They'd gone.

'Oh balls, Zoe, we've lost sodding Philip.'

But it didn't matter that they lost him and got marked down for it, or that Jerry looked at them with disappointment. Because somehow that afternoon changed everything.

From that day on Zoe accepted Allie completely.

The spate of warm weather didn't last and the sound of rain lashing against the windows accompanied Allie a few days later as she walked with Carter down the stone stairs to the basement training room talking about what had happened the night before. The weather had been fierce then, too. So instead of going for a run they'd been given a word problem to work out.

Written in Eloise's neat, square handwriting on a white board, it had confounded them all.

A runaway train, packed with passengers is about to crash. You can save all the passengers by switching the train to another track, but if you do that, one innocent person will die. Is it right to sacrifice one to save the lives of many?

As usual, all they'd been told was that this was the sort of decision they might have to make some day, and that there was no right answer and no wrong answer. Instead, they were to make their own decisions.

It drove Allie crazy.

'It's horrible. I mean, what kind of question is that?' she said now, as they walked under the flickering fluorescent lights of the basement hallway. The air smelled musty; it felt cool and damp against her skin. 'And how can they not tell us what right is?' She shook her fist at the ceiling. 'I need to know what right is!'

'You'll get used to it,' Carter said. 'They're always asking us things like that.'

'What are they trying to teach us?' Allie asked. 'How to be evil?'

'Maybe.'

Allie watched him out of the corner of her eye as his expression clouded. She didn't say anything but she was glad he wasn't always OK with the things Night School demanded of them. That he could look at it all and wonder, as she did, *Is this fine? Or is this really not fine at all?*

'Well, it won't work. We're too nice for them. They will never succeed.' She pushed open the door to Training Room One. 'They'll learn . . . ' But as she looked inside she lost her train of thought. The blue mats were gone. A table stood at one end of the room, faced by metal folding chairs arranged in rows.

Looking over her shoulder, Carter murmured, 'What the hell . . . ?'

Exchanging a worried look, they walked in together, slipping into two free seats.

'What's going on?' Allie whispered, but Carter shook his head. He didn't know either. Worry chilled Allie like a cool breeze. The room had the ambience of a church sanctuary before the sermon began – everyone sat in poses of subdued reverence. She got the feeling nobody knew what was happening, but they all knew it wouldn't be good.

By the time the doors swung open ten minutes later the air fairly crackled with tension. The Night School leaders walked in together like they were heading into battle – Eloise, Isabelle, Zelazny, Jerry and Raj, all dressed in black and matching each other stride for stride. They didn't look at the students until they'd taken their seats at the front of the room, then their eyes swept the room impassively.

Allie twisted the edge of her shirt around one finger so tightly it cut off the blood flow.

Raj spoke first. 'What you're going to do this week isn't easy, but it is critical. Each of you will be assigned one person to interview. You are to ask your subject about every aspect of their life and produce a written report. In that report you will decide whether or not the person you investigate is telling the truth. Throughout the week you will each receive one-to-one training in lie detection. By the end of the week we expect you to be able to identify all the signs of falseness – vocal tics, mannerisms, tells. You will use those to determine the truth.'

He leaned back, and Eloise took over. 'Assigned subjects will, in many cases, be someone you already know – in fact, somebody you know well.' A dismayed murmur crept through the room. 'Through this you will learn how to separate your emotions from your work. However, you should know that your subject will never see the report you write for us. This will be completely confidential and should, therefore, be the unvarnished truth.'

Placing her palms flat on the table, she emphasised the next words. 'Lying to your interviewer is grounds for expulsion from Night School and Cimmeria Academy.'

As Zelazny took over, Allie felt herself move back in her chair, as if to get further away from them all.

'Subject assignments are secret – only you and your subject should know you are investigating them. Do not reveal these to anybody else.' His icy eyes surveyed them. 'Anyone found to have revealed this information will be punished.' Reaching into a briefcase on the floor beside him, he pulled out a stack of thin black folders. 'When your name is called, please come forward to collect your assignment. Anderson . . . '

As a tall, slim girl walked to the front of the room for her folder, Allie and Carter exchanged a quick despairing look.

While the stack of folders dwindled in front of Zelazny, Allie watched as first Lucas then Jules collected their assignments.

When Zelazny called out, 'Glass!' Zoe strode past them, visibly fuming. She snatched the folder from his hands. 'This is *lame*,' she muttered as she passed Allie on her way back to her seat.

Finally, Zelazny barked, 'Sheridan!'

Taking a steadying breath, she walked to the front of the room. She kept her face blank although her hands curled into fists at her sides. She made herself meet Zelazny's frigid eyes as she took the cool folder from his hands. The entire process of walking from her seat to the table and back again must have taken less than a minute. It felt endless.

Carter's was the last name called. As he stood up he gave Allie a helpless look.

'You now have your assignments.' Isabelle's cool, clear voice rang out after he returned to his seat. 'Your absolute discretion is required with this process.'

While she spoke, Jerry took off his wire-framed glasses and wiped them with a cloth. When finished, he took over for the final part. 'Spend time with your subject. Learn to ask the right questions. And to tell truth from a lie. This is important.' Replacing his glasses on his nose, he studied them all solemnly. 'Somebody in this room is working for Nathaniel. Lying to all of us. You could find that person. The process starts tomorrow. There will be no Night School training this week – we want you to focus solely on this project.'

As the students shuffled out of the room, Allie and Carter caught up with Lucas and Jules.

'Can you believe this?' Lucas looked disgusted.

Shaking her head, Jules glanced up at Carter. 'I don't like this at all.'

Her worried expression made Allie nervous.

Nothing ever bothers Jules.

'This isn't going to end well. Someone's gonna get their feelings hurt,' Lucas joked darkly, trying to lighten the mood. 'And I'll bet it's me.'

But nobody laughed.

Back in her room later, Allie sat on her bed, the folder closed in front of her; a rectangular black hole amid the milky whiteness of the duvet.

Nobody had wanted to hang out. By unspoken consensus they'd all parted at the top of the stairs, everyone going their own way.

Now she knew she had to open the folder and see whose privacy she was going to invade. Whose honesty she was about to doubt. And who would probably hate her before the week was over.

Eloise had said the assigned person would be somebody they knew well.

A horrible sixth sense told her she already knew what she would find inside that folder. Still she looked at it for a long moment, her hands refusing to move.

Finally, closing her eyes, she reached out blindly for the folder. She could feel the cool smoothness of the cover beneath her fingertips, then the sharp ridge of the edges. She flipped it open.

Saying a silent prayer, she opened her eyes.

Two words stared up at her, written in neat black letters against the white background of the page.

'Carter West.'

TWELVE

Picking up the paper, Allie glared at it fiercely, as if the intensity of her gaze could change its contents. But no matter how long she looked the same message glared up at her. She flipped it over and back again. Aside from those two unwanted words the page was blank.

Behind it, though, was another piece of paper – a short sheet of instructions, neatly typed.

Now that your subject has been assigned, you are required to inform this person that you will be investigating them. Try and do this in an unthreatening fashion. For example, offer them tea first. Or meet them for lunch. In that relaxed environment, tell them that they have been assigned to you, and that you'd like to conduct your first interview as soon as possible.

During your meetings, take thorough notes. Along

with your final research document, all of your notes must also be submitted for review. Keep no copies for yourself.

Keep this folder safe. Allow nobody to see it or its contents. Any breach of this rule could result in your disqualification from Night School or, in some cases, in your expulsion ...

A light tap at the window stopped her mid-sentence. Carter peered at her through the glass from his perch on the ledge outside.

Allie scrambled to close the file folder. For a moment she thought about telling him to go away.

Feigning illness or exhaustion. Anything.

When she didn't move, he pointed at the window latch and gave her an 'any time now' look.

Reluctantly, she climbed off the bed and pushed open the latch. The shutter-style window swung out and Carter climbed on to the desk in a rush of cool air, unfolding his long legs with difficulty. It was still raining out, and his dark hair hung lank; water dripped on to his blue jumper. The cold had made his cheeks red.

He looked amazing. But he was a bit cross.

'What took you so long? It's freezing out there.'

'Sorry,' she said, gesturing vaguely. 'I was working on a ... thing.'

Glancing at the folder on her bed, his eyes darkened. 'Yeah, I've been working on that thing myself.'

'I hate that thing,' she said. 'Do we have to do that thing?'

'Yes,' he said. 'But it doesn't have to ruin our lives. We just do the thing and then we go and do some other thing. It's just a thing.'

'You say that, but what they're asking us to do is invade each other's privacy.' Her eyes flashed. 'Tell each other all our secrets. Reveal all the embarrassing or weird or bad crap we never tell anybody. And, basically, accuse each other of being spies and liars. How do we do that and still stay . . . ' remembering that he didn't know yet who she'd been assigned, she finished weakly, '. . . friends?'

'You just do,' he said. 'Because everybody has to go through it, so we're all in the same position.' He pulled her closer. 'Don't worry, Al. It'll be fine. Who'd you get anyway?'

Instead of answering him, she stood on her toes and kissed him. Kissed him until his hands moved down to her hips and pulled her closer. Kissed him until his breath came in short gasps. His hair was wet between her fingers and his lips cold against hers but she didn't care. His warm breath filled her mouth and she was as close to him as she knew how to be.

Then without warning, he stopped and looked down at her, realisation clear in his eyes. 'Oh hell, Allie. You got me, didn't you?'

She nodded.

Carter swore under his breath. 'Those *utter* bastards.'

'So what you're looking for are physical signs – sweating, for example,' Eloise explained.

'Gross.' Staring at her shoes, Allie slid further down in her seat. She twisted the hem of her shirt around her fingers. Then untwisted it. And twisted it again.

'Also fidgeting.' The librarian glanced at her pointedly. 'But these are very obvious indicators and, frankly, I would expect more from Carter.'

Allie bristled. 'What does that mean?'

It was late morning, and Eloise had taken her out of her maths class for her first training session on interview techniques and lie detection. This was her area of speciality and Isabelle had insisted that she spend extra time with Allie, training her.

Normally cutting maths would have filled Allie with joy, but she was still too angry about being assigned to interview Carter to find any happiness in it.

'It means,' Eloise's voice was patient, 'that he's had a lot of Night School training. So he's probably quite skilled at deception.'

Her words chilled Allie as if they'd been chipped from ice.

Carter is the least deceptive person I know. He would never . . .

'Right. Let's try something different.' Leaning back against the vividly painted wall, the librarian pulled her notebook on to her lap and flipped through the pages. They were in one of the study carrels at the back of the library. All the little rooms – each about the size of a small office with barely room for a desk and two chairs – were completely covered in seventeenth-century murals. This was the one Allie thought of as 'Peace', as the people in it were smiling. The cherubs fluttering near the ceiling seemed adorably plump and jolly. Nobody was killing anybody else like they were in the other rooms.

'You tell me,' Eloise continued, 'what signs are you going to look out for in your next interview with Carter?'

Allie thought about Carter looking at her with those eyes, his long lashes sweeping downward when he was upset ...

'Sweating,' she sighed. 'And if he touches his ...' she waved a hand at her own face 'you know ... nose or mouth.'

'Good. And do you know why people cover their mouth when they lie?'

Allie did know but, her lips set in a tight stubborn line, she shook her head anyway.

Eloise wore a stylish pair of narrow glasses that barely covered her eyes. They sparkled in the light as she spoke. 'Some believe it's a subconscious effort to hide the lie.' She flipped a page in her notebook. 'You should also be looking out for eye movements.'

'Seriously?' Allie frowned at her. 'Like, if he looks shifty?'

'Actually, the opposite,' Eloise said. 'You're looking to see if he makes too much eye contact. When people lie they often concentrate on looking you in the eye, not realising they don't normally do that.' She pointed at Allie. 'For example, just now when I said you should watch his eye movements, before you spoke you looked up to the ceiling. Why did you do that?'

'I did?' Allie squirmed in her seat. 'I don't ... Did I really?'

Eloise nodded. 'We do that when we're thinking of an answer to a question. It's like we're trying to check our brain for the information we need.' She leaned forward. 'If Carter doesn't do that when he's thinking, he probably prepared the answer in advance.'

Sighing, Allie looked down at her hands, which were now twisted into a tight knot in her lap.

'Great,' she said, miserably.

'Here.' She handed Allie a sheet of paper with three questions written on it. 'When you interview Carter, you must work these questions in. They have to be in your final report with his answers.'

Taking it, Allie stared at the first question. 'Have you ever talked about me to Nathaniel or anyone who works for him?' Her stomach churned.

When she spoke, her voice was sharp with tension. 'Eloise, you know and I know that whoever the spy is, it's not Carter. This is a waste of time. Why can't we concentrate on finding who it really is? What if it's Zelazny or Jerry? What if it's you? Who's interviewing *you*?'

Her voice rang out in the quiet room, and Eloise didn't immediately respond. Instead she walked around to be closer to Allie. She took her glasses off, set them down and leaned forward. Her long dark hair was pulled back loosely. Not for the first time, Allie noticed how young she was. As she leaned forward, her face unlined, her brown eyes clear, she could have been another student.

'Look, Allie,' she said, her voice more gentle now, 'I know you're having a rough time with this. And we all knew you might. That's why we've asked you to do it.'

Resentment made Allie's heartbeat rush. 'What? You all wanted to ruin my life?'

'No,' Eloise said. 'We want you to learn how to keep yourself safe – even from people who seem like your friends. Don't forget Gabe. He was your friend, too. You trusted him – we all trusted him – but he wasn't what he seemed. We were always going to have you interview the person closest to you.'

'But why Carter?' Allie's voice was anguished. 'He's not my friend. He's my boyfriend. That's different.'

Reaching out to untangle her tightly knit fingers, Eloise squeezed her hands. 'Because the person closest to you can do the most harm.'

That was a horrible thing to say. Furious, Allie wrenched her hands free. But when she opened her mouth to argue Eloise held up one hand to stop her.

'Look, before you say it, I know. I know Carter is a good person. We know Carter very well and it's extremely unlikely he has any secrets from us. But Carter might not always be the closest person to you. And you've got to learn how to assess the people you care about dispassionately. You've got to be able to separate what you want people to be from what they really are. Even if you love them.'

At the mention of the word 'love', Allie flinched. 'That's stupid.' She kicked a foot against the leg of her chair. 'Nobody can do that. Nobody can investigate their boyfriend and then, like . . . make out with him after class. Nobody.'

'People do,' Eloise said simply. 'All the time.'

That evening after dinner, Allie sat alone in her room, pretending to read her English assignment, but as she stared at the words they seemed to float on the page in no particular order, as meaningless as a code for which she had no key. Her thoughts were elsewhere. The seeds of doubt Eloise had planted that morning were taking root and winding through her mind.

How would I feel if Carter lied to me? she wondered, flipping a page. Then, horribly: *Would he do that?*

Keep moving and you won't die.

Allie ran through the frozen woods repeating those words in her head – over and over.

Keep moving.

Blue moonlight suffused the forest, glinting off her white pyjamas.

You won't die.

Nine hundred and seventy-one steps ... Nine hundred and seventy-two.

She was so cold she couldn't believe she was still moving. Her frozen fingers clenched into fists that pumped at her sides. She could hear nothing except her ragged breathing and the sound of her sodden slippers crunching through snow.

In the moon's day-for-night glow, she could make out pine trees and frozen ferns as she skidded along the forest path. Her breath puffed in a crystalline cloud.

She didn't know where to go. And she was so cold. A sob welled in her throat and she forced it back.

Not now.

Then a sound – something moved through the frozen brush nearby. A bush shook off its mantle of snow.

She skidded to a stop, then crouched in a defensive stance.

As she held her breath and waited for attack, the undergrowth parted and a fox slunk out and stood facing her.

His lush fur was a flash of elegant carmine against the white snow.

Gazing at her with fearless, predatory eyes, he sniffed the air.

Tears sprang to Allie's eyes, and she dashed them away.

'You're so beautiful,' she whispered, reaching out a hand – blue with cold – to touch him.

His lips curled up to show his white teeth. Before she could withdraw her hand he crouched.

Then, with a snarl he leapt for her throat.

Her breath burning in her throat, Allie leapt out of bed. By the time she was fully awake, she stood shivering, her bare feet on the cold floor, clutching the corner of the duvet. Her eyes wild, she swatted at the desktop lamp until the light came on, then she searched the corners of the empty room.

Finally satisfied that she was alone, she closed the open window, latching it tight. When she climbed back into bed, she pulled the duvet up across her chest like a shield.

'Thank you, my subconscious,' she muttered, 'for ensuring I never sleep again.'

She stayed awake for a long time, and when she did sleep, she left the light on.

THÌRTEEN

After the nightmare, Allie slept only fitfully, and it was still dark when she woke for good. She made her way downstairs before seven and sat in the dining hall watching the kitchen staff set up the hot plates and coffee urns. She was staring into the distance when Rachel walked up a few minutes later. Allie hadn't seen much of her lately – she'd been too busy with Night School.

'You look like hell,' Rachel announced, dropping her books on the table. 'Let's stuff ourselves. And you can tell me all about it.'

Now they sat in the still mostly empty dining hall with steaming cups of tea and piles of scrambled egg and toast that Allie hadn't wanted but was nonetheless devouring. Somehow, she felt better just being with Rachel. She'd missed her. There was so much she couldn't tell her – things she longed to talk about. But bantering with her over breakfast felt good.

It felt like the old days.

'I'm famished,' Rachel announced. 'Dinner was too weird last night for actual consumption. They should have just, I don't know ... framed it. Called it modern art. What are you doing up so early anyway?'

'I couldn't sleep.' Allie yawned. 'I had this messed up nightmare where I was running and then a fox ate me.' She took a scalding sip of tea.

'A fox ate you?' Rachel looked impressed. 'Was it gory? Did it hurt?'

Remembering standing shivering and alone in her bedroom, Allie said, 'I woke up when it started eating my face.'

'Yum. Eating.' Rachel took a bite of eggs. When Allie didn't laugh, she tilted her head to one side. 'Foxes don't usually eat people, you know. Actually, they never eat people and I think I should be precise about that. Foxes do not eat people. Your dream self was probably just too delicious for that particular dream fox to resist. It just means he likes you.'

Even as grim as she felt, Allie had to smile. 'He? What if it was a girl fox?'

'Lesbian fox dreams – you naughty vixen! I wonder what Freud would say about that,' Rachel said.

'I wish it had been a sex dream,' Allie grumbled at her plate then she glanced up at Rachel. 'Hey, speaking of sex ... You and Lucas. What's up with that? Is something up with that? Because I think something's up with that.'

Rachel blushed. She *actually* blushed.

Allie's eyes widened. 'Something's up with that – I can see it in your face! You tell me everything right now.'

Rachel looked over at her shyly. 'Well, Lucas and I . . . are together. It's official.'

'Oh. My. God.' The words rose to a small scream as Allie jumped out of her chair and hugged her.

Breathless with laughter, Rachel pushed her away. 'Get off. You're squishing my toast.'

'Oh, Rach, I'm so psyched for you! When did this happen?'

'Last weekend. Didn't you notice I disappeared after dinner?' Rachel asked. 'And then on Sunday I was all giddy and stupid. It was disgusting. I hope you didn't see.'

A rush of heat coloured Allie's cheeks. She hadn't noticed. Not at all.

She'd been busy last weekend, training with Night School, hanging out with Carter and Zoe. She hadn't noticed Rachel acting giddy because she'd hardly seen Rachel in days.

Last weekend? That was ages ago. And she didn't tell me?

It seemed inconceivable that Rachel wouldn't have rushed to her room and jumped on her bed, eager to tell her everything.

As Rachel chattered happily about moonlight and kissing by the stream, Allie nodded and smiled in all the right places, but in her head she was thinking that Night School was driving them apart.

Even after lingering with Rachel over breakfast, Allie arrived early for history class, but Jo was already there, waving at her across the otherwise empty room.

Her gamine short fair hair made her look pale and thinner. Or maybe she just *was* pale and thinner. Allie studied her critically as she sat down.

'Hey! Quick, before everyone gets here,' Jo whispered. 'Who did you get?'

'Who'd I get? Who'd I get for what?'

Jo seemed jittery, overexcited. Her eyes were too bright. 'You know what.'

'I don't . . .' Her voice trailing off, Allie felt anxiety twist her stomach as she realised what Jo meant.

She stared. 'How do you know about . . . ?'

'Oh, Allie,' Jo giggled. 'My contacts are everywhere. I know all. So tell me. Who are you assigned to interview?'

Her laugh seemed too high-pitched, her reply too glib, and Allie tried to hide the suspicion that had nestled in her chest like a shard of ice.

This was Zelazny's class room. Zelazny hated her. Jo knew that. Why would she ask something so forbidden somewhere so dangerous?

'I can't . . .' Allie was horrified. 'I just . . . I can't tell you, Jo. You know that.'

'What? Seriously?' Jo seemed affronted. 'I won't tell anyone.'

Thinking about the word 'expulsion', Allie shook her head emphatically. 'Jo, I can't,' she said.

But even as she said that, she knew that somewhere deep inside, she just didn't *want* to tell Jo. She didn't trust her. If she told her and word got back to Zelazny . . .

'How nice to see students so eager to learn that they come to class early.' Zelazny's icy voice cut through Allie's thoughts.

Both girls spun around to face the front. The teacher stood by his desk in a military stance, feet shoulder-width apart, hands loose at his side, eyes alert.

How long has he been standing there? Allie wondered.

Luckily, Jo was never at a loss for words for long. 'We just wanted to get a little studying done before class, Mr Zelazny.' She dimpled cutely. 'We didn't think you'd mind.'

As angry as she was at Jo right now, Allie had to admire her smoothness.

'Far be it from me to deny students a place to study.' His voice dripping sarcasm, he pulled his books out of a briefcase and began arranging his desk. 'Please continue your work. Don't let me interrupt.'

He said the last word of each sentence as if it tasted bad.

Jo and Allie exchanged another loaded glance before looking down at their books. After just a minute, though, Jo sprang to her feet.

'I'm just going to dash downstairs before class to get something to eat,' she announced as she hurried to the door. 'I'll be right back.'

'If you are late you will be given detention,' Zelazny called after her. He added in an almost panicked tone, 'And don't bring food into my classroom!'

After Jo abandoned her, Allie busied herself reading over the short history essay due that day but she was acutely aware of Zelazny's presence a few feet away. She could hear him breathing and it made her muscles tense. She found she was reading the same lines over and over. Still she didn't look up.

When he spoke she nearly jumped.

'Is there anything you'd like to ask me?'

Slowly, Allie raised her eyes from her paper to find him watching her fixedly.

'Ex . . . Excuse me?'

'I said. Is there anything you'd like to ask me?'

Something about the way he said it was menacing. Allie's skin crawled.

What had he heard?

She shook her head vigorously. 'No . . . Sir?'

'Are you certain?' He leaned forward, his fingertips resting on the desktop.

The colour drained from Allie's cheeks but she held herself steady. She was starting to get angry, but she knew that was probably just what he wanted.

What is he so pissed off about? All he could have heard was me refusing to talk about Night School. So why is he being such a wanker?

She spoke coolly, her voice more confident than she felt. 'There is nothing I want to ask you right now, Mr Zelazny. Thank you.'

Lowering her eyes to her book, she pretended not to notice the sharp intake of breath and the sound of a drawer slamming shut.

Just as she thought she might have to flee the classroom, Sylvain walked in. 'August,' he said to Zelazny without waiting for a hello, 'I have a quick question about the assignment . . .' He seemed to notice Allie and the tension in the room at the same moment; his voice trailed off.

Desperate, Allie caught his gaze, and tried to plead for help with her eyes. Her heart rate accelerated as their eyes locked.

He did have the most ludicrously watercolour-blue eyes.

'What's your question, Sylvain?' Zelazny snapped impatiently. 'I'm busy.'

But Sylvain seemed suddenly uninterested in being rushed. 'The essay you assigned for tomorrow ... Can you explain exactly what you're seeking from it? I found the assignment a little vague.'

'I think I was quite clear,' Zelazny said. 'I've got it right here.'

As he flipped through the papers piled on his desk, Sylvain caught Allie's eye again. And winked.

All day Allie expected to hear from whoever was going to interview her. Each time someone called her name or tapped her on the shoulder, she expected to hear a voice asking her questions she didn't know how to answer. Everybody else was preparing for their interview, but she had still not been contacted.

She'd come up with a variety of conspiracy theories to explain the silence. Maybe, knowing what she knew about her family, Isabelle had kept her out of it altogether. Or maybe she was going to conduct the interview herself.

Either way, she wasn't going to talk about it to anyone except Isabelle. And she wasn't in a huge hurry to do that.

After the incident in the classroom she'd avoided Jo. That whole conversation had been strange. She hadn't told anybody about it because she didn't want to seem paranoid. But she still didn't understand why Jo would have put her in that position.

At dinner, she made sure she sat between Lucas and Carter. Both in Night School. Both safe.

When Lucas suggested a game of night tennis, she looked at him doubtfully. 'I am so behind on my work—'

'Let's do it.' From across the table, Jo cut her off. 'Defo. It's been ages. Who's in?'

Everybody raised their hands except Allie and Carter.

'I can't.' Carter shrugged. 'I've got a meeting with Zelazny to talk about an assignment. There's no escape.' He glanced at Allie. 'You should do it, though. You'll like it.'

'Yeah, come on, Allie,' Rachel said. 'You really should. It'll be fun.'

The others' enthusiasm was hard to resist so, later that evening, she walked out into the cold with Rachel. But she still wasn't convinced.

As they pulled equipment out of a utility closet, Allie shivered. 'It's *freezing*. Why are we doing this?'

'Don't be so wet.' Jo handed Lucas a racquet and a box of balls. 'We're doing it because it's awesome.'

Guiltily, Allie wondered if Jo had noticed she'd been trying to avoid her. Even now she stood three people away from her.

'Yeah, Allie.' Lucas threw her a tennis ball, but her reflexes were too slow and it bounced off her shoulder and rolled back across the ground to him. 'Aren't you supposed to be some kind of hardened athlete? I can't believe you think this is cold.'

When she sighed, her breath puffed out in a visible irritated cloud. But she didn't want to be a wimp.

'I'm not saying we shouldn't do it at all.' She swung her racquet awkwardly.

As they hooted at her change of tone, Rachel put a loyal arm across her shoulders.

'It *is* cold. But that makes it even better,' she said. 'Wait and see.' As she turned to grab some netting though, she seemed to remember something. 'Oh, one thing. I forgot to tell you that—'

'Well, are we playing or just standing around?' Katie Gilmore's crystalline voice preceded her across the frozen grass. Her long red hair was pulled up in a smooth ponytail, and she wore a ski-style headband that covered her ears.

With betrayal in her eyes, Allie turned to Rachel. 'You must be joking.'

'She invited herself.' Wincing apologetically, Rachel hurried off with her equipment as Allie stared after her.

'Oh, Allie. You're not playing too, are you?' Katie eyed her with mild disdain. 'Where did you learn to play tennis? Do they even play tennis in Brixton?'

'Oh piss off, Katie.' Allie turned to follow Rachel across the lawn, but Katie stuck right on her heels.

'No need to be vile, although vile does seem to be your speciality.'

Allie glanced at her. Her ponytail was bouncing, the cold had brought colour to her cheeks and she looked quite cheerful.

She loves this.

'Why are you following me, Katie? Why aren't you off eating brains with your friends?'

Katie's perfect lips curved up. 'Oh, Allie. You're so adorable. You know, I heard a rumour – probably a lie – that you're in Night School now. It isn't true, is it?'

'I admire your optimism.' Allie's reply was as icy as the weather. 'But if you think for one second I'm going to discuss this with you—'

'It's just,' Katie cut her off, 'I'm surprised you'd do it. I thought you hated it after what happened last year.'

She sounded almost reasonable – maybe even genuinely curious – and Allie turned to look at her in surprise. 'I have my reasons,' she said slowly. 'Whatever I've done, whether I'm in or I'm not in, I did it because I thought it was the right thing to do.'

She could tell from Katie's face that she knew perfectly well she was in Night School. The redhead arched one eyebrow as if to say she didn't think it *was* the right thing to do, but she said nothing more. Allie glanced around – nobody was paying any attention to them and now she was curious.

'Why didn't you ever join . . . you know what? Surely you'd qualify.'

'Because I'm already rich enough and I don't like getting dirty.' Katie started walking again, her expression enigmatic. 'Let's go and play some tennis.'

It was a clear, starry night, and even colder than the night before. The wind had stilled, and the air felt frosty. Allie shivered – her thin jacket couldn't handle these temperatures. The others were much more bundled up. Her parents hadn't packed a scarf or gloves in her suitcase – maybe they thought the school would provide them.

As they gathered on a flat section of lawn at the edge of the trees, Sylvain walked up, a striped scarf tied jauntily around his throat. 'Room for one more?'

'Absolutely not,' Lucas joked, tossing him a racquet. The French student caught it easily. It looked comfortable in his hand – Allie got the feeling he'd handled a lot of tennis racquets.

In fact, she was certain they all had. They seemed so completely at ease with the rules and equipment. She'd never have admitted it, but Katie was right about Allie's lack of tennis background – she could only remember playing it as a child in the school gym on a rainy afternoon in PE class.

Others began to join them now that the net was being set up. Zoe showed up at Allie's side, wearing fluffy white earmuffs and matching gloves. 'Frozen night tennis. I am so in,' she said without being invited.

'I know somebody else who would love to play,' Sylvain said. 'I'll be right back.'

Allie stood alone, watching as Lucas and Rachel strung a net between poles and connected wires to power outlets she hadn't noticed before. When everything was connected, Lucas flipped a switch.

On the other side of what was now a tennis court Zoe whooped and waved her racquet in the air. 'We have lights!'

One hand over her mouth, Allie turned around in a circle to take it in. Each thread of the net was strung with tiny fairy lights. It looked like a dew-covered spider-web caught in dawn sunlight. Around the court, all the trees were similarly wrapped in hidden webs of lights that now illuminated each branch with cool white light.

As vivid racquet-shaped lights appeared around her, Allie turned hers over and realised there was a switch at the end of the handle that caused them to light up. Each was a different colour. Zoe's was green, Jo's purple, Lucas' red.

When she pushed a button on the base of her own racquet it instantly came to life, glowing blue.

Across the court a glowing orange orb was suddenly whacked with a red racquet – the lighted tennis ball flew through the darkness. The players on the opposite side were virtually invisible – the lighted racquets and the ball seemed to operate of their own accord.

Delighted, she laughed out loud. 'This is *crazy*!'

'This,' Jo said, returning Lucas' volley with the smooth ease of somebody who has been coached, 'is night tennis.'

'Come on.' Rachel nudged Allie. 'Let's warm up.'

'I'm not that great at tennis,' Allie admitted reluctantly.

Rachel pulled her on to the court with a laugh. 'We don't care, Allie. You're not auditioning for the Olympics. You're playing tennis in the dark in the freezing cold.'

A glowing tennis ball whizzed by their heads and they both ducked.

'My bad!' Zoe's voice called, but all Allie could see was her green racquet waving apologetically.

'See?' Rachel said. 'We all suck.'

But Allie knew that wasn't true.

While she tried swinging the racquet a few times, Sylvain returned, standing just outside the glow of the lights. 'Does everyone know Nicole?'

Allie squinted into the dark but couldn't see the person with Sylvain.

'Of course,' Jo called. '*Bonsoir*, Nicole.'

Musical laughter came from the general direction of Sylvain, and then a husky French voice responded, '*Bonsoir*, Jo. Your forehand is lovely.'

'Ta muchly,' Jo said whacking the ball hard at Lucas, who lobbed it back with ease.

As Sylvain and Nicole stepped into the light cast by the net,

155

her full lips curved into a smile. She wore a creamy cashmere scarf around her neck and an expensive-looking white wool coat. Sylvain's hand rested lightly on her back, and Allie was staring at them open-mouthed when the ball hit her on the side of the head hard enough to knock her down.

Everyone rushed to her at once.

Lucas vaulted the net. 'Allie, are you OK? I'm so sorry. I thought you were ready.'

Rachel held Allie's head in her lap as Zoe knelt beside them asking, 'What day is it? Who's the prime minister?'

'Sorry,' Allie said. 'I think I was more surprised than hurt. But then again, it *could* be brain damage.'

She could hear a collective relieved sigh from the group. Rachel smiled at her and squeezed her fingers.

'Don't fall asleep,' Zoe said urgently.

Everyone turned to her.

'I read an article,' she explained. 'If it's a concussion you have to stay awake.'

'I'm awake,' Allie joked feebly, as Rachel and Lucas helped her to her feet. 'But if I fall asleep playing tennis please call an ambulance.'

'Yay!' Zoe said, racing to the other side of the net. 'Allie's alive and we can play!'

Rachel studied her face with worried eyes. 'You really OK?' she asked.

Although she was still a little dizzy, Allie nodded. 'I'm good. In a blindsided, cracked-skull kind of a way.'

'That's less good than usual,' Rachel said.

'True,' Allie agreed. 'So . . . I think I'll sit out the first game.'

'Somebody has to sit with Allie and make sure she stays awake and knows who's prime minister,' Zoe called from across the grass court.

'What is your obsession with the prime minister?' Lucas asked.

'It's a question people get asked when they hit their heads,' Zoe said. 'In films. I mean they're usually American films and they ask who the president is. I guess brain damage knocks all the politics out. But this is England so there's not a president. And you can't exactly ask them who the Queen is, can you? She's just ... the Queen.'

'I know who the prime minister is,' Allie said sitting down on the frozen grass. 'So you can all relax.'

'Is it still that same man?' Nicole's voice came out of the dark right beside her and Allie jumped. 'The one with the funny face?'

'Yeah,' Allie replied. 'It's still that one.'

'I like him,' Nicole said. 'He seems very good with children. And that is a proven sign of kindness.' As she spoke, Allie glanced over at her furtively – her expressive brown eyes were surrounded by thick lashes; her bone structure was as fine as a fawn's. 'I'm sitting out this game, too.' Nicole's French accent was more delicate than Sylvain's; it seemed to curl around each word lightly before letting go. 'I will help keep you awake. Sylvain will sit with us when he reappears. I don't know where he's gone.'

But at that moment, he walked up with a bottle of water, which he handed to Allie before sitting on the cold grass beside Nicole.

'How do you feel?' He studied her with concern.

Her head was starting to throb, but she knew if she said that they'd make her go and see the nurse. 'OK, I think. A bit fuzzy maybe. But I think that's an I-just-got-hit-on-the-head thing,' Allie said.

Rachel had been talking to Jo and Lucas on the court but now she joined them. 'How are you feeling?'

'Seriously, everyone.' Allie held up her hands. 'I'm totally fine. Except that I'm asleep and I've forgotten the date and the prime minister.'

'That's it. I'm calling an ambulance,' Rachel said mildly, as the first ball of the game flew across the net, glowing like a meteor.

It was entrancing to watch the disembodied, lighted racquets move in the darkness – hitting the star-like ball back and forth across the glittering spider-web net. Occasionally the ball would spin out of reach and the unseen players would laugh or groan. But beautiful as it was, it was freezing, too. And the cold seemed to penetrate to Allie's bones.

Shivering, she pulled her thin denim jacket tightly around her. 'It's so cold.'

'You should be wearing gloves.' Rachel looked critically at Allie's clothes. 'And a scarf. And . . . a coat.'

'Here.' Sylvain unknotted the scarf from his neck and reached across Nicole to hand it to Allie. 'Wear this. I am fine without it.'

As Nicole looked up at him with an approving smile, Allie realised they must be together. Like . . . *together* together. They were so close to each other. And now that she thought about it, they sat together at dinner almost every day, didn't they?

The pounding in her head was worsening – it made it hard to think. She considered saying that she wasn't really cold. Or she didn't really need it. But she was shivering, so she accepted the scarf and wrapped it around her neck and shoulders.

A wave of his distinctive scent – coffee and spice – enveloped her and she had an instant flash memory of kissing him and breathing in that smell.

She felt dizzy.

'Thanks.' She avoided his eyes. 'I think my parents forgot to pack mine.'

'Now you must sit closer to me,' Nicole purred to Sylvain. 'Because you will turn to ice.'

He moved so that she sat between his legs, leaning back against his torso. He slid his hands inside her coat pockets.

'There,' she said. 'Now I will share my body heat with you.'

He replied in French, and she laughed that tinkling, musical laugh. Like champagne glasses clinking.

Even with the scarf, Allie's teeth began to chatter. She felt colder than she thought she really should under the circumstances. Cold from the inside out.

Her thoughts whirled. *When did they get together? Why didn't I know? And why do I even care? Maybe I do have brain damage . . .*

The pain in her head seemed to be getting worse – her ears began to ring.

Suddenly Allie decided she'd had enough cold pain and hot French girls for one day, but when she jumped to her feet the ground seemed to rock a bit. As she wobbled unsteadily, the others looked up at her in surprise.

'I feel a bit funny,' she said, steadying herself. 'I think I'll go inside and have a cup of tea and a brain haemorrhage.'

Sylvain's face creased with concern. 'Do you want me to come with you?'

Allie shook her head so hard she nearly lost her balance. She also thought she might throw up. 'Rachel?' She turned back to where Rachel had been sitting on the grass but she was already at her side.

'Let's go, girlfriend.' She hooked her arm through Allie's. 'I'll keep you awake, and you can tell me all about the prime minister.'

The nurse greeted Allie like an old friend. 'What on earth have you done to yourself now?'

At least her injuries last term had been memorable.

After shining bright lights in her eyes, taking her blood pressure and considering her temperature, the nurse told her all she really needed was something to eat and a cup of strong tea, but she told her not to fall asleep, and gave her something for the headache before sending her to the common room.

Later, Allie and Rachel sat on a deep leather sofa in one corner, wrapped in blankets, drinking steaming cups of spiced tea and eating fresh cookies.

'You should get hit on the head more,' Rachel said cheerfully. 'They give you things.'

'Injuries are brilliant,' Allie agreed. The pills had kicked in and her head was less painful. As she relaxed in the warmth, she wondered why it had felt so weird seeing Sylvain with Nicole. Yes, she'd forgiven him for what happened the night of the summer ball. She believed he was genuinely sorry, but she didn't think she'd ever trust him like that again.

So why should I care who he dates?

She didn't like that she cared.

When Carter rushed in a few minutes later, she jumped to her feet in a guilty rush, wobbling unsteadily.

'Whoa,' he said, lowering back down. 'You're still a little shaky.'

'I'm fine,' she assured him with the confidence of a doctor. 'The nurse said I'm fine.'

'Actually, she said you should sit and rest for a while. And not go to sleep,' Rachel said. 'Zoe's going to be so psyched that she was right about that.' Turning to Carter, she added, 'She doesn't think Allie really has a concussion. She's just being careful. But we're supposed to keep an eye on her for a couple of hours.'

Carter brushed Allie's hair back to look at the faint red mark on the side of her head. 'But you feel OK?'

'Yep. No permanent brain damage,' Allie said, leaning against him.

'I'm sorry I wasn't there.' His lips brushed the place on her head where the ball hit her. 'To pick up the pieces.'

The light touch made Allie quiver, and she looked up into his eyes.

Rachel stood and stretched. 'I'm not sure my medical talent is needed now that you're here, Carter. Are you fine to stay with her?'

Carter's eyes crinkled when he smiled. Allie liked that crinkle. 'I'll stay with her,' he said.

When she'd gone, Allie and Carter curled up together on the sofa. Lying in the crook of his arm, she told him what had happened.

'Lucas feels terrible,' Carter said. 'I saw him before I came up here. You'd think he'd shot you. But I'd still be furious with him if you weren't OK.'

With a finger on her chin, he tilted her head up until she was looking into his eyes. Then he lowered his lips to hers.

'So, I see you're feeling better.' The nurse's dry voice might as well have been hands pushing them apart given how quickly they separated.

'Thank you,' Allie said. 'Yes.'

Looking amused, the nurse glanced at her watch. 'Remember, we need you awake for a while longer. I suggest another cup of tea.' As she walked away, Allie thought she heard her add, 'And a cold shower.'

Laughing soundlessly, Carter stood up. 'I'll go and get you some fresh tea.'

'I don't need any more tea,' Allie protested. 'I slosh when I walk.'

But he was already on his way out the door. 'Maybe I want a cup, too,' he said over his shoulder.

As she waited, Allie picked up a magazine someone had left on one of the tables. She was studying an actress in a £2,000 dress when a sound caused her to look up.

Sylvain was leaning against the door frame watching her. In the split second their eyes met she saw something in his that took her by surprise. A kind of sadness. But almost immediately the look disappeared, replaced by his usual well-cultivated blankness.

'You look better,' he said.

'I'm really fine.' Her hand rose to her temple instinctively. 'Thanks.'

'Good,' he said. 'Nicole sent me up to check on you.'

Dropping the magazine on to a coffee table, Allie affected a casual stretch and yawn.

'She seems nice,' she said after a second. 'How long have you two been together?'

'We've known each other for ever,' he said carelessly. 'We are old friends.'

'Oh.'

Allie concentrated on not finding his accent charming. Her eyes shot up to meet his for a second then flitted away. She found it a little hard to focus with him just standing there, watching her as if he knew what she was thinking.

A possible distraction occurred to her. Sitting up straight, she rooted around the sofa underneath her jacket. 'Here's your scarf back. Thanks for loaning it to me.'

Sylvain took the soft cashmere scarf from her hands but instead of walking away, sat down on the chair across from her. 'I need to talk you about something else. I've been trying to see you alone.' He fidgeted with the scarf and she studied his long slim fingers with their neat oval nails; so different from Carter's strong, solid hands. 'There's something I have to tell you. I have put it off too long because I think you won't like it.'

A chill ran through her and her eyes flicked towards the door through which Carter would be walking any minute. When she looked back at Sylvain he was studying her curiously. She didn't like the way his gaze could still unsteady her.

'What is it?'

'It's just that . . . I have you.' His electric blue eyes held her gaze.

Glancing again at the door, she drew back. 'What do you mean, you have me?' she whispered. 'Have me how?'

Leaning closer he lowered his voice.

'To investigate. For Night School.' He held out his hands, palms up. 'I have you.'

FOURTEEN

'Nineteen twenty-five was a particularly fertile year for literature.' Isabelle leaned against an empty desk as she lectured. 'That year *The Great Gatsby* was published, among many other works. Fitzgerald thought *Gatsby* was his greatest work. He described it as a "sustained imagination of a sincere and yet radiant world". But I see it as a morality tale. A book about a good man seduced by corrupt people.' She straightened, and began walking around the circle of desks. 'What I want you to tell me is whether that good man is really a good man at the end of the story. And was he truly good at the start?'

Allie, who was just enduring the class today, circled the title in her notebook and put a star beside it. As Isabelle continued to talk, though, her thoughts wondered back to what happened last night. And how furious Carter had been when he found out.

Sylvain had left by the time Carter returned, carrying two

steaming cups of tea and looking comforting and normal and ...
Carter-like.

Allie waited for him to sit down before she told him. When
it came to Carter, she didn't care about the rules. He was so
jealous of Sylvain. If she didn't tell him and he found out later,
he'd never forgive her.

As she explained what Sylvain had said, Carter didn't shout
or rage. It was worse than that. He went quiet and pale, and the
tendons in his neck were taut.

After a long pause he said in a low voice, 'I'll talk to
Zelazny.'

'The thing is ... Sylvain says ...' Carter twitched, but she
continued. 'He says he already asked Jerry and Zelazny to
change the assignment. They refused. That's why it took him so
long to—'

'Great.' Cutting her off in mid-sentence, Carter shoved his
hands deep in his pockets and looked down, his gaze so icy
Allie marvelled that the floor didn't frost.

'It'll be no big deal,' she'd said, trying to make things better.
'It's just an interview – it's one afternoon. Then it's over.'

But Carter hadn't been mollified. 'They really are,' he said
through gritted teeth, 'messing with us right now.'

Isabelle tapped Allie's desk sharply with a fingertip, making
her jump. Without interrupting her patter, the headmistress
shot her a warning look before continuing her journey around
the circle. Allie sat up straighter and tried to pay attention. But
her chest felt tight, as if the anxiety that curled up there had
left less room for her lungs.

After class, she and Carter were going to do their interview.

She wished the class would last for ever. But it was already over.

Isabelle's parting words had to fight through the sound of students gathering their things: 'Please collect your copies at the library – Eloise has them ready. And I'd like you to read the first three chapters by tomorrow's class so we can discuss them. You're free to go.'

'Allie, I'm going to a kick-boxing class, want to come?' Zoe looked up at her expectantly as they walked through the door.

God yes.

Beating something up was about the only thing she wanted to do right now.

'I wish I could. But I've got plans.' The regret in Allie's voice was so tangible Zoe gave her an odd look as she turned away.

'No worries – see you later.'

Carter was waiting for her outside the door, leaning against the wall out of the crowds of students filling the hallway.

'Hey,' she said, her heart heavy.

'Hey back.' His dark eyes held hers just long enough for her to see the worry there.

'So ... Shall we meet there?' he asked, as they joined the throng of students surging from the classroom wing through a heavy wooden door into the main school building.

'Sounds good,' she said, with a tentative smile.

Pulling her close, he gave her a reassuring kiss before loping off towards the stairs to the boys' dorm to drop off his things.

Her tennis headache had been mostly gone by morning,

although the purple-tinged bruise on her temple was still sensitive to touch.

In her room, she changed from a skirt to trousers. After pausing at the mirror to check her hair, she grabbed her jacket and turned to go, but something stopped her. Draped over the back of her chair was a wool scarf in dark blue. Hesitantly, she reached out to touch it – the fabric was finely knitted wool, soft as a hug.

Where did that come from?

Running the scarf through her fingers, Allie decided Isabelle must have heard about what had happened last night from the nurse. It wasn't that unusual for things students needed to just appear in their rooms. Like the slippers that appeared the first night she'd arrived at Cimmeria. And the fresh towels and clean sheets that showed up every few days.

After a moment's hesitation, she wrapped the new scarf loosely around her throat and looked at herself in the mirror by the door. She was pale – nerves probably – and set against the dark scarf her skin looked like porcelain. Her dark, wavy hair had grown long – she hadn't cut it since last spring and now it hung down to her shoulder blades. Sweeping berry-red gloss on her lips she threw her book bag over her shoulder and headed out.

As much as she dreaded it, she was glad they were doing it now rather than waiting – she just wanted it all over with.

For her part, she still hadn't decided how much to reveal to Sylvain.

Should I tell him about Lucinda? And who I really am? Do I have a choice? Lying would get her expelled. But if she told

Sylvain, she'd have to trust him with her whole life's story. With secrets only Carter knew. And with some secrets nobody knew.

On the ground floor, she made her way along the wide hallway, threading through the busy afternoon crowd of students heading to the library and common room, their feet pounding on the polished wood. In the entry hall the wood floors gave way to stone, large tapestries covered the old stone walls and the crowds thinned.

Grabbing the iron door handle, Allie pulled the heavy front door open. Cool air flooded in, redolent of the rain that had fallen that morning. She stepped out on to the wet stone steps as the door closed behind her with a solid thud.

As she crossed the sprawling lawn, her shoes squelching in the mud, she could hear the shouts of students playing football in the distance. Two breathless boys returning from a run said hello as they passed her heading the other way – she recognised them from Night School. This was nothing like the quiet of the summer term – these days the grounds buzzed with activity until curfew. But still, even now, the world hushed when she entered the woods. Walking along the familiar footpath – mostly dry, thanks to the canopy of trees – she noticed the ferns beside the path were already dying from the autumnal cold. There was little breeze to stir the branches today, so the trees stood silent around her. It was just after three o'clock, but already the sunlight was beginning fade; Allie hastened her steps, breaking into a jog as she made her way down the path towards the chapel. She ran so much for Night School these days she rarely ran for fun any more. Even now her steps felt mechanical, unsatisfying.

When she reached the old limestone wall, she followed it to the arched gateway that opened on to a peaceful churchyard. In the watery light, the old tombstones looked disconsolate amid the thinning autumn grass. With the trees denuded of their leaves, the graveyard lost the sun-dappled charm it held in the summer months – now it just felt spooky.

Out of instinct she crossed to the gnarled yew tree where she and Carter had met often over the summer but it was empty; its bark slippery and darkened by the rain.

She headed back to the chapel, where the ancient arched door was so heavy she needed both hands to pull it open. It creaked ominously as it swung outward.

Inside it was colder – the air smelled of incense and wood polish. Stained glass windows gave the daylight a lavender hue. As always, the elaborate medieval wall paintings drew her eyes to their depictions of suffering sinners in hell being jabbed by demons with pitchforks, and dragons soaring upwards. And above the door the painted phrase *Exitus acta probat*, 'The result validates the deed.'

Carter stood in front of the altar lighting the candles in an iron candelabra that stood taller than his head.

'Hey,' he said without turning around.

'Hey back,' Allie said, shivering as she closed the door behind her. With stone floors and walls, the unheated chapel felt colder than the outside. 'I thought we weren't allowed to play with fire any more.'

'The lights aren't working.' The match burned down towards his fingertips and he cursed as he shook it out. He sucked his fingertips to cool them before lighting a fresh one. 'And it's going to be dark before too long so I thought I better make us some light.'

'Cool.' Allie sat down on the front pew.

Glancing at her over his shoulder, he gave her that sexy half-smile of his that sent tingles down her spine. 'I'm nearly done.'

'After that, let's set fire to one of these pews.' Allie rubbed her arms. 'It's freezing in here.'

'Yeah,' he said. 'No electricity equals no heating.'

'Lame,' she said.

But when the candles – at least two dozen in all – were glowing the light created a false sense of warmth. And he sat down beside her, pulling her close for a kiss. Her mouth opened to his unhesitatingly and she felt his pulse speed as his fingers tightened on her back.

We could forget everything, she thought. *And just do this . . .*

Then, with a regretful sigh, she pulled herself free.

'We'd better stop,' she said pointing at a tall cross. 'Jesus is watching.'

Carter chuckled, the colour still high in cheeks, but he sobered quickly as the task before them loomed.

'Right.' She pulled the notebook out of her bag and opened it to the page where she'd put her prepared questions. 'Let's just get this over with. And then we can get back to reality.'

Scooting away from her until his back rested against the high arm of the pew, Carter raised his eyebrows expectantly.

'Hit me,' he said.

'Full name,' she said with an unhappy sigh. 'Birth date. Parents' names. Grandparents' names.'

'Carter Jonathan West,' he said, with a casual attitude she could see right through. 'Twenty-fourth of September . . . '

She gasped. 'Wait,' she said, staring up at him. 'Your birthday was *last month*? You didn't say anything.'

He shrugged as if it didn't matter. 'I hate birthdays. I don't celebrate mine.'

'How can you not celebrate your own birthday, Carter? That's horrible.' She felt unaccountably wounded. He'd kept it from her. He'd had a birthday and he hadn't told her. He was seventeen now. 'You didn't say anything. I didn't give you a present or bake you a cake . . . '

He tried to calm her, as if her reaction was unreasonable. 'I'm sorry, Al. I just . . . I don't celebrate it. I haven't, you know, ever since my parents . . . '

But Allie shook her head, her lips tight, and dropped her eyes to her list of questions.

This was starting badly.

'Parents' names?' she said, not looking at him.

'Mother, Sharon Georgina West. Father . . . '

His voice trailed off and she looked up from the page to find him staring into the distance.

He cleared his throat. 'Father, Arthur Jonathan West.'

She couldn't be mad at him.

'You have the same middle name as him,' she said. 'That's nice. Like you still share something.'

He nodded.

After a second she continued. 'Grandparents' names?'

They went through the required list of family names and dates, towns where people were born, jobs they worked so long ago that she couldn't imagine it being real.

'None of your family ever went to school here? Before you, I mean?' she asked at the end.

He shook his head.

They'd now reached the point of the interview she'd been dreading. She and Eloise had argued about whether she really had to ask it, and Eloise had insisted.

'If you're doing this, you have to ask,' Eloise had said. 'And you must forget your relationship to him, no matter how compassionate you might feel. Write the answer down and then ask the next question.'

'But he's never told me about what happened,' Allie had protested, feeling increasingly aggrieved. 'He doesn't ever talk about it. It seems cruel to force him to talk about it.'

But Eloise had been unbending, and now Allie knew she had to say the words.

'I know . . . ' she began and then faltered. Taking a calming breath, she tried again. 'I need to know what happened to your parents and how you ended up here.'

When his dark eyes shot up to meet hers she saw a warning in them.

'I know,' she said quickly. 'And I hate to ask you this. But if I don't, they'll just make us do this again until I do. I'm so sorry, Carter. Can you tell me very quickly, maybe? I won't ask for any details.'

He was so still for so long she wondered if he was going to

just get up and walk away. She could see conflicting emotions in his face.

Finally, as if he were giving in to the inevitable, he raked his fingers through his hair. When he spoke his voice was low, and he looked away from her into a dark corner of the chapel.

'My father worked in a car factory, but he lost that job before I was born when the factory closed. He couldn't get another. There just ... weren't that many factories around. He saw an ad, I think, in a paper. Isabelle told me once but I can't quite remember everything ... My parents lived near here, I think. Before.'

Allie was having a little trouble following his tangled narrative but she said nothing. She sat as still as she could, barely breathing. She didn't take notes – she knew she'd remember this.

'Anyway,' Carter continued, 'at some point he was hired here to be the handyman, taking care of the boiler and the electrical system – anything you could fix with a screwdriver or a spanner. This place must have seemed like a godsend, you know?' He looked up at her briefly then returned his gaze to the distance. 'My mum worked in the kitchen – cooking and cleaning. They got a place to live rent free on the grounds; they were putting money in the bank. For them, even though the work wasn't, like, thrilling, I guess it was a perfect set-up.

'When my mum got pregnant they were really excited. They didn't have any other kids and I think maybe they thought they couldn't or something. I guess it was a big deal. When I was born my mum took some time off for a while but then she went back to work.' He stopped to think. 'It's hard to explain but, because they lived on the grounds, it was kind of like I was raised by everyone. Nobody else here had young children. The teachers and other staff took turn babysitting me. I was, like, a novelty.'

Her hands still in her lap, Allie watched his face.

'And you lived in that cottage?' she asked. 'The one we saw that night in the woods – with the roses?'

He looked surprised, as if he'd forgotten the night they'd come across the little stone cottage with the lush flower garden. He nodded. 'Bob Ellison lives there now.'

'It looked like a beautiful place to grow up,' she said.

He shrugged as if it were a silly question, although she could see in his eyes that it wasn't.

'Were your parents happy here, do you think?' she asked.

A wistful smile flittered across his face. 'I think so. I remember us being happy. My dad was really good at what he did – he could fix anything, you know? He was a genius with anything technical or mechanical. Everybody relied on him, and Isabelle says he liked that. Knowing he was needed. And Mum . . .' He stopped to rub his eyes.

Allie felt horrible. She wanted to hold his hand, hug him – do something aside from just sit there. But he sat stiffly, with his body turned away from her. She knew he didn't want that right now. So she stayed still.

His voice was steady when he started again. 'Mum was, I think, kind of like a mother to everybody. She'd make sandwiches for the kids if they got hungry after class. Make scones for the teachers' meetings. She fussed over everybody.' He stopped again for a long moment. 'So yeah,' he said finally. 'I think they were happy.'

Allie could feel tears prickling the backs of her eyes. She rubbed her nose fiercely as if it itched.

I don't want to do this.

'Carter,' she said quietly, 'what happened?'

The silence between them was like a physical wall. She felt as if she could touch its cold edges. The muscles in his jaw worked, and his hands were twisted into a knot in his lap.

'So,' he said as if she hadn't spoken, 'one day, my dad was sent out to collect some parts from a distributor in Portsmouth.' His voice was strangely steady. 'It was something he did all the time. This time, though, my mum wanted to go along too, you know? It was a sunny summer day. She thought we could have a day by the sea. So she made a big picnic, and they packed me into the back seat of the car and we all headed out. But ...'

This time when he paused, Allie held her breath.

'A lorry lost control on the motorway,' he said, his eyes on some invisible point far away from her. 'They say the driver fell asleep, came across the central divide and hit us.' He flexed his fingers, then squeezed them into fists. 'Everyone said they wouldn't have felt a thing. It happened so fast.'

A tear slipped down Allie's cheek. 'What about you?' she asked, striking it away. 'Were you hurt?'

'Bruises. A few scrapes.' He sounded almost angry. 'Nothing serious.'

'That's incredible.' Allie allowed herself a moment of gladness that he'd survived. 'What happened then? I mean ... You were just a little kid.'

'Bob Ellison and my parents were really close friends. They'd made him my godparent. He came to the hospital and got me. Neither of my parents had close family so I think it was all settled really quickly. I don't really remember.' He shrugged. 'Guess nobody else wanted me. He moved into the cottage with me, and I lived there until I was old enough to move into the boys' dorm.'

He met her eyes. 'And here I am.'

Resisting the urge to wrap him in her arms and squeeze the pain out of him, Allie cleared her throat. 'This is all so ... huge, Carter,' she said. 'I can't believe I didn't know this already.'

He arched a sardonic eyebrow. 'Yeah well, it's not something I go around telling people.' He held out his hand. 'Hi, I'm Carter. My parents were killed in this awful car accident when I was little but I'm handling it remarkably well under the—'

'Stop it, Carter.' She interrupted him sharply. 'That's not fair. And it's not real. I'm your girlfriend – not just "people". And you can be real with me.'

'I know,' he looked chagrined. 'I'm sorry, Al. I just don't know how to ... you know ... say this stuff. It's hard. Not talking about it makes me happier than talking about it. So I don't talk about it.'

Spontaneously, she leaned over to hug him. 'Thank you for telling me,' she whispered into his shoulder. 'I know it was hard. And I'm so, so sorry.'

His arms were like bands of iron around her ribs. Behind her back, she could feel his hands clenched into fists.

They held each other like that for a long moment.

When he leaned back, he rubbed his eyes before straightening.

'Right.' His voice was gruff but he forced a half-smile. 'This is really great so far.'

'Just a few questions left,' she said, flipping through her notebook. 'Are you now or have you ever been sympathetic to Nathaniel? Do you want to destroy the school? Are you plotting against Isabelle?'

'No. No. No,' Carter said, stretching out his legs. 'Anything else?'

'I don't think so.' Looking down at her list, Allie made a few quick notes. Then she noticed a question she'd forgotten to ask. 'Oh, here's one: Have you ever told Nathaniel's people anything about me?'

Holding himself oddly still, Carter tilted his head to one side. 'That's a strange question.'

'Yeah. Eloise wanted me to ask that one. No idea why.'

Busy writing notes, she didn't really clock Carter's hesitation, but when he replied, something about his tone caught her attention.

'Not that I know of,' he said.

She glanced up at him, her pen poised between her fingers. 'What?'

'I said "Not that I know of",' he said. 'I haven't told anybody in Nathaniel's group anything as far as I know.'

She squinted at him, confused. 'I don't understand. What do you mean "as far as you know"? How could you tell them about me without knowing it?'

'Well, I talked to Gabe, didn't I?' He shifted in his seat uncomfortably. 'And now he's one of them.'

Allie felt her pulse accelerate. She kept her voice as calm as possible. 'What did you tell Gabe about me?'

He shrugged. 'You know ... Stuff.'

'Stuff.' A tiny seed of suspicion flowered in her heart. 'What kind of stuff?'

He shrugged. 'You know ... Guy stuff. Come on, Allie. He was my friend. We talked about stuff.'

Sitting up straight, she fixed him with a disbelieving look. 'No, Carter, I don't know. What kind of stuff about me did you discuss with Gabe?'

'I don't know.' With a stubborn look, he crossed his arms across his chest. 'He used to ask a lot of questions about you. I didn't really think about it at the time. I just answered them, I guess.'

'And you never mentioned this to me before?' Her voice rose, and she paused to take a calming breath before continuing. 'Did you tell Isabelle?'

'No.' Under questioning, he sounded increasingly defensive. 'I guess I didn't really think about it until now. Allie, would you mind not treating me like a murder suspect?'

'OK,' she said evenly, 'I'm sorry. Can you remember any of the things he asked you?'

Exhaling loudly, he stood and walked across the room to where an ancient wall painting of a yew tree stretched up towards the ceiling. Its elaborately tangled roots spelled out the words 'Tree of Life'. It was one of Allie's favourite things in the 900-year-old chapel but right now she barely glanced at it.

'He asked me,' he said after a long pause, 'about your family.

Where you lived in London. Who your friends were there. You see?' He looked over at her.

'What did you tell him?' she asked.

'What I knew,' he said, 'which wasn't a lot. South London. Some crummy school you hated. Some guy named Mark, and another one named Harry. That you didn't get along with your parents.'

Allie was trying very hard not to feel betrayed. But it felt as if he'd told Gabe everything he knew about her life before Cimmeria.

I don't know how to handle this.

She remembered something Eloise had said about keeping it like an interview.

'Think like a reporter,' she'd said in their one-to-one training session in the vividly painted library carrel. 'What would a reporter ask if they were interviewing him? Keep your emotional distance and you'll find it easier to separate what's important from what isn't.'

So now Allie tried to think of what she would ask if she wasn't Carter's girlfriend. 'Was there anything he asked that you thought was especially strange? Anything that weirded you out a little?'

Walking to the altar, Carter turned so his back was to her. His hands were shoved deep in his pockets. When he spoke, his voice was so low she wasn't certain she'd heard him right.

'He asked about your brother.'

'What?' A tingle of electricity ran through her fingertips. 'Did you say he asked about Christopher?'

His back still to her he nodded. 'And the thing I couldn't

figure out was . . . ' he turned so she could see the worry in his eyes, '. . . how did he know you had a brother in the first place? You never told anybody about him. And even if he did know, why did he care? He asked me about him a lot.'

Suddenly the room felt colder. Allie swallowed hard. 'Maybe Jo told him?' she suggested hopefully, drawing the scarf closer to her neck. 'I told her about Christopher, and she was Gabe's girlfriend at the time. What did he ask about specifically?'

Carter walked closer to her, his footsteps echoing in the empty chapel. The sun must have dipped low outside, because the glow from the stained glass windows had disappeared. The room suddenly seemed gloomy; dancing shadows cast by the candles jerked nervously on the white walls.

'How close you two were. Whether or not you talked about finding him.' He stood in front of her, his dark eyes filled with concern. 'Once he asked if you'd ever mentioned looking for him. And where you might go if you did.'

Allie wrapped her arms tight around her torso.

'That's so creepy,' she said, her voice low. 'I don't like it.'

'No,' he said, and the candlelight flickered in his eyes. 'Me neither.'

FİFTEEN

All that night, Allie went through the paces of normal Cimmeria life. But in her head her thoughts swirled in a tornado of worry. Everything seemed all tangled up and horrible. Carter and Gabe, the spy among them, Nathaniel ... Somehow she had to figure it out. Why had Gabe asked Carter those things? What was he hoping to learn?

The one person she thought would understand – the one person who would know what she should do – was Rachel. And she couldn't tell her. In fact, she couldn't tell anyone at all.

Except ...

She could tell Isabelle. But if she did that, what would happen? Would Carter get into trouble? She couldn't bear it if she was the reason Isabelle lost faith in Carter – she was the closest he came to having a mother on this earth.

Her thoughts tormented her. She couldn't focus on her studies. She couldn't focus on anything.

After dinner, as the other students settled into their normal routine of studying in the library or playing games in the common room as the rain continued to fall outside, she paced the wide hallway near Isabelle's office. Her footsteps were soft and rubbery on the polished oak floor as she walked from the common room to Isabelle's office and back again, over and over.

What he said wasn't that big a deal. We know Gabe was with Nathaniel and we know Nathaniel has a thing about me. So I don't see why it matters so much.

Turning, she paced the other way.

But what if it did matter? Isabelle said she wanted any information about Gabe that might help them understand when he joined with Nathaniel and why.

And again.

'You'll wear a hole in the floor.'

Standing at the foot of the main staircase, Sylvain stood watching her. She had no idea how long he'd been there – she couldn't remember the last time she'd looked up.

Even in his school uniform blue sweater and trousers, he managed to look sophisticated. He'd pushed the sleeves up to the elbows, and the sweater looked as if it had been tailored just for him.

As she fumbled for a response he added, 'And then the builders will have to come back with all of their equipment and rebuild it, and everyone will blame you.'

Allie's eyebrow arched. 'Your pessimism ... Is that a French thing?'

'Not pessimism,' he said. 'Pragmatism. It is a French word, you know. *Pragmatisme.*'

'Isn't pessimism a French word, too?'

'Yes.' His shrug was eloquent. 'But then, all the best words are French.'

She smiled, despite herself.

He tilted his head to one side, his expression open. 'So tell me, Allie. Why do you pace the floor like a prisoner? Are you working something out in your head?'

His eyes held such open curiosity and concern she had to fight off the urge to tell him everything.

I trust him again. When did that happen?

All this term he'd been nothing but thoughtful and kind. And heaven knew she needed help now.

'There's a thing.' She rubbed the toe of one of her sturdy school-issued loafers against the other. 'I've got to decide what to do. And whatever I do, I think it could be misunderstood by someone I care about. It might hurt him ... or her,' she added hastily. 'So, I guess what I'm deciding is ... which misunderstanding would be best.'

'Ah.' He leaned against the wall. 'That is the worst kind of problem, I think. The kind where there is no right answer. Only two wrong ones.'

'Exactly! So then how do you decide?'

'I suppose you trust your instincts.'

'Trust *my* instincts?' she scoffed. 'Nightmare.'

He studied her thoughtfully. 'I think, Allie, you make the right choice more often than you know.'

She started to make a joke, but then realised he was serious and the words died on her lips. For a long moment she stood still, staring at him without seeing him. 'I have to go and to talk to Isabelle.'

Without another word, she turned to walk away, intent on seeing the headmistress as quickly as possible. Then, just as quickly, she spun back towards him. He hadn't moved – he was watching her with such an affectionate smile, it threw her off-kilter.

'Sorry,' she said, flustered. 'I shouldn't walk off without saying goodbye. That's rude. And . . . We're still doing our thing tomorrow, right?'

'Yes.' She could see the amusement in his eyes. 'We will do the interview after dinner.'

'Cool.'

Light on her feet, she dashed under the staircase to Isabelle's door. Knocking, she turned the handle without waiting to be invited in; it sprang open at her touch. The room was empty. But the headmistress must have just stepped out – the light was on and the warm room smelled of her Earl Grey tea.

As Allie waited, her eyes moved from the tapestry of a maiden and a knight with a white horse to the neat, low cabinets where the student records were kept. Though she tried not to think about it, her mind kept returning to the night when she and Carter had broken in to search for information.

At the thought, she twisted the hem of her jumper nervously.

'Oh, hello, Allie.' Isabelle breezed in, a pale blue pashmina loose around her neck. Her crisp white polo neck top and black pencil skirt were balanced by a pair of sensible, rubber-soled shoes. After setting a file down on her desk, she looked up with an enquiring smile. 'Is everything OK?'

'There's something I need to ask you,' Allie said. 'Something kind of weird.'

Shutting the door, Isabelle gestured to the leather chairs in front of her desk. As Allie sank into one, the headmistress sat in the other.

'Now,' she said, 'what is this weird thing? And does it require tea?'

Shaking her head, Allie talked quickly, explained what Carter had told her about Gabe. As she spoke, she watched Isabelle's cheerful expression fade.

'Why didn't Carter ever tell us about this before?' she asked, when Allie finished. 'Did he explain that?'

Allie thought she sounded wounded.

'I don't know. He said he didn't really think about it.' Hurriedly, she added, 'Because . . . There was a lot to think about at the time. A lot happened. He kind of thought it didn't matter any more once we all knew Gabe was with Nathaniel.'

'I don't know why he would have thought that,' Isabelle said shortly. 'It doesn't make sense.'

Allie didn't know either but she couldn't say that. Worry made her stomach churn, and she started to explain more but the headmistress cut her off. 'Please don't worry, Allie. I understand completely. I was just thinking aloud. I'll speak with Carter myself to find out if there's anything else he might be able to tell us.'

Allie's mouth went dry. 'Don't be angry with him. I feel strange about telling you this stuff. But I didn't . . . I mean, I just thought you should know because it's information about Gabe.' She leaned forward in her seat. 'You know Carter's not working for Nathaniel, right? I mean, he's not the one?'

Isabelle held her gaze. 'I do not believe for one second that Carter would intentionally betray us to Nathaniel.'

Intentionally?

As she tried to figure out what the headmistress was really saying, Allie's panic grew.

What have I done?

'Thank you for telling me,' Isabelle said, ushering her out. 'You did the right thing.'

But as Allie headed up the stairs to her room a short while later, she didn't believe her. She was completely lost under a heavy shroud of worry when a hand grasped her arm. With a startled squeak, she wrenched her arm free, only to hear a familiar deep chuckle.

'Sorry, did I scare you?'

Carter stood on the step just below her, that sexy half-smile she so loved curving his lips as he reached out for her hand again.

Oh balls.

'No,' she said. 'Just surprised me.'

'I've been looking for you all evening,' he said, lacing his fingers through hers. She wondered if he'd notice her palms were sweating. 'Where've you been?'

Allie thought carefully before answering. 'Oh, I was studying and then I kind of went for a walk, chatted with Isabelle, you know . . .'

'Oh yeah?' His expression didn't change. 'What were you chatting about?'

The sounds around them – students talking, feet thumping on steps, laughter – seemed to fade into the distance. She couldn't tell him. She couldn't bear to see the look on his face – the hurt and betrayal.

'Nothing,' she said, blood like ice water in her veins. 'I'm behind with my maths work and I was hoping she could buy me some time.'

'Tsk.' He waved a chiding finger. 'Behind on your work, Miss Sheridan? I'll bet she didn't like that.'

'Yeah.' Allie could hear the falseness in her own brittle laugh. 'She told me to catch up. Fast. Without her help.'

'Sound advice, young lady.'

He was standing one step below her and she had to look down to meet his eyes. Guilt seared through her.

I just lied to Carter for the first time.

Impulsively, she freed her hand from his and ran her fingers through his soft dark hair; instantly, his hands moved to her waist, pulling her closer. She bent over to kiss him.

'Curfew!' Zelazny's voice sliced through her confused emotions.

'Bugger,' Carter whispered against her lips.

The rush began almost instantly as crowds of raucous students hurried past them up the stairs towards the dorms. But Carter wouldn't let her go. His hands roved up and down her back sending sparks through her nervous system.

'I wish we could go somewhere. And be alone.' He pulled her towards him until his lips were against her ear. 'If you're not tired, I could come to your room later?'

Allie swallowed hard. She'd just betrayed him. Could she pretend nothing had happened while making out with him?

'People do,' Eloise had said. 'All the time.'

But Allie couldn't.

'Seriously, Carter,' she said, 'I'm so behind on my maths work. I've got to catch up or I'm so profoundly screwed.'

Lie number two. Which he bought completely, of course.

Because he trusts me.

As she ran up to the girls' dorm, her heart was so heavy in her chest it seemed to slow her down. Moving one foot after the other was difficult.

Lying to Carter. She'd never imagined she could do that. How had everything got so tangled?

In the relative safety of her room, she closed the door and leaned against it. Catching her reflection in the mirror next to the door, she frowned at herself.

What have you done?

She had to tell him the truth, of course. He'd figure it out soon enough after Isabelle met with him. And when he realised she'd lied ...

A sudden chill made her shiver, and she walked over to close the window. Wind was making the shutter thump against the wall, and rain had blown in and dampened the desktop.

Two things happened at the same time: she remembered she hadn't opened the window today and she saw the envelope on her desk.

It was of thick, heavy paper – the kind used for invitations. Her name was written on the back. In Christopher's handwriting.

SİXTEEN

Allie scrambled away from the desk so rapidly her feet tangled and she nearly fell. Reaching out for the wall, she caught her balance, all the time staring at the envelope on her desk as if it might get up and chase her across the room.

He's been in here, she thought with a mixture of horror and excitement. *Christopher's been in here.*

Her heart pounded so loudly in her ears she couldn't hear herself think, and she forced herself to calm down while she tried to decide what to do. Should she run straight to Isabelle? Try and find Carter or Rachel?

Or just open the envelope and see what's inside?

With tentative steps she made her way back to the desk, approaching the envelope as one might a caged panther until, reaching out a shaking hand, she picked it up.

The creamy paper was unmarked aside from the word 'Allie',

written in the familiar handwriting she hadn't seen in more than a year. She ran her fingertip across the word as if it would give her some sense of what had happened to him – why he'd run away. Why he'd left her.

Slipping her finger under the lip of the envelope, she pulled it open. Inside, a single sheet of thick, ivory paper had been neatly folded. She held it to her nose wondering if it would smell of her brother. Of home as it had been before he left.

But it smelled of nothing.

Unfolding it, she found her name written at the top in Christopher's distinctive left-slanting handwriting.

Dear Allie,

I can't believe I'm finally talking to you after all this time. I've missed you so much! Staying away from you has been the hardest part of everything that has happened.

When I saw you that night last summer, I knew I had to get back in touch with you. You've changed so much I almost didn't recognise you. You're all grown up now.

I am so proud of you.

I know you don't understand why I'm with Nathaniel. But I haven't gone crazy or joined a cult, or whatever Mum and Isabelle told you. I just learned the truth about our family. And I made a choice.

I want you to have the same chance I did to make a choice based on the truth about who we are. We **Meldrums**.

So will you meet me so we can talk? I'll be down by the stream, next to the chapel, Friday at midnight.

I know you're probably angry with me, and I wouldn't blame

you if you didn't come. But I'll be there. Please come. I can't wait
to see you again.

Christopher

Standing stock still, Allie gazed out of the window into the
dark autumn evening.

Christopher was right here. Standing where I am now. Hot
tears flooded her eyes. *If he wanted to see me so badly, why
didn't he wait until I walked into the room? Why leave a note
and sneak away?*

With effort, she forced herself to read the letter again. This
time she noted the way he'd underlined their grandmother's
name, writing over the letters twice until the word stood out on
the page. He'd pressed his pen so hard against the paper it had
nearly gone through.

As she stood holding the letter, one thought reverberated in
her head: *What am I going to do now?*

Allie didn't sleep that night. She read the letter over and over
again until she didn't need to read it any longer; she'd memorised it.

At about three in the morning, convinced that there was no
hidden message in it and no part she might have missed, she
lay back on the bed, her hands covering eyes, counting her
breaths.

She had few options.

If she told anybody about the letter they would insist on
telling Isabelle out of a desire to protect her. Then the matter
would be taken out of Allie's hands.

They'd never let me see him, and they might do something to him. Have him arrested. Or something else. Something worse.

But the other alternative was to lie to everybody she knew.

Thinking about that made her feel sick.

The way she'd felt lying to Carter tonight . . . *How could I do that again and again?*

And on and on her thoughts went until, at some point, just before dawn, she must have dozed, because the alarm woke her before seven.

All that day, she moved in a fog of exhaustion and panic; her classes passed in a blur. When Rachel commented on the dark circles under her eyes, Allie lied again. 'I think I'm coming down with something.'

Lying was getting easier, but when Rachel tutted like a mother hen and insisted on getting her tea with honey she felt like a monster.

All day – every minute of the day – she worried about what she was going to do.

At dinner, she stirred the food on her plate, not touching it, avoiding Rachel's sharp gaze. She was meeting Sylvain later for her interview and everything was so complicated now she had no idea what to do, what to say.

She was too tired to spin some sort of elaborate lie. But if she told him the truth . . .

Suddenly she *did* feel ill, and she pushed her plate away.

What am I going to do?

*

Just after eight o'clock, Allie stood at the foot of the stairs, her arms crossed tightly, helping to hold her upright. Her head was so cloudy – sleeplessness and stress were taking their toll. Nothing felt real.

'I'm sorry I'm late.' As he ran up to her, short of breath, Sylvain smiled disarmingly. 'I had a last-minute meeting with Jerry that went on so long, I thought perhaps I would be there for the rest of my life.' Running his fingers through his ruffled hair, he nodded towards the classroom wing. 'I have an idea of where we can go, if you want to try it?'

He took the stairs two at a time; she followed him silently. (*Sixty-six steps.*) The second-floor hallway was dark as they walked through the shadows (*sixteen steps*) past empty classrooms. Their footsteps echoed hollowly.

'In here.' Opening a door near the end of the hall, he flipped the light switch and the fluorescent lights flickered on. The room was small (*ten desks arranged in five rows of two, four windows . . .*). Sylvain turned two desks so they faced each other then, directing her to one, slid into the other, giving a slight groan as he stretched his long legs out into the aisle.

'This has been a long day,' he said, reaching into his bag. 'Jerry was really on my case today. He's been in a terrible mood lately.'

Allie found it hard to imagine Jerry, the kindly science teacher, on anyone's case. He'd always been patient with her.

Sylvain set a notebook in the middle of the desk in front of him and produced a slim, silver pen.

'Listen,' he began, a serious line dividing his azure eyes, 'I must tell you again that I'm sorry they chose me for this.' He stopped, studying her face for the first time. 'Are you OK? You look terrible.'

'I'm fine,' she said, but her words came out a whisper. Clearing her throat, she tried again. 'Just ... coming down with something, maybe.'

'I want to say first that you can trust me.'

Colour rose in her cheeks, and she looked away.

Two breaths in, one breath out ...

'I mean ...' He was studying her closely and she got the feeling he'd observed her reaction. 'I know you may never trust me, and I don't blame you for that. But you can trust me not to tell anybody what you tell me today. I will only write it down and hand it in. OK?'

She had to force herself to meet his eyes, and she knew her cheeks were burning with the heat of all the unspoken words between them – how angry she'd been after the summer ball, and the confusion that had dominated her feelings towards him ever since; how he made her feel both safe and threatened.

'OK,' she said, her voice steady. 'This wasn't your idea, any more than it was mine. And I'm fine with it. I really am. I'd rather it were you than ... well, a lot of people. So let's just do this.'

I'm glad it's you, she thought, and then wondered where the thought came from.

'Good.' With a relieved smile, he opened his notebook. 'Let's do it.'

His first few questions were the same ones she'd asked Carter. When he asked her grandparents' names, she quickly reeled off the names of her father's deceased parents. Then she paused.

He glanced up at her enquiringly. 'And your mother's parents?'

'I . . . I'm afraid I don't actually know my grandfather's name on that side of the family,' she said finally. 'I've never been told.'

A puzzled frown crossed his face but he said nothing, making a note in his notebook. 'And your grandmother?'

Rain pattered against the window in a staccato rhythm. It sounded like small pebbles being pelted against the glass.

'My grandmother's name is Lucinda Meldrum.' Her voice was calm.

He'd started writing as soon as she began talking but now his pen froze, and he looked up at her. 'Your grandmother has the same name as the chancellor?'

'Lucinda Meldrum, the former chancellor, *is* my grandmother.'

Setting down his pen, he frowned in confusion. 'Is this a joke, Allie? Because I don't understand . . .'

'No joke, Sylvain,' she said. Now that she was talking about it, saying the words felt liberating. Another person was now in on the secret. Each person she told made it seem more real. 'It's completely true. I am Lucinda Meldrum's granddaughter.' She pointed at his notepad. 'Write it down.'

'I don't understand.' He still hadn't picked up his pen. 'If this is true, why doesn't anyone know about it? I thought you weren't a legacy student at all, but first generation.'

'Yeah, I know that everyone has always wondered what that nobody Allie Sheridan is doing at super-amazing Cimmeria, the billionaire's academy. Well, Sylvain, now you know.' When he started to speak, she held up her hand. 'Seriously. Just write down her name. And ask me the next question.'

After a long pause, he picked up his pen and wrote three words: 'Grandmother: Lucinda Meldrum'.

The incident seemed to throw him off his game, and he referred to his notes distractedly.

'Uh ... OK, so my next question is ... Who in your family attended Cimmeria?' His expression quizzical, he glanced up at her. 'But I'm not sure I need to ask ...'

'My mother attended Cimmeria.' Allie's cool words overrode his. 'And my grandmother.'

As he made notes, it occurred to her that she was getting used to saying the word 'grandmother'. It no longer felt so odd. But she found she said it in a commanding way, as if she were saying 'the Queen'. Just talking about Lucinda conveyed power.

She was still feeling the thrill of that when Sylvain asked his next question.

'So what led you to come to Cimmeria? I believe you were brought here as punishment.'

The thrill of power practically made a sizzling noise as it died.

Sliding down in her chair, Allie launched into the story of her brother's disappearance and all that happened after: Her parents losing interest in her. Her arrest for breaking into the school and spray-painting obscenities on the walls. How this arrest had followed two other arrests for vandalism and petty theft. How Mark and Harry had stepped into her brother's place in her emotions – only instead of helping with her homework they taught her the fine art of rebellion.

As she talked, Sylvain took notes in his neat, precise

handwriting, occasionally looking up at her with a bemused expression but never interrupting. She wanted to gloss some of it over to make herself sound better, the way she did when telling Jo or Rachel about it, but found she couldn't. She told him *everything*. And the more she talked the better she felt, as if the story were leaving her. With every word the weight on her chest seemed to lighten.

When she'd finished, he studied her with overt curiosity. The silver pen glittered in his long fingers. 'This Allie you describe, she doesn't sound like the Allie sitting in front of me. I don't recognise that girl.'

'Yeah, well.' She shrugged. 'When your life falls apart sometimes you fall apart with it. Hasn't that ever happened to you?'

'No – not like that. I just . . . ' He paused as if trying to think of the right words. 'I admire your strength, Allie. It's not possible for me to say what I would have done if I were in your feet, but I think I would not have handled it as well.'

'Shoes,' she corrected him automatically. 'If you were in my shoes.'

But even as she spoke, a rush of unexpected emotion flooded through her. She didn't know what it was – maybe it was just dredging up all that stuff again – but for some reason his words touched her heart.

'By the way, have you heard from your brother?' As his words sliced through her reverie, her eyes shot up to meet his. 'You know,' he said, 'since the fire?'

Reflexively, her hand slid into her skirt pocket, touching the now familiar thick paper of Christopher's letter. She tried to speak, but no words came out.

Three breaths in, two breaths out . . .

'Allie?' Frowning, Sylvain cocked his head to one side. 'What's the matter? *Have* you heard from him?'

'No,' she said, her voice hoarse. 'Never. Not until . . . last night.'

SEVENTEEN

'You have to go to Isabelle and Raj.' Sylvain handed the letter back to Allie, who folded it carefully and put it back into her pocket.

'No.'

'Allie . . .'

But the warning in his eyes only made her more determined. 'What will happen if I tell Isabelle?' she asked.

'She will have Raj's people intercept him,' he said.

'And do what with him?'

His shrug told her he didn't know. Maybe didn't care either.

'Don't you dare tell Isabelle. I won't let them kidnap my brother and use him as some sort of bargaining chip in their crazy war.' Rising panic made it hard for her to breathe. 'I'll go by myself, Sylvain, I swear to God. I'll warn him. I'll run away with him,' she threatened wildly. 'Nobody is kidnapping him.'

'Allie, no!' Her reaction had clearly taken him by surprise

and his words tumbled out in a rush. 'Don't – you could be hurt.'

'Christopher wouldn't hurt me.'

His eyes darkened. 'Christopher nearly burned this school down with seventy-five people inside. Including you.'

'You can't . . .' All of a sudden, her lungs felt compressed, as if the air had disappeared. It was hard to speak. The room swayed sickeningly. '. . . tell.'

She could see the puzzled alarm in his eyes. 'Allie? Are you OK?'

The walls moved closer; her breath came in short gasps. A clammy sweat coated her skin. She struggled to get air.

It's happening again.

'I can't . . .' For a long minute she struggled to breathe, her heart thudding so loudly in her ears she couldn't hear what Sylvain was saying to her. Then, leaping to her feet, she fled from the room. Without looking back, she clattered down the stairs to the back door (*thirty-seven steps*), and out into the cold rain.

Then she just ran.

The icy air was like a slap in the face as she hurtled through the darkness as fast as her feet would move, with rain lashing at her skin, fighting off the panic attack that threatened to overwhelm her.

As she ran, the cold and the movement seemed to make her lungs work again and she could feel the tension in her chest loosen. But still she didn't stop. Her wet hair stuck to her scalp and face. Rain blinded her. Mud splashed up her bare ankles to her knees.

She was nearly to the treeline when hands grabbed her shoulders, yanking her back.

Flailing, she spun around, punching blindly. Her fist connected with Sylvain's flesh and she was glad. For a moment she slithered free, her wet skin sliding through unwanted fingers, but she hadn't gone three steps when she was wrapped in arms as strong as bands of iron. Only when she realised she couldn't run any more did a sob finally shake her body.

'Let me go!' The words burst out of her in a scream.

'Allie. Stop fighting!' Sylvain was panting from exertion. 'What the hell is wrong with you?'

'I'm going to go and wait for Christopher,' she sobbed irrationally. 'If you're going to Isabelle, I've got to warn him.'

Muttering something in French – she didn't know the words but she was pretty sure he was swearing – he held her so close she could feel his breath against her ear.

'I won't tell, OK?' he said. 'I won't tell Isabelle. Now please. Stop this.'

Instantly, she stopped fighting, and after a second he loosened his hold on her. Pushing wet hair out of her eyes, she searched his face for signs of deception.

'Promise me,' she said, raising her voice to be heard above the rain. 'Swear you won't tell anybody.'

'You have my word.' His eyes never wavered. 'Now please.' He held out his hand. 'Come back inside.'

She believed him.

Suddenly exhausted, she allowed him to take her hand; his skin wet and cold against hers. In silence, they walked back towards the building. The adrenaline that had stopped her from feeling the cold flooded away as quickly as it had arrived and she trembled violently. Casting a sideways glance at Sylvain, she saw that he was shivering, too. His jaw was set as he led her to a small door in the east wing.

When he opened it, though, she balked. 'Where are we going?'

'If we go in through the main entrances looking like this, people will ask questions you don't want to answer,' he said. 'This is another way in.'

The door opened on to a short stairway down into a part of the cellar she'd never seen before. It seemed unused – old chairs were stacked haphazardly against the walls. Flickering lights in wall sconces cast moving shadows that chased them down the corridor. About halfway down the hall, he opened another door and flipped a light switch, revealing a narrow, winding staircase. Allie's teeth were chattering so loudly she was sure he must be able to hear them.

'It's one of the old servants' staircases,' he explained. 'They're everywhere. We used another one the night of the fire.'

They climbed several storeys, finally emerging into a warm hallway. Sylvain led her past two closed doors before opening one. It was a spacious, neatly kept bedroom.

Instantly she knew just where they were. Her heart thudded three quick beats.

I cannot be in his bedroom – Carter would kill me. This is so not a good thing. I've got to get out of here.

But when he handed her a thick warm towel, instead of throwing it on the floor and running out of the door she began drying herself, looking around curiously. It was like any other dorm room, except for the extraordinary painting in an ornate gilded frame, of angels carrying an unconscious man.

Following her eyes, Sylvain gave an embarrassed shrug. 'A gift.'

Yanking open a drawer, he pulled out an armful of T-shirts and jumpers, dropping them on the bed. 'Here. Take off your wet clothes and put these on. They will all be too big but they will do.'

Through the tangled mass of wet hair covering her face, Allie glowered at him. 'You think I'm taking my clothes off in front of you? Good luck with that.'

A flash of amusement sparked in his eyes. 'Don't be such a child. I'll turn my back if you prefer, but you will not get warm if you keep those wet clothes on. Plus, you will make a spectacle walking back to your room.'

Without waiting for her to agree, he turned around to face the door.

For just a second she didn't move.

Her soaking wet top made a slapping sound when it hit the wood floor. She wanted to leave her bra on, but it was wet through.

'Don't you dare turn around,' she said through gritted teeth as she unhooked it.

His chuckle surprised her. 'Hurry up or I will,' he threatened. 'I want to change, too.'

Dropping her soaking bra on top of her wet shirt, she pulled on one of his T-shirts. It hung to her thighs. She put a jumper on top of it, then a pair of pyjama bottoms with a drawstring waist.

'Done.'

'Thank God,' he said. 'I'm freezing.' As he turned, his eyes skittered across her body. 'My clothes look better on you than they do on me,' he commented. She felt colour rise in her face, but he'd already turned to rifle through the T-shirts and jumpers she hadn't put on.

'Now, I need to get out of my wet clothes,' he said in perfectly reasonable tones. 'I won't make you turn around, though. I am French, so I'm not shy.'

'I will turn around ...' she said, but before she'd finished the sentence he'd peeled off his wet shirt.

So there was no point.

Right?

His torso was leanly muscled, and his latte-coloured skin held a Braille pattern of goosebumps. Shivering, he dried himself quickly before pulling on a clean T-shirt identical to the one she wore. Then, without any hesitation, he peeled off his wet trousers and dropped them into the pile with her wet clothes.

Turn around, Allie, she told herself. But she didn't move.

He had the long, muscled legs of an athlete, she observed, as he pulled dry trousers on over his dark blue boxers.

'You're very good-looking,' Allie heard herself say as if from a hundred miles away.

Oh good. I've gone completely insane.

Surprised, he looked up at her.

'Thank you,' he said simply. 'You are beautiful.'

'I'm a mess.' Allie sat down on his bed, wondering with only mild interest what she would say next.

When she glanced up, he was holding a towel out for her. She looked at it blankly.

'For your hair,' he explained.

But the stress had taken its toll and, when he handed it to her, she just held it loosely in one hand, thinking about Christopher and Carter and Gabe ...

And ...Shut up brain! Please God, let my brain just shut up.

When she didn't move, Sylvain lowered himself on to the bed next to her and began drying her hair with gentle hands. 'I read somewhere,' he said, 'that when you are cold you lose most of the heat from your head. So even if the rest of you is perfectly warm, you can still feel freezing if your head is cold. I think that is very strange, don't you?'

His hands felt cold when they touched her neck, and she shivered.

'What happened, Allie?' he asked. 'Why did you run away like that?'

She closed her eyes. 'I get these panic attack things. I can't breathe.' She gestured vaguely. 'Claustrophobic. But ... ' she opened her eyes again '... you mustn't tell.'

His hands quit moving. 'Tell what? Tell someone about your panic attack? Of course not.'

'No. Sylvain,' she said with such passion it startled them both, 'please don't tell Isabelle about Christopher's letter.'

Dropping the towel, he moved until he could see her face. 'I have promised. And I won't. But now you must promise me that you won't go off to meet Christopher by yourself.'

'I have to see him.' She held his gaze. 'I have to know what happened. He's the only one who can tell me. Sylvain, he's my *brother.*'

He held up his hands. 'Then take Carter with you. And Lucas. And Jules.'

She shook her head. 'If I tell Carter he'll go straight to Isabelle. He won't listen to me.' Only when she said those words did she fully understand why she hadn't told Carter about the letter. She didn't trust him. And he didn't trust her.

'Because he'll want to protect you,' Sylvain said. 'It is the right thing to do.'

'I can protect myself,' she said.

His reply was chilling and instant. 'Not from Nathaniel you can't. Not from Gabe.'

'I have to go, Sylvain.' She leaned towards him intently. 'I have to.'

Their eyes locked – his clear blue eyes sparkled in the lamplight.

'What are you asking me, Allie?' His voice was low.

'Will you go with me?' She held her breath.

For a long moment he studied her face. Then he sighed. 'I think this is a very bad idea,' he said. 'But I won't let you go alone.'

EIGHTEEN

Now all she had to do was get through Friday.

That morning, she explained away her disappearance the night before with an imaginary illness. Nobody doubted her. Rachel plied her with herbal tea while Carter checked her forehead for signs of fever and asked if she'd seen the nurse.

Her whole day was one lie after another. And it was easy.

I'm a natural, she thought bitterly on her way to the dining hall for dinner. *It must be in my blood.*

She glanced at her watch. Five minutes to seven.

Five hours until she'd talk to Christopher again for the first time in nearly two years. Five hours until she'd learn the truth.

Nervousness sped her heart rate, and she took calming breaths before walking into the busy dining room. Sliding into her normal seat next to Carter, she smiled at the group already assembled at their usual table.

Rachel mouthed, *You OK?* at her from her seat next to Lucas. Allie nodded and smiled to show she was fine. Carter draped his arm loosely across her shoulders and pressed his lips lightly to her temple.

Guilt stabbed like a needle prick, and she smiled broadly to push it back.

I'm going to do something, Carter, she thought, watching him chat with Lucas. *I hope you'll forgive me.* And, horribly, *I don't think you will.*

Zoe had taken to sitting with them lately and she was chatting earnestly to Jo about a complex chemistry problem she was working on with her tutor. Jo looked baffled but was nodding politely.

On the next table, Sylvain sat next to Nicole with a group of international students. They appeared to be deep in conversation but, as if he sensed her gaze, he looked up. When their eyes met, she could feel the connection their secrets had made between them.

'So.' Jo interrupted her thoughts by tapping her spoon against a glass until everyone at the table was looking at her and laughing. 'I've decided it's time.'

'Time?' Rachel said doubtfully.

'Uh-oh,' Lucas muttered. 'I think I know what's coming.'

'Time for what?' Zoe asked, cocking her head to one side.

'Time to start talking about the ball.'

The chorus of derision was instantaneous.

'I knew it,' Lucas said, dropping his head back against the top of his chair.

'It's a month away, Jo,' Carter pointed out. 'And all we have to do is get dressed.'

'Don't be absurd, Carter.' Jo dismissed him with a wave. 'It's much more than that.'

'Isn't it just like the summer ball?' Allie asked.

'No, it's totally different,' Zoe said before Jo could reply. 'Everyone comes to the winter ball.'

'She's right,' Jo said. 'Alumni come back, the entire board of directors usually comes. And I've heard a juicy rumour about this year.'

'Oh God,' Carter murmured, sipping from a glass of water.

'Just say it,' Lucas said. 'You know you won't rest until you've said it.'

'Go on then, Jo.' Rachel sat forward eagerly. 'Spread the goss.'

'Apparently,' Jo leaned forward and lowered her voice, 'lots of international politicos are coming this year. As in presidents. Prime ministers. Chancellors.'

As soon as Jo said the word 'chancellors', Allie felt her blood temperature drop.

She cleared her throat. 'Any names?'

'Totally.' Jo looked delighted. 'Henry Abingdon, Joseph Swinton and Lucinda Meldrum were the names I heard.'

Carter and Rachel, who both knew about Lucinda, were careful not to meet Allie's eye. She sat stunned, staring at Jo.

Lucinda is coming here? For the ball?

The grandmother she'd never met – who never even travelled across London to meet her – would be at Cimmeria. They'd be in the same room.

The others were now all talking at once in excited tones.

'President Abingdon!' Zoe sounded breathless. 'I wanted him to be my other dad.'

Under the table, Carter took Allie's hand and squeezed it gently. When nobody was paying attention, he leaned over and whispered into her ear, 'Did you know she was coming?'

She shook her head.

Before he could respond, the doors at the end of the dining hall swung open and the staff streamed in carrying heaping trays of food. The students gave their customary cheer, but this time Allie couldn't even fake a smile.

Everything was too messed up.

As soon as dinner ended, Carter disappeared. When he turned up in the common room twenty minutes later, he looked pale. Allie was on a sofa pretending to read *The Great Gatsby* as somebody pounded on the piano, each note sending a shard of glass into her tired head.

'Allie.' His jaw was tight. 'Can I have a word?'

Frowning, she looked up at him. He didn't sound right and, when she met his eyes, she saw anger there. Fear uncurled near her heart.

Has he found out about Christopher?

She followed him into the hallway. His muscles tense, he took quick, jerky steps, shoving open the door of the great hall. When they walked into the vast dark room he didn't turn on the light. His eyes glittered in the faint ambient glow from the windows.

'Did you tell Isabelle about what Gabe said to me?'

Her heart seemed to stop. Swallowing hard, she nodded. 'I didn't want to, Carter, but I had to.' She took a panicked step towards him. 'Not to get you into trouble but just in case the information was useful to the work she and Raj Patel are doing.' Her words sounded weak and pathetic to her own ears.

'Bloody hell, Allie.' He walked a few steps away then turned back to face her. 'Why didn't you at least warn me? Now I look like a . . . I don't know. Liar? Murderer?'

Aghast, she shook her head with fierce insistence. 'No, Carter. Isabelle would never think that. They're just surprised you didn't mention it – they know you're not . . .'

'Do they?' He crossed his arms. 'Thanks to you I think they're not so certain of that any more.'

Her shoulders slumped and the pounding in her head grew exponentially louder. She'd messed this up, too. Why couldn't she do anything right?

'I'm so sorry, Carter. That was the last thing I wanted to happen. I just didn't know what else to do.' She tried to read his expression to see how much trouble he was in. 'What are they going to do to you?'

'Nothing,' he muttered. 'I mean not really. Isabelle was angry. And she told me she was disappointed in me. That I should know better. The usual. But you're right. I don't think she suspects me of anything.'

The tightness in her chest eased – he wasn't in real trouble. 'I'm sorry, Carter. It's all my fault. I did the wrong thing. I know it sounds stupid but I was trying to help.'

And I trusted my instincts. Always an idiotic thing to do.

'Damn it, Allie.' He seemed to be calming down now and he walked back towards her. 'Just be careful, OK? You can do a lot of damage trying to help.'

She nodded miserably. 'Do you believe me, though? That I didn't mean to get you in trouble?'

'Of course I believe you.' The question seemed to puzzle him and he pulled her into a rough hug. 'You wouldn't lie to me.'

After that, the throbbing in her head was making it hard to think, so Allie escaped to her room. When the door closed behind her, she glanced at the clock.

Eight-thirty. If she was going to be any use to Sylvain tonight she needed to get some rest. Setting her alarm for eleven-thirty she lay down on the bed.

But the moment her eyes closed, last night's events played out for her like a film. She'd stayed in Sylvain's room for hours while they plotted out what they would do tonight. It had been odd to feel so comfortable, curled up across from him on the bed, wearing his pyjamas, as he sketched out for her on a piece of paper her precise route for tonight. But the longer they talked the more relaxed she felt.

She didn't realise she'd fallen asleep. Just, one minute she was awake and Sylvain was sketching the forest on to the map and talking about footpaths and the next minute she was sitting in the dining room, and Gabe was staring at her through the window.

The room was completely empty aside from her, Sylvain and Carter. Turning to Carter, Allie grabbed his arm, pointing at Gabe.

'There! He's right there!'

But he couldn't see him, and he shook his head, a worried look on his face. 'What are you talking about, Allie? There's no one there.'

When she looked back to the window, Gabe wasn't there any more. Instead, he was inside the dining room.

Walking towards them.

Her heart pounded in her chest as she spun to face Sylvain, her nails digging into his arm. 'Can't you see Gabe? He's right there.'

'Of course I can see him, Allie,' Sylvain said calmly. 'He's standing right next to you.'

She didn't know if her own scream woke her or Sylvain, who held her by the shoulders, shaking her. 'Wake up, Allie.'

'Sylvain?' Her eyes scanned the room wildly. 'Where am . . . ?' Then she remembered and her speeding heart slowed. 'I fell asleep.'

The overhead light was off, although the desk lamp still cast a soft circle of light. At some point he'd put the papers away and covered her with a blanket.

'You were talking in your sleep.' Sleep and worry thickened his accent. 'Were you dreaming about Gabe?'

At the mention of his name, she shuddered. 'He was in my dream. Nobody could see him except you and me. He was going to kill us.'

Propped up on his elbow beside her, Sylvain smoothed her hair out of her face. 'It was just a bad dream. You're safe.' His fingers were soft against her skin as her heavy eyelids fluttered shut.

This is wrong.

She sat up. 'I have to go back to my room.'

He hadn't tried to talk her out of it. Instead, he'd walked with her down a staircase, through empty narrow corridors she'd never seen before and up another servants' staircase to the girls' dorm. Their bare feet padded conspiratorially on the cold wood floors. She was terrified of being caught but he'd seemed undaunted. 'Nobody ever goes this way except students sneaking into each other's rooms,' he'd said. And she wondered how many girls' rooms he'd visited.

Just outside the door to the girls' dormitory wing, they'd stopped, and she'd looked up at him. He leaned in close – she could feel his breath warm on her cheek.

'You're certain you want to do this?' he'd whispered, his eyes serious.

Not trusting her voice, she nodded.

'OK then. Until tonight.'

At eleven-thirty the alarm woke Allie from confused dreams. She was instantly alert; her heart thudding in her ears.

It's time.

Moving efficiently, she pulled on the warm clothes she'd set out earlier, wrapping a dark scarf around her neck and buttoning up a navy blue pea coat.

The hallway was silent and dark when she opened her bedroom door at ten minutes to midnight. She crept silently down the hallway towards the same narrow staircase she'd used the night of the fire.

Her hand was on the doorknob when a sound behind her made her freeze.

'Allie?' Jules clicked on a flashlight, momentarily blinding her. 'What are you doing?'

Allie scrambled for an excuse; an explanation. A lie. But her mind was blank.

Where on earth could she legitimately be going at this hour, with one hand on the stairwell door?

'Jules, please don't tell anyone,' she said. 'But I have to go.'

The prefect's eyes narrowed. 'Allie, you must be joking. You know The Rules. You can't leave the dorm after eleven without special permission. Where are you going?'

'I have to meet someone.' Even as she said the words Allie knew how bad that sounded and she hastened to add, 'It's not what you think; it's very important.'

Jules took a step towards her and Allie marvelled that her perfect white-blonde bob was smooth as silk, even at this hour.

'Is it Carter?' she whispered. 'Are you going to meet him?'

Allie shook her head, mutely.

A suspicious frown lined Jules' forehead. 'Then who is it?'

'Sylvain,' Allie whispered. As soon as she said his name, colour flooded her cheeks for some reason, as if she were on her way to an illicit assignation.

Puzzled, Jules lowered the torch a little. 'I don't understand. Why are you sneaking out to see Sylvain?' Her eyes widened. 'Are you two . . . ?'

'No!' Thinking about last night, Allie could hear the panic in her own retort. 'No, he's just . . . helping me with something. Jules, listen, I know you'll need to report this and that's fine but please don't do it until morning. I'll take my punishment then. I promise you we're not doing anything wrong or totally weird. He's just helping me.' She searched Jules' eyes for understanding. 'Please, Jules.'

With a click, Jules turned off the torch. 'I hope this is worth it, Allie. I won't say anything until morning. But that's all I can do. And, later, I'd really like one of you to tell me what the hell is going on.'

Allie took a deep relieved breath. 'Thank you, Jules. I owe you.'

'Yes, you bloody do,' the prefect said tartly. 'Pay me back by not getting into trouble tonight, OK?'

The twisted truth had come so easily, Allie didn't even feel guilty. If everything went to plan, Jules would never know a thing. Nobody would. Nobody would get into trouble. Everything would be fine.

Allie dashed down the narrow staircase, emerging several storeys later in the crypt. Using the small, light pocket torch Sylvain had given her, she crossed the darkened, ancient chamber. Alone and in the dark it was much creepier than it had been in a crowd of girls with the lights on. Quickly, she found her way to the short staircase leading outside.

The whole time she was fighting the fear that threatened to squeeze her heart until it couldn't beat any more.

When she located the low door and her shaking fingers turned the handle, she stumbled out into the cold night air, the tightness in her chest loosening with relief.

I've done the hardest part, she reassured herself. But she knew that wasn't true.

She and Sylvain had plotted out every step she would take, but they both knew Raj's security guards patrolled the grounds nightly. And there was no way to predict where they would be. Sylvain believed Christopher had chosen this night and this time for a reason.

'I think he is certain Raj's team won't be there, or at least they won't encounter us.' He'd frowned as he said it. 'In a way that worries me more than anything.'

Still, they couldn't be certain of any of that, and Allie crouched low as she darted through the darkness into the woods. With her torch tucked away in her pocket, her instincts guided her through the shadows.

She followed the path Sylvain had told her about – around the east side of the property, near the fence line. This footpath wasn't as heavily used as the main path to the chapel and Allie was forced to move slowly to avoid tripping over the rocks and branches that cluttered her way.

The rain had ended at last. The night was cold and clear – a crescent moon shone brightly in a sky dusted with stars. But moonlight couldn't penetrate through the tree canopy, and the path was muddy, and Allie cursed silently as she splashed into a puddle she couldn't see. An icy breeze blew through the trees, and high above her head night birds grumbled. In the distance a fox screeched.

The noises were normal, but still, Allie felt a prickle of fear raise the hairs on the back of her neck. She had the strangest sense of being watched.

Picking up her speed, she tried to put the bad feeling behind her. Sylvain was out there somewhere, she knew. Maybe it was him.

They'd agreed that they would leave the building separately – he would depart before her and then watch for her from a hiding place. Once she was in the woods, he said, 'I will be with you all the time. You won't be able to see me, but trust that I will be there.'

I trust you, Sylvain, she thought. And then, conflictingly: *Please be there.*

As she rounded a bend, she was forced to clamber over a downed tree blocking the path. Her heart pounded – until she got across it, she was vulnerable. Panic made her careless and she crashed through the branches on the far side.

Once she'd made it to the other side, she could see the church wall ahead. Turning off the footpath before the church-yard, she made her way through the trees, moving carefully. Dried ferns brushed her fingertips like feathers, rustling softly with her every step. She could hear water rushing nearby.

As Sylvain had promised, on the far side of the church a narrow path led down to the stream and she followed it down to the water's edge. As she neared the creek bank, the trees opened up and moonlight illuminated the muddy shore. She was standing where Isabelle had stood last summer to meet Nathaniel.

Now she stood alone, peering into the darkness for any sign of her brother but the woods stood silent. The stream itself was swollen to nearly three times the size it had been the last time she'd been here. The heavy rains had fed it nearly to the break-ing point; now it was a mini-river, whose waters rushed by her feet.

Down the stream a stepping-stone bridge was almost com-pletely submerged. As she watched the water rush past it in a violent torrent it occurred to her that it would be fun to hop across that bridge on a hot summer day; the kind of day when you secretly hope to fall in.

'Allie.'

Christopher stood on the far bank, watching her with steady grey eyes exactly like her own.

'Oh.' Seeing him, she felt real, physical pain. Covering her mouth with her hand, she fought back tears.

He looked so much older. His unruly, light brown hair had been cut severely short, and he seemed taller, she thought. When she knew him, T-shirts and jeans had been his constant uniform. Now he wore a suit and tie, and the dark suit jacket covered the broad shoulders of a man.

Then he smiled and she could see the sixteen-year-old who'd helped her with her homework and met her after school. 'I knew you wouldn't let me down.'

'Christopher, I've missed you *so much*.' Through tears, she smiled back at him. 'I had to make sure you were OK. Your hair is ... so short.'

She couldn't believe that was what she'd come up with to say to her long-lost brother, and colour flooded back into her face.

But he didn't seem to notice. 'You've grown up into such a beautiful girl,' he said. 'No wonder all the boys are in love with you. And I hear your grades are aces. I'm so proud of you, Allie-cat.'

As he spoke, Allie wondered how he knew those things about her, but then he used his old pet name for her and all other thoughts flew away.

'Oh, Chris, I miss you,' she said, reaching out towards him with empty hands. 'Why did you have to go?'

The smile disappeared from his face. 'You know by now, don't you?'

She shook her head. 'I have no idea. I mean, I know Lucinda

Meldrum is our grandmother, and that Mum went to school here and didn't tell us but that's . . . '

'So you know she lied to us our whole lives.' The recognisable Christopher was gone now, replaced by an angry man who glared across the water at her. 'And that she and Isabelle conspired to keep us in the dark about our own family. And that now our grandmother . . . ' he spat the word out with contempt '. . . is denying us our family heritage. You do know that. Right?'

'Christopher, wait a second. Wait, wait, wait.' Allie tried to cut through the stream of vitriol. 'I don't . . . How is Lucinda denying us our heritage?'

'She refuses to acknowledge us as her family, Allie,' he said. 'How can you not know this? It's all because of Isabelle. You see, Allie,' he took a step closer to the water's edge – moonlight turning his face ghostly pale – 'Isabelle has a plan. This is what I need to tell you. She's wheedled herself into Lucinda's good graces, effectively replacing our mother. The last thing Isabelle wants now is for two kids to come along – real blood relatives – and take their rightful place as Lucinda's heirs. So she's keeping you at Cimmeria where she can control you completely.'

His face was twisted with rage, and she held her breath as she watched him. He looked deranged, she thought, her heart heavy in her chest.

'Well, I'm not going to be a part of their little game,' he continued. 'Nathaniel has a plan, Allie. A good one. He's going to take the power back from Isabelle completely. Get her out of the picture. He's going to get rid of the people who've run the organisation for the last twenty years and then . . . ' He squeezed his hands into fists. 'Then things will change around here.'

Sickened, Allie was suddenly glad of the water running between them.

'Are you sure he's the one to trust, Christopher?' She kept her tone cautious but steady. 'I mean, why trust him and not Isabelle? I find it hard to believe Isabelle's power hungry like—'

'Oh, Allie, don't be ridiculous.' Christopher cut her off. 'Look around you. Where are you? You're at a preparatory school for kings, prime ministers, bankers ... These people will run the world one day, and Isabelle is their figurehead and you don't think she's power hungry?' His voice rose in disbelief. 'Bollocks. She's power hungry all right. She's hungrier than anybody.'

Stubbornly, Allie shook her head. 'You don't know her, Chris. She's not like that. She really cares about me ... about our family.'

'Oh she does, does she?' The heat that had fired his previous words was gone, replaced by ice. 'Then ask yourself this: Why did she lie about Ruth's death? And whatever happened to Ruth's body anyway? And if you died, what would she do with yours?'

All the oxygen seemed to leave her lungs, as if he'd punched her. The one thing she couldn't explain away – the one thing she couldn't understand about Isabelle – was Ruth. Ruth was murdered at the summer ball, by Gabe. And Isabelle had covered it up. She'd knowingly – willingly – told everyone it was a suicide. Ruth's parents had either believed her or gone along with it. Everybody for ever would think Ruth killed herself, and Allie could not accept it. It just wasn't right.

But ... how did Christopher know that?

Suddenly grief crashed over her like a wave. Must everything she cared about be taken away from her? Must everyone she trusted be a liar?

'Why should I listen to you?' She nearly screamed the words. 'You abandoned me. Isn't *that* betrayal? Then you just show up here, siding with some arsehole who kills people and . . . what? I'm supposed to go with you? I'm supposed to trust you?'

His expression changed, and he held out placating hands. 'I know you're angry at me. I'm sorry for what I did to you. But don't trust Isabelle, Al, she's a liar. She's cheating you out of your inheritance and you don't even realise it. She's cheating you out of your whole family. She doesn't really care about you. But I do.'

Allie crossed her arms across her torso. Her heart felt compressed into a tiny cube, cold in her chest. Every instinct in her body told her to run away. But she couldn't go now. She had to know everything.

'What exactly do you want me to do, Christopher?' Although she felt breathless with anger and pain, her voice held steady. 'Leave Cimmeria and come with you?'

'Not yet.' He seemed pleased by her question, perhaps thinking he was making headway with her. 'But soon.' He glanced over his shoulder; when he turned back he seemed almost apologetic. 'Look, Al, we don't have much time tonight. But we should meet again. I want to tell you about our plans.'

When he smiled, he looked so much like the boy Allie remembered it almost made her cry. The older brother who always made her feel safe. The one who always looked out for her.

'Eventually, you'll see what I mean about all of this. Nathaniel is a good guy.' Her disbelief must have shown in her face because he added quickly, 'I know he's had to do things . . .

It was hard for him, too. But this is a war, Allie. And he's right about the organisation.'

'What do you mean?' She kept her voice light and conversational. 'At least tell me something, here. What does he want to do?'

'Oh, Al.' His eyes shone with passion. 'He's going to change everything. Fix all the things that have gone wrong in the world because the wrong people are in charge. Put the right people in charge. You know what Cimmeria is, right? I mean, what it's part of? If he ran the organisation, he could really do it, Allie. He could change everything. *Fix* everything.'

Allie didn't understand what he was talking about. *Change everything? Fix everything?*

But Christopher was looking over his shoulder again and she got the impression someone was speaking to him, quietly. When he turned back, he looked almost sad.

'God I've missed you, Allie-cat.' From across the water, he studied her face as if he were memorising it. 'Sometimes I thought I'd never see you again but here we both are.'

'Yep.' Allie fought to stay in control as her lower lip trembled. 'Here we are.'

'Hey,' he said with sudden brightness, 'remember that time I taught you to ride your bike and I forgot to show you how to use the brakes before letting you go?'

'I went careening down the pavement in front of the house and crashed into the postman's cart.' For just a second, Allie smiled at the memory. 'Letters flew everywhere.'

'He was furious,' Chris chuckled. 'He went to Mum and Dad and . . .'

The mention of their parents seemed to bring him back to reality and his smile evaporated. He took a step back from the water's edge. 'I have to go now, Al. Take the same path back that you took down here and you'll be clear of Patel's guards.'

How can he be so sure of that?

He held up his hand. 'Goodbye, Allie. And don't worry – we'll be keeping an eye on you. We've got someone on the inside.'

'Who?' she called after him.

But he was already disappearing into the trees.

As she made her way back up the rocky trail to the churchyard (*thirty-three steps*) she moved with mechanical efficiency. But while she pushed her way through branches her brain fought to make sense of what had just happened.

'*You know what Cimmeria is? What it's part of.*' When he'd said that his eyes had fairly glowed with excitement. She needed to talk this over with somebody. But who? Nobody knew she was here. She couldn't tell Rachel or Carter – not without word getting back to Isabelle.

And then Sylvain would be in trouble.

She'd almost made it to the main footpath. She was stepping around a large branch half blocking her way when a shape hurtled out of the woods, hitting her so hard she went sprawling, winded. Then, before she could recover, he wrapped her in his arms and dragged her into the forest.

It happened so fast there was no time to react. No time even to scream. No time for a neck lock or a defensive left flip. Just one minute she was walking on the path. And the next she was gone.

NINETEEN

llie was half dragged through the trees by someone she couldn't see – a muscular arm was tight across her chest, a strong hand held her brutally by the upper arm and hair. Her feet barely skimmed the ground and she was immobilised – she could neither move her arms nor grab on to anything. Because he was behind her, she couldn't see her kidnapper but she could feel the hardness of his torso against her back, smell his sweat, hear his harsh breathing.

Rising panic made it hard for her to focus.

Come on, Allie. Think! What would Mr Patel have told her to do?

But fear seemed to have rendered her brain inoperable. Her own breath had shortened to gasps. When she struggled, the arms around her tightened to the point where she thought her ribcage would crack.

'Your body is a weapon,' Mr Patel always said. *'Use it.'*

But how could she when she couldn't move? Her arms were held tight, her legs . . .

Her breath caught as she realised: her legs were free. And her kidnapper's most vulnerable point was right behind her thighs.

He probably had help somewhere nearby, she needed to act fast.

Saying a silent prayer, she lifted her legs up, forcing her kidnapper to shift as she curled into a ball against his torso. He grunted in surprise but before he could react she'd swung backwards, aiming the soles of her shoes at his crotch.

He cried out and dropped her at the same moment – she hit the ground hard, rolling into the brush beside the path. She scrambled to her feet, already running, but strong fingers grabbed her ankle yanking her back to the ground.

She kicked hard at the hand with her free foot but his grip didn't lessen and she couldn't get free. As his hold tightened and she realised she wasn't going to get away, she screamed.

Then she heard a sharp crack and a thud from somewhere in the darkness around her.

The hands let go.

Without waiting to see what had happened, Allie jumped to her feet, poised to run away. But then the moon came out from behind a cloud and she saw everything.

Gabe and Sylvain were on the path, facing off. Blood poured down the side of Gabe's face from a wound to his head. Sylvain held a thick stick in one hand, and circled Gabe like a panther.

Everyone had always told her how good Gabe was at Night School. How he was the best of all of them.

This is my fault. If anything happens to Sylvain ...

At that moment in a move so quick Allie could barely see it, Gabe ducked and spun, grabbing the branch in Sylvain's hand and twisting it sharply in an under-and-over manoeuvre.

Now it was Gabe's club.

For a fleeting second, Sylvain's gaze met hers. 'Run, Allie.'

She shook her head. 'I'm not leaving you.'

Anger flashed in his eyes. 'Run. *Now*.'

'Yes.' Gabe didn't turn around to look at her; his tone was sardonic. 'Run, Allie. You don't want to see this. I'll come and get you in a minute. And I will pay you back for kicking me in the balls.'

As Allie watched in horror he swung the club at Sylvain's head. At the last second, Sylvain feinted to the right but the branch clipped his shoulder. His cry of pain seared her. But Sylvain stayed on his feet and responded with a vicious elbow to Gabe's gut.

A sob burning her throat, Allie turned and ran into the woods. Behind her she heard Gabe's voice, as confident as ever. 'She's gone now. You can relax. I can't believe you're messing with Carter's girl, Sylvain. That's not like you. Usually you like them all fresh and unsullied.'

A sound like meat being slapped on to a countertop followed. But Allie was searching for something now and she tried to block the sounds from her mind. Seeing Sylvain's makeshift club had reminded her of a Night School class on found weapons. At the time, she'd thought it all a bit ridiculous and fairly simple. But nobody had been trying to kill Sylvain then. Suddenly it wasn't simple at all.

Whispering to herself, she crashed through the undergrowth with her torch, searching. She found what she was looking for at the exact moment Sylvain cried out in pain – a tormented sound she felt in her bones.

She switched off the torch.

It took a second for her eyes to readjust then, moving stealthily, she made her way back to the footpath. The sounds of their fight grew as she neared them. Whatever had just happened, Sylvain was still on his feet.

Seeing a hiding spot behind a young oak tree just off the path, she headed towards it. They were too absorbed in their fight to see her. She was almost in position when she skidded on a stone. As if he knew it was her, Sylvain spun towards the sound and in that split second of inattention, Gabe wrapped his forearm across his throat, tightening it with his other hand.

Stricken, Allie stared at them from her hiding place. She knew this move well. With Gabe's greater height and weight there was no way Sylvain could escape. She and Zoe practised it all the time – Zoe could never get free.

All Mr Patel ever said was 'Don't get yourself in this position.'

'An amateur's mistake, Sylvain,' Gabe whispered. His arm cut off the air through Sylvain's windpipe – his face was already turning purple. His hands grasped feebly at Gabe's arm. Without oxygen he'd be unconscious in seconds.

Dead in minutes.

For a fleeting second the realisation that he could actually die froze her in place. But she had to move. Now.

This isn't real, Allie, she told herself. *It's just Night School practice. None of this is real. Just do what you have to do. Raj Patel is watching.*

Busy taunting Sylvain, Gabe hadn't noticed her. Maybe he hadn't heard the noise that had caused Sylvain to lose focus in the first place.

Gripping the slender, sharp stick she'd found in the woods, Allie steeled herself. When she sprang out from behind the tree a second later she held it like a knife and, without a second's hesitation, she drove it with all the force she could muster into Gabe's shoulder.

She'd thought it would most likely scratch him and bounce off. Or break.

But she'd chosen her weapon and her target well and, instead, horribly, the muscle and flesh gave way.

Gabe screamed and, as he reached for the stake protruding from his skin, Allie grabbed Sylvain's hand, pulling him free. He was bloodied and struggling to breathe, but he was alive.

'You little bitch,' Gabe gasped. 'You stabbed me.' Grasping the stake, he tried to pull it out then screamed again, letting go. 'You little . . .'

'Yeah I know, "bitch",' Allie snapped. 'You said that already.'

Adrenaline coursed through her veins like alcohol and she wanted to hit Gabe again and again but Sylvain was pulling her away. He was saying something she couldn't make out – his voice was faint.

'What is it?' she asked, leaning closer to him.

Up close she could really see what Gabe had done to him, and her heart ached – he was bleeding in so many places she didn't know where a doctor would even start. But then she heard what he'd been trying to say.

'*Run.*' Limping, his breath rasping, he pulled her with him, and they rushed into the darkness.

Sylvain clung to her hand so fiercely it hurt but she didn't care; she didn't want to let go of him either. He knew these woods well – he seemed to know exactly where they were all the time, pausing only to wipe the blood out of his eyes. As the saplings whizzed by inches from her body and twigs tore at her hair and clothes, Allie found herself surrendering to the situation – fearless. The further they ran the better she felt. Her muscles were loose and strong – she was powerful. She had a strange desire to laugh.

When they broke through the treeline and sped out on to the smooth grassy lawn in front of the school building she did laugh. They'd made it.

But as they crossed the grass, a cluster of shadows broke loose from the trees and ran into their path.

Their footsteps slowed and Allie looked around, bewildered; Sylvain pulled her closer as the shadows approached them and became people – Raj's security guards.

They were surrounded.

'You did *what*?' Raj stared at her in disbelief. 'Do you have any idea how dangerous that was?'

They were crowded into the school's entrance hall; in one corner, one of Raj's men tended to Sylvain's wounds. Others were gathered around openly watching them argue.

'Yes.' Her voice was cold. 'I do.'

He was not mollified; small white lines of rage had appeared beside his mouth. 'This is the most irresponsible thing I can imagine any student doing. You could have died. Sylvain could have died.'

'But we're alive.' An errant sense of pride made her stand taller. 'And I want to say right now, this was all my fault. I made Sylvain come with me. He tried to stop me.'

'Sylvain,' Isabelle's voice rang out from the doorway where she stood like an angel of vengeance in a white dressing gown, her hair flowing loose over her shoulders, 'will take responsibility for his own actions. Raj, Allie, in my office now.' She pointed at the medic helping Sylvain. 'Take him to the infirmary.'

'I'm fine.' Sylvain struggled to his feet with obvious effort. 'I'm coming with you.'

'The *infirmary*.' Fury crackled in Isabelle's voice.

But he didn't back down. 'I'm coming with Allie,' his words were slurred, as if he spoke through a mouthful of ice, 'Isabelle.'

When he said the headmistress' name it sounded like a threat. Or a reminder. Puzzled, Allie's gaze moved back and forth between them.

Closing her eyes, Isabelle took a calming breath. 'I'd really rather you didn't haemorrhage in my office. Please do me that favour.' She snapped her fingers at the medic. 'Give him a towel. Then you three, with me.'

With Isabelle in the lead they walked down the hall, Sylvain limping beside Allie, and Raj Patel making up the rear guard.

In case we try to flee, Allie thought.

Inside her office, Isabelle handed them bottles of water. Allie poured hers on to the towel and gently dabbed Sylvain's wounds. Most appeared superficial, but his face was swelling alarmingly; she wondered if Gabe had broken his jaw.

All the while he sat still, stoic. As if the pain didn't matter. Then suddenly he looked up and their eyes met. Allie's hand stilled as the enormity of what had happened hit her. He'd nearly died for her tonight. Again.

She searched his eyes as if she could find the answer she sought there.

Why? Why would you risk your life for me?

'Sylvain, you will see the doctor when you leave this room or as God is my witness I will put you on the next plane to France.' Isabelle's angry voice jerked Allie back to reality. She turned to Mr Patel. 'What do we know?'

'On-the-ground shift change was at midnight tonight – two members of incoming staff received messages from my phone telling them they weren't needed.' His tone was brisk and businesslike. 'They followed protocol – alerting me via our alternative messaging network. That's how we knew something was planned for tonight. We trebled our staff and we are certain Nathaniel's people got nowhere near the building.'

'Have you identified how many of his people were on the grounds?' Isabelle asked.

'We know of three.'

Three. There was another. Allie tried not to think about what would have happened to Sylvain if the third person had stopped her from stabbing Gabe.

'Where are they now?'

Mr Patel cleared his throat. 'My team believe they've left the grounds but I'm not convinced. The building is surrounded by my guards, and there are four inside the building patrolling.'

'So we don't know where they are.' Her tone was unforgiving. 'Allie.' When the headmistress turned to face her, Allie could see that she was pale and her skin was tight across her sharp cheekbones. 'Tell me what happened.'

Talking quickly, Allie explained the letter, the meeting, everything Christopher had told her about Nathaniel and somebody working 'on the inside'. She told her what he'd said about everything except Isabelle herself – she couldn't bring herself to say that right now.

As she spoke, Isabelle's face changed. Colour flowed into her cheeks and her golden brown eyes glittered with rage. She and Raj Patel exchanged a look heavy with meaning.

'I am so angry with you two right now . . . ' She rubbed a hand across her forehead as if to clear her thoughts. 'We will talk later about the way you both broke The Rules. And the chances you took, especially you Sylvain.' She fired a glare at him. 'You more than anyone should know better. I'm putting it off until then because I do not trust myself right now not to expel you both for this. Dammit!' She slapped one hand down on the desk with a bang. 'You put yourselves and the school in danger,' Isabelle said. 'And you both know better.'

For a long moment, she gazed over Allie's head at the tapestry of a knight and maiden that took up one whole wall. When Allie tried to speak she raised a hand in a warning.

'Not one word,' she snapped.

For what seemed like a very long time they all sat still. The only sounds were the occasional creak of an old beam settling and their breathing.

'OK.' Isabelle's voice had returned to normal. 'Allie, you broke every rule I hold dear and you betrayed my trust. You are on very thin ice right now. Sylvain ...'

The anger in her eyes was so raw Allie felt a wave of fear for him.

'I will need you to debrief the others about what you've learned. I'll set up a meeting in the usual place for first thing tomorrow – that's presuming you are able to attend.' Their eyes locked as she added, 'You'll be lucky if Jerry Cole doesn't try to have you expelled from Night School. But you knew that.'

'*What?* You can't throw Sylvain out,' Allie protested, sliding forward in her chair. 'I made him ...'

'That is no excuse for somebody as experienced as Sylvain to do what he did tonight.' There was no sympathy in Isabelle's voice, only resignation. 'He risked both of your lives. He knows The Rules better than anybody here. He knew what punishment he would face if he did this.'

Shocked, Allie turned to Sylvain, but he was watching Isabelle through swollen eyes.

He went with me, knowing he could lose everything? Guilt and confusion did battle in her mind.

'I think it's best if you don't go to that briefing, Allie,' Isabelle continued. 'Zelazny will have to be talked out of expelling you. If you're there it will be worse. I'll send for you later.'

'I want to be involved,' Allie said, sitting up straight. 'Whatever happens next. I want to help.'

'I rather think that you needn't worry about that,' Isabelle said icily. 'At this point you're in it up to your eyebrows whether you like it or not.'

TWENTY

'**A**re you OK? You really should go and see the nurse.' As they stood in the hallway near Isabelle's office, Allie studied Sylvain's battered face worriedly. He'd stopped bleeding, but one eye was swollen shut, and his jaw was so bruised his mouth barely worked.

'I will.' His good eye blinked at her.

'How's your . . . ' She gestured at her neck.

He gave a weak shrug, and then winced. 'Fine, I think.'

Talking seemed to hurt him and, as they stood in awkward silence, Allie could think of a thousand things she wanted to say but she didn't know how to say them. Or whether if she did it would convey what she really felt.

And what did she feel anyway?

Thank you for nearly dying for me. Thank you for risking everything for me. Thank you for being there for me. What are we going to do now?

Instead she said, 'Do you want me to come with you? Do you need help?'

'I'd rather do it,' he said painfully, 'myself.'

'OK.'

'Well,' he said after a long pause. 'Bye.'

As he turned in the direction of the infirmary, her hands curled into fists so tight her nails dug crescents into her palms. Was she really going to let him just walk away after all that happened tonight without saying anything? He'd nearly died for her. She'd nearly killed someone for him.

What's happening here?

'Sylvain!'

Her tone was sharp and, creakily, he turned to look at her.

'Thank you.' Frustrated by her own inability to say what she meant, or even to know what she meant, she held her hands up helplessly.

For a brief second his battered gaze held hers. Then his swollen lips tried to curve upwards.

'Any time.'

The sound of footsteps and voices in the hallway woke Allie late the next morning. For a brief moment she didn't know where she was and she sat up in a panic.

She was in her own room, her own bed.

After watching Sylvain make his way to the infirmary last night, she'd trudged up to her room and tumbled into bed, stopping only long enough to strip off her dirty clothes and pull on a T-shirt. She'd been sure she'd never fall asleep, but exhaustion had taken over so quickly she hadn't even dreamed about Christopher.

Christopher.

Now bright sunlight flooded the room, and she pushed her tangled hair out of her eyes so she could see the alarm clock.

Nine o'clock.

Jumping to her feet, she grabbed a towel and hurried down to the bathroom, not even seeing the girls she passed in their uniforms, who glanced at her curiously.

After rushing through a shower, she threw on a clean uniform and clattered down the stairs; a worry headache had already begun to throb. She had to know what had happened while she slept. Had Sylvain been expelled? Had they found Christopher or Gabe?

And Carter . . . At the thought she skidded to a stop.

She had to find Carter before he learned what had happened last night. Either way he was going to be so angry when he found out she'd gone with Sylvain.

Her stomach contorted and she grabbed it with one hand. When was the last time she'd actually eaten? Not yesterday. Maybe the day before?

Isabelle's office was her first stop, but it was empty, the lights turned off. The common room was busy, but nobody she recognised was there.

She was halfway to the library when she spotted Jules walking towards her.

'Hey, Jules, do you know where Carter . . .' she started, but her voice trailed off when she saw the anger in her eyes.

'Allie, what the hell were you thinking?'

'I—' she tried, but Jules cut her off.

'I've just been given a vicious bollocking by Isabelle. She

says you sneaked out last night and met your brother and Gabe,' Jules hissed, looking around to make sure nobody was listening. 'All the senior Night School students have been called into a strategy meeting about what to do next. Frankly, I can't believe you haven't been expelled yet.'

The injustice sent heat rising to Allie's face.

Met Gabe? MET Gabe? I tried to kill Gabe . . .

'After all that happened last term, how could you?' Jules continued, clearly furious. 'How could you invite Nathaniel's people here?'

Allie tried not rise to the bait. There were things she needed to know and getting angry wouldn't help.

'I know you're angry, Jules, but, first, has Sylvain been expelled?' she asked crisply.

'Not yet,' Jules said gracelessly.

Allie ignored the last comment. 'Is he OK? Have you seen him?'

'He's a mess, but he's alive,' Jules said. 'No thanks to you and your brother.'

Closing her eyes, Allie allowed herself a moment of relief. Then she squared her shoulders and faced the prefect.

'I'm sorry you got in trouble because of me. I would never put Cimmeria in danger knowingly. I didn't invite Christopher – he just came. And, yes, I wanted to see my brother. I had to know . . . ' Her breath caught and she paused. 'I just had to.'

Jules did not seem placated. 'Sometimes it seems like all you do is put Cimmeria in danger, Allie. Everything was fine until you came here. And, maybe it's unfair of me to say this, but sometimes I really wish ...' Allie flinched, and Jules stopped, biting her lip. 'I'm sorry. I shouldn't ...'

'No. Don't apologise.' Allie said, straightening her spine. 'I deserve that. You know, I am trying ...' But her voice trailed off. What was the point? Nothing she said would make things different. 'I'm just ... sorry.'

As she said the last words she was already walking away; her ribs felt tight around her lungs, and she had the awful sense that everything had gone horribly wrong.

If Sylvain was fine and hadn't been expelled then there was one thing Allie needed to do before finding Isabelle and facing whatever happened next. She needed to talk to Carter.

As she walked down the wide hallway through crowds of chatting students, relaxing on a Saturday morning, her steps were slow and reluctant. If Jules knew what had happened, then Carter probably did, too. He knew she'd kept Christopher's letter a secret from him, and shared it with someone he hated. That she'd lied to him.

He'll never forgive me, she thought. *And why should he? I'm a liar. Like everyone else in my family ...*

So lost was Allie in self-incrimination that Jo had nearly walked past before she'd spotted her.

'Hey, Jo, have you seen ...' Her voice trailed off as she got a good look at her friend; Jo's face was red and raw from tears, her short blonde hair rumpled, her uniform buttoned up crooked. 'Are you ... Jo, what's the matter?'

'Is it true?' Jo stared at her with red eyes. 'What everybody's saying. Is it true?'

'I don't . . . ' Allie's mouth went dry and the pounding in her head grew louder and more insistent. 'What is everyone saying?'

'Did you see Gabe last night? Here?' Jo's voice rose, and Allie could see people stopping to look at them.

Taking Jo's hand, she tried to pull her out of the hallway towards the kitchen but Jo recoiled, yanking her hand free and slapping hard at Allie's wrist. The slap stung and Allie pulled her hand back before she could hit it again.

'Jo, calm down.' She looked at her friend with concern, and chose her words carefully. 'Yes, I saw Gabe last night. He was sneaking around the grounds.'

'What . . . ' Jo stared at her as if she were trying to focus. 'What was he doing here? Why did you see him?'

Allie didn't know how much of what happened last night was freely known and she lowered her voice. 'Christopher came to see me.' The memory of Gabe carrying her brutally through the woods made her stomach churn. 'Gabe was with him.'

'Why didn't you tell me?' Jo's accusing tone was unexpected, and Allie stared at her blankly.

'Tell you what?'

'You went to see Gabe and you didn't tell me.'

'Jesus, Jo.' Allie fought to keep her temper. Jo clearly wasn't herself and getting angry wouldn't help. She didn't know what had happened, and anything involving Gabe made her irrational. 'I went to see Christopher and only Christopher. I just wanted some answers. I didn't know Gabe would be there. He showed up without an invitation. And we shouldn't be talking about this.'

For a long moment Jo's eyes searched hers. 'You wouldn't talk to Gabe without telling me, would you?'

'No, Jo,' Allie said sadly. 'I wouldn't do that. But you need to stop thinking about Gabe. He's not good for you. He's not good for anyone.'

'I know that,' Jo snapped. '"But . . . Don't you see? I never got to ask him why he did what he did.'

Allie thought about her own driving need to ask Christopher why he left her family and for the first time she thought she understood Jo's irrational attachment to Gabe.

'I promise you,' she reached for Jo's hand and this time she didn't hit her, 'if Gabe ever gets in touch with me, I'll tell you.'

A short time later, her hand shook as she raised it to knock lightly against Isabelle's door. The pounding in her head had worsened now, and was more like a jazz drummer beating away at the inside of her skull. But she had to keep going.

'Come in.'

When she stepped into the room, the headmistress didn't look thrilled to see her. Her glasses were shoved up on to her head, and she had a stack of papers in one hand.

'I told you I'd call you when I was ready for you.'

'I'm sorry, Isabelle.' Allie leaned her head against the door frame as if resting it would make it stop hurting. 'Sorry – I seem to be saying that a lot today. I just feel like I should be doing something. I feel like everything's my fault and I want to, I don't know, make it better.'

Isabelle pointed at a chair. 'Sit.' As Allie sat down, the head-mistress studied her appraisingly. 'Have you eaten today?'

Allie shook her head.

The headmistress' eyes narrowed. 'Yesterday?'

Too numb and tired to lie, Allie held up her empty hands.

'I thought as much,' Isabelle said. 'You look awful. Stay here.'

Turning the kettle on as she passed, she walked out of the door.

Sitting still in the empty office, Allie stared into the distance as the kettle rumbled to life. As steam poured out in a curling cloud, she flipped through her mental list of options, her lips moving slightly, betraying the intensity of her concentration.

A rush of air stirred her hair as the door opened. Isabelle handed her a plate holding a cheese sandwich before turning to fill the two teacups. Allie nibbled at the edge – even though she was hungry, she didn't feel like eating.

Isabelle handed her a cup of tea and then curled up in the deep chair next to hers.

For a while they sat in silence that could have been misconstrued as companionable. But Allie could sense the tension between them.

'I'm afraid,' the headmistress said, 'that August Zelazny has demanded a tribunal be held to hear the case for expelling you. This will happen tomorrow.'

The news didn't surprise Allie but it hurt nonetheless. It was entirely possible that, after everything she'd been through, Cimmeria would just throw her out like all the other schools.

'OK.' Her voice was dull. 'I guess I deserve that.'

'I'd like to say you don't, but yes, you do.' Isabelle's voice was peevish, but when Allie sat staring glumly at her hands, she added, 'Eat your sandwich.'

Allie took a dutiful bite, avoiding the headmistress' eyes.

'There's something else,' Isabelle said with a sigh. 'And you're not going to like it either.'

Allie swallowed hard. 'What is it?'

The headmistress rubbed her eyes. 'We need you to talk to Christopher again. When he next gets in touch with you, you'll make a date and set a meeting point.'

'And then you'll ... what? Grab him?' Allie set her plate down with a clatter. 'He has people on the inside, Isabelle. He knows everything about me. My grades. Who I'm dating ...' She slid down further in her chair. 'If he knows that kind of stuff, he'll know all about your plan. And he'll use that against us.'

'We will have two plans.' Isabelle said the words so quietly Allie almost missed them. 'One that we tell the staff and senior Night School students. And one that I tell you, Sylvain and a handful of people I trust.'

Allie covered her mouth with the fingers of one hand. 'Do you know who it is, Isabelle? Who's working for Nathaniel?'

Isabelle shook her head. The conversation seemed to be ageing her – she looked drawn. 'I wish I did.'

'It's somebody high up, isn't it?' Allie said. 'Somebody close to you.'

'And to you,' Isabelle said.

They stared at each other for a long second, the enormity of the situation reflecting back to Allie from Isabelle's worried eyes. In the corner the kettle ticked as it cooled.

And that's when Allie decided she didn't care what Christopher said. She trusted Isabelle. She would side with

Isabelle and fight with Isabelle against whatever it was he believed.

'I'm sorry I didn't tell you about Christopher.'

The headmistress regarded her coolly.

'I couldn't, Isabelle.' Allie knew she sounded desperate, but she needed her to understand. 'I knew what you would do. I knew you'd set him up and grab him, and he'd know I turned him in. I couldn't do that without talking to him first. I needed to hear what he had to say.'

'And now?' Isabelle's voice was heavy.

'Now ...' Allie clutched her cup again so tightly she was surprised it didn't burst. 'Now I know my brother is gone. I don't recognise the person who's replaced him. He's changed. And I don't want anything to do with him.'

Isabelle leaned towards her. 'I care about you, Allie. But you must have faith in me. I know a lot about how Nathaniel works.' She was close enough for Allie to see the green flecks in her light brown eyes. 'And I am afraid if you don't learn to trust me, one day you're going to get hurt.'

After her meeting with Isabelle, and unable to find Carter anywhere, Allie fled to her room. Exhausted, she fell asleep, and didn't wake up until it was nearly dinner time.

Just before seven, she was walking down the stairs towards the dining hall when she saw Sylvain walking a short distance ahead. For a split second, her heart leapt and she hurried her pace. Then she saw that he wasn't alone – Nicole held his arm. Her long dark hair swung with each step and from time to time she glanced over at him, worry clouding her big dark eyes. As

Allie watched, Sylvain fell slightly behind her. When Nicole turned to see why he'd slowed, her gaze met Allie's. Leaning towards Sylvain, she whispered something – he turned to look at her and Allie felt a charge of electricity.

He was the only one who knew what had happened last night. The only one who understood.

She didn't want to feel like this, but she did.

He said something back to Nicole and they stood still, waiting for her.

Faking a casual smile, Allie waved as if she'd been hoping to see them together and hurried down to them.

'I've been looking for you everywhere, Sylvain. Oh, hey, Nicole.' She was pleased her voice sounded normal. 'Are you feeling better?'

But even as she cheerfully uttered the words, her eyes skittered from wound to wound, silently assessing him. He was covered in cuts and bruises. One eye was still thoroughly swollen, but his jaw looked better – no longer puffy.

'I'm alive,' he said. 'But this is not the best I've ever looked.'

Nicole slid her hand down his arm to his hand. 'I told him it looked like he crashed his motorcycle without a helmet, but he says only that there was a fight and that you helped him.'

Allie tried to imagine him, not in his uniform, but in jeans and a T-shirt, riding an expensive motorcycle. It wasn't that hard to do.

Sylvain was still watching her. 'Sit with us at dinner,' he said.

Allie hesitated. If he was dating Nicole again she didn't want to be a gooseberry. But Nicole interceded. 'Yes,' she said, leading the way. 'Please do.'

As they walked towards the dining hall, Allie waited until Nicole wasn't looking then leaned close to Sylvain.

'Have you talked with Jerry and Zelazny yet?'

Nodding, he looked away.

She frowned at his reaction. 'Is everything OK?'

When he didn't reply, something in the way he avoided her eyes told her it wasn't.

Before she could say anything else, Nicole glanced back at them, her gaze sharp and curious.

Quickly, Allie stepped away.

Carter didn't come to dinner. His continuing absence left Allie with a growing sense of dread. Wherever he was, he knew what had happened. And he wasn't taking it well. After a tense meal during which she couldn't talk about anything that mattered, she fled the dining hall at the first opening, determined to track him down.

A quick search showed he wasn't in the library or the common room. She was considering crashing the boys' dorm when it struck her that she knew exactly where he was.

With a steadying breath, she opened the door to the great hall and stepped inside letting it swing shut behind her. She squinted into the dimness; dust motes seemed to hang still in the air in denial of the laws of gravity. In front of a fireplace so big she could easily have stood upright inside it, she surveyed the space – a few empty tables, a scattering of chairs.

She was turning back towards the door when a scuffing sound made her turn back around again.

'Carter?'

No answer. But, from the far corner of the room, the sound came again. Like a chair moving on the wood floor as someone stood up.

Weaving her way between odd pieces of furniture, Allie walked towards the sounds. She was about halfway across the room when she sensed motion to her left.

'Why didn't you tell me?' He was standing in the shadows, one hand on the back of a wooden chair.

'Carter.' Her throat seemed to close on her words. 'I . . . '

She'd thought so hard about what she should say, but now that she was standing in front of him, she knew there could be no excuses.

'I knew you'd go to Isabelle,' she said at last, 'regardless of what I wanted. And I needed to talk to Christopher. I couldn't let them kidnap my brother.'

'So you told Sylvain instead.'

His grip on the chair was so tight she could see his knuckles bulge.

He looked so hurt and angry; her shoulders sagged under the weight of her guilt. 'I had to tell him, for the interview.' When Carter shot her a dubious look her tone became more defensive. 'He asked if I'd heard from Christopher and I had. I couldn't lie. So I told him. I told him I was going to go and meet him. He didn't want me to go alone.'

'Why didn't you tell someone else? What about Rachel?' When he spoke, his voice was low and steady, but she could see how he fought for control over his emotions. 'Don't you trust her?'

'She doesn't have any training.' Allie's voice was dull. She felt like she'd lost this argument already. 'I couldn't bear it if she got hurt.' She took a step towards him. 'Carter, it killed me not to tell you. You're the one person I would have wanted to tell. But . . .'

'But you didn't *trust me*.'

With a move so sudden she didn't have any time to react, he picked up the chair with one hand and flung it across the room. It crashed to the floor with a shattering sound that echoed through the ballroom.

'Carter,' she breathed, staring up at him.

'Tell me the truth, Allie.' Clenching his hands at his sides, he breathed heavily. 'Look me in the eye and tell me you don't feel anything for Sylvain except friendship. Tell me you're not attracted to him at all.'

Allie opened her mouth to say, *Don't be ridiculous. You're the only one.*

But nothing came out. She'd lied enough. And her feelings for Sylvain were so conflicted she no longer knew how she felt about him.

She hadn't thought it possible Carter's eyes could get darker.

Crossing the space between them in three rapid steps, he grabbed her arms, pulling her close. His body pressed up against hers until she could feel his heart beating through his shirt. She could see nothing except his dark eyes.

'I would,' he said through clenched teeth, 'have done anything for you.'

Allie stared at him, stunned. This was not Carter. He never acted like this. Reaching up, she touched his temple lightly with her fingertips – he flinched away.

'I'm so sorry I hurt you,' she whispered, her lip trembling. 'I just . . . I hoped you would understand how important it was for me to see Christopher. And I care about you so much . . .'

He didn't wait for her to finish. Shoving her away roughly, he stepped back.

'And I hoped you would understand how important it is for you to trust me. But you don't. And I'm starting to think . . .' To her horror she realised there were tears in his eyes. 'I think you never will.'

When he walked out of the room, he didn't look back.

TWENTY-ONE

The next morning Allie felt numb.

Numb to pain, numb to danger. Numb to anything the world had left to throw at her.

When Isabelle called her to her office to tell her a tribunal was scheduled for that evening to consider her punishment, she just nodded.

Of course that was next.

'Tell them the truth,' Isabelle said, 'the way you explained it to me.'

'Will they kick me out?' Allie asked. She only half cared what the answer would be, but Isabelle's simple reply stung.

'I don't know.'

After that, Allie retreated to the forced quiet of the library where, in a dim corner, she tried to bury herself in work. There was nobody for her to turn to. She couldn't even really tell

Rachel why she and Carter had had the fight – not without getting into more trouble, anyway.

Besides, what was the point? She knew what everybody would say. They'd say, *Why didn't you tell Carter instead of Sylvain?*

And now that she thought about it, that was a perfectly good question. Why didn't she? Over and over again Carter's words resonated in her head. *'Look me in the eye and tell me you don't feel anything for Sylvain . . .'*

As she flipped through the pages of her history textbook, it was images of Carter's face she saw. The intensity of his reaction had frightened her. It was the first time it ever occurred to her that he might really break up with her over Sylvain.

Tears stung her eyes and she swiped them away with the back of her hand.

What's the point in crying? she asked herself bitterly. *It won't help anyone.*

'Hey, are you OK?' Jo slipped into the chair next to hers, looking at her with concern. She seemed better than yesterday – her face wasn't red.

Still, Allie really didn't want to talk to her right now. So she lied. 'I'm fine.'

Jo ran a nervous hand through her short blonde hair. 'Look, I wanted to apologise for losing it – anything to do with Gabe makes me completely mental.'

'You shouldn't apologise,' Allie said, setting down her pen with a sigh. 'I'm the one who caused all the trouble.'

'You were doing what you had to do,' Jo said, surprising her. 'I don't think anyone would have done differently. But I've

253

heard they're planning some sort of stupid tribunal for you and that pisses me off so much. I've already told Isabelle how freakin' stupid it is, but she won't do anything.' Jo kicked a leg of the table. 'As bloody usual.'

Allie stared. 'How do you know about that?'

Jo made a dismissive gesture. 'That doesn't matter. What matters is this: I've told Isabelle if they expel you I'm going, too. OK? And I just wanted you to know that.'

'Jo . . . ' Allie didn't know what to say. She was horrified and pleased in equal measures. 'You can't.'

'I can and I will.' Jo's tone was emphatic. 'I want to leave anyway. It hasn't been the same since everything happened over the summer. Maybe I'll go to that finishing school Lisa's at in Switzerland. I could meet some handsome Swiss prince and live happily ever after. Anyway,' she didn't wait for Allie to respond, 'I just wanted you to know. Especially after what they did to Sylvain.'

Allie's mouth went dry. 'What do you mean? What did they do to Sylvain?'

'Haven't you heard?' Surprised, Jo blinked at her. 'He had his tribunal yesterday. They've put him on probation and suspended him from senior Night School activities.'

The rush of relief made Allie feel lighter. He wasn't expelled.

The day crept by at an achingly slow pace. By nine o'clock, when Allie's tribunal was due to take place, she longed for it to just happen. Whatever the verdict.

Just before nine, she walked down the cold basement stairs alone. She didn't know what to expect but told herself she no longer really cared. Nonetheless, the corridor seemed longer than usual and darker. She'd never felt more lonely.

When she saw Sylvain ahead of her, she instantly panicked, rushing to his side. 'What are you doing here? Is something wrong?'

His bruises stood out in stark relief. One eye was still nearly swollen shut, and the cut on his lip looked raw. But he tried to smile anyway. 'I just wanted to wish you luck.'

A sudden surge of emotion made it hard for her to talk; she bit her lip. 'I heard what they did to you. I'm sorry.'

'Don't be sorry.' He held her gaze. 'I'm not.'

'But it was my fault, Sylvain,' she said passionately. 'And now you're in trouble.'

'It was worth it,' he said. When she prepared to protest again, he reached out and lifted her chin until her eyes met his. 'Allie. It was worth it.'

She'd worked *so hard* not to care about any of this, but now one tear escaped, betraying her. He wiped it away, his fingers gentle on her skin.

'*Courage*,' he said, pronouncing it the French way. 'Don't let them see you cry.'

Then he walked to the door, resting his hand on the handle, waiting until she'd composed herself. Taking a steadying breath, she nodded to show she was ready.

He opened the door.

Inside, a table had been set up with four chairs, as it had been arranged the day Night School students began their interviews. This time, though, only one chair faced it. For a split second Allie imagined running out of the room. Out of the school.

She walked inside.

The room was chilly and smelled faintly of dusty concrete and stale sweat. Zelazny, Jerry Cole, Eloise and Isabelle sat at the table, watching her.

'Please sit, Allie.' Eloise looked sympathetic as Allie lowered herself stiffly into the folding chair, its metal cold against her thighs. The others were expressionless.

'You're here today because you broke The Rules by going out after curfew without permission to meet a member of Nathaniel's team.' Isabelle's hands were crossed in front of her. Her light hair was pinned back severely, and her narrow glasses made her face look angular. 'You were accompanied by Sylvain Cassel, who has already verified all of this to the tribunal. Do you disagree with any of these allegations?'

Allie held her gaze steadily. 'No.'

'Allie, this is your opportunity to make your case against expulsion, from Night School and from Cimmeria Academy, the most serious penalty this tribunal can issue.' Eloise's voice was gentle. 'Tell us any mitigating circumstances – any reasons why what you did was justified. Please start by giving us your account of what happened that night. Why did you break The Rules?'

As Allie recounted the events of that night, her voice started out shaky but gradually steadied until her words rang out clear and confident. When she reached the part where Gabe grabbed her off the path and explained how she'd freed herself from him, a half-smile flickered across Isabelle's face before it was suppressed. Again, though, she left out everything Christopher had said about the headmistress.

When she'd finished she said simply, 'I take full responsibility for everything that happened that night. None of it was Sylvain's fault. He wouldn't have been there if I hadn't threatened him and refused to follow his advice. He was trying to protect me.'

Zelazny spoke immediately. 'And why did you not follow his advice?'

Keeping her expression blank, Allie turned her eyes to his. 'Because I knew you would kidnap my brother to get to Nathaniel and I didn't want that to happen.'

'Knew?' Zelazny's tone was sarcastic. 'How could you possibly know what we could do? Can you read our minds?'

'Fine. Tell me I was wrong then.' Allie's gaze challenged his, but he waved the comment away with a dismissive gesture.

'I'm not the one on trial here,' he said. 'And you'd do well to remember that.'

'Nobody's on trial here.' Jerry Cole moved in to calm the situation. His wiry brown hair was more rumpled than usual, and his glasses lay on the table in front of him as he rubbed the bridge of his nose. 'Allie, was your sole motive to protect your brother?'

She nodded vigorously.

'You had no interest in helping Nathaniel?'

'No.' She looked at him with confusion. 'Why would I want to help Nathaniel?'

'From what you've told us,' Jerry said, 'your brother made a fairly thorough case for following Nathaniel. Were you not convinced at all?'

'I think . . . ' Allie's stomach twisted, and she swallowed hard.

'I think my brother's lost it. I disagree with everything he said. But I had to see him. I had to find out what happened to him. I had to know he was really alive.'

'Nobody can argue that there's anything irrational in that,' Eloise interjected. 'There is a special bond between siblings. Anyone would have done the same thing.'

'It's that special bond I'm asking about, though,' Jerry said. Eloise shot him a strange look but he didn't seem to notice. 'You felt so bonded to him that you would break The Rules and risk everything to go and see him. Would you break The Rules again for him? Would you still put your brother before your school?'

Allie hadn't considered such a situation and for a second she stared at Jerry, imagining Christopher calling for her help, asking her to throw everything aside for him.

'No,' she said, with sadness. 'Not any more.'

'May I ask why not?' Jerry peered at her across the table.

Tears burned the backs of Allie's eyes and she remembered Sylvain's words. *Don't let them see you cry.*

She took a deep breath. When she spoke her voice was steady. 'Because I don't trust him.'

TWENTY-TWO

After questioning her for several more minutes, Isabelle called an end to the proceedings. 'I think we've gathered all the information that we need to make our decision,' the headmistress said. 'Allie, please wait outside. We'll call you when we're ready.'

As Allie crossed the room, her legs felt heavy. Outside, the corridor was empty. She leaned against the wall in the leaden silence and waited.

After ten minutes, she slid down the wall to sit on the floor and dropped her head to her knees, counting her breaths. But even that became tedious after half an hour. Occasionally she'd hear raised voices from inside the room, but she couldn't make out words.

Allie was half dozing when the door opened at last, and Eloise gestured for her to enter. 'We're ready for you now.' Scrambling to her feet, Allie stumbled after her into Training Room One.

This time she stood in front of the table like a condemned prisoner awaiting her sentence. She tried to take deep breaths to steady her nerves, but her lungs refused to cooperate, and her breath came in short panicked gasps. She gripped the back of the folding chair so hard she was surprised it didn't bend in her hands.

'What you did was wrong, Allie,' Isabelle said. As she talked, Jerry polished his glasses, avoiding her eyes. Eloise watched her supportively. 'It violated rules that bind all students at Cimmeria. But it was worse than that, as it put your own life and Sylvain's at risk, not to mention the lives of Raj Patel's team. This cannot go unpunished. However, we understand the connection between siblings is strong, and it's hard for any of us,' she shot a look at Zelazny who was staring angrily away from her, 'to say that we would not have felt bound to help our own family members in a similar situation. For that reason, we are not expelling you.' Zelazny slammed his pen down on the table in disgust and the headmistress flinched. After a second, she continued. 'Instead, we're placing you on probation for three months.'

Allie's eyes flickered between them. 'What does that mean?'

'It means,' Isabelle said, 'that as long as you don't get into any more trouble – as long as you don't break The Rules again – in three months it will be off your record. But if you are found violating any rules at all – even very minor ones – you will be expelled without further discussion. Do you understand this decision?'

Allie nodded.

'We appreciate your honesty.' Isabelle leaned forward to hold

Allie's gaze. 'We hope you've learned from what happened and that if you are contacted by anybody connected with Nathaniel again, you will come to us. And trust us to help you.'

All the next week, Carter avoided her completely. At first, Allie wanted to talk to him, to explain and apologise and make things better. But she knew she couldn't make things better. Not this time. So instead, reluctantly, she left him alone.

His absence left a hole in her life. Each night at dinner, she missed the warmth of his arm draped across the back of her chair. When she sat in the common room or the library, her eyes automatically scanned the room for him.

They'd been given another week off from Night School training to finish their interview reports, so at least she didn't have to train in the same room with him – watching him laughing and acting normal with Jules and Lucas.

But there was a price to pay for that, and writing the story of Carter's life was a kind of delicate torture now that he wasn't a part of her life any more. By the time she finished, she'd drawn a complete picture of a teenage boy alone in the world, trying to make his own way.

It broke her heart.

'I believe Carter West is the most trustworthy person I have ever met. And every word he told me was the truth ... '

As she wrote the last words in the report it was after midnight on Saturday night. Tears streamed down her face and, dropping her pen, she pulled her knees up on to the bed and wrapped her arms around them, rocking herself gently.

When she heard Rachel knock something over in the room

next door, something just snapped. She missed her friend too much. She needed her advice. Without allowing herself to think it through further, she flung open her door and ran out into the hallway where, resting her hot cheek against the cool wood of Rachel's door, she closed her eyes and tapped twice with her knuckles.

A rustle of papers and then, 'Enter,' said in Rachel's most commanding voice.

'Rach, I don't know what to do ...' Allie tumbled into the room in mid-sentence, waving a tissue and looking, she was certain, insane. But Rachel just cleared a place beside her on the bed and patted it.

'Tell me.'

'There's things I can't say,' Allie hiccoughed, the damp tissue compressed into a ball in her hand.

'Tell me the other things.' Rachel handed her a clean tissue, her almond-shaped eyes sweeping Allie's face as if she searched for clues.

'Carter and I ...'

'You broke up.'

Allie stared.

'Everyone's talking about it,' Rachel explained. 'I wanted to ask you but ...' She held out her hands, and Allie thought the gesture said *We don't really talk any more.* This brought a flood of fresh tears, and for a while Rachel just patted her shoulder until she could speak again.

'He's just so angry,' Allie said finally. 'And I did some things he can't forgive me for.'

'Is it Sylvain?'

Allie knew Rachel was trying to keep the disapproval out of her voice, but she could still hear it curling around the edges of her words.

'People are saying you and Sylvain – when he got beat up – you were out in the woods ... you know, together. Basically, they're saying you were having a thing with Sylvain behind Carter's back.'

An invisible knife twisted in Allie's stomach as she imagined Carter hearing that gossip. She'd known word of what had happened had got out – Sylvain's bruised face alone was enough to get people talking. But she hadn't realised it had all been tangled up like that.

Poor Carter. Poor me.

'We weren't doing anything like that, Rachel.' She was almost breathless with the need to be believed. 'Sylvain and I aren't ... we weren't ... He was helping me ... with something.' Her own inability to explain what she and Sylvain were doing made it sound like she was lying. She needed to tell the whole story.

Can I tell her about Christopher? It wasn't Night School, so it wouldn't be breaking The Rules. *Would it?*

Once she'd made up her mind, it was such a relief her words blurred together as she explained in rapid-fire sentences what had happened. The note from Christopher. Carter's obsession with protecting her. Her decision to go to Sylvain.

'Oh, Allie,' Rachel whispered when she got to that point.

'I know.' Allie twisted the tissue between her fingers. 'Maybe it was a mistake. Maybe it wasn't. But Sylvain nearly died for me. And then Carter dumped me.'

Saying those words aloud made her want to cry again, but she seemed to have used up her allotment of tears for the day and her eyes stayed dry and burning.

For a moment that seemed to stretch on too long Rachel studied her. Allie knew she didn't like Sylvain after what had happened at the summer ball. Knew she didn't trust him.

But she doesn't really know him.

'What's really going on with you and Sylvain, Allie?' Rachel asked at last. 'Do you fancy him? I mean, nobody would blame you. What happened between you – the way he saved you from the fire and now,' she swirled her hand, 'all of this. It must have created a connection between you. A kind of bond. And that can be hard to resist. Anyone could confuse that in their head with love.'

'No,' Allie said instantly, although her heart sped up, and she wasn't certain anything she was saying was true. 'No. I don't fancy him.' And then ... 'Oh God. I don't know.' Pulling her bare feet up on to the bed and wrapping her arms around her knees, she said, 'I feel attracted to him, I guess. But that's not why things went bad with me and Carter. I think ...' She stopped to really consider how she actually felt. 'Rach, I miss Carter so much but at the same time I feel like now I can breathe. When he's around I can't breathe.'

'Why? Because he's too overprotective? He suffocates you?'

Allie nodded miserably. 'I love him, I really do. But he tells me what to do. He argues with me all the time. I think he doesn't believe in me and it makes me doubt myself. And I know why he does it – I've been thinking about it a lot and I know. He doesn't have anybody. No parents, or brothers or sisters, no aunts or grandparents. He's alone and I'm all he's got and so he hangs on to me. He wants to protect me. But when he does that I can't breathe.'

'It was that bad?'

'I don't know. Yes . . . No . . . ' Allie held up her hands helplessly. 'I'm making it sound worse than it is. There was so much good stuff too. But as much as I miss Carter – and I do – I feel free without him.'

Rachel let her breath out slowly. 'Then you have to stay broken up, Allie. If you feel like that, no matter how hard it is to move on, I think you have to do it.'

'But I don't know how.' Tears returned as suddenly as they'd left. 'All I do is think about him. All day I'm like, *Carter and I stood here* and *Carter and I laughed here*. It's so stupid.' She dashed the tears away with an angry gesture. 'But I can't stop. It's like my mind is obsessed with him.'

'This is why breaking up sucks, Allie.' Rachel's tone was gentle. 'This is why people don't like to do it. It takes time. And I think you need to distract yourself. All you ever do any more is work. So do some things you didn't ever do with Carter. Hang out with Jo, even if she's as mad as a box of chickens. Or me. Or Zoe. Avoid Carter . . . and Sylvain,' she added hastily. 'The last thing you need is a sloppy rebound. You need to find out who you are now so you'll know what you want. Maybe you do want Sylvain, I don't know. But maybe that's just your heart looking for a replacement model. And I don't think replacement models ever work out as well as the real thing. So, take some time to row your boat down the River Allie.'

Almost laughing through her tears, Allie said, 'I can't believe you just freakin' said that.'

'Me neither.' Rachel grinned. 'This therapy session is over. I'll invoice you later.'

Allie tried to take Rachel's advice. Forcing herself to hang out in the common room playing chess with Jo. Or, rather, losing to Jo at chess. Going to a kick-boxing class with Zoe, who passionately loved kicking things. Sitting with Rachel and Lucas at dinner talking about classes she didn't really care about.

She practised not searching for Carter in every room. Getting through classes they had together without once looking his way. Not looking up until he'd walked out the door.

It helped that Carter had taken to sitting across the dining hall with Jules and her friends. But everybody still walked on eggshells around the two of them, trying not pick sides, though loyalties were inevitably divided.

'I'd really hate for things to become Team Carter and Team Allie,' she told Jo one night as she lost a speedy game of chess in the crowded common room after dinner. 'But that's happening anyway.'

They were sitting on the floor around a low chess table, hidden away on one side of the room. At the piano, a boy was playing a jazz version of a rock song. Some students were dancing in front of the bookcases. The room was cacophonous. And Allie found herself almost enjoying the anarchic feel.

'It always happens,' Jo said loftily. 'Check. You really need to learn to use your rook. It's just sitting there. But this isn't the worst case I've seen. When Lucas and I broke up ... Oh my

God. What a mess. Because we were really mad at each other, so it was like ... *Palestine* around here.' The drama in her voice made Allie smile. Jo had been holding steady for a week now; it was nice to see her acting like herself again. 'Everybody picked a side and people didn't talk to each other. Grimness. But you guys ...' As instructed, Allie moved her rook and Jo rolled her eyes. 'Checkmate – Jesus, Allie, you're pathetic at this. You two don't seem so mad. Mostly you just ignore each other, which makes it easier. For your friends, I mean. Sucks for you, I know.'

'Have you,' Allie helped reset the board, 'talked to Carter?'

'Of course! I talk to him every day. That's the crappy thing about break-ups – the only people not talking are you guys.'

This had never occurred to Allie. She sat still, holding her king in one hand. 'How is he?'

Jo's eyes were sympathetic. 'Sad. Lonely. But totally fine. He's like you – he's getting on with things. Lucas is helping him. He wants to kill Sylvain but Jerry Cole is keeping them apart.' As she finished arranging the pieces, though, she brightened. 'Hey, are you going to the party next week? Up at the castle ruins?'

Never had Allie wanted to do anything less, but she tried to sound like she cared. 'What party? I haven't heard anything about it.'

'It's a thing – they do it every year. It's next Friday. I'm definitely going. It's fun and spooky up there. We'll have a bonfire. Roast marshmallows. Drink wine, tell ghost stories ...'

'Is it ...' Allie bit her tongue. She'd almost said, *Is it safe?* Meaning, safe from Nathaniel, safe from Christopher. Approved by Raj Patel. But she couldn't talk about that with Jo. 'Is it legal?' she asked instead. 'You know, is Isabelle cool with it?'

'It's for all advanced students.' Jo's tone was evasive. 'Of which you are one. Everyone will be there. You should definitely come.'

'I'll think about it,' Allie said, not wanting to think about it.

Every few days she met with Isabelle. Each time, Allie asked about Nathaniel and, each time, Isabelle told her there was nothing new about him or the spy among them. In return, Allie could tell her that there'd been no word from Christopher, either, even though, every single time she walked into her bedroom, her eyes were drawn first to her empty desktop, searching for the envelope in thick ivory paper with her name written in left-slanted handwriting. But it never appeared.

Throughout it all she stuck zealously to the rules. In her room by eleven every night. Never late for any meal or class. And as Night School resumed, she focused on training and strategy – her back straight and her eyes on Raj Patel. Blocking out Carter and Sylvain and anything that could not be used to save her life in the woods, in the dark. She poured her sadness, confusion and anger into learning to fight with her hands and feet. It was satisfying.

This was just what Isabelle wanted and, little by little, Allie thought the headmistress was beginning to forgive her.

As she made her way down the grand staircase to meet Isabelle one afternoon, she saw Katie Gilmore's distinctive red ponytail bouncing in her direction. As always, Allie moved to avoid her but, to her surprise, Katie made a sharp turn to intercept her.

'Hey, Allie.' Her bright smile showed off her even, white teeth.

Jesus, Allie thought, *even her lipstick is perfect. How does she do it?*

'What's up, Katie?' She tried to keep the suspicion out of her voice.

'A few of us are going to go out on Friday, up to the tower for a bonfire,' Katie said. 'It's a tradition for senior students. You should come.'

'Let me get this straight.' Allie stared at her in disbelief. 'You're inviting *me* to a party?' She paused for drama. 'Katie, are you off your meds?'

'Oh, Allie, don't be silly.' Katie's smile was disturbingly angelic. 'It's a big party. I know you and Carter are having problems so I just wanted to make sure you weren't just sitting around moping. Will you come?'

At mention of Carter, Allie bristled. Something about the way Katie said his name set her nerves on edge. She said it with intent, as if she had plans for him.

Remember you're on probation, Allie told herself, and from somewhere she produced a bland shrug.

'Maybe. I've got some studying to do.'

'Brilliant.' Katie looked pleased. 'We've even got special dispensation to stay out past curfew. I hope you'll come. It'll be fun.'

As Allie watched her go, suspicion uncurled in her belly.

What are you up to, you evil red-headed cow?

TWENTY-THREE

When she walked in to Isabelle's office that afternoon and asked the usual question with her eyebrows and, looking at her over the top of her glasses, Isabelle gave the usual answer with a shake of her head, Allie plopped into the chair in front of her desk with a sigh.

'Katie Gilmore wants me to go to that party at the castle on Friday night. I guess that means I shouldn't go.'

Isabelle took off her glasses and set them down on the stack of papers in front of her. 'I don't think,' she said, 'that you should set your social calendar so that you only do what Katie Gilmore doesn't want you to do.'

'She says it's legal,' Allie said. 'Is it? For girls on probation, I mean?'

Isabelle waved her hand. 'It is "legal", as you put it, in that nobody is punished for going. It's a tradition. The students are trusted to go up and not burn the entire forest down. Teachers don't go up and hover. Students are given an extra hour after curfew. If everyone minds their manners, it happens again next year. It's been going on ever since the castle fell down; we certainly did it when I was a student here.'

Allie tried to imagine a sixteen-year-old Isabelle hanging out with her own sixteen-year-old mother and failed. 'But is it,' she shrugged, 'you know ... safe?' It still felt weird talking about security and she mumbled the words. 'Like, will Raj Patel be there?'

A melancholy smile flashed across the headmistress' face. 'It is both a sign of your progress and our lack of progress that you ask that question. But the answer is yes. Raj's guards will be all around it. He's calling in extra people for the night. It will be very safe.'

'Doesn't matter,' Allie muttered, contrarily. 'I probably won't go. It'll all be happy clappy campfire bollocks.' Isabelle shot her a look. 'Pardon my language.'

'I'm going to say something that might shock you, Allie.' Fixing her with a firm look, Isabelle leaned forward. 'I want you to go to that party.'

'Oh God.' Allie slid down low in her chair. 'Not you, too?'

Isabelle continued as if she hadn't spoken. 'The last few weeks have been so stressful for all of us, but especially for you. And with what's happened between you and Carter ... ' She walked around to the front of her desk until she was right in front of Allie. 'I think you've handled everything incredibly well. Your work has been exemplary. But I'm worried about what's going on in here.' Gently, she tapped her forefinger against Allie's heart. 'And I'd like to see you have fun. Promise me you'll go.'

Squirming, Allie looked to one side. 'Isabelle . . .' She really didn't want to go now.

But Isabelle wasn't going to be put off. 'Promise me, as a condition of your probation, that you will go to this party and *try* to have fun.'

'OK,' Allie said with deep reluctance. 'I'll go. But I'm not promising to enjoy it.'

'Good.' Isabelle walked back around her desk. 'But stay away from Katie Gilmore. You're not good for each other. And you're not allowed to fight.'

Allie glared at her. 'Awesome.'

When Allie walked into the common room a few minutes later, she found Zoe was curled up on the sofa reading *Mrs Dalloway* with a baffled expression.

'I don't get it,' she said, tossing the paperback on to the table beside her. 'Everybody in this book lies all the time. It's stupid. Nobody ever says what they mean. And why was everyone so depressed in history?'

'War?' Allie suggested, sitting on the other end of the long, leather couch.

'We have war,' Zoe pointed out. 'But we're not miserable.'

'True.' Allie thought about it. 'I don't know. Maybe it was . . . diet.'

That seemed to mollify Zoe. 'Vitamins.' She nodded knowingly.

'What are you two talking about?' Rachel carried a stack of books so tall it reached her nose. It wobbled as she set it down gingerly on a table nearby.

'Vitamins,' Zoe explained.

'Of course.'

Rachel shuffled the books in a complex system, like a thick deck of cards. Allie and Zoe exchanged puzzled looks. 'Tea?' Allie suggested hopefully. 'Possibly with food?'

Rachel looked up, a dusty, leather-bound book dangling from one hand. 'Absolutely.'

It was still several hours until dinner, and the kitchens were empty. Loaves of bread dough had been left to rise on one counter, covered in white cloths like tiny corpses. The room smelled sweetly of warm yeast.

There were two large refrigerators – one the students were allowed to open for milk and snacks. The other they weren't meant to touch.

'Let's see . . . ' Opening the students' fridge, Rachel peered inside. 'Ooh, leftover sandwiches. Score!' She pulled out a tray covered in plastic wrap with sandwich quarters neatly arranged. They were pouring tea when Jo walked in.

'Great minds . . . ' she said, grabbing a mug.

'So, about this stupid party . . . ' Allie sighed.

'Don't look at me.' Looking almost panicked, Rachel stepped back. 'I'm definitely not going. Behind on everything.'

Jo raised her hand. 'I'm definitely going,'

'I want to go.' Zoe spoke through a mouth full of cheese, and Allie looked at her dubiously.

'Are you allowed? It's senior students only.'

Zoe glared at her. 'I may be small, but I'm as senior as you are.'

'It's true,' Jo interceded. 'Zoe can definitely come.' She turned to Allie. 'Look, why don't we all go together?'

'I don't want to go at all.' Allie sank back against the counter glumly. 'Isabelle's making me.'

'It won't be so bad,' Jo said. 'We can be each other's dates.'

'No kissing,' Allie said.

'Holding hands?' Jo's voice was hopeful.

'Deal.'

'Am I wearing enough layers?'

Standing in the hallway by the back door, Jo was swathed in a pale pink pashmina, heavy white boots, a quilted jacket and thermal leggings, It was nearly nine o'clock and they were heading out to the party but she seemed more prepared for a Swiss ski slope than a hill in England.

'I think you might survive,' Allie said dryly, buttoning her pea coat. She wore her uniform skirt with two layers of tights and her red Doc Marten boots, which reached all the way to her knees.

Eyeing Allie's boots, Jo said, 'Are those insulated? Your feet will get cold.'

'I don't care.' Allie knotted her scarf. 'I'm donating my toes to science.'

'Hey, wait up!'

Allie glanced back to see Zoe hurrying down the hall, pulling on her coat. A bright blue bobble hat perched on her head.

'Come on,' Allie said. 'We're holding hands on the way up and later we're going to make out.'

'You said no kissing,' Jo reminded her as she opened the door.

'I meant no *tongues*.'

Outside the night was dark and clear; a nearly full moon illuminated the path ahead of them so thoroughly that until they passed into the woods at the base of the hill they didn't need a torch.

Walking single file, they followed a nearly overgrown footpath that wound steeply upwards from behind the walled garden.

Allie could see her breath hanging in the air in the moonlight. She didn't want to go to this party but she had to admit it was nice to be out doing something that wasn't work or Night School.

'I've never been up there,' she said, pointing up ahead of them. 'Is it cool?'

'It's supposed to be haunted,' Zoe said.

'Everything's supposed to be haunted,' Jo scoffed.

'Yeah, but this is really supposed to be haunted.' Zoe seemed to find the idea of ghosts both amusing and absurd. 'Apparently some lord lived there who was Catholic. He was tortured brutally by Henry VIII and executed.'

'So does he haunt the tower?' Allie asked.

'No. His wife was totally pissed off after Henry had her husband chopped up, so she started supporting the rebels. They say she allowed them to hide around here – maybe even in the old house that used to be where the school is now.' As Zoe talked, their pace slowed. 'Finally, Henry's soldiers came to get her too. But she wouldn't give up. She and all of her supporters fought them off for days. Eventually, though, the soldiers killed all of them except her. She fought like a wildcat – they say she killed at least five men – but there were too many of them. They cornered her in her bedroom at the top of the tower.' She pointed up the hill where the shadowy outline of the old stone building could just be seen, leering down at them like a vulture. 'When they got her sword away from her, they used it to flay her skin off a little at a time while she was still alive.' She whispered the last line. 'They took her eyes last.'

'That is so unnecessarily grim,' Jo murmured.

'Nobody has ever lived in the castle since then. They say you can see her on moonlit nights, walking on the top of the tower looking out for Henry's soldiers. Which is super creepy because there *is* no top of the tower any more.' Zoe had lowered her voice to a whisper. 'So she must just be floating there . . .'

'Hi, guys.'

Lucas' voice came from nowhere and they all screamed.

'Jesus.' He turned on his torch, blinding them. 'What the hell is the matter?'

'Zoe was just telling us a horrible story.' Jo sounded defensive.

'Oh.' He grinned at Zoe. 'Did you tell them about the Floating Lady?'

She smiled back. 'Totally.'

He high-fived her. 'Awesome. I love that story. Scary as hell.'

'They fell for it completely,' Zoe said, with satisfaction.

'Where is everyone?' Shining her light in a circle, Allie saw trees and little else.

'We're not there yet,' Jo said.

Up ahead, Allie heard the faint sound of laughter carried down on the breeze.

'Is the fire going yet?' Jo asked as they began walking again.

'They were lighting it when I left.' He looked uncomfortable. 'I came back to look for Rachel. Have you seen her?'

'She's not coming,' Allie said, puzzled. 'Didn't she tell you?'

'Yeah.' His hands shoved deep in his pockets, he kicked a pebble until it rolled down the hill. 'I was hoping she'd change her mind.'

'Sit with us,' Zoe said. 'We're going to kiss with tongues.'

He blinked. 'Excuse me?'

'Without tongues, Zoe,' Jo corrected her primly.

'Well,' Allie said as they headed up the hill, 'tongues are optional.'

The slope lessened as they neared the top of hill, and Allie could just make out the old tower. The sweet smell of woodsmoke filled the air, and she could hear voices laughing and shouting.

The tight invisible string of nervousness Zoe's story had strung around them loosened now as they headed across the stony hilltop to the castle.

Lucas led them to a spot where fallen stones had made natural steps up to the top of the old castle wall. At the top, it was about three feet thick, and for a moment they all stood in a row, looking out over the other side where a giant bonfire blazed. Students sat around it like a coven, talking and laughing.

As they walked up to the group, Katie bounded over to Allie. 'Hey, you made it.' She wore a ski jacket and white cashmere hat. 'Welcome. There are drinks passing around and marshmallows, of course.' Her smile was disarming. 'Come on over.'

As she hurried back to the fire, Allie dropped behind to whisper to Jo. 'Katie's broken. Fix her.'

'When did she stop hating you?' Jo looked as baffled as she felt. 'Why didn't I get the memo?'

'I don't like that girl,' Zoe said before spotting somebody she knew and running off.

As they reached the fireside, Allie instinctively glanced around for Carter but didn't see him. As her eyes swept the crowd they alighted on Sylvain. Aside from a few marks, his face had largely returned to normal. The bruise across his throat had taken the longest to heal. He sat with Nicole, who looked glamorous in a long black coat and earmuffs. Seeing them together made Allie's chest hurt – they seemed perfect together. And now she wasn't perfect with anyone. When Nicole saw her looking at them across the flames, she waved a champagne bottle at her and smiled.

Allie held up her hand in a tentative wave.

Jo pulled her to the front where the fire was warmest and they sat on a large flat stone that had once been part of the castle structure. Zoe joined them and they watched as someone nearby held a long thin stick into the fire. When the marshmallow on the end toasted, the air began to smell of candy. Allie breathed in deeply, inhaling the scent of camping trips and childhood.

'Want,' she said, in a piteous voice.

'Lucas,' Jo called over authoritatively.

Glancing over at her he arched one eyebrow.

'Marshmallowy stick thing, please.'

From the stack on the ground behind him, he pulled a

whip-like length of freshly cut twig. Someone passed a bag of marshmallows over.

Bottles of wine and champagne made the rounds as well. Some people had plastic cups; others swigged directly from the bottle. When one was handed to Jo, Allie held her breath. But to her relief Jo waved it away.

'I'm like a saint now,' she told the person who'd tried to give it to her. 'Haven't you heard? St Jo of Not Drinking.'

Allie passed on the wine as well. After what had happened at the summer ball she wasn't interested in losing control.

Jo stabbed another fluffy marshmallow on to the end of the stick.

'They're so good but I can only eat three,' she said pleasantly. 'And then I want to vom.'

Someone threw more wood on the fire and it flared brightly, casting the woods around them into darkness. Its heat seemed to curl soft woolly tendrils around them. Leaning back, Allie looked up at the ruined castle tower that loomed over them, its crenellated roof like jagged teeth and tiny archers' window slits like eyes.

'I wonder if there's any truth to it,' she murmured, thinking aloud.

Jo looked over at her enquiringly. Allie could just make out the blue of her eyes in the firelight.

'The story of the lady being murdered, I mean,' Allie said. 'I wonder if it really happened.'

Jo held her marshmallow just above the dancing flames. 'My brother said he saw her ghost when he was at school here.'

Allie leaned back doubtfully. 'He was just trying to scare you.'

Looking uncomfortable, Jo shrugged. 'Maybe. But I don't think so. Tom isn't scared of anything, but whatever he saw that night, it did seem to scare him.'

Other students were listening to their conversation now.

'What exactly did he see?' Lucas stood next to her, a champagne bottle in one hand.

'He said he and some friends were up here for the winter bonfire – just like we are now – only they were actually in the tower. At midnight, they heard footsteps above their heads. He said the wood floor creaked clearly with every step. Only there are no wood floors, no floors at all. Just empty space.'

The group had fallen silent now. Allie swallowed hard.

'So they all decided to get the hell out, you know?' Jo continued. 'They took off running. But just before they went down the hill they looked back and they could see her.'

'See what?' somebody asked.

'A woman in a long grey dress standing and watching them go.' She pointed at the top of the tower. 'Right up there.'

There was a collective exhalation, like a long sigh. Someone giggled nervously.

'He probably imagined it,' Katie said, pouring champagne into a plastic cup.

'Maybe, but ... Oh, bugger!' Jo's marshmallow was on fire and she blew on it fiercely, but by the time the fire went out it was a blackened lump. She scraped it into the flames. 'He never came up here again.'

Lucas took a swig from the bottle before passing it to a

friend. 'I've been up here plenty of times and I've never seen ...'

At that moment a log in the fire popped so loudly it sounded like a gunshot and they all jumped. Several girls screamed then dissolved into giggles.

'I do not like ghost stories.' Nicole sounded disapproving. 'It disturbs the dead when we speak of them. It's dangerous. They should be left in peace.'

'Do you believe in ghosts then?' Lucas asked.

'Of course!' She seemed to find the question absurd. 'I am from Paris. The city is full of spirits. It would be arrogant to say something doesn't exist simply because you don't understand it. I don't understand how the television works and yet I still admit that it's there.'

A murmur swept through the group as they considered her logic.

'This conversation is a total buzz killer,' Katie said. 'Let's play a game.'

A burst of derisive laughter followed. 'What should we play?' somebody asked. 'Snakes and ladders?'

'How about Truth or Dare?' she replied without missing a beat. 'I haven't played it in ages.'

'That is a risky game.' Nicole leaned back against Sylvain.

Allie noticed how his arm rested with familiar ease around her narrow waist. But when her eyes drifted to his face she saw he was looking at her. Something dangerous fluttered inside her.

When she tuned into the conversation, Katie had taken command. She stood up on a fallen stone so everyone could hear her. Her hair was the same colour as the flames behind her.

'OK, here are the rules. Anyone who has been asked a question can ask someone else a question. You can decide after the question is asked whether you want Truth or Dare.' A roar of dissension followed but she raised her voice to be heard above it. 'This makes it safer. I know it's kind of cheating but . . . I'll get the ball rolling,' she said. 'Alex. Have you ever been given a blow job?'

'Gross.' Zoe wrinkled her nose.

Glancing at her, Allie remembered that she was only thirteen and wondered if she should suggest they leave together before this all got out of hand. It was making her uncomfortable, too. This wasn't how she remembered Truth or Dare. But Zoe seemed more curious than disturbed and she didn't want to embarrass her.

A tall blond boy who Allie recognised from Night School stood up, a bottle of wine loose in one hand.

'Truth,' he said. The crowd fell silent. 'Yes.'

They hooted in disbelief and someone threw marshmallows at him, which he swatted away. 'Once,' he insisted. 'I swear to God.' He grinned lasciviously. 'I can't tell you the details because I'm a gentleman.'

'I doubt that. Now you ask a question,' Katie said, taking the bottle from him.

'Pru,' he called out.

'Present!' A giggling blonde girl stood up.

'Is it true that you lost your virginity on a yacht?'

Laughter and gasps greeted the question as, wobbling a bit, Pru considered her options.

'Dare,' she said finally. Her friends howled with laughter.

Alex considered what to ask. 'Take off your top and go into the tower alone for three minutes.'

Pru looked nonplussed. 'I don't want to go to the tower.'

'It's Truth or Dare, Pru,' Katie said, her voice stern. 'You know the rules.'

With a sigh, Pru unzipped her ski jacket then pulled off her thick sweater. Underneath it she wore a tight, pink T-shirt. Without the slightest indication of inhibition, she pulled it over her head revealing a lacy white bra. The boys cheered.

'For God's sake, girl,' Jo muttered. 'Have some self-respect.'

'Bra goes too,' Alex insisted but he needn't have, she was already taking it off.

'To the tower! To the tower!' the crowd chanted.

As she disappeared, weaving and laughing, breasts bouncing, into the dark depths of the stone building, Allie decided she would leave and take Zoe with her as soon as everybody was too busy to notice. This wasn't her kind of party.

'Somebody really should go with her to make sure she's safe,' Alex said. 'I volunteer.'

'Don't be vile,' Katie said above the jeers. 'This isn't a porn film. I'm timing this.'

As they talked and laughed and passed bottles around, Allie leaned towards Zoe.

'If you want to go, say the word,' she said, giving the younger girl a significant look.

'It's kind of fascinating, in an anthropological way,' Zoe said. 'I haven't ever done anything so I would always take Truth.'

'Time,' Katie shouted. 'Pru? You may return to your clothes.'

A long moment passed, and everyone fell silent, as if they thought she wouldn't reappear. But she bounded out of the tower and ran back to her seat, shivering. She wasn't smiling now.

'Bloody hell it's freezing in there. I should have taken Truth.'

'Your turn, Pru,' Katie said.

'Lucas.' Pru zipped up her coat and pulled her hat down over her head. 'Have you ever shagged someone inside the school building.'

Allie felt Jo flinch beside her and glanced at her curiously; she was staring down at the ground.

'Truth,' Lucas said, without smiling. 'Yes.' The boys around him applauded sardonically. He didn't look at Jo.

'My turn.' Lucas swiped a bottle someone held up to him and took a deep drink. 'Katie.'

The crowd cheered wildly as the redhead stood up, her expression fearless.

'Truth or Dare,' Lucas said. 'Have you ever shagged some-one on the school grounds. In, for example, the summer house, after curfew?'

'Truth,' she said, a hand on one hip. 'Definitely.'

The group laughed.

'My turn,' she said, turning towards the fire. In the light of the flames her face looked unearthly. 'Allie.'

Allie was so surprised she jumped. With a sympathetic look, Jo squeezed her hand.

A chorus of 'oohs' greeted the choice.

Slowly, Allie stood up and turned to face her. Dread formed a tight knot in her stomach, as she kept her eyes on Katie's fire-lit face.

I knew I shouldn't have come.

She waited to be asked about sex or blow jobs or all the things she hadn't ever done. But Katie's question was completely different.

'Are you Lucinda Meldrum's granddaughter?'

Time seemed to stop.

A puzzled murmur swept the fireside. Allie was aware of the hot fire cracking and snapping behind her. Jo's fingers slipped from her hand.

Stunned, she stared at Katie in disbelief – all she saw in her face was triumph – she knew the answer already. Finally, Allie found her voice. 'Dare.'

Whispers swirled around her. She wished Jo was still holding her hand.

'Kiss Sylvain.' Katie's words hit her like icicles. 'Passionately.'

TWENTY-FOUR

'No!' Allie took a startled step backwards. 'That's not ...
He's with Nicole.' She felt sick. Like she'd stumbled
into one of those reality TV shows where you're forced
to do things you don't want to do.

'It's OK,' Nicole called out merrily. 'It won't bother me.'

Katie didn't take her eyes off Allie. 'You have to. Or everyone will know you're a coward as well as a liar.'

A hiss of concern passed through the crowd. When Allie
turned towards Sylvain she saw he was staring at Katie with
open contempt.

She didn't know what to do. Whatever happened now, she
knew would stay with her for as long as she was at this school.
It seemed as if everyone held their breath, waiting for her to
move.

Her legs felt numb, and it took all her strength to make them
carry her through the crowd to where Sylvain and Nicole sat.

Students moved to clear a path, as if she were royalty. Or tainted.

Standing in front of Nicole, she held out her hands helplessly.

'I don't want . . .' she said, before stopping and trying again. 'He's your boyfriend, this isn't right.'

Leaning forward, Nicole placed her lips against Allie's ear to whisper. 'Sylvain is not my boyfriend.' She sounded a little tipsy. When she straightened she gave Allie a significant look. Then she spoke loud enough for everyone to hear: 'I know what to do.'

She leaned towards Allie again. Confused, Allie at first thought she was going to whisper something else but, instead, Nicole grabbed her scarf and pulled her closer, kissing her on the lips. Allie was so stunned she stood stock still. Nicole's lips were soft and tasted of champagne. She smelled like jasmine and roses. Being kissed by a girl wasn't bad exactly, it was just . . . peculiar. Especially when Nicole's long hair swung down and brushed her cheek like feathers.

After a second, Nicole stepped back and turned to face the crowd with a sophisticated little shrug. 'Now it is fine for you to kiss Sylvain, because I have kissed you.'

As she sat down, appreciative applause and laughter greeted this gesture, but Allie could sense the confusion beneath the noise. She knew everyone was thinking about Lucinda Meldrum and why Katie had asked that question.

She could hardly breathe as she turned to face Sylvain. His anger was clear in the tight set of his shoulders and the way his hands clenched at his sides. 'It's a foolish children's game,

287

Allie,' he said. 'We don't have to do it. Katie,' he raised his voice, 'is just causing trouble as usual.'

Looking into his eyes, sapphire in the darkness, she thought her heart would explode with pain and longing. Trust Katie to devise the most perfectly focused torment for them both. Of course she would know there was attraction between them; she would have heard the gossip. She would also know how much this would hurt Carter if he found out, but she wouldn't care about that.

Tears of confusion stung Allie's eyes. Stepping closer to him, she whispered so quietly only he could hear. 'I can't ... Carter ...'

At Carter's name, he recoiled as if she'd slapped him. Allie's breaths were shallow and her heart pounded with rage and shame and loss.

I have to get out of here.

If she didn't, she was going to kiss Sylvain or hit Katie or have another panic attack. None of those things would be good.

Pivoting she strode back to where Zoe stared at her, open-mouthed. Next to her Jo watched the fire, avoiding her eyes.

'Come on, Zoe,' Allie said hoarsely. 'We're going. Neither of us belongs here.'

There was a split-second pause as the younger girl seemed to process this, then she scrambled to her feet and hurried to follow Allie away from the fire.

As they walked into the darkness, Katie called after them, her voice echoing off the castle rocks.

'You should have chosen Truth.'

*

'I thought you were kidding about kissing with tongues.' Zoe hopped to keep up with Allie's pace as they headed down the hill away from the castle.

They moved so quickly the beams from their torches swung wildly, bouncing from rocky path to tree branches to dark sky.

'So did I.' Allie's reply came through gritted teeth as she skidded on a stone. Taking a deep breath to steady her nerves, she slowed her pace. After that they walked for a while in silence, the sound of their feet on the earth the only noise in the silent forest.

'Allie?' Zoe's voice was quiet.

'Yes?' Allie said, although she knew perfectly well what the question was going to be.

'Is your grandmother really Lucinda Meldrum?' Zoe was looking at her with something like awe.

An owl hooted in the woods nearby – Allie stopped walking. 'Did you hear that?'

'An owl.' Zoe nodded. 'Somewhere close.'

'I love the way owls sound.' Allie had lowered her voice to a whisper as she peered at the branches above them. 'They sound like they know so much.' Silence fell between them as they waited. The owl hooted again. 'Yes,' Allie said, still staring at the trees.

'Yes?' Zoe looked at her, puzzled.

'Yes, Lucinda Meldrum is my grandmother.'

Allie started walking again. After a second, she heard Zoe follow.

'But how . . . ' Zoe hopped over a root that bulged in her path.

'How could nobody know you're her granddaughter? Everybody knows who everybody's families are.'

They were at the base of the hill now, making their way around the walled garden.

'I really don't want to talk about this right now,' Allie said, her voice grim.

Zoe seemed to accept this, and she changed the subject. 'You kissed a girl.' There was admiration in her voice.

'Oh God.' Allie thought of Nicole whispering, 'Sylvain is not my boyfriend.' 'Yes I did.'

'You're going to be famous,' Zoe said as the school building appeared in front of them.

Rachel was half asleep when she answered her bedroom door to Allie's light tapping. Her white pyjamas seemed too big for her, and her normally glossy hair hung across her shoulders in tangled curls.

'Allie?' She looked bleary-eyed. 'What's the matter?'

'Allie kissed a girl,' Zoe said.

'What?' Rachel blinked.

'She's going to be famous.' Zoe sounded pleased.

Rachel's eyes moved up to Allie's face and her eyebrows arched skyward.

'You know that thing you didn't come to tonight?' Allie said. 'That was smart of you.'

Rachel held the door open. 'Inside. Both of you.'

She must have fallen asleep reading – books were still piled on the bed near the pillow. Now she swept them out of the way as Zoe sat cross-legged on the floor, eyes wide as if she were watching an exciting film. Allie sat backwards on the desk chair, leaning her chin against the tall back, while Rachel climbed back into bed, pulling the duvet up to cover her bare feet.

'Start at the beginning.'

Speaking quickly, Allie told her about the night. When she got to the part where Katie asked her about Lucinda, Rachel's breath hissed between her teeth.

'How did she find out?' she murmured mostly to herself. 'I haven't heard a thing.'

'Well, everybody knows you're my friend,' Allie said. 'Maybe they don't talk to you about me any more.'

Rachel waved that away. 'Yeah, but I eavesdrop.'

'You're the most important legacy student at the school now,' Zoe said matter-of-factly. 'More important than Sylvain.'

Allie looked at Rachel. 'There's no way this doesn't spread to the whole school, is there?' Futile hope suffused her voice, but Rachel's look told her to give up.

'Sorry, babe. You're outed.' Rachel stretched out her legs under the covers. 'Now tell me the rest. Did Pru get her tits out again? She's so predictable.'

Walking into the half-empty dining hall late the next morning, Allie kept her head high and her eyes straight ahead. Selecting a table in a far corner, she pulled a book from her bag and pretended to immerse herself in studies as she ate her cereal. She could feel eyes on her. Hear whispers. She didn't know how much was real and how much of it was in her head but it didn't really matter – the impact was the same.

When someone pulled a chair out across from her and sat down a few minutes later she froze, her spoon halfway to her mouth.

'Allie.' Reluctantly she looked up to meet Jo's blue eyes, which today looked clouded and serious. 'I think we should talk.'

Balls.

Setting her spoon down, Allie clutched her tea mug like a shield. 'Sure.' She kept her voice diffident. 'What's up?'

'Why didn't you tell me who you are?'

Allie's head dropped until her chin touched her chest. *And so it begins.*

'It's true, isn't it?' She could hear the hurt in Jo's voice.

Allie nodded. Jo's quick intake of breath was audible. 'That's huge. And you never told me. Why, Allie? I'm supposed to be one of your best friends.'

'I didn't know,' Allie said, knowing how unbelievable it sounded – how much like a lie. 'Until I went home after summer term. And then I promised not to tell.'

'But you told some people.' Jo's voice was accusing. 'You told Rachel, didn't you? And Carter.'

'I told only those I had to tell. Only a very small number of people know.'

'A small number of people,' Jo said. 'But not me.'

'Jo, please,' Allie said. 'It wasn't personal. I didn't want anyone to know at all until . . . '

But Jo didn't wait for her explanations. 'I'm so glad it wasn't personal.' Pushing her chair back with a squawk, she stood up, her shoulders stiff. 'That makes me feel so much better about everything.'

As she walked away, Allie dropped her head into her hands.

My whole day, she thought glumly. *My whole day is going to be like this.*

A few weeks ago, she would have gone to Carter for refuge. They would find somewhere to be alone and he would have shielded her from the worst of the attention. But those days were over.

She was going to have to take care of herself.

When she walked down the grand hallway she moved in a cloud of whispers, curious sideways glances and stares.

In the end, she retreated to the library, where the thick Oriental rugs absorbed the rumble of gossip. At the librarian's desk, Eloise was staring at a document, a pen in one hand.

'I'd like to use one of the study carrels, please.' Allie tried to sound casual, as if she asked this sort of thing every day.

'Technically those are for final-year students,' the librarian began, but seeing Allie's desperate expression she changed her mind, 'and good students like you who helped clean the library after the fire.'

Reaching into a drawer, she pulled out a small key on a silver ring. 'The third carrel is free. Use it for as long as you like.'

'Thank you.' Allie could hear the relief in her own voice. The librarian had obviously heard it too, and she looked at her with concern.

'Is everything OK?'

'No,' Allie said, turning away. 'It really isn't.'

Getting the key turned out to be the easy part. The carrel doors were virtually invisible, tucked into the heavily carved oak panelling on the library walls so skilfully no join could be seen. She felt along the carved squares, acorns and roses until she found a straight crack that had to be a door frame. From there she could find her way down the wall slowly looking for similar cracks until she found the one she thought was the third doorway.

Then she had to find the lock.

By the time she finally found it tucked in the heart of a flower, she was frustrated and angry. Angry at herself. Angry at Carter and Sylvain. Angry as hell at Katie. And not thrilled about the stupid panelling.

The door opened with a nearly silent click. When she flipped the light switch the room sprang into life – vibrant colours from the mural that covered the walls formed a rainbow of rage that suited her mood.

This mural showed people facing each other with swords and pikes at the ready alongside a stream flowing through a verdant field. Clouds roiled overhead, with menacing cherubs holding vicious-looking golden bows and arrows. Everybody was shouting at everybody else.

Flinging her bag to the floor with a reverberating thud, Allie paced the confines of the small room, her hands tugging her hair. 'What am I going to do?' she muttered to herself. 'How do I deal with this?'

She dropped into the chair behind the desk and lowered her head on to her arms. Everything seemed to have fallen apart. How had Katie found out about Lucinda? Nobody would have told her. Certainly not Isabelle, Rachel or Carter – and they were the only ones who knew.

A knock at the door interrupted her fretful thinking. It was most likely Eloise; some more senior student probably needed the room. She was already arguing her case when she opened the door. 'Eloise, I've only been in here a few minutes . . . '

When she saw Carter on the other side, her words faded away. She hadn't been this close to him since the night they broke up. Somehow seeing him was everything she wanted and the last thing she needed, at the same time. For a split second she wondered if, by some miracle, he'd forgiven her and things could go back to the way they were before. Then she saw the jaded look in his dark eyes and she knew that was just a dream.

As she stared at him, stunned, he gestured at the room behind her.

'Can I come in or do you just want to stand here?' The impatience in his voice jarred her and she jumped away from the door.

'Sorry. Come in.'

He looked around the room as he stepped past her, taking in the bag she'd hurled earlier, which now spilled books and papers on to the floor. Glancing up at the furious mural around them, he muttered, 'How appropriate,' before throwing himself into the chair in front of the desk.

His straight dark hair fell forward over his eyebrows and he shoved it back with an absent gesture she'd always loved. For a moment she thought her heart would shatter in her chest, like glass dropped on stone. But it kept beating for some reason.

Standing with her back against the door, she took a deep shaky breath. His eyes flickered up to her. 'I thought we should talk.'

His calm but distant voice chilled her as she walked to the desk and sat down across from him, her back held very straight.

'How ... How are you?' Such a stupid thing to say but she really did want to know.

'I'm great, Allie, thanks.' His smile was sardonic. 'My girlfriend is running around in the woods with other guys and doesn't trust me enough to be honest with me. But otherwise things are good. I aced my history essay.'

'Carter, I—'

'I didn't come here to hear your explanations,' he said, cutting her off. Then he stopped. 'Or maybe I did ... I don't know.'

For a second she saw a raw pain in his face that matched her own. Unable to bear it, she looked down at her hands and noticed they trembled slightly. She shoved them down on to her thighs.

'I just saw you walk in here and I had to come and talk to you.'

She was still staring at her hands and he raised his voice just a little.

'Look at me, Allie.'

Reluctantly, she raised her eyes to his. The pain she'd seen was gone, replaced by icy blankness.

'I heard what happened at the bonfire last night.'

She felt ill. 'I ... But nothing ...'

'I'm not talking about you making out with Nicole and having some sort of scene with Sylvain, although we can discuss that if you want,' he said coldly. 'I was talking about what Katie said about Lucinda. I wanted you to know that I never told anybody about Lucinda, and I never would.'

She looked up at him, eyes wide with surprise. 'I never thought you did.'

The strength of her reaction seemed to catch him off guard, and for a second his eyes flickered. But all he said was, 'Good.' Then he moved as if he were about to stand up. 'Well, I guess that's it.'

'Carter, wait.' Without thinking she leaned forward across the table, reaching out as if to hold him back. He recoiled from her touch and, cheeks flaming, she withdrew her hand. 'Can we just talk for a second?'

'I'm not sure that's a good idea,' he said but he stayed in his seat.

'I know I haven't been completely fair to you and I'm so, so sorry. But you haven't always had faith in me either. We're such good friends, but . . .' She held his gaze. 'I've been thinking a lot about this, and I think we weren't the best couple. You don't trust me to make good decisions. And I don't trust you enough to tell you things. And I know that's caused our problems.'

'Not just that,' Carter snapped. 'There's also Sylvain.'

A hole seemed to open in her chest. 'Yes.' Her voice dull, she leaned back in her chair. 'There's also Sylvain.'

'The thing you never realised is that how you feel about him is written all over your face. You go . . . still, when he walks in the room. Your whole face changes.' He laughed bitterly.

'Carter,' Allie said, 'Sylvain saved my life. If I . . . care about him, it's because of that. Not because I fancy him or whatever it is you think.'

'You know what's sad?' Carter looked tormented, 'It's just so bleeding obvious to everyone except you that you like him.'

He stood suddenly, and walked to the door, then stopped with his hand on the doorknob. He spoke his last words with his back to her. 'You'll have to forgive me if I don't enjoy watching this little love story play itself out.'

When he was gone, Allie dropped her head into her hands. All she wanted to do was cry. But the tears wouldn't come.

By the time Allie ran into Katie that afternoon, she was poised for a fight. When she saw that familiar red mane ahead of her in a quiet hallway she ran to catch up, grabbing her by the sleeve.

'How did you find out?' Allie asked before Katie had even turned to face her.

'Like I'm going to tell you.' Jerking her arm free, Katie took a step away from her.

Her lips were painted a warm shade of apricot that perfectly suited her colouring. Allie hated that Katie's beauty made her feel insecure even now.

'The fact is, you lied to people,' Katie continued, 'and now people know you lied and you have to deal with the consequences of your own action. I don't see how that's my fault.'

Anger made Allie shake. 'How is not telling people something private about my family a lie? What business is it of yours or anybody else's?'

At first other students swirled past them as they argued but then a few, clearly sensing a fight was brewing, stopped to watch. Soon a crowd grew.

Katie looked bored. 'You were asked more than once whether or not you were legacy and you said no. Darling, it doesn't get any more legacy than Lucinda Meldrum and I find it hard to believe you didn't know that. So the real question is: why did you lie?'

When Allie hesitated, she smiled, sensing victory. 'You can tell us, Allie.' She gestured at the watching crowd. 'We won't tell a soul. Why did you keep your family connections a secret?'

'Because it's none of your bloody business,' Allie snapped, her cheeks burning.

Katie rolled her eyes. 'That's hardly an answer. And it's everybody's business now.'

'Thanks to you.'

'Yes.' Katie smiled. 'You're welcome.'

Looking in her eyes, Allie knew this argument was pointless. She would never reveal her source – she was enjoying this too much.

Defeated, she turned to walk away, but Katie's parting words sliced through the air after her. 'Why don't you run and cry to Sylvain? Oh wait.' She covered her mouth. 'Should I have said Carter? No. I'm sorry, which one of them is it this week?'

When Allie whirled back towards her, fists clenched, Katie's green eyes widened. 'Oh no! Are you going to punch me?' Her laugh was patronising. 'Grow up, Allie. You're pathetic.'

'*She's* pathetic?' Nicole's silky voice took them both by surprise and Allie whirled to find the French girl standing beside her, eyes flashing at Katie. 'I think you're mistaken, Katie, about who is the pathetic one here.'

Somebody sniggered. Flustered, Katie glanced at the watching crowd before regaining her equilibrium. 'Oh, Nicole, this is ridiculous. I know you snogged her but what's going on here? Are you actually in love with her or something?'

Nicole tilted her head, her glossy dark hair falling over one shoulder as she studied Katie as if she were slithering across the floor. 'I think the problem here is not who I kissed or who Allie kissed, but who you want to kiss. And who doesn't want to kiss you.'

An ugly red flush crept up Katie's neck to her face; she stared at them, open-mouthed. All her vindictive rhetoric seemed to have left her.

Allie too had lost the gift of speech, and turned to Nicole, wide-eyed. The brunette smiled as cheerfully if they'd just been chatting about the weather. 'Come on, Allie,' she said, stepping away. 'There are more interesting people to talk to.'

'Uh ... Thank you, Nicole.' Allie said lamely as she stumbled after the brunette. Nicole's gait was light and quick – despite her tiny size, she moved fast and they'd left Katie far behind in seconds. 'I might have punched her.'

'Oh, Allie.' Her smile was angelic. 'It was my pleasure. I despise Katie Gilmore.'

They walked through the crowds of students purposefully, although Allie had no idea where they were going. 'Listen,' she said, 'about last night ...'

'It was fun, wasn't it? Everyone was shocked.' Nicole giggled. 'But it's so easy to shock English people.'

'The thing you said ...' Allie cast a sideways glance at her '... about Sylvain. He's not your boyfriend?'

Stopping, Nicole turned to face her, full lips curved up. 'Sylvain and I have been friends since we were six years old. Our parents have summer houses near each other. We played together in the sea when we were little then we went to school together. And when we grew up we ...' she made a vague gesture '... experimented with dating. But it didn't work out. It felt strange kissing him, you know?' She wrinkled her nose. 'It was like kissing my brother. So now we are best friends.' Her dark eyes seemed to miss nothing. 'I thought maybe you would like to know that.'

All around them students talked and laughed in the busy hallway but Allie couldn't really hear them any more.

'You think ... I should ...' Her voice trailed off.

What am I asking?

But Nicole answered her unfinished question without hesitation. 'I think sometimes it's easy to think too much about things. Sometimes you just need to listen to your heart. Trust your instincts.' She pointed at the door next to them. 'Now, I have to go to a science seminar. Do you want to come?'

Allie shook her head. 'No thanks.' Her tone was absent. 'Thanks again for ...'

Nicole shrugged, pushing open the door. 'I told Sylvain the same thing.'

'It was Katie's parents.' Isabelle poured boiling water into two cups as Allie draped herself, morose, across the chair in front of her desk. A bergamot-scented steam filled the room. 'She spoke to them on the phone yesterday, ostensibly about the winter ball. They must have told her then.'

'But how did they find out?' Allie accepted the cup of milky tea Isabelle handed her, holding it absently as the headmistress sat down in the chair next to hers.

'That's where it all gets a bit complicated.' Isabelle's tone made Allie nervous. 'You see, the entire board knows, Allie. Lucinda has decided not to keep it a secret any longer.'

'What?' Allie's hand jerked and hot tea spilled on to her leg. Swearing under her breath, she wiped it away with her hand. 'Why?'

'After Nathaniel's latest attempt, Lucinda decided to tell the board what he's been doing – *everything* he's been doing.' When Allie stared at her blankly, she sighed. 'There's a lot going on within the organisation that you don't know, Allie. What's happening with Nathaniel is bigger than this.' Her hand swept around to take in the room. 'Bigger than Cimmeria. Bigger than anything you can imagine. We're just a tiny part of it. Tiny, but crucial.'

Hoping she might actually find out what was going on, Allie held her breath. She had to play her cards right. 'I don't get it,' she said after a second. 'How does telling this to people help Lucinda?'

'She didn't do it just to help herself. She did it for you.' Isabelle's golden-brown eyes held hers. 'She did it to protect you.'

'How does it protect me?' Allie frowned. 'It just seems to mess me up. Now everyone thinks I'm a liar and a freak.'

'It protects you by letting the people who matter know how important you are to her.'

I'm important to her?

The idea seemed foreign to Allie, who hadn't felt like she mattered to anyone in a long time. And she couldn't really accept that it was true, that a woman she'd never met would care about her.

'I still don't really understand.'

'Allie.' Isabelle was as serious as Allie had ever seen her. 'There's a spy here, working for Nathaniel. For all we know this person could try to kill you. Or me. Lucinda has done all she can to protect us from somebody coming at us from the outside. But somebody who's already here? Hiding in plain sight? We need more help for that.'

Goosebumps rose on Allie's skin.

'So,' Isabelle continued, 'Lucinda has decided to try something different. Telling people within the organisation what's been happening here. Hoping that the attention will intimidate Nathaniel and whoever is working with him.'

This didn't sound like the greatest plan. Allie crossed her arms across her chest.

'Do you think it will work?'

Isabelle dropped her gaze. 'I don't know. You see, she's in a bit of a situation right now – we all are. Nathaniel is trying to get high-ranking people within the organisation to side with him and help him force Lucinda's hand. To make her change The Rules of the organisation in a way that could ... ' She stopped herself. 'Well. That could ruin everything. And Lucinda is trying to show these same people just how untrustworthy he is. How irrational his methods have been. How ruthless he can be. How dangerous.' She sighed. 'I know Nathaniel well, so I know he will stop at nothing. But some members of the board, they can't see that. They just see him as somebody who says things they want to hear.'

'You know so much about Nathaniel,' Allie said, 'do you know him personally? Or did you at some point? Who is he, Isabelle?'

The headmistress thought for a long moment before answering.

'I did know Nathaniel very well, once.' She spoke slowly, as if she were choosing her words with great care. 'You see, Nathaniel is my step-brother.'

Allie froze. 'What?'

'And that's why,' Isabelle continued, 'I understand what's happening with you and Christopher. Because I've been through something like it myself.'

Allie felt betrayed. Why had Isabelle never mentioned this before? But she tried to focus on the conversation at hand. 'Were you and Nathaniel ever ... close?'

'Once, a long time ago. But Nathaniel always wanted things he couldn't have and he blamed me when he couldn't get them.'

Allie stared at her blankly.

With clear reluctance, Isabelle explained. 'When he died, my father left everything to me. The money, the houses, the companies. Everything. He thought Nathaniel was too unstable to be responsible.' Her hand toyed with her glasses. 'It is in the will that I must give Nathaniel a sizeable annual allowance – he's well taken care of. But that didn't matter to him. What mattered was the humiliation. The rejection. Nathaniel never forgave me for it. It's that simple. And now he wants more.'

'Isabelle.' Allie's voice was low. 'What exactly does Nathaniel want?'

For a long moment the headmistress thought. When she spoke, her tone was resigned.

'Everything.'

TWENTY-FIVE

When Allie thought about it, her life at Cimmeria Academy could be divided into clear epochs: before the summer ball, and after. Before Carter. And after. And now: before Truth or Dare, and after it.

Before Truth or Dare, she was a nobody. An interloper.

After it? She was a star.

When she walked into a room, people turned to look. When she spoke, they listened attentively. People she'd never met before were incredibly polite.

Only those who knew her well weren't affected.

'This is ludicrous,' Rachel said one day, after a star-struck junior student insisted on bringing Allie a cup of tea and a biscuit in the common room after overhearing her complain that she was hungry. 'It's going to go to your head.'

'Or my arse, more like,' Allie said, munching.

'Oh, Allie, can I carry your books? Is there anything you'd

like? Can I apply your lip gloss for you?' Rachel simpered. 'Your hair must be so heavy. Let me carry it for you.'

'Don't be jealous.' Allie offered her half the biscuit, which Rachel accepted grudgingly. 'It doesn't suit you. Besides, it won't last, will it?'

'I bloody hope not,' Rachel replied with her mouth full. 'Although this biscuit is delicious. I wonder if he could get us some more.'

'Wow, you corrupt so quickly,' Allie said. 'You're like, "Instant Tyrant: all it takes is one biscuit".'

'Two,' Rachel corrected her. 'I'd become a tyrant for two biscuits.'

But only Rachel and Zoe could make her laugh right now. Jo was still angry with her. And the rest of her life was tension and fear. And sadness.

There'd still been no word from Christopher, despite his promise to get in touch with her again. And she still hadn't told Rachel or Zoe what was really going on. She couldn't tell Rachel, and Zoe was just a kid. As the weeks passed, though, not telling them grew harder, if only because she had nobody left to discuss it with.

And still she couldn't cry. She hadn't been able to since that day in the library with Carter. It was as if all her tears had abandoned her right when she really needed them most.

'Something must be wrong with me if I can't cry,' she told Rachel. 'Maybe I'm actually ill. I could have some disease.'

'Sjögren's syndrome.' Unsurprised by this change of subject, Rachel, who hoped to be a doctor someday, didn't look up from her advanced chemistry textbook.

Allie blinked. 'I beg your pardon?'

'It's a disease where you can't make tears.' Rachel studied her critically. 'But you haven't got it.'

'How do you know?'

'It's excruciating.' She flipped a page in her book and wrote something in her notebook. 'You have to practically peel your eyeballs off your brain every morning.'

'Gross.' Allie returned to her own work. 'I'm glad I haven't got that. How would I look in a fancy frock with peeled eyeballs?'

Rachel's brows arched. 'Like an alien. Actually, an obsessed alien. You're obsessed with the ball, Allie. Get help.'

Before the biscuit-bearing student had appeared, they'd been talking about the winter ball. Or rather, Allie had been. Because she was, in fact, obsessed. It was only two weeks away. Aside from Allie's lineage, the buzz in the hallways, the dining hall and class was about nothing else. Everybody talked about the ball, the ball, the ball. What to wear. Who to go with. But all Allie thought was ...

Lucinda will be there.

At the very thought of meeting her grandmother – of asking her the questions that had tormented her for months now – Allie's heart sped up. She would do anything to make that meeting happen. Including putting on a posh gown and twirling on a sodding dance floor while a string bloody orchestra played.

But the awful night of the summer ball was very fresh in her memory. And with Lucinda, Allie and Isabelle all in the same place at the same time, why wouldn't Nathaniel do something horrible?

307

Lucinda will be there, she thought again. *And something bad will happen.*

That night, Allie stretched out on the floor of Training Room One, extending her hamstrings until they ached. Beside her, Zoe bounced on the balls of her feet.

'I hope we go running.' Her voice vibrated as she hopped. 'I feel like running.'

'Me too,' Allie said, lowering her head to her knees.

At that moment Zelazny's sharp voice rose above the din. 'Tonight we'll start with a four-mile run.'

'Yay,' Zoe whispered and dashed for the door.

Allie hurried to follow but Zelazny called her name and, turning back, she saw him motioning for her to come over.

Zoe stopped by the door to wait for her.

'Can I have a word?' His voice was calm and unthreatening. 'Zoe, you can go on ahead. Allie will only be a minute.'

As she left, Zoe raised her eyebrows; Allie responded with a helpless shrug.

Zelazny waited to speak until the students had all gone. As they stood in awkward silence she could see the perspiration glistening on his forehead. He tugged at the collar of his exercise shirt as if it constrained him.

Crossing her arms across her chest, she looked down at the floor.

'I've been meaning to speak with you, Allie, for a week or so.' He cleared his throat. 'Just to clear the air between us.'

She glanced up at him suspiciously.

'We've had our difficulties over the months you've been here, and I ... Well, I feel I haven't been entirely fair with you.' He coughed. 'So I wanted to ... to apologise if I was too stern with you at times. And to say I hope you'll work with me going forward. I believe we can have a good working relationship. You've got a great deal of promise and, at times, I think I haven't made that clear.'

If he'd said he'd just seen a green Martian eating chocolate in the common room, she couldn't have been more stunned.

He gazed at her expectantly, his expression pure humility. She had to say something.

'Uh ... Sure, Ze— *Mr* Zelazny,' she said. 'That would be great. And thank you, I ... I guess.' Watching him as if he might bite her, she took a step towards the door. 'I should probably ...'

'Oh yes,' he said. She thought she could see a glimmer of resentment in his small blue eyes but his voice held nothing except beneficence. 'Go and join the class. If you need extra time, do take it. No hurry.'

Allie fled the room so quickly she nearly stumbled over Zoe, who was outside with her ear pressed to the door.

As they jogged away into the freezing darkness, Zoe said, 'He is so unbelievably lame.'

The whole thing made Allie's skin crawl. 'He ... grovelled.'

Zoe stopped running to pogo with malicious joy – it was a clear night, and in the moonlight she looked like a manic forest imp. 'It was *awesome*. He thinks you'll tell your grandmother bad things about him.' Pausing to think, she added, 'Blimey, considering how he treated you he must be terrified.'

'I need to take a shower.' Allie increased her pace. 'Right now.'

But there was no time to wash away the memory of that meeting. Instead, after their run, Raj Patel put them through a particularly brutal series of martial-arts style manoeuvres. No matter how painful it was, Allie didn't mind the work; his training had helped her escape from Gabe.

Stopping to rest, she watched as Sylvain and his training partner practised a complex escape move. Sylvain's partner attacked with a flying leap, but Sylvain parried him as easily as if he were a child, flinging him on to the mat. Afterward, he leaned over to help him up with an apologetic grin.

As if he'd felt her gaze, his eyes darted up to meet hers. For a long second she froze. He studied her curiously, as if he wondered what she was thinking. Colour flooding her cheeks, she dropped her eyes and crouched down to tighten her shoelace.

'Your attention, please.' They all turned to look as Zelazny walked to the centre of the room. 'Raj Patel would like to say a few words to you about some things that will be happening over the next few weeks.'

Mr Patel walked to the centre of the room with a confident stride and turned in a circle to see them all. 'As you know, my firm has been maintaining security at Cimmeria throughout the autumn term. You may also know that a meeting of the G8 is scheduled to happen outside London in two weeks, and we will be providing security for that. At the same time, the winter ball will be held here attracting a number of international dignitaries. So our resources are going to be stretched.'

His eyes met Allie's for a second and she felt a chill of fear. *Something's wrong.*

'I'm pulling in extra staff for this period but we'll need your help. We're putting Night School back on its regular patrols. You've been training towards this for months now, and you're ready. You'll be working directly with some of my team, who will be staying behind while the rest of us are away. These are skilled, highly trained security experts, and I think you can learn a lot from them.'

A twist of ice had formed in Allie's chest. All his words about how safe they'd be, and how ready they were, rang hollow as she stared at him.

Lucinda will be here. Raj is going away. And something bad will happen.

TWENTY-SİX

As she walked out of Training Room One, Allie was utterly unaware of the burble of conversation swirling around her. As soon as Mr Patel had stopped speaking the students had erupted in an excited buzz.

'At last.' Zoe grinned. 'We get to go out and *do something*.'

Across the room she saw Jules clap Carter on the back, and Lucas high-five his training partner. Like Zoe, they were thrilled to be involved at last. But Allie felt like the bottom had dropped out of her world. Whatever Mr Patel might have actually said, all she'd heard was, *You will be all alone when Nathaniel comes.*

In a stunned daze, she made her way to the stairwell, propelled by the crowd. When she reached the ground floor she stopped, staring into the distance, her mind a whirl of worry. When a hand touched her arm she looked up in surprise to see Sylvain's blue eyes.

All he said was, 'Let's go and see Isabelle.'

It was after midnight and Isabelle had already gone to bed, so Allie waited in the corridor while Sylvain went to fetch her – as a prefect, he could go into the teachers' residential wing. All other students were forbidden.

When they arrived a few minutes later, Isabelle was casually dressed in leggings and a long cardigan, her hair pulled up loosely. 'Right, you two. What's this all about?'

Sylvain looked at Allie and she took the lead, explaining what Mr Patel had told them.

'I know this already, Allie,' Isabelle interrupted her, sounding tired and a bit snappish. 'I wouldn't let him go if I didn't think it was safe. He's leaving us some of his best people – very highly skilled – and he's sending in some associates of his to help as well.'

'But . . .' Her reaction caught Allie off guard. She'd expected at least some sympathy; a smidgen of concern. 'What about the ball? And Lucinda?'

'I think Allie has a point,' Sylvain interjected. 'This is not an ideal time for him to go.'

'Look, both of you,' Isabelle said in her most soothing tone, 'as important as we are, we are not as important as the prime minister. So I cannot ask Raj to stay when he's been called in for something like this. But I promise you we will not have less security while he's away. We will have more. We've planned for this. His people will be everywhere – inside and out. All of them highly trained, very skilled. If I thought it mattered that Raj wasn't going to be here to oversee this personally I would never have agreed to him going. I genuinely don't think it does.

I think we will be safe.' She turned her gaze to Allie. '*You* will be safe.'

Her words were comforting, and Allie nodded to show she understood. But every instinct she had told her to be afraid.

After the meeting, Allie walked out with Sylvain into the now silent hallway. In the quiet, their trainers made a sticky sound on the polished floor. Somewhere in the building a door closed too loudly.

The heat was off, and the air felt cold and heavy – as if it were waiting for something to happen.

'Sylvain . . .'

'Allie . . .'

They both spoke at the same time.

Stopping at the foot of the grand staircase they laughed awkwardly, their voices echoing.

'You first.' Shivering, she wrapped her arms around her torso for warmth.

'I think Isabelle is probably right,' he said. But something about the way his eyes searched her face told her this wasn't what he'd wanted to say. 'Everything will be fine.'

'Of course,' she said, not meaning it. 'I'm sure she's right.'

'We can still talk to Raj or Zelazny if you're worried?' he continued, and she shook her head.

'No, it's fine. Isabelle made sense.'

Dropping her gaze to her feet, she thought about all the things she wanted to tell him. To explain about Truth or Dare. How torn she felt. How she couldn't bear to hurt Carter and yet . . .

Against her will, her eyes darted up to meet his.

And yet.

For a long moment they looked at each other; the moment seemed frozen in time. Allie was steeling herself to speak when they heard footsteps. Turning, Allie saw Jerry Cole walking towards them.

'What are you two still doing out?' he said, his tone sharp. 'You know The Rules. Allie, aren't you in enough trouble already?'

Instantly, she took a step towards the staircase. Jerry was usually the most laid-back of the teachers so his anger caught her off guard. A puzzled frown crossed Sylvain's face before he smoothed it away. 'Sorry, Jerry. We were just going.'

But Jerry's reply startled them both. 'Do it quicker.'

The science teacher stood at the bottom of the stairs, watching as they walked up side by side.

'What's wrong with him?' Allie whispered without looking at Sylvain.

His reply was equally stealthy. 'Not sure.' At the landing they glanced back – Jerry was still there.

As they separated to head to their respective dorms, Sylvain caught her eye, arching one expressive eyebrow; she responded with a tiny bewildered shrug.

They both nearly smiled.

Amid all that was happening, Allie still worried about Jo. Two weeks after Truth or Dare she was keeping Allie at arm's length, and the schism left Allie feeling lonelier than ever. She was determined to fix it – not just for herself but for Jo.

Much as the idea of the ball frightened Allie, she imagined it must be worse for Jo.

So she decided to do something about it. After supper the next day, she tracked Jo down in the library where she studied alone at a table, her short blonde hair backlit into a halo by the glow from the brass desk lamp.

'Hey,' Allie whispered to a student nearby, 'can I borrow a piece of paper?'

Looking thrilled that she'd spoken to him, he handed her a sheet.

'And a pen.' Allie gestured impatiently.

Without a hint of hesitation he handed her the one he was using and waited as she scrawled out a quick note.

J

Come and talk to me outside. PLEASE. I miss you.

I'm sorry.

Ax

'Thanks,' she told the star-struck student, handing him back his pen. 'Do me a favour. Go and hand this note to that girl.'

As she pointed at Jo he leapt to his feet so quickly he nearly knocked his chair over.

'Steady.' Allie arched one eyebrow. 'Nobody needs to get hurt here.'

Then she hurried out of the room and waited in the hallway, chewing on her thumbnail.

But when Jo still hadn't appeared ten minutes later, Allie's heart sank.

She's not going to do it. She'll never forgive me.

Her head dropped to her chest, and she leaned back against the wall, propping one foot up behind her.

'Posture fail.' Jo's cut glass accent was so familiar, Allie smiled at her shoes. This sounded like old Jo. Sane Jo.

'You came.'

Crossing her arms across her chest, Jo scowled at her, but for the first time in weeks Allie saw a glimmer of amusement in her eyes.

'I wanted to hear your grovelling apology.'

'It was all my fault,' Allie said. 'I'm an idiot. You should refuse to be my friend and become very good friends with evil Katie instead. She deserves you more than I do.'

Jo fought to keep a straight face. 'That's an excellent start. Please continue.'

'If I told anybody, I should have told you. It was insane of me not to, and I promise,' Allie held up her right hand as if she were swearing in court, 'that I will never keep an important secret from you again.'

Jo dimpled at her. 'Now we're getting somewhere.'

'Will you please, please, *please* forgive me?'

'Of course I will,' Jo said. 'I'm not a monster.'

'Thank God.' Allie launched herself at her, pulling her into a hug. 'I couldn't have taken it much longer.'

'It is hard to live without me,' Jo agreed. 'I missed you, too. But no more secrets, OK? Tell me things. I'm not going to, you know, go mad up on the roof with a bottle of vodka or anything.'

'Like that'd ever happen,' Allie agreed.

*

In Training Room One, a rota for student patrols had been posted on the wall. They were working in shifts, alongside Raj's hired security guards. When they weren't out on patrol, they were trained relentlessly. The lessons were intense but practical: how to escape; how to raise an alarm; when to stay together and when to divide; how to fight someone with knife; or a gun.

Allie was asked to demonstrate the move she'd used to stab Gabe with a stake. One night all the Night School students dispersed in the woods trying to find a sharp stick like the one she'd described, which they could use as a weapon.

Even with all of that, her sense of unease hadn't lessened, and each night she focused intently on the training – she knew better than almost anyone how important these skills could be.

The night of Allie and Zoe's first patrolling shift, they were so nervous they both showed up early for their nine o'clock shift, arriving at the changing room to find their patrolling gear hanging from hooks on one wall. It was bitterly cold out, so the clothes left for them were black thermal leggings and tunics, black silk long underwear for additional warmth. Black hats and gloves. Black running shoes.

As she changed into the unfamiliar clothes in front of a full-length mirror, Allie studied the changes all the exercise had made to her body. The muscles in her upper arms and shoulders were defined. Her stomach was taut and flat. Her leg muscles had always been long and lean from running, now her upper body matched it.

I don't even look like me any more.

Ten minutes before their shift was due to begin, angry voices rang out from a room across the hall. She leaned closer to the door until she could make them out.

One of the voices was Jerry Cole's. The other belonged to Carter.

Humming to herself in a changing cubicle, Zoe didn't notice as Allie slipped out the door.

In the narrow basement hallway, she could hear the heated discussion clearly.

'They aren't trained enough.' Carter's voice was sharp. 'I think this is unacceptable. I can't believe Isabelle's allowing it. They shouldn't be out there on their own.'

'This is Zoe's second year in Night School,' Jerry replied. 'She's as highly trained as you.'

'But she's physically small.' Carter sounded as if he thought the science teacher was being intentionally obtuse. 'Just look at her. Her head barely comes to my chin. And Allie's only been training a few months. No other Neos are going out. I just don't think they should be out there alone. They should be with a more experienced student.'

Leaning back against the dressing room door, Allie stared unseeing at tiles on the floor as she listened. She could tell that Jerry was trying to calm him down.

'Carter, I'm sure that they'll be fine,' he said. 'They'll always be given the earliest shift, and they have to check in every hour. We'll keep a close watch on them.'

The door swung open so quickly Allie didn't have time to react – Carter stood in the doorway, his back to her, still arguing with Jerry. He hadn't seen her.

'I'm sorry, but I think it's dangerous. If one of them gets hurt . . . '

As he spoke, Allie scrabbled at the door behind her, finally finding the doorknob and diving back into the changing room just as he turned around.

Standing behind the closed door, she closed her eyes for a second as she steadied her breathing. Heat rose in her face.

'What's the matter?' Across the room, dressed all in black, Zoe was watching her quizzically. 'You look strange.'

'Nothing.'

With a shrug, Zoe turned back to the mirror.

The overheard conversation bothered Allie as she finished getting ready. Carter hadn't given her a clue that he was worried about what was happening. He'd acted as if he hated her. The fact that he was still trying to protect her made everything harder.

Yanking on a hat, she stared into her sober grey eyes in the mirror as she argued with herself. Because, wasn't this just another example of his suffocating overprotectiveness? *They aren't trained enough . . . They shouldn't be out there on their own.*

Her eyes darkened. *He doesn't believe in me. He never believes in me.*

A few minutes later, she and Zoe stood in front of the school building, looking out into the dark night.

'You ready for this, partner?' Allie asked.

'I am so ready.' Zoe's reply was fervent.

I hope you're right, Allie thought. But all she said was, 'Let's do it.'

They followed the path assigned to them by the security guards, their feet crunching on the icy ground. Their breath froze in the air like puffs of smoke as they ran into the dark forest, where the moonlight disappeared. It was a still night – no wind stirred the treetops. Their footsteps were the only sound. As their training dictated, they ran in silence.

Their first check was the fence, which they followed to the main gate, looking for signs that anybody had tried to get over, under or through. But everything was just as it should be. The fence seemed solid and impregnable. The gate was locked tight.

From there they ran through the woods to the stream. As they neared the place where Allie had met Christopher, she felt her heart speed up, but the stream ran by them innocently and empty. There were no footprints in the mud – nobody had been down there in a while.

The churchyard gate squawked unhappily as they passed through it on their way to check the chapel – it, too, was closed up tight. No flitting shadows to scare them. No flickering lights inside.

Each hour they met with one of Raj's security guards near a side door to the school building to check in, and each hour they reported nothing.

They were hurrying back to make their last report when something moved just off the path. 'Did you see that?' Allie whispered, pointing.

They skidded to a stop.

At first, all was still. Then the dried bracken began to sway, as if something behind it moved.

'What is it?' Zoe spoke so quietly Allie could almost not hear her. She shook her head.

When the thing moved again, she gestured for Zoe to approach from the left. She circled around to come at it from the right.

Lowering themselves to a crouch, they moved as quietly as possible but the brush beside the path was dry and brittle, and it crunched with every step. To Allie, the sound seemed deafening.

The thing must have heard it, too, because it quit moving.

For a long moment Allie and Zoe stood very still, each trying to see what was hidden in the darkness. Then, out of nowhere, a strange snuffling sound – almost a snort – made them both jump. Zoe's eyes widened. When the sound came again, her lips quirked up in sudden amused recognition.

'Oh my God,' she said. 'I know what it is.'

No longer trying to hide herself, she stalked over to the dried ferns and pushed them aside. Allie hurried to her side, arriving just in time to see a small, spiky creature curl up into a ball and cover its eyes.

'Oh! A hedgehog,' she cooed. 'I've never seen one before in person. It's adorable.'

'You can touch it,' Zoe said. 'It won't bite.'

Lowering her hand, Allie brushed one finger lightly over the hard shell-like spikes. At her touch, the hedgehog quivered and tightened its curl.

'It's scared,' Allie whispered. 'We should leave it alone.'

'Sorry, Mr Hedgehog.' Zoe moved the dried ferns back into place. 'We didn't mean to spook you.' As they tiptoed away, it snuffled to itself consolingly.

And so their night went.

Whatever he might have expected, Carter's fears proved to be unfounded. They encountered nothing more frightening than the hedgehog while patrolling.

Each night after that was the same: no Nathaniel, no Christopher.

Nothing at all.

In the days before the ball, the mood at the school changed markedly. Most students had already turned in their final papers and essays for the term so classes, which up until then had been frenetic with last-minute work, took on a relaxed atmosphere. Even so, when the students walked into English class they were stunned to see a television in a corner.

As she followed the others into the room, Allie's jaw dropped when she saw what they were all looking at. With technology forbidden at Cimmeria, the sight of even an old box-shaped TV filled them all with excitement and something like wonder.

Watching their reactions from across the room, Isabelle seemed positively gleeful.

'I thought for a bit of a treat we could watch a film,' she said, laughing as they broke into raucous applause. 'It's a film version of a book we read earlier this term – *The Age of Innocence* – so don't get too excited. It's not exactly MTV.'

Zoe was practically jumping out of her seat with joy, and Allie laughed at her reaction. Then, as always, her gaze floated to Carter, who sat as far away from her as possible. Talking to a friend next to him, he looked as if he were trying to summon a smile and failing.

Sliding down in her chair, she dropped her eyes to her notebook as all the excitement fizzled out. Just looking at Carter made her feel awful, every time.

When Isabelle turned down the lights and switched the television on the students fell into instant silence, gazing at the glowing screen, rapt.

'I've missed this so much,' someone whispered.

Though the film was slow and the story complicated, the technology-starved class became engrossed in the tale of a young man who marries the wrong woman. Although her own worries and fears were whirling in her mind, after a few minutes, Allie found herself lost in the story, willing Newland Archer to run off with Ellen.

When Ellen asked him, 'How can we be happy behind the backs of people who trust us?' Allie unconsciously covered her mouth with her fingers.

Sensing someone watching her, she glanced up. Across the darkened room, she caught Sylvain's gaze, the flickering lights of the screen reflected in his blue eyes. For a long moment their eyes locked. The confused emotions coursing through Allie's body were like nothing she'd ever felt before. She was drawn to him, angry at him, longing for him . . . all at once. She felt as if they were speaking to each other through that one long look. Communicating things they didn't dare say aloud.

Finally, she couldn't bear the tension and forced herself to turn back to the film. Only then did she notice her hands had been clenched so tight her nails had dug pale crescents into her palms.

TWENTY-SEVEN

The day of the ball dawned clear and cold. With snow forecast for later, nobody knew whether to be more excited about the dance with its array of international political leaders and corporate billionaires, or the mass snowball fight that would inevitably follow any snowstorm.

Students were free from classes and many of them spent the time packing, as most were leaving for Christmas break the next day. Allie had no reason to pack. She and Rachel were staying at the school until Christmas Eve, and then only spending a few days at Rachel's house before returning to Cimmeria. Allie's parents had agreed with Isabelle that London for Christmas wasn't really possible this year. Not after what happened in August.

Downstairs, a giant Christmas tree had been installed in the entrance hall, while a smaller tree stood in the common room near the piano, draped in red and gold fairy lights and so weighed down with baubles it looked buried. The whole building smelled of pine and cinnamon. Students played Christmas carols on the piano in the common room. But Allie, who felt not even slightly festive, had so far ignored the impending holiday. No cut-out snowflakes or baubles hung in her room.

Her main goal right now was to meet Lucinda – to ask her all the questions she'd been longing to ask.

Her other goal was to stay alive.

She still believed Nathaniel would try something during the ball, and she wasn't convinced they were ready for it.

But there was no way to stop the ball from happening. And when she knocked at Jo's room that afternoon, holding her dress in her arms, Allie was determined to put on a festive face for her. If Jo knew she was worried, she'd be worried, too. And that was rarely a good thing.

In stark contrast to Allie's room, Jo's embraced the ethos of the holidays in a borderline fanatical fashion. An LED Christmas tree glowed on the desk, fairy lights were draped across the bookcase, and a glossy gold ribbon had been wrapped around the chair and tied into a gigantic bow. From his perch on a bed pillow, a stuffed Santa Claus surveyed the room doubtfully.

'I think,' Jo said, 'we should do something special for the ball.'

'What do you have in mind?' Allie hung her dress from a hook on the back of Jo's door and dropped casually on to her bed next to Santa.

Reaching into the wardrobe, Jo produced two small boxes and held them up. 'Since neither of us has a date, which in my case is unprecedented, I think we should look particularly amazing tonight,' Jo said. 'Let's show everyone what they're missing.'

She tossed one box to Allie.

As she turned it over in her hands, a broad grin spread across Allie's face. 'You're a genius.'

'I know.' Jo grabbed two towels. 'I loved your hair when you first came here. It inspired me. Come on. You and me. Loos. Now.'

Ignoring the curious stares from two girls standing at the sinks, they ducked into a shower cubicle together, giggling.

Without ceremony, Jo took off her top and draped a towel across her shoulders. Allie did the same.

Jo pulled on rubber gloves with a loud snap and shook a plastic bottle in one hand. 'I think I should do yours and then you do mine. It's hard to do your own.'

Allie leaned over as Jo streamed purplish goo on to her hair, working it in with the rubber gloves.

Allie shivered deliciously. 'I love someone else doing things to my hair.'

'I know. It's like a headgasm.'

'Where did you get this stuff?' Allie asked.

Working on the back of Allie's head, Jo said, 'My brother's girlfriend sent it to me. I called her last week.'

The room smelled so strongly of chemicals Allie's eyes watered. 'You were planning this all the time?'

'After we made up, it just came to me.' Jo squished the goo through to the ends of Allie's hair with a satisfying squelch. 'Like a vision.'

One hour and two ruined towels later, the job was done. Back in Jo's room they admired their handiwork.

Hanging in wet strands below her shoulder blades, Allie's hair was vivid, almost metallic red. Jo's short blonde locks were now shiny pink.

Dimpling prettily, Jo shook her damp locks. 'I look like a pixie.'

A wave of melancholy hit Allie as she studied herself. 'I look like old me.'

As if she knew what she was thinking, Jo's eyes met hers in the mirror. 'Old you is just as beautiful as new you.'

Someone knocked at the door. 'Whatever you're selling . . .' Jo said, yanking it open.

Zoe and Rachel stood on the other side, their arms full of clothes.

At Allie's insistence they were all getting ready together. After everything that had happened to drive everyone apart, she wanted – this one night – everyone to be together. Where she could keep an eye on them.

Zoe stared at Jo's pink hair with her mouth open.

'Oh my God, you look *amazing*.' The fabric in her arm rustled as she jumped up and down in excitement.

'Enter.' Jo stepped back from the door. 'And prepare to be fabulous.'

'Leave my hair alone.' Rachel's eyes flickered to Allie's head. 'Vivid,' was her only comment.

Allie shrugged helplessly. 'Something came over us.'

'Can my hair be purple?' Zoe dropped her dress on the bed.

'Sadly, your very young hair will have to stay its natural

colour as we used up all the dye I had,' Jo said. 'But you can hang out with us and bask in our reflected, many-coloured glory. And I'll put makeup on you.' She added the last sentence hastily when she saw Zoe's face fall.

Zoe looked up at them hopefully. 'Lots of makeup?'

'As much makeup as your heart desires.' Holding up a golden tube of lipstick that sparkled in the light, Jo smiled.

First, she styled Allie's hair into glossy red curls. Next, she wound Zoe's straight brown hair between ribbons, pulling it back off her face and brushing it smooth until it shone like a sheet of dark glass. Then she lined Zoe's eyes with dark blue liner and applied a lavish coating of mascara. As she painted Zoe's lips with strawberry pink gloss, Rachel glanced over at her doubtfully.

'She looks like a midget prostitute.'

'I like it.' Zoe pouted at herself in the mirror. 'I think I look older. More mature.'

'It's the Cimmeria Ball. She'll be fine.' Jo motioned for Rachel to sit in front of her. 'It's not like Gary Glitter will be here.'

'Who's Barry Glitter?' Zoe asked.

The others ignored the question.

As Jo began working on Rachel's mane of dark curls, Rachel watched her suspiciously. 'I don't really do anything with my hair.'

'I won't do much either.' Jo waved curling tongs. 'Just a bit of this and a little of that.'

Rachel hunched her shoulders. 'That's what I'm afraid of.'

By now it was dark outside – the stars had disappeared

behind a bank of cloud, and the air had that heavy, silent feeling that portends snow. For the last hour, Bentleys and limousines had pulled in steadily, crunching their way down the gravel lane. Now the drive was full, as far as they eye could see.

As she finished with Rachel's thick mane, Jo glanced at the clock on her desk, currently covered in sparkly gold tinsel. 'It's time, ladies.'

After makeup touch-ups, they zipped each other's dresses then stood in front of the full-length mirror to take it in.

'We look like angels,' Zoe breathed, staring at them.

'More like fairies, I think.' Jo's pink hair glittered in the overhead light and her black velvet minidress showed off her long, slim legs. 'Or film stars.'

Zoe's dark green taffeta dress had a high neckline and a circle skirt. Her heavy eye makeup gave her an oddly charming punk look. Rachel wore a matte red dress that left one arm and shoulder bare. Her thick dark hair had been pulled back from her face with a gold braided band that made her look like an exotic princess.

But they were all staring at Allie.

'Allie, darling,' Jo said, 'you really do look amazing.'

'*So* amazing,' Zoe agreed.

'Even with that hair,' Rachel conceded.

Allie's vintage blue silk dress clung to her waist and swung out into a full skirt ending at the knee. The sleeves hugged her arms to just below her elbows. Her henna-red hair contrasted with it perfectly, making her fair skin glow. She'd loved this dress since it first appeared in her closet during the summer term – one of Isabelle's mysterious, well-chosen gifts.

Allie blushed. 'Well, all I can say is: who needs boys? I just want to snog us.'

'Not again,' Zoe muttered, heading for the door.

'Seriously, Allie,' Rachel said, 'this kissing girls thing seems to be becoming a habit.'

'I'm convinced if I were a lesbian dating would be easier.' Allie followed them out. 'Boys are the problem.'

'I don't know,' Jo said mildly. 'Sometimes boys can be the answer too.'

'I don't know what either of you is talking about,' Zoe said.

'Me neither,' said Rachel.

By the time they reached the top of the main staircase they were all laughing. Down below the wide, oak-panelled hallway had been draped in velvet ribbon and filled with bouquets of red and gold flowers. The ban on candles had clearly been lifted, because they glowed in sconces and on every table and windowsill.

Classical music filtered out of the great hall and down the corridor, accompanied by a low roar of voices. The hallway was packed with people – most of them adults; their glossy hair glittered in the light. The men were all in tuxedoes while the women wore designer dresses and clutched tiny bags.

'I don't remember inviting all these people,' Jo murmured dryly as they walked down the stairs side by side.

'Oh my God. Is that *President Abingdon*?' Zoe zipped ahead of them and threaded her way through the people, soon disappearing into the crowd.

'Our little girl,' Jo sighed.

'All grown up,' Allie said. 'Or at least her face is. Jo . . . '

'I know,' Jo laughed. 'But she wanted it.'

Spying Lucas looking dapper in a tuxedo, Rachel slipped away. Allie watched as his face lit up when he saw her. He bent low over her hand and kissed her fingertips.

She loved how happy they were together. But seeing them like that reminded her of all she'd lost.

Inside, the great hall was even more crowded. Tables draped in red linens spiralled out around an empty dance floor. Each table was topped with a centrepiece of dark green ivy. The room was warm and smelled of candle wax, hothouse lilies and expensive perfume. In one corner an orchestra played a waltz. Throughout the ballroom, staff in white tie carried trays of champagne and mulled wine.

At the edge of the dance floor, Isabelle stood in a flowing black dress, snug at the waist and threaded through with gold. Her hair was pulled back in a loose chignon and she was laughing, surrounded by well-wishers.

Allie turned a slow circle, looking for a woman with a distinctive head of white hair.

'Blimey,' Jo said, standing on her toes to look for a seat. 'Bit crowded.'

'Much worse than the summer ball.' Allie's voice was distracted but Jo didn't notice.

'It always is. Because the board's here and all the influential parents . . . I think I see a couple of seats over there.' Jo pointed at the far corner of the room, and they began making their way over.

Lucinda Meldrum would stand out in a crowd, even one as

thick as this. Allie knew if she were here she'd see her. Since she didn't, she began to relax a little.

She must not be here yet.

But whenever she tried to imagine how she was going to get close enough to her grandmother to speak with her she couldn't think of what she might say. 'Hi, Grandmother, why haven't we ever met?' seemed a bit of a weak start.

'Why aren't your parents here?' Allie raised her voice to be heard above the crowd as they seated themselves with their backs to the wall and a wide view of the room. 'Aren't they rich and important?'

'Very,' Jo said without a hint of embarrassment. 'But they're busy and they don't like to come back here often. Dad always says, "Next year, darling. Next year."' She affected a deep dismissive tone. 'And Mum is busy with Olivier, her toy boy *du jour*.'

'Gross.' A waiter appeared at their table, and Allie and Jo ordered Diet Coke.

'Exactly.' Jo crossed her legs, revealing the red soles of her stilettos. 'Oh, look, Sylvain's parents are here.'

She nodded in the direction of an elegant couple who stood chatting with Isabelle near the dance floor. Leaning forward, Allie studied them with hungry curiosity. The man had fair skin and greying sandy-blond hair. He looked suave in his perfectly tailored tuxedo. The woman had tawny skin and a mane of dark hair that fell in waves and curls down her back. She wore a bronze silk gown that clung to her trim hips. A necklace heavy with diamonds encircled her throat.

Nearby, Katie Gilmore stood with an older couple who must have been her parents. She was stunning in a dark green dress – the colour made her skin shimmer like milk. With a touch of bitterness, Allie wondered if it was a coincidence she was standing so close to Sylvain's family.

As she watched, though, Sylvain walked by Katie without seeing her and up to his father. Allie willed herself to feel nothing, but her heart beat faster nonetheless; his perfectly tailored tuxedo emphasised his leanly muscled shoulders. His father turned to greet him and, even from across the room, she could see the brilliant blue of his eyes.

'So that's where he gets it from,' she murmured.

'Hmm?' Jo, who had been looking elsewhere, turned to follow Allie's gaze.

'His dad,' Allie said absently. 'Sylvain has his eyes.'

The waiter returned with a tray of drinks; Jo looked thoughtful as he set them down, waiting until he was out of earshot. Then she leaned forward tapping a glossy silver nail against the tabletop. 'OK, out with it, Allie. What's going on with you and Sylvain? I've seen the way you look at him. And the way he looks at you. Frankly, a blind person could see there's something happening between you two.'

Flushing, Allie tore her gaze away from Sylvain's family. 'No. I mean ... What?'

'Come on, Allie.' Jo's cornflower blue eyes studied her knowingly. 'This is me. I can see it in your face. You fancy him.'

Panic made it hard to think. She'd tried so hard not to like Sylvain. *So hard*. And she'd failed.

'I can't like him, Jo.' Allie's eyes pleaded with her.

But Jo seemed confused. 'Why not? He's sex on legs. And he sure likes you.'

'It's just, Carter . . .' Allie fumbled her words, trying to think of a way to explain this that didn't sound absurd. 'He hates Sylvain and we haven't . . . I don't want to hurt him.'

Resting one hand on Allie's arm, Jo pointed across the room; her narrow diamond bracelet caught the light, fracturing it into a million bright sparks. Allie followed the line of her slender arm to . . . Carter and Jules. He looked tall in his tuxedo, and she wore a tight black dress that suited her perfectly. They were kissing.

'What?' Staring, Allie ordered herself to close her mouth.

'This is the thing.' Jo leaned forward to catch her eyes. 'Don't ever let your ex-boyfriend decide who you date. OK?'

'How long have they . . . ?'

'Does it matter?

I've been so worried for so long about hurting Carter and he just . . . What? Got over it and forgot to mention it? Let me keep on feeling guilty while he made out with Jules?

Anger flared in her chest as she glanced over at the dance floor again. They'd been slow-dancing, but now the band switched to a different tune – an Eastern song Allie remembered from the summer ball – and Carter swirled Jules out on to the dance floor. They were both laughing.

As she stared at them, a boy walked up to Jo and bowed from the waist. 'Miss Arringford, might I have the honour of this dance?'

He had a Spanish accent and a courtly manner; Allie wondered why she hadn't seen him around before.

'Hello, Guillermo.' Jo fluttered her eyelashes. 'I think so. Let me just check with my date.' She turned to Allie. 'Do you mind, darling?'

Guillermo was tall and lanky, with brown hair in irrepressible curls. He looked like a Spanish prince. Jo's eyes were aglow.

How could Allie say no? 'Have fun, kids.' She smiled as they walked away.

Guillermo was so tall he had to lean over to hear Jo talk. Jo's cheeks were pink. They looked adorable together.

As Allie watched the others dance and laugh, an overwhelming sense of loneliness threatened to subsume her. She wanted to sit at the table and cry, but that wouldn't do anybody any good.

I'll go and look for Lucinda.

She threaded her way through the crowd, snippets of mysterious and uninteresting adult conversations floating around her like flotsam riding on waves of noise.

'He's with a hedge fund now, of course . . . '

'Five under par! At St Andrews!'

'I told her that dress was unacceptable but she won't listen. She never listens . . . '

'We're thinking of selling the house in Saint-Tropez, actually . . . '

When somebody rested a hand on her arm she flinched. But when she looked up Sylvain was smiling at her. 'Allie. My parents would like to meet you.' Taking in her bright red hair, his eyebrows winged upwards. She responded with an apologetic shrug as he led her over to where his parents waited expectantly.

'Madame and Monsieur Cassel, may I introduce Mademoiselle Allie Sheridan,' Sylvain said.

Shaking her hand, they studied her with frank interest.

'Uh ... Hi ... Or *bonsoir*.' She'd never felt less sophisticated.

They exchanged pleasantries and she responded in her schoolgirl French. Then his father spoke in English.

'What is it like,' he asked, 'to grow up as the granddaughter of Lucinda Meldrum?'

'Papa, that's personal,' Sylvain protested, looking horrified.

But Allie was getting used to this; she decided to answer. 'It's strange,' she said leaning forward confidentially. 'But we're not close.' This seemed to intrigue them, so she added, 'She's very busy you know. Travels all the time.'

Looking down, Sylvain hid a smile. His parents seemed fascinated.

'Of course,' Mr Cassel said. 'We don't see Sylvain as much as we would like because we're busy, too, so we understand completely.'

Syvlain's mother placed her arm across her son's shoulders with obvious affection. 'We are always trying to convince him to come home to us more often.' Her voice was throaty, her accent as smooth as the silk dress she wore. 'But he always says, "No, Maman, I have work to do."' She gave a resigned smile. 'He is like his father.'

Her perfume was heady – she had the insouciant elegance of a model. Allie was dazzled.

'Well, they work us very hard here.' She glanced up to find Sylvain watching her with open affection. A smile flickered across her lips and a flock of butterflies swirled in her stomach. She lost her train of thought.

'You must come and visit us.' Mrs Cassel stepped into the silence smoothly. 'We would love to host you.' She turned to

Sylvain. 'Invite her to Antibes in the summer, darling. Wouldn't Henri and Hélène adore her? She is adorable.'

Adorable? Allie looked at Sylvain desperately.

'That's my aunt and uncle.' He apologised with his eyes. 'And, please consider yourself officially invited.'

'Thank you very much,' she said in her most polite voice. 'That's very kind of you. I would love to see your home.'

'Allie must go and see her other friends now,' Sylvain said to her relief. 'We can't keep her here all night.'

'Oh but she is so charming!' they chorused, as she hurried to say her goodbyes, smiling politely until her cheeks hurt.

The party spilled over into the dining room, which had been set up much like the great hall with tables and candles. There was no sign of Lucinda there, but a delicious smell distracted her and she followed her nose to a buffet table in one corner where she liberated a mini crab cake.

Popping it in her mouth, she turned and nearly collided with Carter.

'I'm sorr—' he started, and then he saw her. She saw the surprise on his face. 'Allie.'

Tensing, she waited for the icy rage that seemed to accompany him these days like a frozen cloud. But instead he looked stunned. His eyes swept her body, taking in her hair, the dress, the high heels she'd borrowed from Jo.

More than anything at that moment she regretted the crab cake, which she was now trying to swallow, but her mouth had gone dry. She turned away quickly to grab a glass of water from a nearby table and took a quick swallow – if she didn't she feared she might throw up all over her pretty dress.

When she turned back around he was gone.

Baffled, she looked at the space where he had stood. If only she knew what she was supposed to feel. The confusing signals he sent were torturous.

I'm over you. I'm not over you. I want you. I hate you . . .

Maybe Jo was right. Maybe she should stop letting Carter decide who she dated.

Setting the glass back down, she made her way through the crowd. There must have been hundreds of people there. They filled the main hallway, the grand stairwell and even the entrance hall. Their conversations and laughter echoed off the high ceilings and reverberated in Allie's head. Despite the cold night, the building felt stuffy, as if the guests were using up all the oxygen.

So when Allie found herself standing by the front door, it seemed the most natural thing in the world to turn the handle and slip outside, into the dark night.

TWENTY-EİGHT

After the heat inside, the icy air felt good as it chilled the perspiration on her skin. Shivering pleasantly, Allie shook her head so the cold air could reach under her heavy hair and cool her neck.

On the curved driveway in front of her, rows of parked cars were neatly aligned. She could see chauffeurs gathered by the west wing with newspapers and cigarettes. They didn't seem to notice her as she headed around the end of the building, wobbling a bit as Jo's delicate shoes rocked on the uneven ground. Camouflaged in the darkness, she followed the unlighted footpath towards the walled garden. In the air she could smell a faint ashy tang of cigarette smoke and hear occasional bursts of muffled laughter from smokers gathered outside the school's back door, but she was nearly at the folly now and hidden by the trees.

And then she stood in front at the small, white marble

structure, with its domed roof. It held only the statue of a woman, draped in diaphanous scarves and dancing for ever. The statue's lips curved up a little, as if she enjoyed dancing in the cold, one bare foot perpetually raised.

Reaching out Allie touched the smooth icy stone as she thought about the night Sylvain found her here, and taught her how to fight.

'You're not wearing a coat, you know.'

For some reason, his voice didn't surprise her, although she hadn't heard his footsteps. For a second she closed her eyes, lost in indecision. Then she turned.

Sylvain stood a few feet away next to the stairs that led up to the statue. When their eyes met, Allie shivered again. She gestured vaguely at his tuxedo. 'You aren't either.'

'Yes, but a tuxedo comes with a jacket, so I at least have this.' He shrugged the black, silk-lined jacket off and held it out to her. His crisp white shirt seemed to glow in the darkness.

'But now you'll be cold,' she pointed out, not reaching for it.

His lips curved up. 'I'll live.'

After a moment's hesitation, she accepted it. As she'd known it would, it still held his body heat and smelled of his cologne.

'You've changed your hair.' His gaze traced the curls over her shoulders. 'It suits you.'

'Thanks.' She touched her hair with nervous fingers. 'It wasn't my idea. Jo can be . . . convincing.'

'So I've heard. I'm sorry about my parents,' he said. 'They really wanted to meet you.'

She shrugged to show she understood parents. 'Your mum is gorgeous.'

'I'll tell her you said so. She likes it when people tell her she's beautiful.' His tone was wry.

Then it seemed they'd used up all the small talk; an awkward silence fell between them. Allie shifted her weight on to one delicate sandal, digging the toe of the other into the dirt. Watching her, he leaned against a stone pillar.

'What are you doing out in the cold, Allie?' His voice was low.

You know what. Or you wouldn't be here, too.

'I don't know ... I guess I just needed some air.' Her eyes challenged him. 'What are you doing out here?'

His shoulders tensed; when he spoke his voice was low. 'I followed you.'

She felt the breath go out of her. 'Why?' The word came out as a whisper.

'*Le coeur a ses raisons que la raison ne connaît point.*' He recited the French phrase too fast, and Allie shook her head.

'I don't understand.' Not knowing what he'd said left her feeling almost panicked. 'What does that mean?'

But when his gaze locked on hers the longing she saw there answered her question. 'It means that I want to be with you. That I can't get you out of my head.' He pounded his fist with restrained violence against the pillar. 'I have tried everything I know how to try, and you're still there.'

Two breaths in. One breath out.

'I ... I think about you, too.' She could barely hear herself speak over the thudding of her heart. 'But ...'

Uncontrollably, her thoughts flickered back to the summer

ball. She could tell by the way his blue eyes flashed that he knew what she was thinking.

'I know I did a bad thing. A stupid thing. But people change, Allie.' His voice was passionate, almost desperate. 'People learn. If they didn't, what would be the point of this?' His arm swept towards the school building they could just see through the trees. 'What would be the point of life? You've changed while you've been here – I've watched you change. Well, I've changed too. And I'm sorry about what I did that night. If there was some way to take it all back . . .'

Suddenly she didn't care about the summer ball or anything else. She'd spent so much time worrying about how Carter felt and what Carter wanted. What about what *she* wanted?

Anyway, she thought, *the horrible truth is Carter has Jules now. He doesn't want me any more.*

So why shouldn't she have Sylvain? No matter what she'd done, Carter thought she wanted to be with Sylvain. Now she could find out once and for all if she did want to be with him.

At least Sylvain cared about her. Sylvain wanted her.

'You can take it back,' she said suddenly. Sylvain stared at her with open surprise. Before she could change her mind, she ran across the space that divided them. His jacket slid from her shoulders, pooling forgotten on the frosty ground.

'Let's just take it all back.'

She could see the doubt in his eyes, as if he didn't believe this was really happening.

Reaching up, she traced the outline of his lips with her fingertips. He closed his eyes. Then, sliding her hands around his neck, she pulled him down to her.

343

At first she was distracted by how differently he kissed than Carter – his lips were softer, more assured. It felt strange. Wrong.

But she wasn't going to chicken out. Instead of pulling away, she leaned into him and the kiss – which had been tentative at first – strengthened as Sylvain realised she was serious about this. Hesitantly, his hands slid down the silk of her dress to her waist – when she didn't pull away he drew her more tightly against him. When her lips parted for him, he groaned softly at the back of his throat; her bones seemed to soften and she leaned into him as his arms tightened around her. She was so close to him, she could feel his heart thudding as if it were beating in her own chest.

Allie poured all the loneliness of the last five weeks into that kiss. The pain of Carter breaking up with her. Blaming herself for everything. The long nights with no one to talk to. Longing for something she wasn't supposed to want.

As if he sensed this, Sylvain cupped the back of her head to kiss her more deeply. Gasping against his lips, she slid her hands up to tangle her fingers in the soft waves of his hair.

Heat radiated from his body as if he had a fever; Allie wasn't cold any more. She wasn't alone any more.

There was no logic to this – no plan. Maybe this was a bad idea. She didn't care any more.

His lips moved down the side of her face to her ear then on to her neck and, breathing in short gasps, she dropped her head back. But something soft and delicate – like feathers of ice – tickled her face, distracting her.

Opening her eyes, she saw white crystals whirling against

the darkness, and she straightened with a small cry. 'It's snowing!'

Still wrapped in each other's arms, they looked up into the infinity of snow falling from a night sky. The world seemed to hush around them.

'It's a sign,' he said. A few snowflakes had settled disarmingly on his eyelashes and his white teeth flashed as he smiled.

'A sign of what?' She wondered if she looked that happy to him.

'That this is right.'

As they walked through the snow to the front door – Allie picking her way carefully in Jo's foolish shoes – she told him her plan to meet Lucinda.

'What will you ask her?' His arm was tight around her waist, his body warm against hers.

'That's the problem,' she said, as they reached the door. 'I don't know.'

'She's your grandmother – she'll understand.'

Inside the warmth that had seemed so claustrophobic before was now welcome. The party had not abated, and the cacophony crashed over them like a wave.

'I'm going to run upstairs just to fix . . ' She gestured at her face.

Smoothing the snow from her hair, Sylvain smiled into her eyes then he brushed his lips against her cheek so lightly it made her shiver. 'Come and find me.'

'Where will you be?'

'In the great hall.' He let her go with a regretful sigh. 'With my parents.'

Dashing through the crowd, Allie ran up the grand staircase hoping she'd get a chance to be alone with him later, after his parents had left. Maybe this time they could go somewhere warmer. And start where they'd left off.

I'll just clean up my mascara and then . . .

She never finished the thought.

At the top of the stairs, Isabelle was talking to someone – even from here, Allie could hear the tension in her voice. Then a strangely familiar, powerful voice floated back to her. Looking up, she saw Isabelle – she was standing next to Lucinda.

Frozen in place on the stairs, Allie felt dizzy with excitement and fear. They were speaking too quietly for her to make out most of the words but she knew they were angry. She was still deciding what to do when she heard Isabelle's shoes tapping out a furious pattern as she walked away.

Holding her breath, Allie stood still to listen. She could hear nobody else up there. Was it possible Lucinda was alone?

Slowly at first, then with increasing speed, she ran up the stairs. But when she reached the wide landing her heart sank. It was empty. Lucinda must have left so quietly she hadn't heard.

Crushed, she was just turning away when a faint sound made her turn. That's when she saw Lucinda, standing in a nook, half hidden by a heavy curtain as she looked out the window.

Closing her eyes to summon her courage, Allie stepped closer to her. 'It's snowing.'

Her voice sounded strange and she cleared her throat.

'Nobody should be surprised.' Lucinda hadn't turned around. 'It was predicted after all.'

'I've been . . . wanting to meet you.' Allie fought to hold her voice steady.

'And I've been wanting to meet you.' Lucinda turned to face her. 'Allie Sheridan. My long lost granddaughter.'

TWENTY-NINE

'Come closer,' Lucinda said. 'So I can see you.'

After a moment's hesitation, Allie did as she said.

'You're very pretty, you know.' Lucinda's cool grey eyes, almost exactly like Allie's own, swept her from her heels to head. 'Except your hair. What on earth have you done to it?'

'It's temporary.' Allie's voice was weak. 'It will wash out. In a few . . . weeks.'

'Thank God for that.' Lucinda had a regal posture – she held her head as if she wore an invisible crown. 'You haven't got any tattoos have you?'

'Not yet,' Allie admitted, a little disappointed in herself.

'Not yet.' Lucinda echoed her words with a light laugh. 'Do think about it before you do it. What looks good at sixteen looks ludicrous at fifty. I see it all the time. Your grades are good. You're excelling.'

Her manner of switching subjects within the same breath

was dizzying; she dominated the conversation with powerful ease, wrong-footing Allie from the start so she could never assert herself enough to ask a question. Besides, she was so busy studying Lucinda it was hard to focus her thoughts. Her grey dress fell to slim ankles under a matching jacket with a raised collar. The emerald ring on her right hand was as big as a pound coin. Platinum and diamond earrings sparkled discreetly beneath her hair. Despite her age, she had an athletic figure and a youthful face.

'I like it here.' Allie was determined to gain some control. 'If I like where I am, I work hard.' Remembering that she wouldn't be here without Lucinda's help she added, 'Thank you . . . for getting me here.'

'It's not just hard work.' Lucinda eyed her sharply. 'You're naturally intelligent. Isabelle told me you were and I see she's right.'

Her praise made Allie's cheeks heat up, but she couldn't be distracted. This could be her only chance. She took a step towards her, pleading with her eyes for understanding.

'Lucinda . . . *Grandmother* . . . ' It felt good to say that. 'Help me understand what's happening. I don't know what to do. Nathaniel has Christopher, and he's trying to take me. Can you protect me? Please?'

As she spoke, Lucinda's gaze softened, just a little. But her words offered little comfort. 'I *am* protecting you. My dear, have you no idea what's going on? Hasn't Isabelle told you?'

Confused and frustrated, Allie held up her empty hands. 'Isabelle said Nathaniel wants to take over the organisation and—'

Casting a tense look over her shoulder, Lucinda cut her off, gesturing for her to follow her into the window nook. On the other side of the glass, the snow fell so fast the outside world seemed to have disappeared behind a frozen veil.

'Things are very dangerous right now.' Lucinda's voice was low and she spoke quickly. 'Especially here. There are people here tonight who support Nathaniel against me. You must be careful what you say.'

'But why? Why do they support him?'

As Lucinda leaned against the windowsill, tension and tiredness made lines that weren't there before appear around her eyes. 'I have worked my whole life to change things in this country. To make things better. But something's changing. Not just here, in the rest of the world as well. Some people have become too rich, too powerful. And that power made them corrupt. Too much became not enough. Limits disappeared. And that's dangerous.' She looked over her shoulder. 'I can't explain it all to you now, Allie. This isn't the time or the place. But I will give you this advice: trust no one. Until we find out who among us is working for Nathaniel, no one is safe.'

As she spoke, Allie's world seemed to grow colder. She didn't know her grandmother at all but she recognised the fear in her eyes. It was like looking into her mother's face when she'd first asked her about Lucinda.

'I wish,' she said, 'that I'd met you before now.'

'I'm sorry it had to be like this,' her grandmother said briskly. 'But it was the way your mother wanted it and I wasn't going to force myself on her. We had an agreement.'

'It must have hurt ... her running away like that,' Allie said.

The look Lucinda gave her then was appraising. 'Life is full of pain, and you might as well get used to that right now, Allie. It doesn't go away. It accumulates. Like snow.' She glanced at the window. 'You just get better at dealing with it.'

On the stairs, footsteps approached them. For the first time Allie noticed the music had stopped.

Straightening, Lucinda stepped out from the window as a team of five men – clearly her security team – appeared at the top.

'Baroness.' The men surrounded her in a protective phalanx. 'We have to go.'

'What's happened?' Lucinda's voice was cool now, and fear-less.

One of them turned away and spoke into a microphone attached to his sleeve. 'Orion protocol two-three-seven. Clear.'

As they hustled Lucinda down the stairs, Allie stayed hard on their heels, so she heard the first one say, 'There's been a security breach.'

Downstairs, all was chaos. Guests poured through the door in furs and diamonds, their bodyguards and chauffeurs leading them through snow that was now five inches deep. Some students were leaving with their parents, others stood around looking bewildered.

Panic threatened to sweep over Allie and she took deep gulps of air to steady herself. She wanted to scream in frustration.

I knew this would happen. Why didn't anyone listen?

Isabelle and Zelazny were nowhere to be seen, but Allie

found Zoe with Jo and Rachel in one corner, watching the exodus. Jo's lips were white with nervousness.

'What's happening?' Allie asked, walking up.

'Someone made an announcement,' Rachel said. 'About the snow, but he gave some code and everyone ran for the door.'

'Where were you? I waited for you.' Zoe fairly vibrated with impatience. 'We have to go *right now*.'

Allie didn't ask where. Turning to Rachel and Jo, she said, 'We're going to ... uh ... ' She tilted her head towards the door.

Rachel gave her a warning look. 'Be careful.'

Hopping on one foot, Allie pulled off her heels before running after Zoe; as they rushed down the stairs their skirts billowed around them like sails.

The basement floor was like gritty ice under Allie's bare feet as they skidded into Training Room One, which was already crowded with Night School students in formal attire – it was such a bizarre scene Allie would have laughed if things hadn't been so serious.

Zelazny and Jerry Cole stood at one end. Zelazny was talking. '. . . the guards found an attempted intrusion near the main gate. Guards are now exploring the rest of the fence line. You will be looking out for anything unusual. Footprints in the snow that are not yours. Signs of damage to the fence. Signs that someone has jumped over the fence – all the things you normally look for.'

Zelazny stepped back and Jerry took over. 'You will each be assigned a quadrant to search. You will travel in groups of four. You will stay together.' His eyes surveyed them sternly to make sure that his words were understood. 'If you see signs of intrusion you will send two members of your team back to report it – the others will continue to search. Your assigned teams are here.' Turning, he taped a single sheet of paper to the wall. 'Get ready. Do it quickly.'

As Allie and Zoe fought their way through the crowd thronging around the assignment sheet, Jules, in a long black dress slit up to the thigh, saved them the trouble of waiting.

'You're with us,' she said, pointing behind her. Emerging from the scrum of students, Carter still had his tux on, although his tie dangled from his hand. His hair tumbled forward over his forehead as he met Allie's gaze dispassionately.

Balls, Allie thought.

'Awesome,' Zoe said. Shoulders squared, she was already headed towards the door, shoving her way through the crowd ahead of Allie like a little tank. 'Let's go and change.'

'See you outside in five, Carter.' Jules tone was brisk as she followed Zoe.

There was no time to say anything; feeling sick, Allie ran after them.

The changing room was mayhem as girls struggled to remove their silk and velvet dresses quickly, replacing them with black thermal leggings. Allie tried not to look at Jules as she changed. Tried not to wonder if Carter thought Jules was prettier.

She had nothing to hold her hair back with so when Zoe ripped the ribbons from her hair Allie grabbed one and tried to use it as a ponytail holder, but her fingers were suddenly numb and she couldn't get it to work.

Standing nearby in a lacy black bra and knickers, Nicole

reached over and handed her an elastic hairband. Allie was starting to learn that the French girl missed nothing.

'This is better, I think,' Nicole said with a wink. When Allie just stared at her tensely, Nicole stepped closer and took the band from her hand. She studied Allie with understanding eyes as she pulled her hair back and tightened it into place with the band. 'Don't be nervous, Allie. It will be fine.'

'I know,' Allie whispered, although she didn't.

When they ran out of the building into the freezing night, Carter was already outside, jogging in place, clad in a warm black jacket and running trousers. As the more experienced pair, he and Jules took the lead, while Allie and Zoe fell into a steady running pace behind them.

The snow fell so heavily now it was hard to see where they were going until they reached the protective umbrella of trees in the forest. Here they sped up, weaving their way through the undergrowth to the stream behind the chapel where Allie had met Christopher weeks before.

Allie's chest tightened when she realised where they were going.

It will be OK. It will be OK. It will be OK ... She repeated the mantra in her head as they skidded down the incline to the stream bed and she looked around with frightened eyes, expecting Christopher or Gabe to jump out at them from anywhere.

But the snow around the stream was pure, unbroken. Nobody had been here for at least an hour or more. They spread out into a line, with five feet between them, sweeping down the stream towards the stepping-stone bridge that Allie had imagined hopping across on a warm summer day.

This was not that day: the stones were covered with snow and ice, and the water looked black and frigid. Jules went first, hopping with athletic grace from stone to stone. She slipped on the fifth step and, catching herself, looked back at them.

'Careful with this one.' Then she made it to the other side.

After her, Zoe ran across with ease.

Carter turned to Allie. 'You next. Be careful.' He held her gaze too long, and Allie hurried to the water's edge.

The water rushing past was louder here, which helped her to focus as she picked her way across. The fifth stone wobbled as Jules had warned and she was ready for it. But when her foot hit the sixth stone it skidded, throwing her off balance. To save herself she rushed to the seventh stone and then the eighth. By the time she reached shore she'd completely lost her balance; Jules reached out for her but Carter caught her first, holding her steady.

He'd been right behind her the whole time and she'd never known he was there.

'Thanks,' she muttered, not meeting his eyes.

They headed to the fence with Jules in the lead, then Zoe, followed by Allie and Carter. On this side of the stream the snow was just as unblemished as it had been on the other – a pure velvet sheet of white.

'Nobody's been here,' Allie whispered to Carter. 'Not tonight.'

He glanced up at her. 'I agree. We'll check the whole area though.'

'Any idea what set this off?'

A magpie, startled by their passage, fluttered out of a tree above them sending a flurry of snow down.

One for sorrow, Allie thought, and she looked at Zoe with concern, but she was too far ahead to see it.

'Somebody saw something,' Carter said. 'One of the guards saw footprints, and he said they weren't his or the other guards'. But they could have been anyone's. Everyone's so paranoid right now.'

It felt strangely familiar walking beside Carter in the woods – like the old days – and Allie's panic began to recede. They fell into an easy rhythm as their feet crunched in the fresh snow, leaving its smooth surface pockmarked.

His next words took her by surprise. 'You looked beautiful tonight.' He cast a sideways glance at her. 'I wanted to tell you that in the dining hall but . . . I bottled it. Things have been pretty messed up between us lately. I'm sorry about that.'

Allie's stomach tightened. He'd been so angry with her for so long she wasn't sure how to take this new attitude.

'I know we've had a rough time,' he continued, slowing his pace so they dropped further behind the other two. 'But I've missed talking to you. And . . . I just wanted you to know that.'

An image of kissing Sylvain earlier flashed into her mind and for a second she flushed.

Carter's not my boyfriend any more, she reminded herself. *I can kiss whoever I want.* But she didn't want to think about how he'd react if he found out.

'I saw you with Jules earlier. You looked happy.'

He stumbled and caught himself. By the time he had his balance again he'd composed his expression. But she knew him too well. She could see the colour in his cheeks. 'Yeah, about that . . .'

'I didn't know you two were together.' Allie was surprised at how calm she sounded. He must think she didn't care at all.

'Yeah, it's . . . new.' When he glanced up at her, his eyes were guarded.

'Well, she's great, so I hope you're both happy. You deserve to be.' It hurt to say it, but she meant it. He did deserve to be happy.

'Thanks.' His tone was gruff.

A long pause fell between them.

'This is weird,' he said finally, with a sheepish smile.

'Super weird.'

'The fence is clear,' Jules called back to them. 'Shall we go over it again?'

THIRTY

'*Carter?*' *Allie was screaming at the top of her lungs but the snow seemed to absorb her words. 'Where are you?'*

There was no answer. She trudged through snow up to her knees, searching through the darkness. Each step was such hard work but she had to find him. He was out there somewhere, all alone. And it was so cold.

A single magpie fluttered right above her head, so close she could see light glinting off its glossy black and white feathers.

'Carter!' she screamed again.

This time she thought she heard a faint reply, and she tried to quicken her steps but her feet refused to cooperate. It was so dark – she couldn't see a thing.

Where had the moon gone?

Then the wind blew his words her way. 'Allie be careful. It's not safe.'

For some reason this terrified her.

'It is safe.' A tear trickled down her cheek. 'It is.'

'Be careful, Allie,' he said. 'And wake up. Wake up.'

Jerking awake with a gasp, Allie sat up so quickly she nearly knocked Rachel over.

'What ... ?' Allie squinted in the sudden brightness. The room was flooded with light. 'What happened?'

'You were screaming in your sleep. I could hear you from next door.' Rachel sat down on the bed next to her and picked up her hand, rubbing it as if to warm it. 'Bloody hell. Your hands are so *cold*. It must have been a nightmare.'

But the dream was already slipping away – trying to remember it was like watching a film through fog.

'What time is it?' Allie leaned over to try and see the clock.

'Nearly noon, you lazy sod.'

Allie stretched. 'We got in so late last night.'

'I heard you didn't have any luck ...' Rachel's voice was hesitant.

Allie shook her head. 'Nothing. It was a false alarm. But they didn't decide that until, like, two in the morning. God, I'm so hungry I could eat that desk.'

'Or you could just have lunch.' Rachel stood up and headed for the door. 'With me. Meet you down there?'

Jumping out of bed Allie glanced at herself in the mirror and winced. 'Bloody hell,' she muttered to herself. 'Forgot about the hair.' When they'd finally come in last night she'd just kicked off her shoes and tumbled into bed. Her makeup was smeared across her face and her bright red hair stood on end as if alarmed.

She grabbed a towel and made her way to the bathroom. The hallway was strangely quiet – some students had left last night with their parents. More would have gone this morning. Soon the building would be almost completely empty again.

After a hot shower she felt better and, returning to her room, she flung open the shutter. Cold white light poured in, brighter than normal daylight, and she peered out into a snow-covered world.

Throwing on her uniform and a warm jumper, she dried her hair and applied a sweep of mascara and lipstick.

The entire time she was thinking about kissing Sylvain. And knowing it had been a bad idea. And hoping nobody would find out about it.

And wanting to do it again.

Zoe and Jo were already at the table with Lucas and Rachel when Allie arrived. Jo's hair was a bright pink crown above her delicate shoulders.

'Feed me now,' she said by way of hello.

'Cheese.' Reaching over, Zoe deposited a sandwich on her plate.

'I love you Zoe Glass,' Allie said passionately, biting into it.

'You should have got up earlier. You missed an amazing snow-ball fight.' Zoe bounced with glee. 'I think I actually hurt people.'

'Borders, Zoe,' Rachel said. 'Remember the borders of normal behaviour.'

'They all lived,' Zoe mumbled defensively.

'This time,' Lucas finished the thought for her.

The others were still laughing when Sylvain sat down in the empty chair next to Allie. She swallowed hard.

'Hey, Sylvain, any news?' Lucas asked, arching his eyebrows.

Sylvain shook his head. 'Nothing – all clear.'

'Cool.' Lucas served himself some soup. 'No equals good.'

Reaching for a sandwich, Sylvain asked about the snowball fight and Zoe launched back into her story. He listened with interest as if it were the most fascinating story he'd ever heard. A knot tightened in Allie's stomach. He hadn't looked at her once.

It hadn't occurred to her that he might think it was a bad idea too. He might be embarrassed by what happened. He probably wished it had never happened.

What if he's sorry? What if it was all some twisted joke?

Just as her paranoia and confusion reached a fever pitch, under the cover of the tablecloth he reached for her hand. Without ever turning his head her way, he laced his fingers through hers until their two hands were tangled up together. Out of sight.

Butterflies fluttered in her stomach. This was so wrong. She and Sylvain could not do this and she'd have to tell him that. But then she remembered what it had felt like kissing him. How she hadn't felt lonely for the first time in ages.

And under the table her hand tightened on his.

As the others caught Allie up on all she'd missed that day – the elaborate snow pirate, complete with tricorn hat and real sword, the chaos of the mass exodus of students – she found herself sneaking sideways glances at Sylvain from underneath her eyelashes. Once he caught her doing it, and his instant half-smile told her he was thinking the same thing.

They were through eating when Allie remembered something she wanted to ask Rachel. 'Hey, did your dad make it back yet?'

The summit was over. He should have been back by now, but Rachel shook her head. 'A lot of roads are closed; he's having trouble getting back from London. He should be here tonight.'

Advanced Night School students were in and out of meetings all day, so Allie never had a chance to talk with Sylvain. Instead she spent most of the day with Rachel and Jo, reading and napping.

By nine that night she was wide awake. All the conflicting emotions of the last twenty-four hours had left her charged with pent-up adrenaline. So as she pulled on her patrolling gear, she was actually looking forward to the work ahead. All the Night School students who hadn't yet left for Christmas were splitting up into shifts. She and Zoe had the first one.

It was even colder out than last night, so they'd been issued snow boots which laced up nearly to their knees, as well as thicker leggings, a bulky jacket and thermal gloves.

Zoe, who already had her gear on, including a black ski mask, was air punching in the corner.

'I'm like an Eskimo Ninja,' she announced.

'That's exactly what you're like.' Allie stood up. 'Blimey, I'm so bundled up I can hardly move. I'm not a Ninja. I'm a Marshmallow Man.'

'Yeah, you have to move a bit to kind of loosen the layers.' Zoe tried to kick high and couldn't raise her leg. 'This isn't going to be easy. I hope nobody breaks in tonight. We'd have to just run at them and try to knock them down with our layers.'

'In this weather,' Allie said as they walked out into the corridor, 'nobody's even going to be able to get anywhere near here, much less break in.'

When they reached the top of the stairs, Sylvain was waiting by the door. He affected nonchalance but Allie knew he was waiting for her. As their eyes met, she melted inside.

'I'll catch you up, Zoe,' she said, her gaze locked on Sylvain's.

Still struggling with her thick layers, Zoe didn't notice anything. 'Cool.' She dashed outside trying to kick things.

Amusement flickered in Sylvain's eyes as he studied Allie's clothes. 'Well, at least I know you won't freeze to death.'

'Don't joke. You'll have to wear this stuff later.' Allie smiled. 'Basically, as long as no actual physical movement is required, we're great.'

He pulled her to him until their foreheads touched. His breath was warm on her face. He smelled of coffee and sandalwood.

'You're going to be careful, yes?' he whispered.

She quivered at his touch. 'Very.'

This is wrong, Allie told herself. *I shouldn't want this.*

Standing on her toes, she kissed him quickly and passionately. When she pulled away his eyes had darkened and he breathed heavily.

'See you in three hours,' she said.

*

'Look at it.' Zoe was trudging through snow that nearly reached her knees. 'It's *beautiful*.'

Snow blanketed every branch of every tree, carpeting the ground, softening every corner. The clouds had cleared away and the moon was out, turning the white world blue.

Allie's breath blew out in tiny clouds as her boots crunched with each step. With so many layers, and in such deep snow, walking was hard work. She was already sweating, and her ski mask hung from her fingers. It made her face itch whenever she put it on.

Zoe still wore hers, but rolled up on her head, like a cat burglar.

'It's weird how quiet it is,' Allie said.

'No birds,' Zoe observed. 'No foxes. But maybe we just can't hear them; snow absorbs sound.'

It was nearly eleven. They'd already made the rounds once, and had begun their second sweep, down along the fence line, following their own prints from earlier. Zoe was in the lead. She'd adapted to her layers at last and was moving with something like her usual grace and speed.

'Almost done,' she was saying. 'I think when we go back in I'm going to have a hot chocolate.'

Allie wasn't really paying attention. She was thinking about Sylvain. His shift didn't start until three. With the school mostly empty, surely they could find some time alone somewhere before he had to go. The thought of kissing him again made her heart race.

But all she said was 'Hot chocolate would be good.'

'Something's wrong.'

Zoe's words seemed so out of context that for a second Allie thought she was still talking about chocolate. Then she saw where the younger girl was pointing.

Ahead of them the school's drive crossed their path before going through the big iron gate. But something about it didn't look right. Puzzled, Allie squinted at the road, trying to figure out what it was.

'Something's missing,' she said. 'What is it?'

'The gate.' Zoe's eyes were wide with fear. 'Someone's opened the gate.'

THIRTY-ONE

'How can the gate be open?' Allie stared at the open drive as if looking at it would close it again. 'I don't understand.'

They were crouched down in the trees, whispering. They'd both pulled on their ski masks.

'It's not supposed to be open,' Zoe said. 'It's a mistake.'

'Could it be Raj?' Allie asked. 'Maybe he came back and left it open.'

Even through her ski mask she could see the scepticism in Zoe's eyes. 'Raj, Allie? Really?'

'No,' Allie said. 'You're right. He'd build a new gate with his bare hands before he'd leave this one open.' She took a calming breath. 'OK, we're trained for this, Zoe. We check this out together. You loop around that way.' She pointed towards the school building. 'Cross the drive further down. Then you search that side of the driveway and I'll search this side. If you find anything, yell. If I don't yell back, go and get help.'

Zoe shot off through the powdery snow and, worry making her heart hurt, Allie watched her until she disappeared in the shadows.

She looked so tiny.

Then she began moving from tree to tree, searching for signs of trouble. As she walked, she thought about the night she went to meet Christopher. The way Gabe had jumped on her from out of nowhere.

She'd never heard a thing.

Her heart beat a staccato rhythm as she moved through the woods as quietly as possible, knowing she was making a perfect trail to follow with every step. But she saw no footprints ahead of her – the snow was smooth.

What am I doing out here? she thought fearfully. *This is crazy. We're just* kids.

When she'd made it to the drive without finding anything, she peered through the open gate, out into the darkness beyond the school grounds.

There was nobody there.

She was just about to walk to Zoe's side of the drive when something caught her eye. There was something in the road, beyond the fence line.

Squinting, she tried to make it out, but it was just a little too far away.

Above her, a heavy clump of snow fell from a branch dusting her with a shower of silvery powder. She was brushing it off her shoulders when the moon moved out from behind a cloud.

In the pale light it cast, she stared again at the thing in the road but she couldn't tell what it was. It was pink. And looked kind of like a doll . . .

Everything went still.

She opened her mouth to call for Zoe but her throat was suddenly so dry words wouldn't come out.

And then she was running. She ran through the gate and down the road, and, as she ran, she found her voice and she screamed for Zoe. But it was like her nightmare – like trying to run through treacle. Her feet wouldn't move like they should. Her ribcage tightened around her lungs and she fought for air.

Jo lay crumpled in the road, her legs twisted under her unnaturally. Her cornflower blue eyes stared up at the dark sky and she was horribly pale.

'Jo?' Allie ripped off a glove with her teeth and pressed her shaking fingers to Jo's neck, whispering a prayer. But her hands were numb and she couldn't feel anything. All she could feel was cold. Jo felt cold.

'Allie, what is it?' Zoe stood just outside the gate, looking out at her. Allie could hear the dread in her voice.

'It's Jo,' Allie shouted. 'Don't come here. Run back to the school as fast as you can. Tell them he's here. Nathaniel's here. Bring help, Zoe.'

'Is she alive?' Zoe asked.

Fear and anger can hurt like burning, and when Allie replied her words roared out of her throat. 'Just *run*, Zoe!'

She said it with such force, Zoe was moving before the last syllable had fallen from the air – she was too far away to hear how the last word turned into a sob.

'Jo, can you hear me?' Kneeling beside her Allie tried to find a wound or cut. At first she could see nothing, but then the moon came out from behind a cloud and she saw the dark stain spreading on the white snow.

'Oh God.'

The sight numbed Allie's brain – for a moment she couldn't even remember how to breathe as she fought back the grief and terror that threatened to overwhelm her.

'Jo, I don't know what to do!' Her voice sounded foreign to her – small and childlike. Her hot tears were cold by the time they reached her cheeks and for a second she closed her eyes, willing herself to get it together enough to think. She needed to stop the bleeding.

'Allie . . .'

Jo's whisper came with obvious effort, and Allie's eyes flew open.

'Oh my God. Jo! What happened? What did they do to you?'

'Allie,' Jo whispered again, her voice so raspy and weak Allie had to lean close to her to hear. 'It's Gabe.' She licked her lips slowly. 'He tricked . . . me.'

Her voice was so weak and she was so pale.

'Look.' Panic making it hard to breathe, Allie fought to keep calm. Jo needed her to keep it together. 'You're going to be OK. They're bringing help. You just hang on, Jo.'

And that's when everything went dark.

Allie's feet left the ground. She couldn't move her arms or legs. She could see nothing. She was being . . . carried.

Screaming inside whatever covered her face, she struggled

with all her strength, kicking out wildly with her heavy snow boots. At one point she made contact and heard the satisfying sound of air being forced out of someone's lungs. Whoever was carrying her lost their grip and her feet touched the ground. Planting her heels in the snow, she nearly pulled free. Then somebody punched her and she fell. Her ribs burned with pain and for a little while she couldn't move.

She was picked up again, and held more tightly now, and with an arm against her throat, choking her.

'Keep fighting and you die, too.' Gabe's voice, so horribly familiar.

She heard a metallic sound and felt herself being shoved into a car. Her shoulder hit the door hard, and she banged her head against something.

'Be careful with her,' a different voice warned. 'He said not to hurt her. You heard him.'

'She's fine,' Gabe snapped as he climbed in after her. 'Drive.'

Allie fought to keep from shaking as the car began to move. It started slowly but soon picked up speed and before long they were speeding down a road Allie couldn't see. But she could feel how icy it was underneath their tyres. The car fishtailed dangerously.

'Watch it!' Gabe shouted, close to her ear and she jumped.

After that the driver slowed a little.

I have to get free. What if Zoe isn't back in time? I've got to help Jo.

'You don't have to do this, you know,' she said reasonably, trying to keep her teeth from chattering.

Gabe laughed unpleasantly.

'You could just let me go. I mean, what does Nathaniel want with me anyway?'

'Shut up,' he snarled, shoving her with such violence her head bounced off the door frame. Her ears rang.

But the movement allowed her to work her hands free from behind her body without being noticed.

For a long while the road seemed unreasonably straight. Allie held her breath, poised. She could hear Gabe breathing next to her. It made her skin crawl.

She didn't know how far they'd gone when the car took a sharp bend just a little too fast; even without sight she could sense the driver fighting for control on the ice. At that moment, she sprang, reaching blindly for where she knew the driver would be. She felt warm hair and hard skull under her fingers.

Then, as she had been taught, she jammed her fingernails into his eyes.

The car swerved sickeningly. Somebody screamed.

Cursing, Gabe grabbed her arms with unbelievable strength, but her grip was solid – he just drove her nails further into the driver's face. As the car spun out of control, Gabe let go of her and leapt over the seat. She could feel him grabbing for the steering wheel but he never had a chance. They hit something with an awful crunching sound and then the world turned upside down.

Allie wondered if she was dead.

She couldn't see anything. Every part of her body hurt.

She couldn't move her left arm. Something hard had jammed into her back.

And worst of all, something wet and cold was dripping on to her face.

Using her right arm, she scrabbled at her face; she felt rough fabric under her fingertips and yanked at it. Her shoulder burned like fire as she pulled the bag off her head.

Now she could see but she couldn't figure out what she was looking at. It was dark and nothing made any sense. She seemed to be looking up at a steering wheel *above her head*.

Staring in blank confusion at the car keys dangling above her, she realised she was lying on the ceiling of a car, which was upside down in the snow.

Turning her head painfully to the left she saw a face, covered in blood and staring back at her with blank blue eyes that reminded her sickeningly of Jo's. The reason she couldn't move was because Gabe lay on her arm. She thought he might be dead but she wasn't certain.

Moaning in horror, she shoved at him, but he was heavy and every time she moved it felt like someone shoved a knife into her shoulder. Using her good arm and both legs, she pulled herself loose a little at a time; it took all of her strength and afterward she lay still, panting. The edge of her vision blackened and she feared she might faint.

Get out, Allie, a voice in her head was screaming. *Get out of the car.*

But it was so hard to move. With effort, she slid slowly to the door. Her left arm wouldn't do anything, she noticed with a kind of distant curiosity. It just hung there.

Using her right hand she fumbled with the door handle. At first nothing happened. Then she pulled harder and heard the latch give. She sighed with relief and shoved it. But it would only open about ten inches. Then it jammed against a wall of snow and branches.

Groaning with pain, Allie turned herself around. Bracing her back against Gabe's body, she rested her feet against the door. Then she kicked the window.

And again.

With each kick she cried out with pain, but each kick also moved the door another few inches. Three kicks, and it was open just enough for her to escape.

Feet first, she crawled through the opening, tumbling on to her knees in the snow with a scream of agony. For a moment she knelt still, sobbing.

Moonlight filtered through the trees around her. Grabbing a branch with her right arm, she pulled herself slowly to her feet, gritting her teeth against the pain.

Bewildered, she turned a slow circle. She couldn't see a road anywhere.

The car was in the woods.

With no idea where she was and consciousness slipping, Allie limped to the back of the car. After pausing to catch her breath, she began to follow the car's tracks, lurching through bushes and trees, and then up an embankment to the narrow country lane.

The way her left arm flopped uselessly at her side scared her so she held it still with her right hand as she stumbled unsteadily along the empty road. She was moving as fast as she could – something told her she needed to get far away from that car.

She could see the skid marks the car had left as it swung from one side of the road to the other before leaving it completely.

But the road was blurred. Something was blocking her vision. When she reached up to swipe her hand against her eyes, it came back covered in blood.

I'm bleeding, she thought unemotionally. *Guess that's no surprise.*

Somewhere she could hear a car engine, but she couldn't tell where it was coming from. She tried to speed up. But as she limped down the road, she knew she was veering from side to side, and blood was now dripping on to the snow with each step, leaving a trail of scarlet behind her.

By the time she saw the car coming directly towards her, she was too exhausted to get out of the way. Standing slightly hunched over from the pain, she held up her good hand as if that would be enough to stop it and stared straight into headlights.

The car skidded to a stop.

She could hear a car door open but all she could see was the blinding light.

The moment seemed to stretch out for ever.

'Who is it?' she tried to say, through gritted teeth, but she didn't know if the words actually came out.

'Allie? Is that you? Oh my God.' A man's voice.

Then he stepped out into the light and she saw his horrified face.

Raj Patel.

As he reached out for her, she collapsed in his arms.

THIRTY-TWO

Golden light. Soft blankets. Warmth. Pain.

Allie could hear voices but she couldn't seem to wake up.

'How is she?'

'Still unconscious.'

'Is it bad?'

'Well, it's not good. Just look at her, for God's sake.'

Someone holding her hand, whispering in her ear.

A pinprick.

Silence.

With a gasp, Allie opened her eyes. They felt gummed together and heavy.

Slowly the room came into focus – all she saw was white. A white bed. White light streaming through white curtains. White walls.

Every part of her body hurt. When she licked her lips, they didn't feel right – they felt swollen and torn. She tried to speak but her mouth was too dry.

She was so thirsty.

With effort, she turned her head to the right. It hurt to move. Sylvain was asleep in the chair beside her, arms crossed protectively across his chest. He looked young and vulnerable.

But when she reached out to him, a shock of pain shot through her and she whimpered. His eyes flew open; the light reflected in them like jewels.

'Allie?' He leaned forward, taking her right hand in his. 'It's OK. You're safe.'

She felt strange. As if she were cocooned. Sound seemed to come from a long way away.

'You were in an accident,' he was saying.

'I know that,' she whispered, although the words sounded fuzzy, as if spoken through a mouthful of gauze. 'I was there.'

A relieved smile spread slowly across his face and he bent down to kiss her fingers.

'Doctor,' he called over his shoulder.

A woman in white appeared behind his shoulder, eyes concerned. 'Hello, Allie. Please don't move.'

Reaching past Sylvain, she took Allie's wrist between her fingers and checked her pulse, looking at her watch. Then she studied numbers on a machine by the bed and wrote down the results.

'How do you feel?' the doctor asked.

'Hurts. Thirsty.'

'I'll give you something for the pain.' She handed Sylvain a cup with a straw in it. 'Tiny sips only. Don't let her have too much. I'll be right back.'

He held it to her lips. The tepid water tasted delicious – she wanted to drink all of it, but he pulled it away. That was OK. It hurt to drink anyway.

Her eyes searched his. 'Jo?'

His face went blank. 'Don't talk, Allie. The doctor wants you to be still. We'll talk soon.'

Panic surged; the heart monitor beside the bed beeped in alarm. '*Jo?*'

Half standing now, Sylvain called over his shoulder, 'Doctor?'

'I'm right here.' She appeared beside him, a syringe in her hand. 'Please don't move,' she told Allie firmly. 'We need you to be still.'

As she injected the contents of the syringe into the drip Allie watched, helpless. Something was wrong but she couldn't quite put her finger on it. Then her brain lost interest.

Everything went dark.

When she woke again, it was night. Her bed lay in a pool of golden light. Now Isabelle sat in the chair next to her, reading a stack of papers. Her glasses were halfway down her nose.

Allie tried to say 'Isabelle', but her throat was too dry again. But the headmistress must have sensed her movement because she leaned forward, setting the papers aside.

'Allie – here.' Isabelle held the glass of water for her.

Her face still felt swollen but the pain wasn't as bad now and Allie slowly turned her head, verifying that her room was otherwise empty. 'Sylvain?'

Isabelle leaned forward, her eyes sombre. 'I sent him to his room to get some sleep, Allie. He's been right here for days. He's exhausted.'

'Days?' She searched Isabelle's eyes. 'How long . . . ?'

'You've been unconscious for three days, Allie. You were very badly hurt – you have a head injury. Your left arm is broken.'

Allie gave a slow shallow nod to show she wasn't surprised. Then her gaze met Isabelle's and held it. 'Jo.'

A long pause followed, but then Isabelle's reply came in a low, steady voice, as if she'd prepared for this moment. 'Jo didn't make it, Allie.'

Somebody moaned and Allie wondered if it was her. Picking up her good hand, Isabelle held it tightly. 'Zoe ran fast; we got there quickly, but she'd lost too much blood.' Her voice caught and she paused for a long moment. 'There was nothing anyone could do. She was already dead when we got there.'

A tear rolled down the side of Allie's face. 'How?'

The headmistress' lips trembled. 'We found some things in her room.'

'What?' Allie asked, although she thought she might already have guessed.

'Letters and notes,' Isabelle said, 'from Gabe.'

Hatred filled Allie's heart.

'They'd been in communication for a while. He told her he wanted to talk; that he missed her and wanted to say he was sorry. He played on her emotions, her unresolved feelings for him. They must have arranged to meet that night. When she got there the gate was open. They argued. She tried to run away. He had a knife . . . '

A sob wrenched through Allie and she let go of Isabelle's hand to cover her face. 'Oh Jo.'

Was it her fault? Hadn't Jo warned her, in a way? She said, '*I never got to ask him why he did what he did.*' Why hadn't she realised Jo wouldn't be able to accept that? That she'd insist on knowing why?

Now Isabelle was crying, too. 'You did everything you could, Allie. Nobody could have saved her.'

But that was a lie, wasn't it?

Early the next morning, Rachel appeared in her doorway with a steaming mug of coffee and a bowl of porridge. Her eyes were red and puffy but she was composed.

'I don't know if they feed you up here,' she said, forcing a sad smile.

Sitting in the chair by the bed, she stirred the oats ('with brown sugar and cinnamon, the way you like it'). Allie's bruised jaw and throat made eating painful but she was surprised to find she was hungry. Rachel fed her small spoonfuls and waited patiently while she forced the food down. When she'd eaten enough, Rachel closed the door to her room, moved the side table out of the way and climbed up on the bed beside her, careful not to jar her broken arm. Then, holding Allie's good hand, she told her everything she knew.

Gabe most likely passed notes to Jo through Nathaniel's spy. The last note probably arrived the night of the ball, thus sparking the panic that the school was being attacked. It must have been his footprints the guards saw in the snow. That person had then slipped the notes into Jo's room at night. It wasn't clear if Jo knew who the spy was, or if they had some system for her writing back.

'Then, just before eleven o'clock, that person, whoever it is, opened the gate,' Rachel said.

Allie's heartbeat seemed unnaturally loud in her ears.

'The gate opens by remote control kept in Isabelle's office,' Rachel explained. 'There is no other way. So whoever opened the gate is close enough to all of us to get into her office and not be noticed. A teacher, most likely. Although it could be a senior Night School student.'

Allie's chest seemed to constrict her lungs and she forced herself to keep breathing.

Isabelle and Raj believed the driver had parked the car off the road in the forest about a hundred yards from the entrance. Gabe then went ahead on foot to meet Jo.

'We don't know why he killed her. Maybe she was planning to tell Dad or Isabelle about her meetings with him.' Rachel's hand was warm against hers. 'Or maybe he only meant to hurt her and it all went too far. Either way, Dad thinks Gabe knew you and Zoe would be patrolling at that time. And that the only thing that would get you to leave the school grounds would be to help someone you loved.'

A tear rolled down Allie's face on to the pillow. She closed her eyes, wanting the story to end.

'After that we think he just waited for you to try and save her.'

Allie's shoulders shook with grief.

'But what he didn't count on,' Rachel was crying now, too; her voice shook as she stroked Allie's hair, 'was how very good you are at fighting back.'

Jo was buried on Christmas Eve at Highgate Cemetery in London. It was a slow news week, so the national newspapers picked up the story. They all reported the tragic death of a beautiful, wealthy teenager in a car accident on an icy country road.

EPILOGUE

*T*en steps, eleven steps, twelve steps . . .

Moving slowly and painfully, Allie walked down the infirmary hallway. It was seventeen endless steps up the hall to the window at the end, and seventeen long steps back down the hall to the stairwell. Her legs were shaky. Her slippers made a zombie-shuffling sound on the floor.

'Still practising?' The nurse stopped to watch her with kind eyes. 'You're getting better, Allie.'

Setting her jaw, Allie took the seventeenth step and stopped to breathe. Sweat poured down her face. 'Thanks.' She tried to smile but feared she'd made a hash of it. She didn't smile much any more.

'Don't overdo it now,' the nurse said as she walked to the stairs. 'Take it slow.'

They'd removed the bandages above Allie's left eye now, and she could just about see out of it, although it was still swollen.

She had a long row of stitches in the hairline, where something had hit her head. Her left arm and shoulder were still in a cast that made her arm stick out at an absurd angle.

'OK,' she replied, turning and beginning her shaky progress the other direction.

... five steps, six, seven ...

'Should you be doing that alone?'

Looking up, Allie saw Carter standing at the top of the stairs, watching her slow progress.

'As long as I don't overdo it.'

'Are you overdoing it?' His eyes were sad.

'Probably.'

'That's what I figured.'

'How are you?' She studied his face with concern. 'You know. Since ... everything.'

Until now, she'd seen him only once since Jo's death, and then he'd been pale and lost looking, but she'd been so grief-stricken and out of it on painkillers she hadn't been able to think of anything useful to say.

'I can't believe you're asking me that question,' he said. 'Haven't they got mirrors up here?'

'No,' she said. 'Doctors can't see their reflections in them. Drives them crazy.'

'I thought that was vampires.'

She shrugged and then winced, remembering she couldn't shrug yet. 'Same difference.'

'Well, I'm not busy,' he said. 'I guess I could take this fascinating tour with you for a while. I like the view: bathroom, bed, staircase, wall ...'

He was trying to cheer her up, like everyone else. But sad people can't make sad people happy.

'I met your parents.' Holding her good arm, he walked beside her down the hall. 'They seem nice.'

'Are you sure those were *my* parents?' Gritting her teeth with effort, Allie lifted her feet. 'Maybe you got them confused with someone else's.'

He almost smiled. 'They called themselves Mr and Mrs Sheridan so I'm pretty sure they're yours.'

'Don't believe their lies.' Allie was breathing heavily from the pain. 'Anyway. I'm trying to get them to go home now that I'm better.'

'Well, it's good that they're here for you,' he said.

She didn't reply.

'Can I ask a question?' he said after they'd made two circuits of the corridor. 'Why are you doing this?'

'They won't let me go downstairs until I can walk up and down the hall ten times without falling down or fainting or something,' she explained. 'I want to go downstairs.'

'How many have you done today?' he asked when they reached the end of the hallway.

'Eight.' Exhausted, she leaned against the wall to rest.

He looked at her with concern. 'Maybe you shouldn't do any more.'

She shrugged and winced again. 'Nah. I'm enjoying this.' Brushing the hair back from her face, she said, 'If *you're* tired though, you know, we could rest.'

Unexpectedly, he leaned over and brushed his lips lightly against the top of her head. 'I'm so sorry, Allie.'

Looking away, she blinked back the tears that threatened never to stop. 'Me too. I can't get used to it. It doesn't seem real. I miss her.'

Turning, she took a step and promptly lost her balance. As if he'd expected that, he caught her easily and directed her towards her room. 'OK, Miss Sheridan, I think that's enough exercise for one afternoon.'

She climbed into bed without argument. He pulled the covers up over her legs, and rolled the side table back into place. When she was settled, he walked to the door. For a minute she thought he'd just leave without saying goodbye.

But at the last second he turned back to look at her.

'Keep breathing, Allie.'

Trying not to cry, she nodded. Then she counted his footsteps as he walked away.

When he was gone she whispered after him: 'Always.'

ACKNOWLEDGEMENTS

No book I have ever written would be as good without long walks with my husband, Jack Jewers, who listens calmly as I freak out and then helps me find the solution, usually before the dog has jumped into the stream and soaked us both. Thank you, my love, for your patience, your thoughtfulness and your genius.

I want to hug everyone at Atom, especially my brilliant editor Samantha Smith, who reads my first drafts, cocks her head to one side and says, 'How about . . . ' and then makes it all much better. Thanks also to Katherine Agar for keeping track of everything and sending me packages filled with books. And all hail Sandra Ferguson, who knows perfectly well I can't spell really basic words, and quietly fixes them.

You would not be reading this were it not for my wonderful agent, Madeleine Milburn, who fights my corner like a tiger. Thank you for being my friend and champion. Together we will conquer the world!

Thanks are due to my muses Kate Bell and Hélène Rudyk and Laura Barbey, who read this book before anyone else did. Thank you for your time, your cleverness and your honesty. This book is better because of you.

To my good friends Mark Lacey and Paul ('Harry') Harrison, thank you for letting me borrow your names. They are very good names.

And finally ... Special thanks to Blacks on Dean Street, London, for providing a haven for writers, and for letting me break The Rules and use my laptop after six o'clock. Chapter twelve is YOURS.

A former crime reporter, political writer and investigative journalist, **C. J. Daugherty** has also written several books about travel in Ireland and France. Although she left the world of crime reporting years ago, she never lost her fascination with what it is that drives some people to do awful things, and the kinds of people who try to stop them. The *Night School* series is the product of that fascination.

C. J. lives in the south of England with her husband and a small menagerie of pets – you can learn more about her at www.cjdaugherty.com